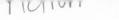

ELIZABETH COOKE

Z E E N A

ST. MARTIN'S PRESS ✻ NEW YORK

Design by Songhee Kim

Library of Congress Cataloging-in-Publication Data

Cooke, Elizabeth.
    Zeena / by Elizabeth Cooke. —1st ed.
        p.   cm.
    A retelling of the story of Edith Wharton's novel Ethan
Frome from the point of view of Zenobia, or Zeena, Frome.
    ISBN 0-312-14775-9
    I. Wharton, Edith, 1862-1934. Ethan Frome. II. Title.
PS3553.O5554Z3 1996
813'.54—dc20   96-20059
                                               CIP

First Edition: October 1996

2 65

10 9 8 7 6 5 4 3 2 1

FOR ALAN

AND OUR MOUNTAIN LIFE

IN MEMORY OF

PHEBE WARREN COOKE

A C K N O W L E D G M E N T S

*D*eena would not have found life without help from Cheryl Higgins, reader, teacher, and friend; Maxine Richmond and Ella Ronco, who remembered their grandmothers' ways; Hope Dellon, Geri Thoma, and Kit Ward, who believed; Kelley Ragland, who read with an expert eye; and especially Don Murray, who lives the writing life and showed me how.

GOODBYE TO THE LIFE I USED TO LIVE—

AND THE WORLD I USED TO KNOW—

AND KISS THE HILLS, FOR ME, JUST ONCE—

THEN—I AM READY TO GO!

EMILY DICKINSON

1 9 0 4

*F*rost clung to the insides of the windowpanes like crusted skin. Needles of icy air slipped into the room through the cracks around its only window.

Zeena lay nearest the window. She'd been sleeping, but now her eyes were open, squinting at the frosted window to blur the diamonds made by the moonlight.

Had it wakened her again? That whimpering?

Wolves is what she'd thought that first time, those years ago when she wakened to the distant moaning, muffled almost. Or maybe a baby what's crying itself to sleep.

The first time, how many years was it? Zeena'd lost track. Twenty-something, was all she could get. Up on the hill, seasons came and went, teasing, making her think time was patient.

There's no patience in time's passing, Father used to say.

There it was again. Little gulps, now. A gasping for air? After all the years Zeena knew it like she knew the morning's first light, that sense of something coming in the darkest part of the night, the expected, come again.

At her back Ethan lay, a stone in sleep. On the nights when the moon lit up the room, she stared at her husband's chest and waited for its quiet rising. It always came, but so slow. Nothing woke Ethan. Not wolves crying, not the ticking of the old clock in the parlor that ticked no longer since he'd sold it, and not the whimpering that plagued Zeena with its insistence.

Zeena squeezed shut her eyes; her flannel rag'd come loose, so she wrapped it round her head and down onto her forehead, then edged deeper under the covers. The night's cold on her face was like the touch of well water just before it froze. There was no way round it. Soon enough she'd start in to wheezing.

As she lay there, it came back to her how, as a child, she'd curled into a ball to stop the shivering that overtook her some nights. Sometimes she woke to Mama sinking down beside her on the trundle bed. Mama's arms round her, Mama's breath always warm, and Mama's voice, "Hush now, Zenobia," chanted like a chorus in her ear to soothe her to sleep. "She needs some flesh on her," Father whispered in the dark. And it was true even now. Zeena's bones showed in her face, her shoulders; her ribs poked at her clothing. High-boned is what Mama'd called it when Zeena was a girl. Bones is what they'd called her in school.

Only once in her life had her flesh filled out and her face taken on the flush of warmth. That first month after she'd come to the Fromes' led to a blossoming she'd not expected. In November's first cold and dark days, Zeena'd found her blood racing in her veins, and when she peered into the looking glass, she saw her own clear eyes dancing with life. Her marriage to Ethan . . . Who'd have guessed her journey into these hills to look after his mother'd turn out as it did? But by the new year's deep frost, it was over.

Zeena lifted onto an elbow now, so as to get the sound of the crying again, but it did not come. Instead she noticed the stillness in the air. This kind a cold is calm, she thought.

Only hours before, the storm had battled on the hill for the second time that day. It'd been snowing at dawn when Zeena got up and found Ethan readying to go to town and fetch the visitor to the Flats to meet his train. All winter the man, an engineer working out at the powerhouse at Corbury Junction, had boarded in town and paid Ethan to take him to the station where he caught the train. "Trains won't be going," he told Zeena. "Not in this," and he gestured to the whirling white outside, adding, "I'll take him clear to the Junction." "Why put yourself out so?" she'd inquired. Ethan turned his blue eyes to her; no pleading for understanding was there, just a cold stare. He stepped from his weak foot onto the other, the strong one. "If you got to ask—" he started, rubbing two fingers against the old scar on his forehead. Till afternoon the snow went on, covering the snow that was already banked up. Then there was a lull. Skies almost cleared before they darkened up again; all through the evening the snow had kept on then. At bedtime they were nearly buried in it. Hills of snow drifted in against the north and east sides of the house, covering the windows. The apple and pear trees were snowy mounds, sentinels rising out of the land. The ridge behind the house was a snowy swirl.

Some said they liked a storm. Least it wasn't so cold, they said. Least it kept the ground warm. Zeena'd just shake her head. The cold weren't something to trade, she figured. You give up one thing for another.

How long would it take now till she'd get to town? Spring wasn't something to imagine in your heart, so far off was it. Those that took a storm over the cold, they lived in town. They didn't listen to their cows moaning nor wonder if their wood'd be froze together.

Only good thing about snow was the cover it provided. She wouldn't have to worry about the spring freezing up, as it'd done twice in the years since the war. Heating snow on the stove grew tiresome before a single day was past.

Out here on the ridge it was different. Here the storm'd end and it'd turn cold and that'd be it. There wouldn't be nothing different now, she thought. A body wouldn't last long if it was to dig a hole and lay there, skin to snow. The critters'd come, prob'ly before the body was altogether gone.

Zeena sighed. Here it was again, another cold night, and the whimpering was started up again. Don't last long. Maybe an hour. Maybe two. Sooner or later, it stops. Nothing changes, she mused.

Then she remembered: the visitor, the man they'd put up for the night. He was sleeping in the birthing room, the same room Ethan's mother'd taken sick and then died in, the same room Ethan'd used for his studies. That's what he called them, his studies. After the smash-up, he never stepped in there again for all Zeena knew. Not till this very night when he brought that engineer fellow back through the snow. Trains weren't going, he'd have been stranded at the Flats, so what were they to do? Hospitality, it was called, but it'd been more years than Zeena could remember since she'd had to offer it.

Zeena wouldn't have used the girl's name with the visitor. But Ethan, he had to speak it after he shuffled his way in through the back passage with the man, stamping his feet on the oilcloth, apologetic as always that the ell'd been taken down so many years ago and was still not rebuilt. "One a' these days," he said, his head shaking, as if it was something bigger than himself that kept him from doing it. "Time," he said, as if that explained it. Then he removed his hat and slapped it against his leg. He brushed his shoulders, sending more snow to the floor, and set the lantern down on the table. Right off he went to the stove, bent down and began to add wood to the firebox. "I'll get this going, it'll be warm soon enough."

Ethan stood then. In the dim light his right side looked more hunched up than usual, and the scar on his forehead showed red. "This is my wife, Mis' Frome," he said to the man.

Zeena lifted her chin. She tried to look the man in the eye, to smile as if it was what she did every day, but how could she? Little did he know of the burdens she'd borne all these years, all the whines and complaints from the girl, all the sorrowful looks from her husband . . . as if that would redeem him. She turned from the visitor to the pine dresser and busied herself by opening a drawer and pretending to look for something. When she glanced back at Ethan, she knew he was preparing for the other introduction. He didn't like to say it either. Even now it pained him. Zeena knew it by the way his head bent, then lolled side to side after speaking it, a mournful kind of motion.

Seconds passed, how many Zeena did not count; she hoped secretly he'd not be able to do it. But, swallowing, his head bent and ready to loll, he said, "And this is Miss Mattie Silver," and he gestured to the figure settled in the armchair.

"So this's Mattie," the visitor said, leaning close.

Mattie's dark shining eyes peered from her pale small face and blinked several times. A slim white hand lifted from the chair's arm. The visitor took the hand in his.

Mattie spoke then, a whining bit of words. "You're nearly froze, though t'ain't much warmer in here, I'd wager." She looked from Zeena to Ethan. "She fell asleep," Mattie told Ethan. "Slep' ever so long, and I thought I'd be frozen stiff before I could wake her and get her to tend the stove."

The visitor coughed into his hands.

"She on'y thinks of herself," Mattie said. "I been setting so long like this," and her head cocked to indicate her slumped position, "when she ties me in, the skin here," and she rubbed at the skin under her arm with her one good hand, "it's got so it's nearly raw."

Zeena grimaced. She bathed Mattie nearly every day, rubbed salve into the sores that formed, massaged her useless limbs. She brushed her hair and wound it up with combs, and kept her clothes clean. Zeena'd long ago given up imagining the girl would acknowledge the care she got; whether Zeena troubled over her or not, all she got was Mattie's sour temper. But she would not defend herself with the visitor there. She brought the remains of a mince pie to the table and set it by the three plates and the milk jug. "There's enough for four," she said.

"It's hardly enough to call supper," Mattie said, looking to Ethan. "She scrimps more'n she needs to, don't she?"

Could the visitor tell? Course he could, Zeena knew. Even though Mattie was an invalid, with her hair gone dry and gray, and her face sallow with discomfort, even though her voice was shrill in its complaints, her eyes sparked, and in that sparking was the thing Ethan'd loved.

THERE WAS THE WHIMPERING AGAIN.

Would the visitor hear it too? Zeena tried to swallow, but it wouldn't come. A pounding started in her head. In the years since the smash-up she'd tried to tolerate her fate, a fate that'd left her with a husband whose shriveled right side kept him only half strong and the girl he loved crippled, and both of them in her care. Ruth Hale was the only one to make regular visits up to the ridge to see them. "You got a lot to bear," she'd told Zeena early on, her head shaking in a gesture of sympathy; on subsequent visits those words hung between them, the only comfort Zeena ever was given.

But now there was no toleration in Zeena, nothing close to acceptance. On this night she knew it was no kindness that she'd take to the girl if she went down those stairs. Something ran through her veins. Her heart raced and thumped. Mama always said hatred was for the godless, but could she ever've imagined what Zeena'd have to bear?

Sometimes it slipped out when she tended the girl's whinings. "How can you complain?" she'd say, remembering the secret Ethan and Mattie thought they shared. That were no secret, Zeena knew. "I'm the one with the secrets," she told Mattie. "You don't know what he done to me before you come here."

But they were just words. Mattie might flinch, her eyes might tear, and she might turn her face to the side, her only escape from Zeena. Zeena might tremble with it, the loathing. But that was as far as it went.

This time was different. Ethan'd introduced Mattie, had said her name to the visitor. It'd all come back fresh as if it'd just happened—Zeena's arrival at the Fromes', her marriage to Ethan, and everything that followed.

The wheezing started in, a rattle in her lungs. Zeena held in the coughing that threatened the silence. She sat up on the side of the bed, pulled her knitted slippers onto her feet. She reached for her shawl at the foot of the bed and pulled it round her shoulders. She stood. A stiffness in her back held her bent, but she eased it by rubbing along the spine, and then straightened. There were the shooting pains down her legs. She drew in her breath against the cold sweep of air up her nightdress. Even with slippers on, the cold floorboards pinched at her feet.

She stood at the top of the stairs with one hand on the railing, the other at her throat; to her left was the door to the room Mattie'd used until the smash-up. Nights, Zeena'd seen a glimmering of light under Mattie's door long after Zeena or Ethan'd blown their candle out. Had Ethan laid there, watching the glow of it too? "Don't she know enough not to waste the candle?" she'd complained to Ethan. "Ain't as if we buy them ready-made; someone's got to make them."

Zeena's mind was lurching. She saw the way Mattie looked the day she arrived, tired and drawn. A cousin of Zeena's, Mattie was to be the hired girl. Ethan took special care to make the girl feel at home through that long first winter by helping with her chores, none of which Mattie completed with any talent. He rose early to get the cookstove going, kept the woodboxes loaded, fetched the water, and was always ready to do for her. By the time summer came, the girl fairly shone with life. It sparkled out of her eyes, off of her cheeks, and into her voice. So the house that had those several years grown silent, it found its life again.

Until the smash-up . . . What would've happened to Ethan and the girl if Harmon Gow hadn't happened by the ridge and found Fly, the old sorrel, standing there alone, a bearskin rug laid across her hollow back, looking confused. They'd've died, sure as night falls.

Harmon's face, when Zeena opened the door, it was something she wouldn't forget. His eyes, shifting side to side, and his mouth working fast, too fast for her to comprehend the words, and yet somehow she knew. "Where are they?" she interrupted him, and then it was silence he gave her as he turned, slanted his head toward the ridge and said, "They was coasting," then looked back at her with the slightest smile across his lips, as if he was just a bit gleeful to be the one to say it, "an' you know the branch of that elm, how it blusters out," so he could watch her go to pieces there in the dooryard because Ethan Frome had chosen the girl over his wife.

Zeena didn't go to pieces, though. She was used to the ground giving way, used to shocks. What she'd found out when they were first married, it'd been more of a blow than she'd ever let on. So when she heard the news from Harmon Gow, she didn't cry out. She knew without thinking it: Death together would ha' been a happier fate than separation. She knew that morning Ethan wasn't going to take the girl to the station and send her back home as Zeena'd insisted, knew he'd not collect the new hired girl at the station. Knew when they turned right out of the gate and onto the Bettsbridge pike instead of left and into town that he had something else in mind. It was in his eyes before he even left with the girl in the sleigh, that looking inward instead of out at the world, and it told her what even he wasn't certain of: Ethan will go with the girl.

Zeena just hadn't figured on the place he would take the girl. She'd heard of other cases where a man'd up and left his wife, headed west. But coasting? Knowing the branch of that elm'd loom up after the second steep slope and hoping the impact'd take them? Zeena hadn't figured on that at all.

Harmon stood before her, his eyes wide. "Ruth," he started, "Ruth Varnum, she's got the girl at her house, and Ethan, he's at Mr. Hartman's. Ned's gone after the new hired girl. Ruth said as how I should come tell you."

Zeena lifted her chin. She felt the shooting pains down her legs. She stepped out onto the narrow porch, one hand pressing a hip to ease the discomfort, and stared into the silver sky, traced the black line of the horizon and the shimmering of moonlight across the sloping fields with her eyes.

Harmon stood there with an expectancy showing in his hunched shoulders.

"Let's get going, then," Zeena told him as she turned to reach for her cape. "For the land's sake, let me see 'em before they join the others at the foot of the hill."

ZEENA ROSE TO HER FEET when the crying started up again.

What if she was to go downstairs this time? All these years, the holding back, the refusing to go to the girl, but now the sound was under her skin like bugs scrabbling, even into her brain so she couldn't think straight.

Zeena pressed her palms to her ears. Even when it wasn't sounding, the crying was there. Inside her ears, in her brain . . . Stop!

Mama was gone, Mama that she loved, Mama that she'd tried to heal so many years ago. But this girl, this girl Zeena loathed, she'd kept this girl alive with hands that'd cleaned and dried and soothed her.

The moonlight on the stairwell made shadows. Was it . . . yes, Mattie was there on the stairs below her, Mattie before the smash-up, she stood holding to the railing with one hand and leaning back like she was standing on the trolley steps and her other hand was waving, delicate as a sparrow, light and fresh and new. Now she was looking at Zeena, her head thrown back. Those dark eyes were flashing as her lids lowered slowly in that way she had of charming folks. And her hair, thick and dark, flowing like a mane. "Do you want I should—" Mattie started. Zeena raised a hand to silence her. Liar! Mean trick, to ask again if you can do for me, just like you used to. I know what you're meaning to do, I know what's in your mind. . . .

It came to Zeena then: If Mattie was to succumb during the night, who'd know it wasn't her heart, a fragile fluttering that could sustain her no longer? Who'd think anything other than this: Poor thing, she died in the night, all those years a cripple, all those years living that way, her spine rotting like an old apple tree, slow and steady.

Zenobia Frome, kindhearted as she was, she looked after her till the end.

1 8 7 3

O N E

$\mathscr{Z}$eena was in the kitchen when Father returned from his morning's work at the icehouse. He came in through the shed, as he always did when his boots were caked with sawdust.

It was Tuesday, so Zeena was ironing. The linens, the ones Mama'd been given at her wedding, were dampened and rolled, awaiting the irons that stayed hot on the back of the cookstove. First she'd done Father's shirts, taking most care with his Sunday white. His dress collar that she'd turned three times already was waiting to be pressed.

Father nodded at Zeena before removing his fedora and hanging it on the hook by the door. Then he unlaced his boots and placed them on the oilcloth, and pulled off his jacket and hung it beside the hat. He walked to the cookstove where the kettle steamed, carried the kettle to the sink, splashed some water into the basin, added some cold water from the jug, and started in to washing his hands and face.

Out of the corner of her eye Zeena watched Father. Men are

curious creatures, she was thinking, noting the way he rubbed behind his ears and worked his wet fingers around the back of his neck, scrubbing his skin, washing down inside his shirt, and then sputtering when he flushed his face. A woman, she kept her efforts at cleanliness to herself. It's a matter of pride for a man to lack modesty, she mused. Zeena looked away. She tested one of the irons with a flick of water. She remembered Mama doing the same and smiled. "Guess that's—" Zeena stopped herself.

"What's that?" Father spoke, his voice muffled into a hand towel.

Zeena hadn't meant the words to be spoken. She'd meant to think it: Guess that's how I learned it. She reached for a hot pad so she could open the oven door. "I'm just checking the muffins."

Father went to his place at the table. The chair creaked as he pulled at it.

"Cranberry muffins," Zeena told him. She'd berried with Cousin Harriet and the children last month, had made sauce and preserves, and saved some for baking. She always went berry picking with the cousins, though it meant ignoring their glances, some of pity, some of scorn, depending on which cousin gazed at her. And it was hard to work that way, on your knees. Zeena's back always bothered after a day of berrying. But Mama'd always said it was fresh air would heal what ailed you, and Zeena preached it herself now, so she had to live by what she told others when they called her to do a healing.

"The mountain berries?"

"The last of 'em," Zeena confirmed, pulling the muffins from the oven and snapping the door closed with her knee. She knew Father preferred the bigger, sweeter cranberries from the bog.

Father was seated now. He spread his napkin on his lap. "Ready any time," he said, pulling something from his pocket, a letter, Zeena noted, even as she turned the muffins into the basket.

Zeena stirred the contents of a pot. Steam rose from its surface. She ladled three cupfuls of corn chowder into a bowl for Father, then two for herself, and carried them to the table. Ordinarily this was the moment when she'd ask if he'd be delivering ice that afternoon or working in the shop, but she was curious about the letter so she merely said, "Yesterday's chowder," and turned to the stove for the muffins. The pickles, the applesauce, they were already on the table, along with the rest of the applesauce cake she'd baked on Saturday.

They ate in silence. Father read the letter, several pages of it, turning it every now and then to get the light on it, squinting at it, drawing it close, in between spoonfuls of chowder and bites of muffin. He frowned now and then, adjusting his eyeglasses, and finally removed them altogether. "Your Aunt Belle, she can't write a clear word," he complained.

"Aunt Belle?" Zeena inquired, hoping he'd say more. Aunt Belle was Mama's oldest sister, the one who'd moved away from the family home in Worcester all the way to Springfield on the Connecticut River when she married Nathan Minton. Mama'd moved away too, but Bettsbridge was nothing like Springfield. Aunt Edith Willis, Mama's other sister who stayed in Worcester, told Zeena she wondered if Mama might've lived if she'd gotten proper care. "Your Mama was loyal to your father's independence," Aunt Edith told her at the funeral. "She wouldn't think of asking him to join the family store." Men's apparel would've been a step up for Father. Cutting ice was better than farming but not as good as shopkeeping.

Aunt Belle was Mama's favorite sister. "Maybe when you're older you'll stay at Aunt Belle's and see the city life," Mama'd told her. "So many opportunities there," she added. "You'd have a finer pick at Aunt Belle's," Mama'd said, and Zeena knew Mama was talking about finding a husband. "They'll be fighting for your affection," Mama added, smiling her even smile and tilting her head. "Not if she don't get some flesh on her," Father interjected from across the room. "She's just a child," Mama reminded him. But try as she did, Zeena did not gain the flesh the other girls carried so easily. Her cheeks did not glow, her eyes did not shine. When she saw her reflection in Mama's looking glass, a stranger peered back at her: What's inside don't show through, she thought.

Father buttered a muffin. He took a swallow of water. Water. Mama'd trained them long ago to drink two glasses of water at every meal. To wash away the bad blood, she'd told them. Water'll keep your teeth strong, she'd said, though it hadn't worked for Zeena; she'd lost half by her twenty-fifth birthday.

"What's Aunt Belle got to say?" Zeena asked.

Father didn't answer. A man need not explain his actions, he'd told her enough times, so Zeena waited. Waiting was something Zeena knew how to do, and the older she'd got, the more patience she had for it. From an early age she'd accompanied Mama whenever she was called for a healing, had sat in many a parlor while Mama tended the sickness in the house, laying her hands on someone's forehead, on a heart, holding to hands when they trembled. The throat distemper, the pox, fevers, pneumonia, there were so many illnesses to heal. "Place your palms like this," Mama'd told her, showing how to rest her hands on the chest when someone's breathing was coming hard. "The Lord'll send the life of your hands into the sickness," she'd explained, and Zeena watched as the breathing slowed. "This's how you'll learn," Mama'd told her. "You watch everything I do, and one day it'll be your hands'll do the healing."

Zeena looked at her hands now. The knuckles were swollen, the skin rough. "Happens faster'n you can blink," Mama'd said when Zeena was a little girl and ran her fingers across her mother's rough skin. It was the only thing about Mama that was rough, though; the rest of her was soft, smooth as velvet. Twenty-eight, Zeena was, and her hands were getting near the age Mama's were when she died. Zeena stared at her palms. Sometimes she thought she might see something different in the lines. Something that would indicate her life was soon to change, that she wouldn't always be Lubin Pierce's spinster daughter.

It pained Zeena to think those words. Spinster daughter. Mama would've turned pale to know it. Mama would've cried for shame.

Mama could've never been a spinster. She had hair the color of pine needles when they turn gold in the autumn, reddish almost, and thick with waves that were bound into a ring around her head. And Mama had eyes blue as the sea, with green specks. A way of laughing that made people want to be close to her. Shoulders that shook when she laughed. Mama loved music; she sang her way through her work, while washing on Monday, ironing on Tuesday, baking on Saturday, all the while singing. Zeena learned all the songs, though she did not have Mama's natural pitch, but she followed Mama's cue and smiled like Mama did while she sang, and laughed when the song was done. Once Aunt Belle sent the money to buy an upright piano, Mama took to playing in the evenings. Zeena learned the notes and they played together. Mama sang the words and Father sat in his chair and read the newspaper and sometimes he looked up, just sat there gazing at Mama like she was an angel. Sometimes Zeena played the notes and Mama pulled Father from his chair and got him to dancing with her. Then he'd be laughing too.

That's when Mama was feeling good.

There were the other times when she couldn't get out of bed. Every year or so, it happened. Another baby, sometimes full grown, sometimes not, but always it came out blue. Days, sometimes weeks, Mama didn't get out of her bed for the sorrow, the pain. It was Father and Zenobia buried the little ones. Father never cried. He kept his back straight. Father stayed away from the house then. He worked past dark while Zeena and Mama waited for him, then he came in on tiptoes after they'd gone to bed. Then Mama would start to crying. "Oh Lubin," Zeena'd hear her moan, and then words, words Zeena couldn't decipher, a flood of words. Zeena took breakfast up on a tray in the mornings; Mama's eyes were puffed and her skin didn't glow. Sometimes Mama didn't eat all day. "Please, Mama," Zeena'd say, "just a bite," and Mama would pick at something with a fork. Then one day Mama would be in the kitchen again when Zeena woke. That was the sign it was over. Mama was back to life.

Until the last one, the last baby—it was a boy baby, Zeena was told—they went together. Zeena was just nine years old when she stood at the side of Mama's bed and tried out her healing hands. Mama's face was smooth as slate. Her hands were still as darkness. The baby lay in the crook of Mama's arm, wrapped tight in a piece of ivory linen, eyes closed tight. The last light of the September day remained in the room, a fairy light. "Hold on, Mama," she spoke.

"That won't do no good, Zenobia," Father's voice came behind her.

Zeena looked at Father. There was something unfamiliar in his face. The dark eyes looked straight through her, straight through Mama, to somewhere Zeena couldn't fathom. His arms hung at his sides like cut branches.

"They're gone, both of 'em," came his words.

Zeena climbed up onto the bed. She placed her palms over Mama's eyes and pressed, like she'd seen Mama do. She made sounds like Mama did, an outletting of small breaths. She moved her palms over Mama's forehead, then down to her heart; she'd work there, just like Mama. "Feel for the beat and place your hand here, like this," Mama'd told her. But Zeena couldn't find Mama's heartbeat. Her hands went to Mama's neck. "Breathe, Mama," she whispered, like she'd heard Mama whisper, but the words came out garbled, more like a lot of crying.

Zeena felt something rise into her throat. Mama, she heard in her head, you didn't teach me good enough. Her hands wanted to close around the neck. A shivering started in her chest that moved down her arms. Her eyes clouded. She couldn't hold her hands still. Her fingers turned jumpy as they worked at the neck, curling, digging into the flesh.

"Get down from there," Father said, his voice like grass, wavering. He stood at the window now, staring out at the dim gray sky.

Zeena's fingers clung, curled still. Baby didn't move, never gave a cry, though Zeena thought to slap it. She reached for Baby, wrapped so still in Mama's arm. She pictured Baby's face turning side to side if she hit it, first with the back of her hand to the right, then with her palm to the left.

"I said get down from there," came Father's words, more insistent now as he turned and came to the bed and thrust out a hand to pull on Zeena's shoulder and then to push her away, off the bed, so she fell loudly to the floor. When Zeena stood, her hands hung in the air like two curls of bark, small and shaking. The shivering was all through her now. Her hands kept up their twitching. She couldn't think, for it. Had she done it, smacked Baby's face?

The sun had died. Zeena and Father stood in the dark for long seconds. Zeena waited for Father to say something, to accuse her of failure, or worse, of an unforgivable violence, but he only stood there, his breath coming hard, as he stared at the figures on the bed. Then, "Go on, now," he growled at her.

"But—" the word quivered from Zeena. She was not sure she could take a step for the trembling that shook her.

"I said get out," and Father shoved Zeena toward the door.

In the dark Zeena stumbled her way to her room over the kitchen where she now slept. She didn't want to feel the cool evening air on her naked skin, but Mama'd always told her it was unclean to sleep in the clothes one'd worn all day so she undressed, shivering wildly. She placed her lace-up boots at the foot of her bed and laid her calico dress, her bloomers, her black stockings, her flannel undershirt, and petticoat across the chest by the window. She pulled on her nightdress, struggling to get her shaking arms into the sleeves without tearing the seams. She wrapped herself in her quilt. She listened to the silence of the house. In her mind was the music from Mama's piano. Mama's voice sang in her head. Zeena's fingers danced in the darkness, curling round Mama's neck. She'd wanted to bring Mama back, wanted her hands to do it, but they'd failed. Or had they done what she'd not meant them to do? She couldn't be sure.

In the morning Zeena woke to rain and the sound of Father's hammer pounding out in the shed. It was still dark. She twisted up in her quilt until a gray light covered everything. She dressed quickly, then went into the kitchen to find the stove cold. Baby's box lay on the floor by the stove; Zeena bent to touch it, ran a hand over the splintered, roughly planed edges. Zeena felt tears way behind her eyes, somewhere in her head, all mixed up with the thing that made her slap the top of the box, whack, like it was Baby's head.

When the hammering stopped, Zeena knew Mama's box was finished. She heard Father struggling with it out in the shed. Zeena had built a fire; the cookstove gave off a glow of heat now, but she couldn't stop shivering, not that day when Aunt Martha Pierce came to do the laying out and packed ice around Mama and Baby so they could be viewed by the relatives and friends who filled the house, not the next when the relatives thinned out and the friends went home, nor any of the days that followed Mama's and Baby's burials when it was just Father and Zeena, the way it was going to be from then on. Zeena went over and over what'd happened in her mind. The music kept playing. Mama's voice kept singing. Zeena's fingers couldn't stop curling. Could she have made Mama go? Or Baby? Maybe it was Baby, Baby who took Mama. But Father never said so. Father never said anything. Zeena looked in his face for blame, but saw only a begrudging.

Nights, Zeena felt Mama's absence. She pulled the quilt over her head and stuffed a corner of the pillow into her mouth; the sobs twisted her into contortions. Mama's voice kept singing, but her face was gone. Her arms, her body wrapped around

Zeena when the cold worked too hard at her, they were gone. Zeena wanted the truth. Why had Mama left her?

Only once in the night did she call his name. "Father," a weak little cry at first, so she mustered all there was in her to call again, "Father," and this time it screamed into the air, shattering the dry and icy silence that filled the night, so loud she knew he'd have heard, knew he'd have come if it was before Mama went, but now Mama was gone and he didn't come.

He didn't come.

Father said nothing the next morning, though he looked at her through slits of eyes as he sat in the rocker by the cookstove and stared at nothing until he went to work, the wide black crepe band around his hat the only outward sign of his grief. Sitting in the rocking chair became his practice. Mornings, it was the sound of the rocker Zeena listened to as she readied herself for school, wearing the black-buttoned gray serge mourning dress Aunt Martha'd given her on the day of the funeral, the dress she would wear for months to come. Sometimes Father's eyes were damp; if she caught his glance he'd snap, "What're you looking at?" Other times those eyes were dry as stones. It made Zeena's throat sore to see those dry eyes. But if his were dry, so would hers be. By squinting she could keep her eyes dry for long periods.

Nights, he kept the paper on his lap and smoked his pipe, but he didn't read it. There was that creaking of the rocker back and forth through the evening. "You get yourself to bed now," he'd tell Zeena, looking above her, past her, anywhere but at her. Zeena didn't answer. She just rose from her place at the kitchen table where she did her reading and figuring, and hurried to her room. Those were the moments when she replayed the night Mama died, when she heard Mama singing in her ear, "Hush now, Zenobia," but there was no one there, there was no Mama to cling to.

Father finally spoke one morning at breakfast as Zeena stirred the cornmeal mush on the cookstove: "You're young yet to take over in the kitchen."

"Not so young." Maybe if Zeena could do it, Father'd forgive her for whatever it was had happened.

"A girl can't do the work of a woman."

"I can," she said.

Father blinked. His whole face turned suddenly soft. "Maybe you'll grow into it," he offered.

It was the only kindness Father had given her since before Mama died. Maybe if she could do everything like Mama, Father would be himself again. Young as she was, Zeena thought she could do it. She would wear Mama's aprons, do Mama's mending and cooking, make soap and candles like Mama.

But her hands. As she stared at her hands, turned them over, looked at the small knuckles, at the tender white of her palms, she wondered: Would her hands ever be as good as Mama's?

THE LETTER FROM AUNT BELLE lay folded on the table by Father's water glass. Zeena tried again, "Is Aunt Belle coming to visit?"

Father reached for one, then a second, piece of applesauce cake. "You know how to bake," he said. He wiped his mouth and leaned back in his chair. From his vest pocket, he withdrew his pipe and a folded-up tobacco pouch. He laid them on the table.

Zeena acknowledged the compliment with a nod. He'd told her so before, but it meant little to Zeena for whom the healings she'd worked were the only part of her life worthy of praise. When she was called, Father usually quipped, "A woman shouldn't be off looking after other people's troubles." When she returned, he never asked how it'd gone, sometimes after days of tending, sitting by someone's bedside. Never said, I heard you brought so-and-so back, days later when word got round. A man, she figured, could no more understand a woman's heart than he could know his own. It was odd, she sometimes thought, that both men and women used their hands to survive; but a man's, his hands went to the practical, to what can be seen, while a woman's went to the spirit and the body, where life lay.

Zeena was credited with numerous healings. In the last year alone she'd saved the Dalton twins when they were born so small they wouldn't barely suckle. She got milk in them by dampening a square of flannel and letting them suck on it, and she showed Minny Dalton how to get her milk going by drinking water in great quantities. And Lillian Harrison, down with a chest cold after birthing a son, Zeena kept fried onions and molasses on the stove for her round the clock and rubbed chicken oil and camphor on her chest till it nearly burned the skin, and Lillian recovered and her son was growing strong.

Father sighed. He rubbed his forehead. Then he took up the letter, unfolded it, and began to read it again.

Zeena watched Father's eyes as they perused both pages of the letter. "Will you be wanting tea?" she asked.

Father shook his head. He cleared his throat. "Cousin Beatrice's taken sick," he said.

"Who?" Zeena knew this was what Father'd read in the letter.

"Your Mama's Cousin Beatrice, what married that fellow Frome who died a couple years back, up to Starkfield."

Zeena had never met them. "How'd he die?"

"Damn fool," Father said. "How a man gets hisself kicked in the head by his own horse."

Zeena waited. The way to learn the most from Father was to say as little as possible. But Father was fidgeting for words, so she asked, "Who tended him?"

"Young Frome. Now he's trying to look after his mother and take care of the farm and the mill. He's got his hands full."

Zeena's eyes squinted as she listened.

"It's too much trouble for one fella. Ol' man Frome, he got to giving away his money 'fore he died so he left 'em nothing but debts. Maybe he took to the spirits too freely in the end."

"Farming's no way to get by," Zeena said, wondering herself how it could be that a man would relinquish his responsibilities so deeply.

"There's plenty a woodland, though, and that's timber, and that's dollars. If young Frome could only get to it."

Why'n't he leave the farm? Sell the property and take his mother away from that place and try a new life, Zeena wondered. So many folks were doing it, up and leaving the hard country life. She liked the idea of a new life. She dreamed of moving south to Springfield and living with Aunt Belle, the closest thing to Mama. There was nothing to hold her in Bettsbridge. But in Springfield a person up and coming like herself'd find opportunities. In Springfield there were other healers, experts. Zeena could work with them and learn.

"You'd best go there," Father said.

Zeena's breath caught. Her eyebrows raised. "Where?"

Father reached for the pipe. "Your mind troubles me, Zenobia." He fingered the pipe, then opened the sack of tobacco. "We're talking 'bout the young Frome fella, his mother ailing."

Zeena lifted her shoulders.

Father went on. "Belle thinks you should go there and stay till the woman's on the mend, or whatever's coming."

Zeena grimaced. Starkfield? Starkfield was farther up in the hills even than Bettsbridge. A world cut off. The opposite direction from that which pulled at her. No fineries in Starkfield. Didn't see as how ready-made clothes'd be in the women's apparel store, if there even was such a store. No opportunities. Course, if she went, then maybe Aunt Belle'd invite her to Springfield to stay awhile. She'd want to hear everything, every single detail.

"There's no money for doctoring," Father added.

Zeena had seen mean living, plenty of it in Bettsbridge. Just last month she'd tended the Strout family out on the Ridge Road, the children all down with typhoid, and no one'd set foot anywhere near the place. Zeena stayed for six days in conditions she found distasteful: unfamiliar odors, no oil for the lamp, food likely to turn her stomach. But she rose above these unpleasantries; she wished to lift the family out of its spare existence, at least restore it to health. The mother, collapsed from exhaustion and starting the fever herself, came close to going. Zeena lost the baby, though. Nothing could be done there. She was limp as a rag when Zeena arrived. No fluids, and that's hard to bring back in an infant and the mother's breasts dry.

"Belle says Cousin Beatrice can't get herself out a bed no more. The rheumatism has her down bad. And her heart's weak."

It was hard for Zeena to turn her back on suffering. Where there was discomfort, Zeena wanted to go. It filled her with satisfaction to watch someone return to the world. But Starkfield, it was so far away, so far in the wrong direction. "How'd I get there?"

"Train don't go to Starkfield. You'd have to go by way a Corbury Junction, then to the Flats. 'Less you took the stage. Belle says a stage goes twice a week till snow comes."

Zeena looked at her hands. She wound her fingers together.

"And that young Frome, he's just one, and no wife. Been tending his mother too long."

Zeena looked up into Father's eyes. "That what Aunt Belle says?"

"It's what I say."

"And what're you meaning?"

"I'm meaning nothing, 'cept you're a spinster and—"

Zeena slapped the table. "For the land's sake—" she started.

"Young Frome, he's got hisself quite a place, Belle says, if he could just get it straightened round."

Zeena folded her arms. She wasn't soft enough, she knew, didn't let a man think she was helpless so as to get him puffed up with the idea of his greatness over her. That's what it took, it seemed. She'd seen the way it was with a man and his girl; she had to be fearful of things, had to chatter when she was nervous, had to giggle at his wit. And beauty. When Zeena looked in the mirror she saw something altogether different from what a man was after. It was true, the central effect was one of bones: high cheekbones, bones poking through the flannel covering her shoulders, and arms and legs that were thin as cattails.

"I'll go for Cousin Beatrice, that's all."

Father pushed his chair back. "Stubborn, is what you are."

"I'm a healer, is what I am, I'm not meant for—" but she stopped. To speak so honestly was to risk hearing something unbidden.

"You're a spinster, is what you are." Father stared directly at her, his eyes darkening. "Your mama'd likely turn in her grave if she knew what you'd come to. You'd best not try to be a healer like her. She was a gold piece, and there ain't many a them in this world. Always put others before her own self, and what good'd it do her in the end? She couldn't heal herself, now could she? I used to tell her, take care of your own, but she didn't listen. You'd best learn from it. And you'd best get used to it: You're a spinster who could do some good by helping out a cousin with an ailing mother. That's enough for you."

Zeena felt a flush deep in her neck, rising. The shame, she was thinking. It's a good thing Mama's gone all these years. What a shame I'd ha' been to her. But she lifted her chin. She drew in a breath. If she could bring Cousin Beatrice back, then sure as spring comes, folks'd know she was a healer just like Mama.

It'd make Mama's heart proud.

And Father, she'd show him. She'd bring Cousin Beatrice to her feet again and feel no sorrow that the son paid her no mind, never even give her a glance.

T W O

*I*t was nearly dark when Zeena got her first glimpse of Starkfield. The sky was pink and gold above the line of hills that rose up around the town. The silhouette of a single steeple and narrow peristyle on the far side of town speared the pink sky. A dozen or so buildings lined both sides of the town's center. Frame houses spread off to the east and west in the valley; smoke spiraled from the chimneys of every structure, sending gray swirls against the evening sky. The arching limbs of the town's elms gave the scene an elegance, along with the regal lines of a row of Norway spruces in front of one house. In the day's last light, October's last colors still shone, firelike.

Zeena saw the beauty, but she did not feel it. Instead there was a slight irritation. There's nothing here, is what she was thinking as she listened to the wheels of the stage on the rutted road. She was picturing the spring thaw and its accompanying mud. Leastways I won't be here then, she knew. A thread of pity ran through her mind. She could guess at folks's dread now that autumn was just past full color. Winter's round the corner. How many times on the stage ride had she calculated the weeks to come? Two, three weeks till snow'd fly. Five, maybe six weeks was as long as she'd stay, she'd already decided, though Father'd said she should stay as long as it took to ease young Frome's troubles.

"I won't be staying once the snow comes," she had told him again at the last moment.

Father shook his head. "Give it the time it requires," was his response.

Zeena didn't wave to Father as the coach veered off around the corner and headed northwest to Starkfield. A man's back is nothing to wave at, she thought, as she watched his steps toward home.

It was like that with Father, had been since Mama died, these nineteen years. It was shortly after the burial that Aunt Belle had taken her aside and told her Father's heart was ailing with the sorrow of losing his wife and that Zeena should be patient. "Men carry their sorrows different than we do," she'd explained. "They don't ask for comfort. But they recover quick." There was no single moment when Zeena realized Aunt Belle was wrong and that Father's sorrow was to be a way of life. Gradually she just came to know he would not return to his former ways. Without Mama there to temper his moods, he sank into his sorrow like a body diving into dark waters with no wish to come up for air. Zeena came to know that any show of feeling might bring Father down.

Zeena soon prided herself on imitating him. If he can keep to himself, so can I, she often told herself as she lifted her chin, a motion that gave strength to her heart. If he was hardened to her, she would harden to him. She was used to waiting and would exercise her stubbornness in this way: She'd wait him out.

Now, when Zeena stood before the general store in Starkfield where the stage had left her, she squinted through the rising darkness at the road that led up into the hills beyond town and at the buildings that rose all around her. She stood beside her valise that held her own belongings, and the satchel she'd filled that morning with her preserves, jars of tomatoes, a meat pie, her best anadama bread, fresh applesauce, and even an apple-sauce cake. She lifted her chin and quelled the question that lurked in her mind: What if Cousin Ethan don't come? It was odd enough, Zeena knew, for a woman to travel alone, as she'd done. Odd, too, for an unmarried woman to wait on a darken-ing road for a man she'd never met to come take her to his home. We're cousins, she reminded herself. Distant cousins.

But what if he don't come?

Zeena's hands went to her back. The fingers worked at her spine and around her hip where the pain was. The stage ride had been interminable; the journey up through the hills had been little more than jouncings and jolts. The woods, endlessly dense, formed a tunnel through which the stage rattled until they came out to the fields and open country outside of town. Now a nag-ging ache nestled in her back and edged down her leg.

"Some people lose their health early," Mama's long-ago words echoed in Zeena's mind, "and there's nothing worse'n that." It sent Zeena's mind to jitters. Did a failing spine constitute a loss of health? She couldn't be sure if it was enough to warrant the sort of attention she gave the folks who called her with their ailments. Certainly she was no invalid. Zeena remembered vis-iting one young woman with Mama; her joints were swollen up, her limbs deformed. She could no longer walk, no longer breathe without effort; yet she never complained. "Bless you," she wheezed to Mama's hands as they worked on her.

"Crippled," was Mama's word. "I can't do much for her. Her will's diminished. Six children, and she can't care for a one."

Even the memory of Mama's words caused a pain in Zeena's chest. She knew Mama's great sorrow had been the fact she'd lost her babies, all but Zeena, her first. "You're Mama's faith," Father had told her in those years when the babies kept dying. Zeena knew it was meant to please her, but it didn't. It left her with a wide emptiness around her heart, an emptiness that twitched whenever it came to her attention that Mama could've had live babies, maybe if Zeena's birthing hadn't been such a trial.

"You started your life with pain," Mama had once told Zeena. "Lord knows you was ready to greet the world. But the cord was a snake 'round your neck. The midwife, she worked in there like she was kneading bread to free you. Wasn't much left of me by the time you first breathed air." The question came to Zeena now: The pain of my birthing, was it hers or mine?

ZEENA DID NOT EVEN HEAR THE WHEELS, groggy in the road's ruts, as a wagon came up beside her. The driver must have recognized the solemn reverie that held Zeena's stare fixed on the last streak of red along the horizon line. He quieted the sorrel: "Hold on there, Fly," he muttered low.

It was only seconds before Zeena exclaimed, "How long you been gawking at me?"

"I—" The man, a dark shadow, fumbled for words. "I weren't, I—"

Zeena squinted in the near darkness at him, couldn't make anything out except his shoulders were broad as an ox's. And he was light on his feet, slipping from his place in the wagon to the ground like a dancer. "I'm beholden." His large hands reached out and took one of hers. "You're nearly froze," he said.

It wasn't that cold. Certainly not the sort of cold that lurked in the hills, waiting for the days to grow dark in the late afternoon. But Zeena's hands were trembling; her fingers were icy. She withdrew them from his and rubbed them, palms together.

"I didn't mean to leave you waiting," he offered.

"I'm used to waiting," Zeena answered him.

A silence settled as sudden as dusk can come. Zeena bent to pick up her belongings.

He reached for them too.

"I can manage," Zeena said, but he'd already taken them in his own hands as if they were feather-light.

He stared at her then. "You're mighty thin, I thought you'd—" and he paused.

"Must ha' been the ride through the hills."

He chuckled. "You're Cousin Zenobia Pierce."

Zeena half smiled. "Which means you're Cousin Ethan Frome."

His shoulders pulled back. "Well," he said, his face turning serious.

"It's going dark."

He tilted his head. "Fly'll get us home. She knows the way," he said, placing Zeena's belongings in the wagon and then offering her a hand to climb up to the seat.

Zeena held on to his arm, not his hand. As she shifted up to the seat, something clutched in her back. She gasped, supported herself with a stiff arm.

He stared up at her, his eyes shadowed beneath his cap. "What is it?"

Zeena rubbed her hip. "It's nothing," she returned, swallowing the pain.

"Is it, is it something I done?" His voice was soft. "I didn't mean—"

"You didn't," she insisted. "Something just cranked up in my spine."

He waited.

So patient, it was befuddling to Zeena. "We going to just set here?" She breathed, in, out, purposeful, while her fingers worked at her hip.

Still he waited, speechless.

"Your mother, we don't want to leave her too long."

They rode past the Congregational Church then; the road dipped down a sharp incline that took them out of town. Then up into the hills, along a ridge. To the left was a steep sloping hill; an elm stood partway down, with one hooked arm jutting out. It was just dark now, but a clear, star-pierced sky stretched above them, and the moon, a day past full, was white as cream.

The lights of the town faded, then disappeared. Through some woods, another tunnel. Past a farmhouse, then another long stretch along another ridge.

Beside her, Ethan Frome breathed evenly, deeply. He held loosely to the reins. Once, he let go one hand. That hand waved in the air as if to encompass all that surrounded them. "These hills," he said, and paused, as if to say more.

Zeena waited, but no more words came. Yet his feeling, the heart behind the words, was plain: Ethan Frome was moved by the sight of the hills, the sky stretching above them, the line of trees along the ridge. Zeena looked away; she did not want to be part of a display she could not understand. 'Sides, her back was bothering. She gripped her hip as the wagon jolted on its way. She wondered just how far up into "these hills" they were going.

"Just ahead," Ethan said, as they veered off onto a hemlock-lined lane at the foot of a sloping hillside.

"I don't see more'n black," Zeena returned. There was no shape, even, that Zeena could make out to be a roof, a barn, a chimney. No light guiding them to a warm kitchen. No scent of woodsmoke in the air.

In the silver light Zeena recognized the scraggy lines of a row of larches, and then they passed through an open gate. To the right and on a rising knoll was a small fenced-in cemetery. The grass grew tall around the iron fence, but inside the ground was well kept. Marble stones leaned at all angles as they gleamed white and gray in the light. Zeena glanced at Ethan, but he did not look that way. In Bettsbridge, Mama was in a cemetery in the churchyard. Zeena visited her often enough, had gone there just the day before, but even after all the years, it pained her to see the delicate marble, mottled now, and all that soft moss covering the ground. It saddened Zeena to see what was left of Mama: those straight letters spelling out her name, Althea Ann Pierce, and the two hands carved above her name to show she was a healer.

Ethan pointed up the sloping ground. "Just ahead," he said again.

Shortly Zeena saw it, the sharp lines of a farmhouse roof, the looming shape of a barn to the right.

"I'll be getting to the ell come spring," Ethan said under his breath.

Even in the darkness Zeena could see the gap between the house and the barn; the ell was a farm's heart, some said, besides serving its practical purposes. To Zeena, though, with or without the ell, it was a lonely spot. The few elms that graced the lane would give beauty to the scene in daylight, she hoped. The apple orchard at the north end of the farmhouse would give it a homey look. The arms of a stand of tall pines rose up behind the house along the ridge; these at least'd offer protection against the wind.

But the isolation. Zeena shivered at the thought of living here. She pitied Cousin Beatrice, these many years alone with her husband and her son. What company would two men be? Farm life was taxing, as anyone knew. Work in the woods, hauling timber, was there anything harder? Today young folk were flocking to the mill towns for steady work and the chance to start up their own businesses; families were migrating west to towns where opportunities abounded, where a man's work was done at the end of the day and he could linger over a pipe and a newspaper, where a woman's work was eased by the latest inventions. She'd heard there was a newfangled machine to replace the washing stick and boiling water, the slow process of putting clothes through a wringer.

Here in the hills outside Starkfield, there was wind and cold and . . . desperation, is how she saw it. A body could spend her life in the kitchen of such a farmhouse, never to see more'n that. A body could suffer pains and never find a cure. A body could be born, live, and die, and no one'd take notice. A simple stone would mark that life. But who would care?

Who would care?

THREE

$\mathcal{Z}$eena stood in the dark kitchen while Ethan fumbled with an oil lamp. "Hold on," he was saying, "I'll get this going in just, in just—" when the wick ignited and filled the room with a sudden glow. Ethan pushed the lamp to the center of the table. He turned and faced Zeena.

Zeena worked loose the buttons on her cape. She felt Ethan's eyes on her, but she did not look at him until she'd finished with the buttons and had slipped her hat off, had stuck her hat pin back in the hat, and then had run a hand over the top of her hair to smooth the loose strands in place. One hand went to her hip, underneath her cape, as she met his dark blue-eyed stare.

Ethan stood tall but stooped; his sloping shoulders showed weariness. His trousers were ill-fitting and worn; a pillow could fit in there alongside the man, Zeena mused. His large hands hung at his sides, a helplessness in the curling fingers. Zeena had expected a youthful vigor, an optimism almost foolish, as she saw in those young men she watched from a distance in Bettsbridge, young men who sauntered when they walked, assuming luck would always bless them.

There was about Ethan Frome something different, an air of uncertainty, as if to take a step or speak a word might undo something. He reminded her of an animal kept too long caged, an animal accustomed to deprivation. Father was like this. His cage was the lonesomeness of losing Mama so many years ago. Other men, they found a new wife, and another, if the second one succumbed. But Father, he stayed in his cage. His sister Martha tried to bring him out until she saw it was no good.

But Zeena saw in Ethan Frome a willingness born of need. This was a man who wanted something but feared the asking. And what's to be done with a man who can't speak his wants? she wondered.

Ethan's face flushed. His eyes were watery-dark when he spoke with deliberate care. "You come a long way," he said, and his hand made an arc in the air. "And you don't even know us."

Zeena stared at him, startled by his forthrightness. She smoothed the folds of her brown merino skirt.

"Like I said in town, I'm beholden to you for coming so far, and I, I—" Ethan's eyes searched the air around Zeena's head, wandered to the ceiling.

Dimly Zeena noticed the room. There were all the things one'd expect to find in a farm kitchen, but the room felt bare, neglected. Behind Ethan and pushed up between the two windows was the table, uncovered and scarred with knife marks, with four chairs, two on either side, pushed in close. A beaten-up pine dresser stood against the wall next to a metal-lined wood sink. There was no hand pump; water had to be carried in. There were none of the signs of a working kitchen; no milk jug by the sink, no breadboard, no jars of jam and honey, no butter churn. The sleeping gray cat in the rocker gave the room its only show of life. "Puss," Ethan introduced. The cookstove dominated the room with its promise of heat and food, but the nickel trim was rusted through and grimy. Beside it the wood-box was nearly empty. "Whyn't I get this stove going," and she moved toward it as she slipped off her cape.

Ethan reached out an arm, held one of hers. "I'll do that," he stopped her.

"I can—"

"Course you can, but—" Ethan's eyes sparked. "I'm telling you," and he paused, still holding to Zeena's arm, despite her effort to pull away, "I'm telling you," and again he paused, then drew in a breath so he could plunge in with the words, "it won't be easy." He released her arm, then, and the flush deepened.

Zeena held her arm, backed off.

"I'm saying, it won't be easy."

Zeena looked around the room. Her eyes landed back on Ethan's shoulders. "It never is."

"But," and he stopped.

Zeena waited.

"Being here, looking after her," and Ethan's head cocked to the side, in the direction of the rest of the house. "And what with winter coming—"

"I won't be staying the winter," Zeena announced.

Ethan sighed. He turned to the cookstove, opened the vent, and scraped at the coals with a poker. Zeena stood tall. "I come to do a healing."

Ethan turned. He blinked, several times.

"That's why Aunt Belle sent me," Zeena said, recalling the letter. Would he understand that she was a spinster because of her calling? That she wasn't just come to do housework, to relieve him of his responsibilities to his mother?

He swallowed. "I, I didn't—"

Zeena held her hands in the air, palms up. "I can do it with these hands," she whispered, realizing as she spoke that this was the reason she'd come. This was where her life had taken her. Some folks never got to such moments; they lived without knowing their purpose. But Zeena felt God's calling her to this point in time. This was the answer to the years of wondering: Why'd Mama go so young? Was it so Zeena'd take over where Mama left off? This healing, it wasn't just to spite Father, she knew now. It was more'n that. Out here in this lonely land sickness can go deep. "I mean to bring her back," she voiced.

Ethan was silent. He gazed at Zeena with eyes nearly black. "What is it that's ailing her?"

Ethan shook his head. He looked up at the ceiling. Then his gaze came to rest on Zeena's hair. "There's the rheumatism."

"Enough to cripple?"

Ethan shook his head. "It's no worse'n it's always been, but a couple years now, she's just—"

"Her heart, is that it?"

Ethan's brow furrowed. "She's gone queer," and he tapped his finger to his temple, "is what some folks say."

"And what do you say?"

Ethan's eyes wandered around the room. "I say her heart's broke." And he sighed, and Zeena sensed relief, perhaps in the speaking of what'd been bottled up too long.

The fire in the cookstove caught; a low roar started. "What, what—" and she paused, realizing she'd taken on his nervous habit of repeating words. "What broke it?" she inquired, folding her arms. If he could get to the point, so could she.

Ethan opened the damper; the roar of the fire increased. He swallowed. "Like I said, it's not easy living on the ridge, so far out of town, and then Pa going like he did, so sudden, it was like the breath was drove out of her, and she's been getting worse every day so some days she just stares and stares but it's like there's nothing behind her eyes, and—"

Zeena waited. He seemed to be on a speaking spree.

"A man shouldn't tend to his mother like I'm doing," and he was shaking his head and looking at the floor.

"Like I said, I come to do a healing."

Ethan took a deep breath. He pulled off his cap and rubbed his head. She guessed he was trying to smile.

She felt a flush go into her cheeks. "I mean to bring her back," she offered, lifting her chin. "Can I see her?"

The smile left his face.

"I mean to bring her back," she repeated.

Ethan stepped to the cookstove. He reached for a candle from the shelf and lit it. He looked at the cookstove, sighed, then turned and said, "This's the way," as he led Zeena out the kitchen and through the dark front passage and on into the parlor.

ETHAN NEARLY TRIPPED ON A PILLOW as he stepped into the room beyond the parlor. The parlor was unheated and held the night's cold, but this room, a tiny space backed up to the center chimney, held some heat from a small woodstove, though Zeena still considered it too cool for comfort. A birthing room, is what Zeena guessed it to be. Where Ethan'd been born and where his mother now lay.

A stale, rank odor was in the air. Zeena couldn't place it. It was more than a lack of cleanliness.

Ethan held the lamp over the bed. A mussed flannel sheet was all that was there. He sighed with irritation. Holding the candle higher, he sent the flame's glow across the room.

Zeena heard an intake of breath before she recognized the shape of a woman hunched on a chair by the dresser, her knees drawn up, a bedcover wrapped around her like a shawl, covering even her head.

Zeena glanced quickly at Ethan. His face held a look of embarrassment.

Under the blanket, a hand came up to the face that peered out. The back of the hand rested on the mouth.

"Ma, you'll take a chill," Ethan spoke. He still held the candle in the air as if he couldn't think of what else to do with his arm.

Zeena bent onto one knee at the woodstove. She waited a

moment, gave her spine a chance to adjust. Then she opened
the door and scratched at the coals. A small pile of kindling lay
in a box. Zeena tossed the kindling in. She was about to ask
Ethan to get some wood in when a sigh came from the figure on
the chair and a finger poked at the air.

"Ma, I told you she was coming, it's Cousin Zenobia Pierce,
from—"

The finger wobbled in the air.

Zeena looked from Ethan to his mother.

"Ma," and Ethan approached his mother now. "You get yourself all twisted up when you sit here. It's not, it's not—"

Zeena noted Ethan's tone. Weariness is what she heard.

The finger pointed at Zeena.

"She come to help us, she come—"

A sudden weeping began then. Gentle weeping, and Ethan
looked at the ceiling, "Ma, don't," but the weeping drew in the
body, loosening the bedcovers from round her shoulders and ex-
posing a graying flannel nightdress pinned at the neck.

"Is she ailing someplace?" Zeena asked, standing. She stared
at the woman, at her gray hair, the slender neck, the wisps of
hair escaping from a days-old braid. Her hands were tiny as
seashells where they twisted in the air. And the smell . . .

Ethan placed a hand on his mother's head. He looked at
Zeena with helplessness.

Zeena smiled. She'd seen women in such a state. She knew
what to do.

"Go right along out and get some wood in," she spoke. It was
not a request, but an order. Ethan turned as if with relief. Zeena
held to his arm. "Don't you fret," she whispered. "I'm here to do
for her now." She smiled at him, and he nodded and stepped
briskly from the room. Zeena slipped onto her knee. "Cousin
Beatrice, I'm Althea's daughter, you remember Mama, don't
you? She's been gone these nineteen years, but you remember
her, don't you?" Cousin Beatrice set in to weeping again. "You
need a woman's care," Zeena told her. She reached for one of

Cousin Beatrice's tiny hands. It was rough and dry and cold. Zeena began to rub the hand between hers. She bent to breathe on the hand, but Cousin Beatrice withdrew it from Zeena's grip. She gazed at Zeena out of a pasty white face with eyes like dark moons, glistening.

"Won't you say something, Cousin Beatrice? It's no good to swallow your words," she said. Zeena reached for the other hand, but Cousin Beatrice just pulled it away.

"Because I'm listening," came a croaky whisper.

"You're what?"

The mouth closed again into a line.

Zeena placed both hands on Cousin Beatrice's shoulders. "You're near froze," she said. "Ethan's getting wood and I'm—"

"Don't you be—" A hand came from nowhere to scrape at Zeena's face from her brow to her chin.

Zeena cried out as she backed away.

"What's—?" came Ethan's voice as the door opened.

Zeena held her hands to the stinging on her face. She heard a thunking, knew Ethan'd dropped the wood in the woodbox. His hands were at her face now, pulling her hands away so he could see, and there was Cousin Beatrice's weeping, almost like laughter, and a kerchief was dabbing at her face, and she tried to pull away, but Ethan's arm held her. "I, I don't know what she was thinking," Ethan said. Up close his face showed lines of worry. His eyes were soft, comforting.

"It were nothing," Zeena said.

Ethan's head shook side to side as he let go her arm.

The weeping continued, pale and hopeless.

Zeena backed to the door and leaned against its frame. Her back was paining again, little stabs in the bones.

Ethan was sighing, over and over.

Zeena held the kerchief to her cheek. She dabbed at the eye that wouldn't stop tearing. "Well," she said, and then repeated it, "well," and then she took a deep breath. "It's too much for her tonight," she offered. "Tomorrow," she said, "in the light of day, she won't mind me so."

Ethan's eyes were pools of helplessness. His mouth opened and closed several times, as if he might speak.

"You'd best get this fire going," Zeena said. "I'll see to the cookstove and get some supper heated. I brought a meat pie. You think she'll eat meat pie?"

Ethan shook his head. "Some warm milk's what she likes. And biscuits to dip in the milk. There's some in the . . . or maybe those're gone," and his voice trailed off.

Cousin Beatrice's weeping had turned to soundless crying. Her shoulders shook. She held her hand to her lips still.

Zeena backed out of the room. She pulled the door to behind her and paused to listen for a moment. There were no voices, though, no words between them. Just the sound of wood being stuffed in the woodstove and the hinge on the woodstove door and then the sound of feet on the floor, Ethan's, she already knew them, carrying his mother back to bed.

FOUR

Zeena had a pan of milk warming on the stove and two slices of bread on a plate for Cousin Beatrice when Ethan came into the kitchen. The meat pie was heating in the oven, and two plates were warming on the shelf over the cookstove. She stood at the sink, the kerchief dampened, and held it against the stinging scrape on her face.

Ethan stepped over to the dresser, rested a hand on its surface. Zeena passed him on her way to the stove. She stirred the milk with a wooden spoon. She sensed his eyes on her back.

"I—" came from behind her.

Zeena waited. The scratch on her cheek was throbbing. Her eye was tearing still. Her heart was going fast. It was hard to think.

"I—" came again.

She stirred the milk.

"I'm awful sorry," he began. "It's what I was sayin'."

Zeena spoke without turning. "I don't think I can judge on

tonight's behavior," she said. "She was nearly froze, for one thing."

Ethan didn't answer.

" 'Sides, she don't know me from Adam."

Still no answer.

"She said one thing," Zeena started as she turned. " 'Because I'm listening,' she said, but—"

Ethan was nodding. "She's waiting."

"Waiting?"

"Out on the porch. She used to sit out there when the rheumatism got too much for her. She'd wait for folks to pass by." Ethan stood with his hands at his sides. "She was a sociable sort, never tired a seeing folks." He shook his head. His hair was fluffed up on one side. He kept blinking, his eyes going open, then shut, then open. "I'll just tend to the animals," he whispered. Seeing the expression on Zeena's face, he added, "The cows. They'll be waiting."

"Yes, I s'pose," Zeena returned, then turned back to the cookstove. She heard the door close, then another door outside. She moved the pot of milk to the side, dipped the ladle into the water bin, and took it to the basin in the sink. She soaked the kerchief in the water and held it to her cheek. A small square of looking glass rested on a shelf above the sink. In the dim light Zeena gazed at her face. There were the same dark eyes, narrowed as they squinted in the glass. One was tearing. She lifted the cloth away from her skin and peered at the purplish scrape on her cheek. I'm a sight, she thought.

"Time for the lard," Mama'd always said when she saw Zeena with a scratch or cut. The one and only time Zeena defended herself against being called Bones as a child had got her a nasty scrape right along this same cheek. "You must rise above it," Mama'd said. "Hold your head high and no one can break your spirit." "But Mama—" Zeena started. Mama interrupted her with, "And don't you never whimper over such foolishness. In your life there'll be many things to cry over. Save your crying."

It's just a scrape, Zeena decided. Won't hardly show in a day or so. She rinsed out the kerchief and hung it on the towel rack over the stove. Zeena found a tin of lard in the cupboard. She dipped a finger in and rubbed it into her cheek.

She pictured Cousin Beatrice, small as she was, dressed in her apron and tending the cookstove as she must ha' done day in and day out when she was young and running the kitchen. Biscuits cooling, a stew simmering, pickles and beans and beets and tomatoes and pears put up in jars from the summer waiting on the table. In the evening, sewing and tatting and crocheting and piecework, whatever mending needed doing. Nothing but work, dawn to dark. A woman shouldn't trouble herself so; everyone knew her constitution didn't lend itself to such labors, day in and day out. She needed hired help if she was to preserve her health. But here in the hills where life was the meanest she knew, there was no help.

Cousin Beatrice had spent her life in this kitchen. Zeena gazed around the room. The low ceiling gave it a cramped feeling. The horsehair plaster was puckered and chipped in places; the paint was faded gray. The floor was covered with patches of oilcloth, all of them dirt-streaked. The stain on the chairs was worn clear through; the legs were scraped up. Such uncleanliness did damage to the spirit as well as the body. The kitchen was grimy, untended, but not so badly that Zeena believed it was Cousin Beatrice's way of things. This was a woman's world gone sour.

A man's comb lay on the shelf beside the looking glass. She picked it up. Unclean, like everything else. She imagined Ethan trying to tend his mother, keep the house clean, do the cooking, and work at the mill. It weren't possible for a man to do all this. Everything's half done.

Zeena sighed. She loosened her hair and placed her hairpins on the table. She ran her fingers through her hair. She'd begun wearing a pug when she was in high school and hadn't changed it since. Except at her graduation when she'd tried something special, a long plait, wound round the back of her head, like Mama wore. The other girls snickered at her and she knew the reason; her hair was too thin to stay plaited.

From her valise she retrieved her brush, part of the set that had been Mama's and her mother's before her. Zeena went to the looking glass. She leaned against the sink. The discomfort in her back tired her. She'd heard about a new treatment, a salve that worked to rejuvenate the joints. Now she wished she'd taken the time to get some before she'd come up here. In the spring Aunt Belle'd sent her a tonic guaranteed to ease the rheumatism and ailing joints. She'd finished that in July with little results, though she'd visited several women in the summer and tried it out on them; one woman gained quick relief and was returned to her household duties within days. Another was bedridden for weeks; her daughters, though young, managed things for her. Zeena gave her liniment rubs and worked spruce gum into her skin, applied hot stones wrapped in wet towels, but she only got worse. Her husband had to hire help finally.

Zeena ran the brush through her hair. One, two, three strokes, she counted. When she was a girl, it was a ritual for Mama to brush it. Eleven, twelve, thirteen. Thin as her hair was, Mama tended it like she had the thick locks that made a girl pretty. Zeena closed her eyes. She felt the pull of the bristles through her hair. Twenty-one, twenty-two, twenty-three. Every night, last thing before Mama tucked her in, Zeena sat on Mama's lap and counted while Mama stroked. All the way up to fifty, then Mama took over the counting.

Zeena guessed Ethan was right about his mother. A heart broke, he'd said. It can make a person's mind twist up, so what was white became black and what was new became old. The whistling of wind through the trees could sound like your own crying, and an apple tree, with its limbs like lace against the sky and its back bent like a cripple, could be your mother leaving you alone to face the night.

Zeena heard a cough. Abruptly she left off with her brushing and turned. Ethan was standing by the cookstove.

Zeena's heart started in to pounding. "I didn't hear you come in," she said as she placed the brush back in her valise, pulled her hair back, and wound it into a pug as she stepped past Ethan to the table where she'd left her hairpins.

Ethan coughed into his hands. "I'll take care of the milk," he said, cocking his head in the direction of the jug that rested on the floor by the door.

Zeena recovered once her hair was in place. "I'll just get the food together," she said, as she rummaged through the drawer for some cutlery. "Will you fetch your mother for supper?"

Ethan blinked. "She don't like to come in here," he said, and coughed again.

Zeena stood, forks in hand, and stared at Ethan. "You mean for supper?"

He nodded, then shook his head. "Any time."

"What're you saying?"

"She likes her room, is all."

"She stays there all the time?"

"These days," he nodded.

Zeena considered Cousin Beatrice's place in life. To've seen her husband go, to've watched the farm fall to disrepair, why it must ha' broken her heart as much as anything. "I suppose she don't want for sociability, not with doing so poorly."

Ethan drew in a breath. "Like I said, it's—"

"It's not easy," Zeena finished for him, nodding. "Course anybody knows it's no good to hole up too long, it can twist a mind like that," and she snapped her fingers. "Maybe that's what made her . . . queer, like they say."

Ethan's mouth went into a line. He stood there, his shoulders lifted. "Maybe."

"It's a shame." Zeena waited, but he didn't seem to have anything more to offer. "Must be hard to watch your mother like this. A woman vital with life, and then this."

Ethan bit on his lip. He nodded.

"Don't she speak anymore?"

"It's like folks say, she's gone queer, she don't know much," he answered.

"You sure?"

Ethan stared back with questioning eyes.

"I'd guess she knows plenty. Clammed up in that room, how's anybody going to get better?" Zeena reached for the tray that hung on the wall by the sink. She held it out straight. "Here, then," she said, smoothing her skirt with the other hand. In the morning, she thought, she'd figure out what was best. She'd bathe Cousin Beatrice, get her up and dressed. It does a woman no good to hole up.

Ethan carried the tray with his mother's supper out of the room. Zeena watched as he balanced the tray so he could pull shut the door behind him. So careful, he was, trying to keep from spilling the milk and close the door quickly so the cold air wouldn't get in. On his face was an intent look, as if, if he put all his concentration into this small task, the other things might fade away.

BY THE TIME THEY SAT DOWN TO SUPPER Zeena was feeling quite tired. The long hours in the stage, the ride out of town with her spine bothering, Ethan's trouble over finding words, and Cousin Beatrice's outburst had all left her tired and short-tempered. Ethan helped himself to the food Zeena'd placed before him; she watched as he stuffed forkfuls of meat pie and spoonfuls of applesauce and hunks of anadama bread into his mouth. The spareness of the room combined with Ethan's unmannered table habits took away her appetite. At home Father always served the main dish while Zeena dished up the stewed fruit and vegetables, and then they waited for a minute or two before they started in to eating, just so they could appreciate the fare before them. It'd been Mama's habit to treat meals as such, with thanks to God for his generosity; her habit had stuck through all the years, though Father'd left off the prayer soon as Mama died.

Here there was only the sound of Ethan's fork clinking against the cracked and mended china plates, of his spoon dipping at the applesauce. There was the sound of water pouring into an empty glass, of swallowings, and the thunk of a glass on the table. And there was the occasional clearing of a throat.

Zeena finally spooned some applesauce into a saucer. She took a taste; it was warm, just to her liking. Father'd turned it away once when it was too hot, didn't even want it on his plate. It spoiled the taste, he'd told her; after that she made sure it didn't get overly warm.

Ethan used his fork to spear several pickles onto his plate.

Finally Zeena spoke: "You're surely hungry."

Ethan's spoon paused in the air, a piece of piecrust balanced. "I was thinking this'd last more'n the one supper."

Ethan's spoon clanked against the plate. He met Zeena's stare.

Zeena smoothed a hand over her hair. "It's just, I thought as how I wouldn't have to do no kitchen work tomorrow if I was going to spend my time getting settled in."

Ethan took a swallow of water. "I just—" and stopped. His face flushed with embarrassment.

Zeena shook her head as she spread a modest bit of butter on her bread. She sighed. "I shouldn't've spoke, it were—" but she stopped. Mean of me, is what was on her lips. "I'm all wore out," she offered. She passed him the plate of bread. "Food's meant for eating, course."

Ethan leaned back in his chair. "Your spine, s'it still cranked up?" He ran his napkin across his lips.

"No more'n usual."

Ethan stared at her, a look of expectancy on his face.

"It comes on when I overdo," she explained, then shook her head. "But won't you take this last slice a pie?"

He shook his head. "It's been two years since this table saw so much good food, 'cept when someone from town come out to give a hand."

"Have folks from town been a good help to you, then?"

Ethan fumbled his napkin into a roll and placed it on the table. "I wouldn't say that. Folks don't have time to spare these days, everyone just gettin' by and all, but there's been one or two come out regular to see to us."

"Oh?" Zeena waited, but Ethan offered no more. "Here, then, finish up this pie."

"I'm full up now."

"I should've held my tongue."

"I had my fill," he said, shaking his head. He reached into a pocket for a toothpick and thrust it in his mouth.

"I brung a cake. Apple."

He shook his head. He pulled a pipe from his shirt pocket and a tobacco pouch, then started from his chair. "I'll get us some tea," he said.

Zeena finished her applesauce. She emptied her glass of water, pausing between swallows. She sighed. She'd learned to hold in her temper around Father; his was always bigger and demanded expression and it'd become easier to listen to him than to speak her irritation and go unnoticed. It was comfortable almost, this unequal balance. Least, it was what she was used to. Ethan was a compliant sort, she guessed. She didn't imagine he'd express his displeasure or his ill will or his suffering or anything. "I'm awful tired," she said, as if to explain her surliness.

She knew Ethan was watching her, even as he brought the teapot, steaming, to the table. Zeena kept her eyes on her plate. "Two years," she mused. "That how long since your mother took sick?"

"It's four years since Pa died," Ethan returned, his voice turning ropy as he held his pipe to his lips, unlit.

There was a startling amount of feeling in those words. Zeena knew it was unlike him to speak so frankly.

"Four years this last May."

Zeena looked up as Ethan withdrew his pipe. A mournfulness was in his blue eyes, dark almost to black in the lamplight that flickered in his face. "How'd it happen?" she asked, though she knew the story; everyone in the family knew the story.

Ethan looked around the room. He held the pipe cradled in the palm of one hand. "That sorrel, Fly, what brought us home," he started, staring at Zeena. "She's temperamental. He never understood her like I did." He shook his head side to side, keeping his eyes on Zeena. "Ma found him in the field. His head'd been butted good. The sorrel was standing there beside him, though. She's temperamental, but she's loyal."

Zeena watched Ethan's hands, the way one held to the pipe with a tremble pulling at it, while the other held to the table's edge.

"One of her shoes was bad. He must ha' tried to fix it. And like I said, she was temperamental."

Zeena noticed the way Ethan's eyes were starting to look through her. She'd seen such gazes before.

"Just lying there in the field," he went on, "the sun beating down like it does. Fly, just standing there." Ethan's gaze turned fuzzy. "Ma got him back to the house, but he wasn't the same after that. I come home, then, from Florida."

"Florida?" She knew he'd been away but hadn't heard where. So many folks went west; she'd heard nothing of Florida.

"I was doing some engineering work, I—"

Zeena interrupted again, "Florida?"

Ethan's eyes focused on her. "I took a year's course in Worcester at a—"

"Worcester? Why, Mama was from Worcester."

Ethan nodded. A brightness came into his eyes. "I studied at the technological college."

"You went to the technological college? I never heard about that." It took more'n money to get to college, Zeena thought. It took a smart mind and ample determination.

"I was meaning to get away."

"Away?"

Ethan's hand, the one holding the pipe, swept a circle in the air, encompassing the room and everything beyond it.

"You'd have left here?"

Ethan sank into some darkness then. He blinked several times, then his eyes went to the window. He rubbed his thumb against the pipe's bowl while he stared, fuzzy eyed, at the window. Twice he opened his mouth, twice closed it.

Zeena waited. It settled on her, then, what had happened. How he'd had to give up his plans once his father died. How his mother took ill, how he struggled under his father's debts. He wasn't clear yet, is how Father'd put it.

But Ethan'd had his chance; he'd been to a technological college, he'd been away, he had a paying position. A body could do it, could actually do it.

Ethan had dreams, she realized. He saw the opportunities that lay beyond these hills, like she did. Like her, he must've felt stifled by the lack of society here in Starkfield. Even Bettsbridge would be too small for him, she guessed. It wasn't enough to live in your ancestors' shoes anymore. Doing what they did, living how they lived, day in and day out . . . it didn't get a body anywhere new. Besides, farming, everyone knew farming kept you always just a little behind and that could wear on a body.

If Ethan'd done it once, though, couldn't he do it again?

Zeena thought about the Frome cemetery. To be buried there, to live with the knowledge of that as your fate, it turned her stomach. It wouldn't happen to her! It couldn't!

Zeena wanted to tell Ethan her dream of going to Springfield where Aunt Belle lived, where there was all the latest in patent medicines. Electricalization, for instance. She'd heard what it could do, had her hopes to try it, but in Bettsbridge she was sure folks'd shy from it. They weren't willing to see possibilities. In Springfield she could do more healings. Folks'd look up to her. In Springfield the importance of cleanliness was understood. Bathing, for instance; folks who kept their health bathed daily in cold water to keep their minds fresh. And everyone knew, least they should know, of the many threats to a woman's well-being. Their weak constitutions made them prey to illness. Their generative organs needed tending through the body and the mind.

It was why she had to bring Ethan's mother back. If she could go to Springfield with this new healing to her credit, why, there's no telling what direction her life might go. Folks'd know her for what she was, a healer of the sick. "It's my hands," she'd tell them. And they'd gaze at her admiringly.

Zeena felt an entirely new hope. Coming to Starkfield wasn't a step away from what she wanted, it was taking her right where she wanted to go. No more would she have to settle for the life she'd been born to. Other folks were doing it. Other folks were getting to the cities and living better. In Starkfield, even in a town small as Bettsbridge, there wasn't enough to go round. It left folks looking hard at one another. One man's plenty was another's want. In the cities there was enough for everyone. Folks could be generous hearted because they had what they wanted. In the city Zeena could be somebody.

"WHERE'D YOU GET THE IDEA to go to technological school?" Zeena asked as she sipped at her tea. Her mind was racing. She was imagining herself telling Aunt Belle all about Cousin Ethan, how he'd done so much and then was cut down. She was picturing Ethan at the college, Ethan turning his back on country ways and facing the possibilities life'd bring him if he could only get away.

Ethan leaned back in his chair. "I seen a science magazine. Lawyer Varnum in town, he had it and loaned me it."

"But all the way to Worcester, why—"

"So many folks're going off. From Starkfield, most of the younger folks're gone. All what we hear of the city, how there's opportunities, lots of 'em, for everybody, it's true. Engineers, there's a call for 'em wherever there's new roads and buildings. Towns're growing, spreading like weeds." Ethan tapped his pipe against the bowl Zeena'd brought him. He reached into his tobacco pouch and filled the pipe again. "I wanted to see what I could do," he said.

Zeena studied Ethan Frome. A large young man, he filled his chair and then some. His hair, all mussed, gave him a rumpled look. Sometimes in his face was a look that said his eyes and nose and mouth didn't go together, like something was off-kilter. And there was a heaviness about him, as if it'd be hard to move those limbs and get himself going. His shoulders slumped, hiding the breadth of his chest. But there was something else there too, an energy that, if tapped, would bring those off-kiltered features and those slumped shoulders to life.

"Pa, he wanted I should stay and keep the place up. Said the mill'd turn vital again if we'd wait it out." The shoulders slumped even farther. He drew on his pipe and exhaled slowly, watching the smoke.

"Your ma, what'd she say?"

Ethan ran a hand underneath a suspender and kept it there, his thumb playing at the suspender. "She said I should do what suited me."

"A good mother puts her son's wishes first, I guess."

Ethan turned to stare at the darkened window over the sink. "Maybe. She didn't take to this life, though, specially not after things changed. Pa, he was born in that room where she's laying, in that same bed. How far'd he ever go? Into town." His gaze turned melancholic so Zeena asked, "College, what was it like?" A bitter half smile came to Ethan's face. He shook his head. "There's things to learn you can't even guess."

"What kind of things?"

Ethan's eyes widened as he leaned forward. "This world as we know now, it's turning on its heels. Every day somebody's figuring a better way to do something." His blue eyes brightened. "There's machines to wash your clothes now, machines to do your drudgery. And roads, they're going everyplace you can think."

"That what you studied?"

Ethan nodded. He took another swallow of tea.

Zeena went to the cookstove where her applesauce cake was warming; she sliced it up and brought it to the table. "Maybe now you'll have room for some cake."

Zeena reached for a piece and took a bite. Again, she pushed the cake in his direction. Ethan shook his head.

His troubles, they planted a sorry soft place in her chest. His sorrow, she felt it in her heart. His flattened hope, it lodged there too. She couldn't think of a body she felt more sorry for. Even all the folks that'd called her with all their suffering, it didn't amount to the mean life Ethan had.

"I'm sorry for all your troubles," she told him. Ethan, he needed her as much as Cousin Beatrice did. She would do what she could. First, she'd bring Cousin Beatrice back. And Ethan, maybe she'd bring him back too.

She looked at her hands. Was there healing enough for two?

FIVE

fter blowing out the candle that night Zeena stood in the dark to undress. It was a clear night; the moon's cold silver brightness touched everything in the room. Once in bed, she heard noises in Ethan's room, as if he was adjusting the furniture, pulling open drawers, walking about. The *clink* of his door handle sounded at one point, and then she heard his footsteps on the stairs. To the backhouse? She heard him return some time later, listened to his slow and ponderous steps on the stairs. A glow of light from his room crept under her door. How long was it until that glow died out? What was he doing, up and about in the night?

At home Zeena slept in the little room over the kitchen; her father was at the front of the house. It gave her the feeling the night was hers. Here, it was distracting to be so aware of someone else, so even after the night was quiet, she lay awake, straining for sounds.

In the dark Zeena remembered what Ethan'd said at the supper table about Florida. Days and days it took just to get there.

It made Zeena's head spin. She'd heard of strange fevers in the warmer climes, of beetles larger than'd fit in a cupped palm, of snakes crawling through open windows to send their poison into some poor soul's throat. But the idea of it, a place so far away, it got Zeena's veins tingling.

Ethan's face came to her. His eyes, troubled in their gaze, registered in her mind. They were an unusual color, not light blue, not bright blue. They were dark blue, dark as a midnight sky, and when they settled into an inward gaze instead of out at the world, they turned almost black. His burdens hung on his shoulders then like a winter cape.

He had too many troubles these last years. Too much responsibility for one man, and a man so sensitive to life's requirements. A body could stay alive while the soul oozed out through the exhalation of a breath if it wasn't allowed to do its calling. Or the body could fade while the soul kept up its yearnings. Either way would be no better'n death. "Leastways your mama went quick. She didn't suffer and linger," Aunt Martha Pierce had said on the day last spring when Mama would've celebrated a birthday.

Zeena knew it now as she'd not known it before: Aunt Martha was only partly right. True, Mama didn't linger; she went quick as the dying light of an oil lamp. But Mama suffered. Her whole life was suffering. When she left Worcester and went to Bettsbridge to be the wife of an ice cutter, she opened herself to a life of suffering. Zeena'd never wondered if Mama ever regretted her choice. But maybe the reason Mama always talked about Zeena going to Springfield was because she didn't want Zeena to end up like herself.

Zeena shuddered: Was she twisting up? Is that what these ailments meant? Were her days numbered, like Mama's? If a spirit was yearning to fly and wasn't allowed to, might the spine shrivel up? There was also the worry about her generative organs. Did spinsters become twisted and cranked if they didn't use their bodies as they were intended?

The pain started in her spine then. A stab of pain, it worked into a full-fledged throbbing. At least her mind could settle then. All she could think on was the pain. There was relief in that, a familiarity.

At some point Zeena fell into a restless sleep, exhausted from tossing to get comfortable. But she woke several times to the throbbing in her spine; she imagined she heard sounds from Cousin Beatrice's room below her. Not a scream or a cry, just a low and gentle whimpering. In the dark Zeena heard Mama's voice instructing her, "You place your hands like this," and Zeena imagined her hands resting on Cousin Beatrice's head, "and then let your fingers glide down over the eyes, like this."

As she practiced the healing of Cousin Beatrice, her own discomfort diminished until finally she fell into a sound sleep.

ZEENA WOKE JUST BEFORE DAWN. She listened to the sounds of the new morning. Chickadees, blue jays, nuthatches, singing for their food. At home she kept a feeder all year long by the kitchen window so she could watch the birds as they collected the seed and suet she left for them. Their singing was an antidote to the long stretch of dark winter days.

When she opened her eyes, Zeena saw pale splashes of color at the window; the last golds and yellows against the early morning gray sky. She closed her eyes again. Some said October was the finest month of the year, but Zeena saw it only in terms of what lay ahead: winter. October's blazes seemed a mean trick. The warmth of the colors, those reds and oranges and yellows, was just meant to taunt her.

The air, it was already cold. Draw in a breath and the cold fingered your lungs. October was a month of teasing.

How many years ago was it she'd tended Nettie Marston on just such an October day? A day whose colors sent false hope through those who waited and prayed for Nettie's life. Nettie was twenty-two, in labor with her first child. "It happens this way," the doctor told Daniel, Nettie's husband, who stood rigid with fear by the door in the kitchen. "The baby's too big and Nettie's small as a peanut," the doctor said as he handed Zeena the necessary surgical instruments. Daniel went to the window, gazed out at an expanse of autumn color as if such sorrowful news could not exist against the backdrop of such beauty. Nettie's screams had echoed through the house since the previous evening, but now, as the second night of labor approached, they were growing weaker; it was just a low sorry moan that came to them. Three other women were there to hold her down along with Zeena when the doctor took the knife to Nettie's belly. Surely there was a better way than to fill a birthing woman with whiskey so you could cut a baby out, Zeena thought, as she watched the writhing body sink into a stupor. When the baby's cries pierced the air, Zeena kept her eyes on Nettie's face, drained white as flour paste. The baby lived—a miracle, folks said later—but Nettie's life faded fast as Zeena held the cleaned and newly wrapped infant in Nettie's arm and coaxed her, "Hold on now, Nettie, this baby needs you." Later Nettie's mother insisted it was the finest way for a woman to go. "She gave herself to her one true purpose," she told Zeena only days after the burial.

That's what an October day'll do, Zeena thought, as the gray eased from the sky, replaced by pale blue. It would be a beautiful day, but she would take no pleasure from it. No sense in giving in to such trickery.

NOW IT WAS MORNING and Zeena looked out the window at the sloping land. She could see the road Ethan'd followed the night before; it weaved along the ridge and down into the valley past the lane to the Frome house. There was the cemetery they'd passed. The sun's new rays clipped the tops of the gravestones. There was more comfort in sun-tipped stones than the mounds of snow that rose in the winter, Zeena told herself.

She listened for sounds, but the house was quiet. She removed her brown knitted shawl, laid it across the back of the chair. Then she pulled off her flannel nightdress and stood naked on the oilcloth by the washstand. She filled the washbowl with water. After dumping the water from the glass that held her teeth into the slop bowl, she poured in fresh water, so they'd soak while she washed. Her skin crinkled at the touch of the cold washcloth. Shivers rippled through her as she rubbed the cloth on her shoulders, under her arms, across her belly. She soaped the cloth and scrubbed her neck, her breasts, her arms. She hated the cold water on her skin but took comfort in knowing she would rid herself of the unhealthy night airs that'd collected on her skin while she slept.

Zeena held the cloth to the scrape on her face; she kept it like that until she was shivering with cold, trembling.

Quickly Zeena slipped in her teeth, then reached for her camisole, her flannel drawers, her black wool stockings, then pulled on her black calico wrapper. She laced up her shoes as she looked around the room at the narrow bed, the pine dresser, the chest at the foot of the bed, and the washstand. There was not one decoration in the room. Not a stitch of embroidery on anything. Certainly there were no curtains; even in Bettsbridge most folks didn't have them, while in Springfield it was the uncommon window that wasn't covered with some finery or other. The walls were whitewashed, leaving a streaked white and gray effect. The meanness of such a life, Zeena thought. Cousin Beatrice'd do better surrounded by beautiful things: lace and polished oak and wallpaper and carpets on the floor, and all the new labor-saving machines. Why, if she could leave here, if Cousin Beatrice could be taken away from all this, maybe she'd find her hold on life returned to her.

Zeena unpacked her valise then. She hung her other flannel wrapper on a hook. She laid the brown merino, her best skirt, and two flannel shirts on the bed. She'd hang them up later. Her extra set of flannel underclothes she placed in the top drawer of the dresser. Wrapped in a flannel square was her brush set, her hairpins and combs. Zeena brushed her hair, wound it into its usual pug, and stuck a comb in to secure it. She pulled her shawl around her shoulders before opening the door.

At the door she paused. She turned and looked around the room. Gray despair is what she saw. Her hand went to her cheek; she felt the scraped skin and sighed. Cousin Beatrice, she thought, I mean to bring you back.

With this determination she started out the door.

ZEENA FOUND THE COOKSTOVE BLAZING. A pot of corn-meal mush steamed on the back of the stove. A tray with a bowl and a cup without its saucer rested on the table. She went to the looking glass over the sink and pulled it off the shelf. Turning her back to the window she looked at her cheek. In the light of day she could see it wasn't much of a scrape, but she drew out the lard and rubbed a little on her cheek with her fingertip.

Zeena made her way to the backhouse, then returned to the kitchen where she had time only to unwrap the meat pie and slice up some bread before Ethan came in. This morning he was bedraggled: unshaven, his thick hair uncombed, his work clothes wrinkled, his eyes holding that watery darkness.

Zeena waited for him to speak, but he just stood there. "I'll be getting breakfast on the table in a moment," she said. She nodded to the tray. "Will she eat same as us, mush?"

Ethan pulled something from a pocket, a folded piece of paper that he unfolded and flattened in his palm. "I thought I'd—" he started, then stopped.

Zeena noted his eyes, narrowed in some point of concentration, and the cocking of his head, as if listening to something she could not hear. The early morning light from the window lay on his hands; there was a slight trembling there, as his first two fingers continued to smooth the paper.

"What is it, Ethan?"

"Since we talked, I, I thought—" and then he stopped.

Zeena felt an impatience. "Thought what?"

"I thought you'd like—" and now he stepped forward as he smoothed the paper between his palms, "to see this."

Zeena kept hold of the wooden spoon as she turned. "What's this?" she inquired, staring intently at Ethan's face, at the paleness of his skin, the slope of his eyelid, and the way when he looked at her now a liveliness came into his eyes.

Ethan held the paper out so Zeena could see it.

Zeena looked at a picture of a lake, with strange-shaped trees lining one side of the water. A lush growth of flowers, shrubbery, small trees filled in the scene. There were small groups of people clustered here and there, sitting on benches, strolling past the water, everyone dressed in Sunday clothes. An open carriage driven by a man with a cap on his head was in the center of the picture; a man and a woman were seated behind him, the woman holding a parasol to shield her from the sun.

"Florida," Ethan said. He pointed to the dots of flowers. "Hibiscus," he said. "Red, like you'd never imagine."

Zeena kept staring at the picture.

"These're called palm trees," Ethan explained, pointing to the lush branches. "And this's an orange tree."

"An orange tree," Zeena repeated. "Palm trees."

Ethan sucked in his breath. "This's a park. Folks walk in the parks on Sunday afternoons."

"Well," Zeena said, shaking her head.

Ethan nodded. "It's a different life."

"I can see."

Ethan's face lighted up. "It's, it's—" and he looked at the ceiling and then around the room as if searching for the words. "So different." The brightness in his eyes dimmed. "There's no burdens on your mind when you wake up. There's just the day ahead of you."

"Are folks as sickly?"

Ethan's eyebrows raised.

"I heard talk of fevers," Zeena started. "From the heat. Is it so hot?"

Ethan nodded.

"Does it make folks sick?"

"Not that I heard, 'less you stayed in the sun too long."

"There's no snow come winter? No cold?"

Ethan shook his head. His mouth pulled in on one side.

In his dark blue eyes Zeena saw a yearning she was certain was the same as her own. A yearning for that different life. A life far from this place in the hills where suffering was the nature of things. It irked her, that folks'd stay where they were when so many opportunities lay just over the horizon.

"Whyn't you go back there?"

Ethan's eyebrows lifted. He cocked his head.

"You could if you wanted," she said, meaning it kindly.

He shook his head and ran a hand over his forehead, straight on back over the top of his head, ruffling his hair. "It's not that easy."

Zeena stared at him.

"Not that easy, doing what you want."

Zeena felt an impatience building. "A body can do what he wants, he just needs the will to do it." Her spine straightened; her shoulders pulled back.

Ethan shook his head.

"It's a matter of will, s'all," she said.

"And what about Ma?"

"Might do her a world of good to get away from here."

"Take her away from—" and he stopped, swallowed. His eyes wandered around the room and rested on the windowpanes that faced the rising sun.

Zeena followed his gaze. There at the foot of the hill were the tops of the gravestones, gray and glistening in the day's early sunlight.

"From here, yes," she told him. "You said yourself it's been hard for her here."

Ethan shook his head, slowly, side to side.

" 'Sides, you want to go. There's no good in staying when your heart wants to go."

Ethan's head kept shaking, his eyes closed now.

"I won't do it, myself," she voiced. "Won't stay where I don't want to be."

Ethan's eyes opened. His brow wrinkled.

"I got my own plans, you know. I don't intend to stay in Bettsbridge just because I was born to it. There's things better'n that."

"There's reasons for staying. I couldn't take Ma from here without someone to look after her. And there's debts." Ethan's hand crumpled the picture in his fist.

"You work harder when there's debts, you—"

"It's other things too. Things—"

"I know what you told me, it's not easy. But nothing's easy."

"Some things're harder than other things." Ethan's face darkened. "You can't come from Bettsbridge and—"

"You ever been to Bettsbridge?"

"I been to Bettsbridge, course. I been all the way to Florida."

"I can tell you Bettsbridge ain't much different from Starkfield," and she turned back to the stove, plunged the spoon into the mush. "This mush's all dried up, you ought'n to leave it like this when the stove's going so hard, you—"

Ethan was beside her then at the stove. He reached out and lifted a stovecover with one hand. Zeena saw what was coming. She lunged at his arm, but it was too late; the picture was gone, sizzling into nothingness, and Ethan was standing by the stove with hollow, shining eyes and slumped shoulders, his chest heaving, and the cover raised in the air like a flag.

Zeena lifted her chin and sighed.

Ethan shifted from one foot to the other. His mouth was a thin line. He lowered the cover onto the stove hole. "Better add some more milk to that mush," he said. "Ma don't like it hardened up."

"You can't burn that dream, don't you know that? A dream don't burn."

Ethan gazed at her, still breathing heavily. "You going to make some tea? Ma likes her tea in the morning." The sun was streaming into the room now. "She'll be wanting her breakfast," he said.

It was like Father. A man changes the subject and there's no getting him back to it. Zeena lifted her chin. "Where you keep that tea?" she asked, gazing evenly at Ethan Frome. If he could play that game, so could she.

S I X

*T*here would be no more of that, Zeena determined, as she prepared Cousin Beatrice's tray. No more telling the man what to do.

He could take all his dreams and throw them to the wind. He could stand on the hillside and wait for the day when he'd be carried in a box down to that graveyard at the foot of the hill so he could join the rest of his family, the folks who toiled their lives away on this godforsaken hillside—and for what? So a piece of stone carved from marble could mark the passing of life.

Zeena slopped some mush in a bowl and filled the fragile china cup with tea. She bent onto a knee and checked the firebox. The coals were dancing with flame, red hot. She put several pieces of wood into the fire and closed the door, leaving the damper wide open.

How long, she wondered as she rose to her feet, till that stone starts to lean, beaten by wind and cold, the shifting rocks under the soil setting the stone off its skyward-bound course? And then how long till that stone lies flat on the ground?

When Zeena turned with the tray, Ethan was gone from the room. She had not heard the closing door. She sighed. It was time to clear her mind. Time for her real work to begin, she determined, as she slipped her arms through the straps of the full-length muslin apron she'd brought with her. Ethan, wasn't much she could do for him.

Zeena closed her eyes and stood still in an effort to rid her mind of the images in her head. Father, stubborn and melancholic since Mama died, failed to see what was there before him. It showed in the lines of his face, in the sorrowfulness of his eyes. Nineteen years now, Mama was gone. And still he persisted in getting that hurt look on his face when Zeena prepared his dinner and something was not quite right and Zeena knew without Father saying so it was something she'd done different from how Mama did it. When she was a girl, she'd voiced what she knew to be so: What's wrong with what I done? Father, he only became more silent, and the hurt in his face only grew deeper as he stared from behind eyes that were granite cold and a mouth that was stone set. By the time Zeena was full-grown she'd learned not to ask it. Not to say it. And never to complain. A word of complaint only got her Father's silence that much longer.

Ethan Frome was no better. He'd tricked her, is how Zeena saw it. Told her about going to Florida, offered that mournful and weary manner about his life, the sorrow of it all, led her to believe she could speak the truth: Whyn't you leave this place, then? She'd thought she could help him, could open his eyes to the truth, but instead she'd discovered otherwise.

He was happier being melancholic, like Father.

ZEENA WAS STILL FUMING when she placed her hand on the knob of the door to Cousin Beatrice's room. She paused. It was time to leave the fuss over Ethan behind her, time to turn her attention to the task ahead of her. The healing, that's what she was here for.

The room was dark still. Zeena drew a breath, noticed that acrid odor again. She stepped past the woodstove that gave off a mild warmth as she continued over to the window. Outside the window were the unkempt branches of a lilac bush, twisted and scraggly. Through those branches and up on the ridge was a row of pines, their thick branches forming skirts around the base of each tree. When she turned, she again drew in her breath. Cousin Beatrice lay motionless, eyes closed, under a thin quilt that left only her face uncovered, and beside her, on a chair, sat Ethan.

Quickly he rose, his large frame filling the room. He leaned over and whispered something to his mother, then he pulled his cap on. Zeena stiffened as he passed by her on his way to the door. "Jotham Powell, my hired man, he'll be waiting for me at the woodlot. We'll get a load on the sledge by noon," he muttered as he left the room.

"I'll have your dinner ready then," she said, staring at his back.

After a couple of moments, Zeena placed the tray on the pine dresser. She clasped her hands as she approached the bed. She stood there, saying nothing for a few moments, acclimating herself to the woman on the bed. The gray hair was in the same braid; wisps fell around her neck. Closed lids covered her eyes. There was a delicate nose. A small sunken mouth, and yellowish skin.

"Cousin Beatrice," Zeena whispered, remaining standing with her hands clasped.

The eyelids fluttered but did not open.

"I told you last night, I'm Althea's girl, you remember Althea," and again the eyelids fluttered. "I hear you been sickly." This time, no response. "I'd like to help you," Zeena added.

Cousin Beatrice's breathing remained even, shallow, but Zeena was certain she was not sleeping.

"I'm Zenobia." Then, "Won't you open your eyes? I'd like to see your eyes."

The eyes remained closed.

"Mama was a healer, you may recall, and she always asked folks to open their eyes so she could see the pupils. There's a lot to be told by the pupils. That's why I want you should open your eyes, so's I can look at your pupils." Zeena waited. Minutes passed. "Your tea'll be cold by and by."

The eyelids flipped up then, revealing eyes blue as a midnight sky, like Ethan's. Cousin Beatrice stared at the ceiling.

Zeena leaned forward. The pupils were narrow holes. This was a good sign. "Let me help you," she started, reaching under Cousin Beatrice's neck with one hand to lift her head so she could fluff up the pillow. She turned to reach for the cup of tea. Sunlight was now filling the room. Patches of sky could be seen through the untrimmed branches, and it was blue, a blue-jay blue, Aunt Belle used to call it. "That lilac needs trimming," Zeena said, and when she turned, Cousin Beatrice's eyes were on her. "You see the likeness to Mama in me?" she asked, smiling.

Cousin Beatrice did not blink; those dark blue eyes kept up their stare.

"Guess you don't remember Mama; she had that reddish hair and that skin like a pearl, soft and white. I take after Father's side. His mama was tall, like me, but not so thin. Father said I get that from my own stubbornness."

Still the eyes stared, almost blue-black and intense.

"Are you ailing?" Zeena asked, now serious.

No response. Just a shining spirited stare.

Zeena held a teacup to Cousin Beatrice's lips. "This'll get you going," she said, still holding the spoon.

It happened so suddenly, Zeena thought later she'd not even seen it coming. One second she was holding the cup, the next an arm flailed out from under the covers, sent the cup flying, grabbed Zeena's wrist and pulled it to her mouth, and then there was a toothless gnawing grip of jaw on Zeena's hand.

There was strength in the grip and in the jaw, but Zeena yanked away her hand, crying out, and through the cries were Cousin Beatrice's blue-black angry eyes staring at her, staring at her with what no one had ever given her: hatred.

"Now look what you done," Zeena said. "Tea all over everything."

The dark eyes did not soften, but they widened.

"It's in your hair even."

The eyes blinked, then squeezed shut. Tears edged out the corners.

"Your cup's all to smithereens." Zeena held her hand. She rubbed at the soreness of it.

Cousin Beatrice's face turned to the side, away from Zeena. Her arm lay limply on the bedcovers.

"You're testing my patience," Zeena told her, standing back and just staring at her with folded arms. "Some women'd leave about now, leave you to your temper." Cousin Beatrice did not stir. "Some women'd say they wouldn't waste their time on someone's so far gone." Zeena waited. Nothing. This woman was the challenge of a lifetime. If she could bring Cousin Beatrice back, she could do anything. "But I don't believe you're as far gone as you're acting. I tended some like you before. I know what's driving you. You're afraid there's no way round this." She waited a moment or two. Nothing. "You been out here so long you forgot what it is to feel your own spirit calling you back."

Cousin Beatrice's closed eyes flickered, just enough to encourage Zeena to go on. "Happens sometimes. A body lets life pass by simply 'cause it's forgotten what it is to be alive. I think this's your trouble. You let in the devilish thought that it don't matter, living."

Zeena pointed to the bowl of mush on the table by the bed even though Cousin Beatrice's eyes'd remained closed through her speech. "Your breakfast is there. You'd best eat it." She stood holding the door open and looked at Cousin Beatrice's shadowed face. This was a woman left too long alone, too long ailing.

"Don't you go nowhere," Zeena quipped, " 'cause I'll be back. With your bathwater." The eyes flickered open this time. Zeena pulled the door closed behind her.

Zeena stood, listening. There was nothing. No crunching in the horsehair mattress to indicate a shifting on the bed. No scrape of spoon against bowl to signify the consuming of mush. No loud sigh or cough. No quiet crying.

Silence was all there was.

TWO TIMES NOW Zeena'd filled a basin with steaming water and brought it to Cousin Beatrice's room. Two times Cousin Beatrice'd knocked it over, spilling the water onto the mattress and soaking the skirt of Zeena's wrapper. One minute the basin was resting on the table by the bed, and the next Cousin Beatrice was flailing again and the basin was sent to the floor.

This time Zeena moved the chair to the foot of the bed and set the basin on it. Mama'd always said you can't fault a body what was sickly for its uncharitable behavior, but this was different. Zeena believed that Cousin Beatrice was clearer in her mind than Ethan'd said she was. She thought Cousin Beatrice'd been so long alone that she'd lost her manners. She was ornery out of loneliness. It was her spirit was ailing more than anything else. Firm in the words she used, Zeena decided was how she would be. Like throwing water in the face of someone having a temper tantrum, she needed to shock Cousin Beatrice out of it. Beneath the firmness, though, would have to be something else: a kindness that comforts.

Giving Cousin Beatrice a bath was what Zeena was trying. A bath to shake the system but soothe the spirit.

She stood this time with her hands on her hips and said, "I'm going to wash that meanness right away."

Cousin Beatrice turned her steady, spirited gaze on Zeena.

"Else I'll get Ethan to hold you down when he comes home at noontime for his dinner."

Cousin Beatrice blinked several times. Zeena saw water forming in her eyes, tears, as she blinked them away.

"Meanness, it don't get a body anywhere."

The eyes closed. The tears spilled out from under the lids.

"Crying's better'n fighting."

The face turned to the side.

Zeena bent to check the woodstove; she added several chunks of wood to the fire. She opened the damper. The room was warm, but she felt a fluttering in her limbs. Something was moving through her. Something was filling her, words she'd never thought of. "It's no good to be so long alone. A body shrivels up without a chance to speak its heart. It's time for you to come back to the world. Time for you and Ethan to do more'n worry over this house. There's more'n this to live for."

Cousin Beatrice lay still as the sky.

"I'll start with your feet," Zeena announced, sitting on the chair at the end of the bed so she could reach under the bedcovers.

In the moment before she reached for those feet, Zeena's hands trembled. They shook like butterflies on the wing, hovering, but ready to fly at any moment, or to rest if that's what was called for, because this was the moment she'd lived her life for. If she could bathe and rub that orneriness out of Cousin Beatrice's skin, then the rest of her life would set out before her like a high road, clear and clean and passable.

As much as Zeena knew it was the touch of her hands that'd do a healing, she'd held back in her callings up till now. Not that she hadn't touched folks with her hands, hadn't held their aching heads or sponged their tired backs. She'd done all that with her hands and had helped restore their health with it. But this was different. This was reaching beyond the body and into the spirit; this was pulling forth what'd been for some time buried, a will to live, to face the day with a strong heart.

73

It'd been so long since Mama'd gone, taking her healing motherly hands, those hands that were always caressing, always giving Zeena what she needed. For too long Zeena'd felt their absence. How could she heal the spirit and then the body when she needed soothing herself?

Now, though, Zeena felt Mama's hands on hers, guiding, shaping her hands around Cousin Beatrice's tiny feet, feeling that dry and cracked skin. The life that once was in Mama's hands, Zeena felt it in her own. She soaped a rag and sponged the toes. She kept her hands moving, working the feet gently but firmly until she could hardly tell where her skin ended and Cousin Beatrice's began. Wasn't that what Mama'd said? A healing occurs when your own hands melt into the body you're working?

Cousin Beatrice kicked a foot at Zeena. Her heel jerked into Zeena's hip. Her toes prodded Zeena's side. Zeena just took the foot more firmly in her hands and worked at it. Her thumbs dug into the heel's pad and worked up under the arch to the toes, pushing, pushing in at the flesh, working the blood and even the life's will. The tears continued, soundless and steady. The foot tried once more to kick; it yanked almost free of Zeena's grip but she held on and worked the arch again.

Zeena's trembling went into Cousin Beatrice's feet as her fingers pressed and kneaded and worked. Cousin Beatrice's legs started to shake with it. Her body flattened into the mattress. She sighed, long and slow.

Zeena towel-dried the trembling feet. Then she pulled a jar of salve from her apron pocket. She rubbed the salve into the skin on the feet. She worked on the heels, rubbing, kneading, pressing, then along the archs. Each toe was treated.

"You've worked hard all these years," Zeena said, as she worked on the ankles. "So many years a hard work out here in these hills." Her trembling was now all through Cousin Beatrice. Her legs, up into her chest, even her eyelashes were shivering, and there was a pulling in at the corner of the mouth.

"Must seem as if it's all gone to nothing, now you're feeling so poorly and Mr. Frome's gone and Ethan barely keeping up."

The eyelids closed more tightly then. The mouth pulled in tighter at the corner.

But Zeena kept on. Cousin Beatrice needed someone to say out loud what her life'd come to; Zeena could see that clear as she could see the lilac branches twisted at the window. "You probably never imagined you'd end your days here in this little bed, 'stead of cared for proper by your husband. Must ha' been a fright to find him down in the field like that."

Now Cousin Beatrice's mouth quivered. She turned onto her side, her face buried into the pillow. The small shoulders started to shake. Zeena worked on the bottoms of her feet with more salve, and up onto the calves.

"You were from Worcester, like Mama; you probably never imagined you'd be so alone, way out here in these hills, no one to talk to."

Now the whole frame was shaking. But not a whimper was heard, not a whine. Just a steady shaking.

"A woman needs someone to talk to," Zeena said then. "A woman, she's not meant to keep to herself."

The shoulders kept up their shaking. The hands tightened into fists that slid under the pillow.

"Mama, she always said of the two—a man and a woman— a woman's the more sociable. A man, he might be content to live his days by himself, talking to no one but the furniture. A woman, she's likely to turn sour with no more'n a chair to talk to." Zeena worked on the calves, up and down. "A woman needs certain things, Mama always said. She needs to stay clean, so her skin can shine. She don't tolerate dirt the way a man do. And she needs someone to brush her hair every so often. And she needs womenfolk to talk to." Zeena felt the words rising in her, unbidden. "Who else's she going to cry to?" she whispered now. Now Cousin Beatrice's shoulders hunched up. "A woman's got to do her crying, else she's like a vessel overfilled." Now there was a series of deep breaths, slow, even. "You been too long alone," Zeena said softly.

Words were muffled into the pillow then: "T'weren't al'ys so."

T'weren't always so? Was that what she'd said? Zeena bent over closer to the pillow. "What's that?" and she laid a hand on the small of Cousin Beatrice's back. She waited seconds, a minute, but there were no more words. One foot kicked out again; the toes pushed into Zeena's side.

"You don't need to fight me," Zeena said. "I'll surely leave if I can't be no help, but fighting's no good, don't you see?"

Zeena worked on the feet some more. Up under the toes, on the tops of the feet, along the tendons. Back to the heel on one foot, then the other, then around the ankles. The minutes passed as she kept to her task. Soon she realized she was perspiring. She rose from the chair, rinsed out the rag and hung it over the rim of the basin. "It's an oven in here," Zeena said. The stove was pulsing heat into the room. She turned then and looked out the window. The sky had a hazy blue look to it, as if it was steaming. She stepped over to the window and looked out. "Well, I'll be," she said, turning to Cousin Beatrice with a smile. "Why, it's Indian summer."

Cousin Beatrice's eyes opened. Deep dark blue, like Ethan's. Like midnight. And sorrowful, like Ethan's.

But the meanness, Zeena thought. It's let up some.

SEVEN

*Z*eena was smiling. Turning her hands over, looking at the palms, turning them back, looking at her knuckles.

"Hands," she whispered aloud, "you done just right."

She sat in the rocker by the cookstove, waiting. She listened to the creaking of the runners against the bare painted boards and felt a whirling of joy in her chest.

"Hands," she whispered again, "you knew just what to do."

Waiting. All these years, you waited, Zeena mused. Time was I doubted you. I thought Mama'd left me everything for healing but the hands. You stayed in my apron pockets when I wanted you to reach out and go to work. When you did touch, it was without the blood what runs through me. It was bones and flesh and skin working together to be hands, regular hands, though. Not healing hands.

The rocker cranked and creaked, back and forth. Zeena smiled and smiled. It was the closest thing to dancing since Mama died.

"Oh, Mama," Zeena said aloud, the words like rain, "if only you could'a been there."

Zeena held her hands out, palm up. There was heat in the palms, spreading out. She clasped her hands together and held them on her lap as she rocked.

"Thank you, Mama," she whispered.

Zeena smiled and smiled and smiled.

THE HOT SUN CAST A PECULIAR LIGHT on the sloping hillside. Every line was fuzzy. Colors, instead of being clear and distinct, were blurred. The newly golden larches, always the last to turn, were shimmering in the wavery light. Down across the valley a patch of red, some birches, flamed less sharply. The sky was blue, but only barely.

Zeena was eating her dinner by herself when she heard the sounds of a horse's hooves in the lane. She put down her fork and looked out the window. The rider was a girl, sitting sidesaddle on a bay. She rode the horse out of view then, over to the barn, Zeena figured, as she went to the back passage and opened the door to what once had been the ell and was now an open area where Ethan stacked his cordwood. The girl came round the corner of the barn and into the dooryard. Tiny, she was, with thick dark hair pulled back beneath a hat, and wearing a cape, unbuttoned, and tiny feet in black laced boots, and carrying a laden basket. She saw Zeena and waved her arm in greeting.

Zeena did not wave back. After all, she did not know the girl.

"Hello," the girl called, coming closer and stopping, looking all around. "I guess Ethan's at the mill?"

Zeena shook her head. "The woodlot," she said, feeling irked that this girl was looking for Ethan. Girls had a way about them. They flounced and trotted and almost danced when they walked. They kept their eyes looking down but Zeena knew they could tell when a fellow was nearby. Their complexions turned pink and they slid their eyes to the side, coquettishly.

"He's never here this time of day, I thought I'd get a chance," and now she stepped to the door and looked up at Zeena who could see she was more than a girl; she was a young woman, but her diminutive size'd made her look younger. "I mean, I was wanting to meet you, seeing as I'd heard you'd come—"

"You know who I am?"

"You're Ethan's cousin, come to look after Mis' Frome."

"Well, I guess word gets round—"

"Course. Folks knew you were coming." She stared intently at Zeena, taking in Zeena's face and looking down at her apron, her wrapper, even to her shoes. She smiled then, an open, generous smile, not like the silly half smiles, the pretended aloofnesses that most girls gave. "We just didn't know when you'd come, but Zeb, he's our hired hand, he told Mother you come in last evening."

She hadn't even introduced herself. Zeena looked at her coolly. Maybe she wasn't like most girls, but why'd she have to come so quick to see Ethan's cousin? Zeena stood tall in the open doorway and looked down at the girl, arms crossed.

"I known Mis' Frome since I was a child and . . ." She looked back to the sloping fields behind her and the lane. "I come several times each week through the summer to set with her while Ethan was at the mill or while he was felling trees at the wood-lot. She was too sickly to stay alone, though he left her the days I didn't come. Course I'd ha' come every day if I could." She had dark brown eyes, large and soft, like a deer's. "Mother said it weren't proper to come every day, and anyway, I ain't come in a while, not since, since the trees started going to color anyway," and she bent her head to brush at her skirt. Then she stood, blinking her eyes, and held out the basket. "I brought you some things."

"I'm Zenobia Pierce." First things first, Zeena thought.

"Mis' Pierce, I'm pleased to meet you."

"And you are . . . ?"

"Oh, my. I haven't said," and she shook her head. "Mother says I'm not well mannered enough, but it's just I forget . . ." and her mouth went into a thin line. Then, "I'm Rebekah. Rebekah Varnum. And I hope you'll call me Rebekah, no need to put on airs here."

At that Zeena stepped back and left room for the girl to come up the steps and into the kitchen. She came slowly, not with the energy Zeena associated with a woman so young, and set the basket by the sink and lifted off the cover. "Some breads and mincemeat and squash," she said, undoing the tie of her hat. "It's not much, but I thought it might help in your first days not to tend to cooking." She took off her bonnet and smiled again, that same generous smile. Most folks were more guarded than this. "And I want to hear everything 'bout Mis' Frome."

"She's coming along," Zeena said.

Rebekah nodded. "I weren't sure. In July she was turning worse. Cranky, and she'd never in her life been cranky. She seemed, well, how's she taking to your being here?"

"Why d'you ask?"

"Seemed like she didn't want anyone but Ethan to care for her."

"No?"

"And Ethan, it was hard for him to watch her. He takes it so hard."

"It's hard to know, him being so quiet."

Rebekah looked at her distantly with eyebrows raised.

Zeena took a chance and asked, "Ethan, he always have so much trouble saying what he means?"

Rebekah's eyes turned serious and sad. "Who's to know what he means," she answered. "He's been tongue-tied long as I known him. Which is why I come out here. I don't want you thinking everyone in Starkfield's as tongue-tied as him and Mis' Frome."

"No," Zeena said, "no, I can see that now."

"You won't be alone here. You need a hand, you tell Jotham Powell and word'll get to me." She leaned closer. "It's a hard life out here on this ridge. Mother says it's not fit for any woman," and she sighed as her eyes roamed round the room, "why, he don't even have running water in the kitchen, and Father says he doesn't see how Ethan can get the place straightened round."

Were the girl's eyes tearing? Zeena saw she was a compassionate soul.

"Ethan, he's done it alone too long and it's a pity, just a pity—"

"You know him well."

Rebekah drew up her shoulders. "You get to know everyone in a small town, least what's on the outside."

"Last summer, you must ha'—"

"I come after he'd gone to the mill. I hardly saw him."

Zeena nodded.

"Mis' Frome, she still so bad off?"

"I mean to bring her back," she said.

Rebekah was silent a moment, staring into Zeena's eyes. Then, slowly, she said, "I believe you will."

Zeena raised her eyebrows. "Oh?"

"I see it in your eyes."

"It may take some doing, but I mean to do it."

"You have a strong will."

Zeena folded her arms and leaned back then and listened to Rebekah talk about Cousin Beatrice, how she'd looked after Rebekah's mother after her lying-in times, how her father'd relied on the Fromes for wood, how Cousin Beatrice'd helped out when her brothers had the scarlet fever. "They both of 'em went with it, but Mis' Frome, she was kinder to Mother than anyone. She understood what it was to lose two sons, is what Mother says, and she's been beholden to her since then." Rebekah's voice was willowy. Her eyes reminded Zeena of Mama's, though Mama's eyes'd been blue and this girl's were dark almost as wet earth. But Zeena had the sense that, like Mama, the girl was not one to pass judgment, and it set Zeena at ease.

*　　*　　*

THE WAGON MAKING ITS WAY up the lane could be seen from where Zeena sat in the rocker. The creaking stopped. He was just at the larches. Rebekah'd left half an hour ago. Zeena'd watched her go, down along the lane and up onto the ridge and then into the woods. "Don't bother Ethan about my coming. I don't want him thinking he owes me a thing." Zeena nodded; she could see as how Ethan'd fret over other folks fretting over him. "He forgets what his family done for mine. I'm just returning what he's already give."

Zeena started to rocking again. Ethan was an hour late for dinner. She'd already taken a tray in to Cousin Beatrice. She'd covered the tray with the only clean dish towel she could find. Applesauce, bread, and warm tea filled the tray, which she left on the chair, saying, "I'll leave this here, lessen you want me to help you with it." After dinner she would see if it had been touched. She had other plans for after dinner that she would speak to Ethan about.

Ethan's dinner was on the table. A single place was set for him. She'd searched for a clean piece of oilcloth to spread on the table but had found none. His was the same fare as his mother's, only more. Biscuits, the last of the meat pie, stewed tomatoes, pickles. All of it brought from home, the jars wrapped in newspapers and stuffed in the satchel.

Zeena watched the wagon make its way up toward the house, the particular creak of its wheels already a familiar sound. It was loaded with unsplit lengths of firewood. The wagon passed under the elms and then disappeared. Zeena felt an irritation. She would have to ask him to help her with Cousin Beatrice and didn't relish the thought. She remained seated, her fingers weaving together, until she heard Ethan's step outside the kitchen door.

The girl, Zeena couldn't help but think of her that way, Rebekah Varnum, she'd let Zeena know that Ethan was a proud man. Rebekah seemed to accept that as part of Ethan's character, but Zeena found it annoying. "If he needs help, he should have the good grace to ask for it," Zeena'd told her. Rebekah shook her head. "But he won't," she insisted. "If you mean to help him, you'll have to do it without his knowing." Zeena thanked her for the advice but admitted she wasn't sure she'd be able to follow it. She was about to inquire how Rebekah'd managed to help out last summer when the girl asked to see Cousin Beatrice. They went together to the room. Cousin Beatrice kept her face turned from Rebekah and her eyes closed. Rebekah patted her shoulder. "You're in good hands," she said. "Mis' Pierce here, she means only to help you." It was a generous statement, Zeena thought, and she asked the girl to call her Zeena as they returned to the kitchen. "We'll be friends, then," Rebekah said, solemnly. Zeena'd never had a friend and felt some discomfort at such proclaimed intimacy, but she nodded.

Ethan pulled on the rim of his cap as he came in the room, a gesture for her benefit, she knew, but he did not look at her as he shuffled in and removed the cap, revealing a dampened head of hair, slicked down, and a stained wet neck. Zeena stepped aside as he made his way to the kitchen sink, leaving the whiff of fresh-cut wood and perspiration in the air. His concentrated gaze stayed on the floor as if he had to watch where he was stepping, but Zeena knew he was avoiding her eyes. She also knew she'd surely die than be the first to speak, so as he filled a basin, she uncovered the foods on the table and busied herself adjusting the placement of bowls, the plate, the glass.

Zeena could not quell her curiosity. She glanced over to the sink. Ethan's suspenders hung from his hips and he was pulling off his overshirt. He gave a quick look in Zeena's direction. She leaned over the table to refold his napkin. When he bent over the basin, Zeena looked back at him. His broad shoulders were to her; she could see the muscles moving beneath his union suit, tightening, extending, as he slathered soapy water over the back of his neck, ran his hands through his hair, soaped his forearms. He cupped the water in his hands, leaned down, and washed his face.

He kept at it so long, Zeena finally coughed. How could a man make such a production of washing up? At the same time, she could not look away for the fascination she felt. Father, the only man she'd ever watched as he washed up, he had a rigidity to him; when he washed, it was with a jerkiness of movement. Ethan was different. His shoulders moved easily; his muscles tightened and loosened effortlessly. His hands had a surprising dexterity.

But as Ethan stood, he fumbled with a towel. He bundled his shirt into a ball and laid it by the sink, adjusted his suspenders, and ran his hands back through his hair. When he turned, his face was flushed, his hair, wet. His hands brushed at his chest, then he held them at his hips, somewhat awkwardly, as he approached the table. His brow wrinkled when he saw the food on the table. His head cocked to one side. "This all for me?"

"I et at noon, when you said you'd be here." She said nothing of Rebekah's visit, as the girl had asked.

Ethan said nothing. He pulled out his chair and sat down. He looked at the meat pie, the dish of stewed tomatoes, the pickles, and the biscuits. His hands rested on his lap now.

"It's what you were wanting, I thought."

Ethan muttered something.

"What's that?" Zeena asked.

"I was saying," and Ethan rubbed the back of his neck with one hand, "I was saying I thought you wasn't going to trouble in the kitchen today."

"T'weren't much. It's mostly what I brought with me." Zeena walked back around the table and over to the cookstove. She checked the firebox. With it being so warm she didn't build it up any more. She turned to the rocker and sat down gingerly, then sank back into the chair. Ordinarily her back'd be bothering by this time in the day; she'd notice it when she bent to sit down, or when she leaned over to clear the dishes from the table. But this noon she noticed no discomfort. This noon her veins were tingling. Her hands, they were practically dancing with life. She breathed in. She would wait till Ethan was done eating to tell him about his mother, how she'd spoken a few words, how she'd relaxed some, how it was time to get her outside while the day was so warm. She rocked as she imagined the words she would tell him. Not overexcited, she told herself. Just matter-of-fact, like it was what she'd known all along Cousin Beatrice'd do.

She reached into a bag and pulled Cousin Beatrice's knitted shawl onto her lap. The stitches were coming loose on one corner; Zeena bent over it and worked with a needle and thread to repair it. From where she sat, if she glanced up, there was Ethan before her. He ate slowly, chewing his food as he stared out the window. His jaw worked as he chewed. His wet hair glistened in the light. The flush in his face glowed. His hands, they were so large. Zeena watched the fingers curl around the fork or grip the glass of water that he filled and emptied twice. The skin of his forearms was reddish brown from working out in the sun. The folds in his neck, where it met his shoulders, were also reddened by the sun.

Zeena tried to work on the shawl, but her eyes kept returning to Ethan. Her hand paused in midair, the needle poised, as she watched his hand spoon the tomatoes into a saucer. As strong as they looked, there was a surprising gentleness to them. They were hands that would hold a baby and know what to do. So many men, their hands stiffened at the touch of a baby. Ethan's were hands that would deftly change a diaper. They would be tender with a woman, they'd . . . She shook her head. Foolishness, she told herself, as she bent farther over the shawl and sent the needle to work.

It was impossible to concentrate, though. She kept thinking of Cousin Beatrice, how she'd shivered and trembled with life when Zeena worked on her feet. The needle jabbed her finger. The thread knotted up. She put the shawl back in the bag with the other things that needed mending. She'd get back to it later. For now she was too agitated. With Ethan right there, every time she lifted her head she saw him and felt distracted. Maybe Rebekah's way was one she could learn. Toleration. Maybe she'd been too short with him that morning. She couldn't expect him to see things as she did. She didn't live up here in these hills. She hadn't been caring for Cousin Beatrice and taking care of the mill. His good sense wasn't working right, she figured. Throwing that picture in the fire, it was just that he'd lost his good sense. It didn't have to mean he'd given up. After all, that's what she'd said—a dream don't burn.

Zeena rose and went to the sink. She rinsed her hands, then unwrapped the applesauce cake. She cut several slices and carried them to the table. "Your mother, she's not so bad as you think," she started.

Ethan's eyebrows raised.

"I know it's early yet to say so, but I think I can do it, I think I can bring her back." She folded her arms together.

Ethan reached for his tea. He held it to his lips, blew on it. He kept his eyes on Zeena. "There's things you don't know."

"Tell me," she started. She sat across from him at the table. "Tell me how she used to be."

Ethan shook his head. Twice he opened his mouth as if to speak. Then he looked out the window. "Folks liked her." He looked back at Zeena, and in his eyes was that yearning.

She waited.

Ethan took a swallow of tea and stared out the window.

Was that all he had to say? Zeena folded her hands together on the table. She would have to ask questions. "She was a sociable sort?"

He nodded.

"How long since she had a woman friend?"

"Mrs. Hale, she used to visit regular. Some years ago . . ." He was still shaking his head. "Ten, at least. Ma went into town then, course. Sundays, to church services. Mrs. Varnum, Ma helped her out. Sewed for her. They was friends of a sort. When Rebekah was born . . ."

"Rebekah?"

"Mrs. Varnum's first daughter. She was a sickly child. Ma looked after her, to give Mrs. Varnum a hand. Mrs. Varnum had three others then. That was before she lost her sons."

"She didn't keep to herself, then?"

Something had turned Ethan's eyes inward. He didn't respond.

Zeena tried again. "Your father's family, there any others in Starkfield?"

He just shook his head. "Most of 'em's gone west. Pa, he was the only one wanted to stay. He said if it wasn't for him then the place'd bush up. Ma heard that and shivered, first time. She didn't want it on her shoulders. She wanted it said she did what she could. . . ."

Zeena stood up. She went to the cookstove to fill the kettle. Just as Zeena replaced the kettle on the stove, they heard it.

A loud clattering, as of dishes breaking.

For a short second Zeena saw in Ethan's face a mixture of feelings. Then it cleared and focused; his fork clattered to the plate as he was up from his chair, saying, "What's it now?" and headed out of the kitchen.

Zeena followed. She already had guessed what'd made the commotion and pictured the tray of dishes on the floor, which it was. The tray was upside down on top of the dishes and food, the teacup smattered. The bedclothes were wet with applesauce. Cousin Beatrice sat at the foot of the bed, small as a child, her bare feet dangling above the floor. She held a spoon in her hand; her thumb rubbed at the bowl of the spoon back and forth, back and forth.

"Ma," Ethan was saying. "Look what you done," down on his knees, already starting to put the broken crockery pieces on the righted tray.

Zeena shook her head as she surveyed the scene. But her

veins were still tingling; the sensation in her hands of dancing was still flowing. "You go on along," she told Ethan, slipping to her knees. "You let me tend to this."

Ethan kept at it. He was picking up pieces of crockery.

Zeena stood. "She's made a mess here, I'd say," she said. She stepped over the tray and around the bed, so she could see Cousin Beatrice's face. She folded her arms. She planted a smile on her face and with her chin in the air, she said, "Didn't like the dinner I brought you?"

"Don't be making fun of her, she don't even understand—"

"She understands plenty. Don't you, Cousin Beatrice."

Cousin Beatrice stayed still as a creature in the woods, frozen.

"Guess we'll be doing some more bathing today," Zeena directed at Cousin Beatrice. "Guess I'll have to ask Ethan for help."

Ethan stared at her. His brow wrinkled up.

"Your mother's not near as far gone as you think she is." Zeena turned and reached for the chair, lifted it, paying no mind to the stab of pain that shot into her hip. "She needs a woman's care, is all."

Ethan was in some kind of paralysis. His eyes darkened, blue-black as his mother's.

"You go right along," Zeena told him, holding to her hip and squinting at Cousin Beatrice.

"I'll just get this off the floor."

"I'll get it cleaned up. I'll talk to her, I'll—"

He looked at her with helplessness. "I don't think you're understanding how she is—"

"I'm understanding that she's knowing everything we're saying." Zeena put a hand toward Cousin Beatrice. She held her shoulder. "Ethan's going to finish his dinner, then he's going to help me get you outside." She looked at Ethan with determination.

"Outside?"

"There's a warm sun out there, from the looks of it. She won't get no more chance for warm after this."

Ethan opened his mouth to speak, but the words did not come. He looked from his mother to Zeena, back to his mother. Still no words.

Zeena gave him time. Then, "Your mother," she pronounced, "she's been in this room too long. Today," she added, "she's getting outside."

ORDINARILY ZEENA'D GONE for the mess first. She'd have filled a basin and set to cleaning right off, knowing the stain on the wall'd stay there if she didn't get right to it. She'd have scrubbed the wall and floor, washed out the bedding.

"This'll have to wait," she said aloud, looking at the floor. She turned to Cousin Beatrice and said, "You think you can scare me off with this devilishness."

Cousin Beatrice sat slumped, her thumb still working at the spoon.

"First things first," Zeena said as she reached for the spoon. Cousin Beatrice jerked it away. Zeena grabbed at one of Cousin Beatrice's hands. She lifted it and started to pull the sleeve away so Cousin Beatrice's arm'd slip back through, but the arm pulled away.

"How'm I going to get you bathed if you won't let me—"

"Get on out. I'll do it myself," and one hand held to her chest.

Zeena drew back. Well. She guessed maybe she was right. Cousin Beatrice could understand just fine.

Blue-black eyes gazed up at Zeena for a couple of seconds. In that gaze Zeena saw trickery. It was an acknowledgment of Zeena's suspicion. Something inside Zeena saw deeper into Cousin Beatrice's eyes. Saw a woman so cramped in her heart that cramping up all the more was her only choice. Without speaking any more words, Cousin Beatrice's eyes told Zeena her life's trouble.

Zeena felt her breath come shallow. A swirling whittled away in her chest. Had she ever come so close to another soul? So close as to feel its sorrow, know its pain? Travel inside its heart and know its palpitations as her own? Zeena felt a softening spread from her chest out into her limbs, into her spine, a tingling, gentle softening.

It's another of Mama's blessings, she thought. Mama's voice echoed in her head along with her own, so when she spoke it was like hers and Mama's mingled into one: "Why're you doing this?"

Cousin Beatrice, small bird of a woman that she was, hunched down so her neck disappeared. Her eyes shone piteously as they looked up at Zeena.

"All right," Zeena replied, still in that feather-soft voice, so even she was lulled by it. "I'll go," as she opened the top drawer of the dresser in search of another nightdress. There was none. A flannel wrapper was the only thing. "This's what you can put on till I can get that one," and she pointed at Cousin Beatrice's chest, "washed."

No response, in words or motions, but Cousin Beatrice's blue-black eyes followed Zeena's every movement. They soaked up Zeena's words, her motions.

"I'll be back," Zeena continued, almost singing. "We'll go on with your bath. It's been so long since you got proper cleaned you don't know the difference. But there is one. There's a difference between feeling clean and feeling dirt." The words came like a song she'd learned when she was a girl, as if Mama'd sung it to lull her to sleep. "You'll be surprised at how good you'll feel once we get you clean."

Cousin Beatrice almost rocked in place. Her eyes glazed over. Her shoulders loosened. She nodded her head. Yes.

MAMA'S VOICE WAS GONE when Zeena found Ethan in the kitchen finishing up his dinner. "I'm going to bathe your mother." He looked at her with blank eyes. "But I'll need your help when it comes time to move her outside," she said as she walked briskly to the cookstove.

Zeena heard the sound of Ethan's chair scraping the floor as he stood. "Ma, she's sickly." He ran a hand back through his hair.

"She's not so sickly she can't get better." She picked up the basin she'd left on the floor by the sink.

Ethan just shook his head.

Zeena carried hot water to the sink and poured it into the basin. "You said yourself, her heart's broke. A heart can mend, can't it?" In her back, then, was a clutching up. Not a bad one, but enough that Zeena's hand went to her hip.

Ethan approached the cookstove. "Look," he said, "it's like I said, I'm beholden to you for coming. If you can help keep the household here going so's I can put in the hours at the mill—"

"S'all you're wanting is a housemaid?" Zeena blustered. There was a pinching in her spine then that went straight down her leg; she shook her foot a little. "I won't be your—"

"If I can just catch up enough to pay what I owe, why," and Ethan coughed into a fist, "there's no telling what I might do. Like you said, I might take her to Florida, I might—"

"I don't believe you." The words startled her as much as they did Ethan. He stared at her with wide darkening eyes. "I mean to say," she started, "I don't believe she's as sickly as you think, s'all."

Ethan drew in a breath. He stared out the window by the table that faced the long slope of hillside that wound down to the family graveyard and continued down the hill to the woods, that dense stretch of dark green that only two generations ago had been an open field. Seconds, then minutes, went by. Zeena waited, holding to her hip.

"Cousin Zeena," Ethan started. "It's more'n you know, why, Ma, she—" and then he stopped.

Zeena saw it was so much more than simple discomfort he was feeling. There was a terror in him, in his eyes. He was as confusing a man as she'd ever met. He wanted her help, but he couldn't say what the trouble was. "What?" Zeena encouraged.

Ethan swallowed. He reached a hand to the back of his neck and rubbed it. His face reddened as he opened his mouth. "She . . ."

Zeena leaned against the basin that she'd rested on the edge of the sink and stared at Ethan, watched as the life drained out of him. He hung his head, shaking it side to side. He mumbled something, but to Zeena it was just sounds. What was wrong with the man? she wondered. He stood there, sighing, his head hanging. "I better finish up in the barn, Jotham, he'll be round."

Zeena could not wait all day. What did it matter, Ethan's confusion? She could tend to Cousin Beatrice despite his sorrows. She could bring his mother round. She started for the door.

When Ethan spoke it was with a deliberateness, as if he'd pondered and practiced the words before speaking them. "There's a chaise I can take out to the south end of the house from the parlor."

Zeena stopped. She forced a smile. "I thank you for that."

"You call me when you're ready." He stepped around her.

Zeena did not answer him. She just watched him shuffle across the floor, open the door as if it weighed too much to move, and then pull the door to behind him. He had his troubles, that much she knew. He'd stayed too long with his mother, the two of them alone, she could see, and his father before that.

What Ethan needed was to get out from under.

Foolishness, Zeena thought, as she lifted the basin and took small steps over to the door. Plain foolishness. He'll never do it. Zeena sighed. It's easier to see solutions to other folks' troubles.

She went through the passage, then through the parlor.

Least I'll never be stuck in this house, she thought, as she opened the door to Cousin Beatrice's room.

EIGHT

ousin Beatrice was lying with her head
at the foot of the bed when Zeena opened the door to her room.
Her feet were stuck beneath the pillow. The bedcovers were on
the floor.

The room was hot. Zeena rested the basin on the woodstove
and knelt to shut down the stove completely. She smoothed the
skirt of her apron as she stood.

Zeena went to the window and looked out past the lilac
branches. In the open area behind the house, four apple trees
stood bent to the south; purple moose grass rose up around their
trunks. The withered tree limbs were like the arms of a decrepit
dancer, arching into position, but they were laden with fruit.
"Looks as if I'll be making sauce tomorrow." She turned and
stared at Cousin Beatrice. "What kind a trees are those?"

Cousin Beatrice did not stir. Her small shell hands curled at
her breast.

Zeena saw Ethan come from round the side of the house then,
dragging a chaise through the grass and on past the window

where she stood, as far as the apple trees. Ethan's hands hung at his sides as he stood and gazed at the pine trees that formed a line on the ridge. He shaded his eyes as he looked to the sun, then up at the trees, following their line that ran north to south, then stared into the sky. He pulled out a kerchief and rubbed the back of his neck; then he stuffed the kerchief into a pocket of his trousers and hurried back to the barn.

Everything about Ethan told Zeena he was discontented. The way he moved with uneven step, the way his shoulders sloped, the way he gazed unseeing at things. A man shouldn't ought to be that way, she was thinking. Father, he did it too. He stood on the edge of things. Long ago Father'd taken to dancing when Mama reached out her hands to him, but no more. Zeena couldn't picture Ethan ever dancing, and though she herself'd danced only occasionally as a child and only in those rare times when she was alone in the house, it was looking out at those pine trees, seeing the leaves dance off their stems and into the currents of air, that gave her the urge to swirl round a room.

Zeena shook her head. Foolishness, she told herself. She turned to Cousin Beatrice. "You ever imagine yourself doing foolish things?" Asking such a question was in itself a foolish thing; Zeena shook her head again. "Something's got into me," she said.

Cousin Beatrice's eyes opened. They followed Zeena as she made her way to the side of the bed. They were not so dark, not so black as they were blue, Zeena noticed, as she reached into the basin for the rag and soaped it. "Where'll we start?" she asked.

Cousin Beatrice's hands folded together at her chest.

Zeena's hands went to the feet again. "I'll start here, then," she whispered, feeling Mama's hands in hers, Mama's voice in hers. This was the most important work she'd ever done. Before, when she was off to do a healing, a doctor was often present, and when he left, she stayed to carry out his instructions. Or if she was alone, she was there to offer advice, to tell someone how to do this or that, what herbs to take, what tonics and remedies. But she'd held something back.

With Cousin Beatrice, there was no holding back. She couldn't even if she'd tried. With Cousin Beatrice, it was a dance. Herself and Cousin Beatrice and Mama, all together in a dance, Mama leading. Her hands and Mama's hands, telling her what to do, her doing it, and Cousin Beatrice following like a young girl just meeting society.

So her and Mama's hands took Zeena to the feet. She began there, rubbing the rag over the toes and along the arches, and kneading the heels. She rinsed the rag, withdrew it from the steaming water, soaped it, and started again on the heels, then the arches, then the balls of the feet, and the toes, and the tops of the feet. Then rinse again, soap, and start up along the legs at the thin calves, the scrawny knees. The thighs, they were like the apple tree limbs, withered. The skin was wrinkled up, loose on the bones.

But to Zeena these legs, this skin, it was all hers.

"You got to get using these legs," Zeena whispered. "They're strong yet, they'll stand you for the years ahead, if you let them."

Cousin Beatrice's eyes stayed on Zeena. They barely blinked, did not waver. They were not warm eyes, but the cold was gone, Zeena was thinking, as she turned Cousin Beatrice onto one side so she could wash her buttocks, her private places.

"These bones, this flesh is all you got," she almost sang, "you got to care for them like they're your baby." The idea startled Zeena. She'd never imagined, nor felt from afar, what it'd be like to love a baby. Babies're life threatening, is all she'd thought. Too many babies took too many mothers' lives. And then the babies, they died too. Look at Mama. And those little twins, Florida and Florilla, born late to Clara Lindstrom some years ago, Zeena remembered. First one baby, then the other, then their mama, they all succumbed to pneumonia, leaving the other children to their father.

Zeena knew, she'd heard it often enough, it was a woman's godly purpose to give life to a baby. But the thought had always sickened her. When Zeena was still in school, she'd listened to other girls and how they talked about wanting to get married, wanting to give babies to their husbands. Zeena wanted no such thing. She'd been certain it would be her death. While the others wished away their days until they'd be old enough for the marriage vows, Zeena drew back. Besides, she felt her own wish to be a healer as one of a higher purpose than those girls wanted. Any woman can have a baby, almost. But a healer, there's only a handful of true healers in the world.

But now, as she cradled Cousin Beatrice, she felt the first doubt she'd ever known about her chosen path. Here she was, knowing it was in her, what Mama had. The power of her hands. At the same time there was inside her at this moment the smallest curiosity, nearly a wish, to mother. Is this what those girls felt? This yearning? It made everything inside her turn soft. And Mama, who'd been gone so long, Mama was with her again, so she kept up her song, "You got to love these legs, love these arms," as she worked the soapy rag up Cousin Beatrice's back, "and this back," she said as the rag went up and down, "you got to love this back."

Zeena'd never heard anyone speak such words. She'd never thought such thoughts. Now, though, they rushed through her like milk must come to the breast when a baby cries. The touch of skin, the feel of someone's back, the legs, the arms, a life held in her hands! Her hands! In Zeena's eyes was a dry stinging.

"It's Saint Lawrence," came at her. Cousin Beatrice'd spoken again. Zeena repeated the words. "Saint Lawrence? What're you saying, Saint—"

"The trees."

"The trees?" Zeena could not think what she meant.

"The apple trees."

Zeena laughed then. "The apple trees out back," she chuckled. "They're Saint Lawrence, and oh, don't that make the finest sauce, just the finest sauce. And cider, I'll start in on cider tonight." She laughed again. Cousin Beatrice was talking, with her eyes and with words. Zeena'd got through to her. No telling how quick she'd come back now.

She turned Cousin Beatrice to her back and started to pull the flannel wrapper apart so she could wash the chest and the shoulders, but the arms clutched together and the shoulders hunched as Cousin Beatrice drew up her knees and began that silent shaking and weeping she'd fallen to the night before.

Zeena's hands held to the shoulders. "No, it's all right," she sang, "you'll feel altogether like new, I just got this little bit of you left to wash, and then your hair, we'll—"

Cousin Beatrice twisted away. Her feet started in to kicking. An elbow gyrated at Zeena.

A struggle started. Zeena pulling, trying to be firm, and Cousin Beatrice rolling and twisting, her body shaking with moans. Zeena would not give in. She held and pulled and yanked until the flannel robe came apart at the shoulder, *zzrippp* it sounded as the fabric shredded first along the seam line and then down across the breast, and then there was a gasp, Zeena's, when she saw it, a layering of gauze across the breast which, when pulled away, revealed an ugly open sore on a flattened breast.

Cousin Beatrice did not try to cover herself. She did not pull away her arm that Zeena still held to. Her moaning ceased. She lay there, still as a critter in the woods what's been found out and shot with a single load, and stared hard at Zeena.

ZEENA FOUND ETHAN in the barn, repairing a wall in the sorrel's stall. The barn door was open and the horse was tethered to a ring on the door; her tail thwacked against it and she nickered. Behind Zeena one of the cows lolled against the door to her stall; there was the sound of feet against hay and the snort of a breath.

Ethan was bent over, measuring for a piece to fit over the hole that'd opened up with rot.

"Whyn't you tell me?" Zeena stood in the light and glared at him.

His head twisted round. In his eyes was a shaded look, a see-ing right through Zeena like she was wind or sky or a cloud.

Zeena folded her arms and tried to gather her wits.

Ethan remained bent, one arm resting against his knee, his eyes hollow now.

"About that sore she's got, that canker. It's a canker, what's open and full a pus," and here Zeena's voice rose, "what's killin' her." She swallowed, then, tried again to rein in her feelings. "And don't tell me you didn't know."

Ethan's mouth closed into a line. He stood, leaving his tools on the floor. His hands disappeared into the pockets of his trousers. He shook his head.

"You knew, whyn't you tell me?" Zeena's insides were on fire. This was the worst, a canker like that, folks didn't survive such. How could she heal a woman with a sore like that, oozing like it was.

"It's like I told you, her heart's broke, she—"

"Her heart may be broke but it's oozing its way to death."

"She just wants to go."

Zeena's hand went to her cheek as if someone'd slapped her. She drew back.

Slowly the words came out: "I know my mother." Ethan's brow wrinkled. "I know what's troubling her."

"She's talking to me, she's telling me about the apple tree, she's telling me how things used to be, she's telling me her whole life—"

Ethan's expression silenced her. It was his eyes, squinted and fearful; his head, cocked to the side in a quizzical turn; his color, blanched. "She's talking?"

Zeena'd seen it in Cousin Beatrice's eyes. That was enough,

surely. The intensity, it spoke of years of loneliness, heartache. "Yes, she told it all."

Ethan breathed in, exhaled slowly. "I wouldn't ha' thought she could."

"I'm saying she wants to be healed. But how can she, when she's fighting something you covered up. How long's it been like that, please tell me."

Ethan looked out the window. "Not so long."

Zeena tried to be reasonable. "I'll do what I can. I seen plenty in Bettsbridge, working with doctors and seeing what they do. But I won't guarantee nothing." She coughed. In her chest was that tightening that meant the wheezing might start up.

"I tried to tell you, but I thought—" he stopped. He was shaking his head again.

Zeena stepped closer. "How'd you think I'd bring her back if I didn't know about this?" Mama ran through her veins and into her fingertips. "Ethan, what is it you want?"

Ethan shook his head. Was he staring straight through her? That hollowness of eye, it gave him a less than human look, more like a horse, or the cow, inadequate in a human dilemma.

"Don't you know?" she asked, stepping still closer.

Ethan stepped toward her, a hand extended. He held to her arm. His head was still shaking. Were there tears in his eyes? "I don't want her to go," he whispered, leaning closer, his voice wavering.

Zeena could hear his intake of breath, could've reached out and touched the rise and fall of his chest. "I wasn't sure," she told him. His eyes widened, watery. "I wasn't sure," she repeated. The pressure of his hand on her arm, it was warm, pleading.

"You want I should go?" Zeena asked.

Ethan's eyes were like the night. They pulled at her with their troubles, their yearnings, their pleadings. He shook his head.

Zeena stepped back. It was the clearest statement he'd made

to Zeena since she'd come to Starkfield. "I'll stay then," she returned.

Seconds passed in which they stood facing each other.

The cat appeared on a rafter above them, rubbing her neck on a hewn beam. The cows made shuffling sounds. The horse backed into the door. The hot afternoon sun, it lay on the worn boards between them.

ZEENA SAT ON THE STRAIGHT-BACK CHAIR Ethan'd brought outside for her the last two days. "How long'll this warm spell last?" she asked him. He shrugged, then said, "Could end when the sun sets today. Or could last a week." He'd settled his mother first on the chaise, carefully tucking a blanket around her before fetching something for Zeena to sit on. He tamped down the grass with his feet, then stood looking to the east and the sloping hillside to the front of the house, his hands in his pockets. Did he have something to say? Twice he cleared his throat and turned to Zeena, though he kept his gaze in the apple boughs above her head, and twice he turned back without saying a word.

Finally he pulled a hand from a pocket and withdrew his kerchief. He wiped his forehead. "It's some warm for October," he said, still looking to the east.

Zeena stared at him. Indian summer, it always seemed warmer than the last one, but it wasn't. Father always said that was the trick of it, the sense of staving off what was to come. He didn't give in to that. He'd taught Zeena more'n to believe in such fancy. But Ethan looked so sincere; for a moment she wondered: Could this Indian summer be different from all the rest?

The apple boughs shaded them from the sun. A bucket of apples rested on the ground by her feet. Zeena was peeling and slicing the apples. The crisp red peels fell to the ground as the apple's flesh was sliced into a bowl in her lap.

"We're going to have sauce to last us a week," Zeena voiced. "And cider . . ."

Cousin Beatrice was wrapped in a blanket, lying on the chaise. Her eyes were open. She watched Zeena's hands at work. Every so often her eyelids drooped, then fluttered open.

"Saint Lawrence," Zeena mused. "Aunt Martha Pierce, she's got Saint Lawrence too. And Red Astrakhan. They come early, August, and they make very fine pies." Briskly her fingers clipped away with the knife. The bowl would soon be filled; she would carry it into the house and dump the apples into the large kettle with the ones she'd already peeled. One more bowl and she'd start the apples simmering. Saint Lawrence was so sweet, there was no need to add sugar. A splash of water was all she'd add. "You must have a strainer," she said, and looked at Cousin Beatrice but was given no answer.

Cousin Beatrice's eyes wandered. Zeena watched them as she sliced. Up into the tree limbs, over along the ridge where the pine trees stood so tall, and back to the bowl in Zeena's lap. Wandering, just like Ethan's'd done. But Cousin Beatrice's eyes were expressionless, while his had almost cried aloud with some sorrow.

On the outside Zeena appeared calm. Her fingers worked deftly. Her shoulders sloped comfortably. Her feet crossed in the tall grass that Ethan'd tamped down. Inside, though, was a swirling of questions. Now she knew the source of that odor in Cousin Beatrice's room. It was Cousin Beatrice's breast, rotting. The skin was mottled yellow. The pus was nearly green, a sickening color.

Zeena'd looked for red streaks that morning when she'd taken Cousin Beatrice her breakfast. Red streaks were a sign the sickness was spreading, but there were none. For now the sickness was confined to the canker. But for how long?

"How long's this been festering?" she'd asked Cousin Beatrice as she soaped a clean towel in a basin of steaming water.

That blue-black stare was all she got for a response. Zeena sat on the side of the bed and laid the towel across the breast and pressed gently. The blue-black eyes did not flinch, though Zeena knew it pained her. Gingerly, Zeena rinsed and cleaned, cleaned and rinsed, until the pus was gone. Then she held a hot compress to it. "This'll force heat deep into the canker," she explained. "It's heat you need to heal."

Cousin Beatrice shook her head side to side. The eyes watered.

"This paining you too much?" Zeena asked.

Her head shook back and forth again.

"Don't you want to get this cleaned up? It'll feel better if it's—"

Her head shook, slowly, left to right.

"I'm afraid you lost your sense of reason," Zeena told her, continuing with the hot compress. "You been so lonely, so clear out of the way of the world, you lost your sense of reason."

The eyes blinked at her, squeezing tightly, then releasing. Tears rose and spilled from the eyes.

Again it came to Zeena. As her hands tenderly continued their work, she felt that softening in her chest. A warmth spread into her limbs. Cousin Beatrice's tears were hers. The sickness in that breast was hers too. The life gone awry was Zeena's. And the heart that was broke.

If I can take it into my heart, she thought, then Cousin Beatrice'll heal.

The song came into her voice. "My hands'll do it, Cousin Beatrice," Zeena whispered. "They'll take the suffering clear away if you let 'em."

Zeena felt a tingling through her veins. She was uncomfortably hot; the air in the room was barely breathable. Tingles in her breast, little sharp shooting tingles, they burrowed deep. "It's mine," she crooned. The pain, it was seeping out of Cousin Beatrice and into Zeena's own breast. Zeena welcomed the pain with the softening that worked through her insides.

It was working. Her hands, they were doing their work. The healing, it was happening, like Mama taught her all those many years ago.

COUSIN BEATRICE'S SKIN was white as milk.

Zeena noticed it when she returned to the apple tree with the empty bowl, ready for more peeling and slicing of apples.

She bent to one knee and felt Cousin Beatrice's forehead. It was cold. Despite the hot afternoon sun, her skin was dry and cool.

Zeena's hands knew just what to do. They went straight to the feet and began their kneading. One foot, then the other. Up the calves, slowly. There in the sun, under the apple tree, Zeena pressed her fingers into the flesh, willing the blood to move again. Then the hands. Working her thumb into the palm of the hand, kneading the flesh. Up the arms. It was working. Cousin Beatrice's face was pink now. Her hands dampened. Her eyes, they shone with moisture.

A small red spot formed on the flannel wrapper at the breast. Even as Zeena noticed it, the spot grew. Zeena opened the wrapper.

The flesh around the canker was swelled up. The sore oozed blood. Had she got the blood going so well it was filling the canker? Blood was better than pus, though. "It's bleeding," she told Cousin Beatrice. "S'it ever done that before?"

Cousin Beatrice shook her head. Her eyes were wild with fear. They darted back and forth from Zeena's eyes to Zeena's hands that worked fast to cover the sore.

"It's a good sign," Zeena told her. "It means it's healing." She was not afraid. It was good the blood was flowing. It meant the old sickness was seeping away. New life was entering Cousin Beatrice's veins.

Zeena fetched another basin of hot water and brought it outside. She held the basin on her lap as she compressed the sore.

"The hot water'll draw the bad blood out," she told Cousin Beatrice whose eyes followed Zeena's hands again as they rinsed and washed, washed and rinsed; they widened as the water in the basin turned red when Zeena rinsed the towel. "Don't be afraid of this bleeding," she told Cousin Beatrice. "It means only good." She trusted her reasoning because Mama was in her. Mama wouldn't tell her wrong.

The sun was hot on Zeena's back. All this bending and leaning, but her spine stayed strong. No pains ran down her legs. No wheezing took over. There was just Cousin Beatrice—her breast, her blood, the canker, her uneven breathing, and her eyes, those fretting eyes, and Mama guiding Zeena. "You'll see, you'll be on your feet again. You'll see your old friends. Word'll get round you're fit for visitors."

Cousin Beatrice's breathing slowed. A calm settled on them. Out of the air, it came. A soothing, tender calm.

"Thank you, Zenobia," came from Cousin Beatrice whose eyes had closed.

Zeena's heart raced. Oh Mama, came the words in her mind, you'd be proud, so proud, to see what I done.

The canker dried in the sun as Cousin Beatrice fell asleep. She kept her color this time. No dryness, no cool skin.

Zeena kept one hand on Cousin Beatrice's shoulder, the other over her eyes; her thumb went back and forth across the eyelids. It's like this, came the words to Zeena's mind. Loving a child, it's like this. Such love as to take any suffering of that child and make it yours. There's nothing between you but air and not even air sometimes. She knew now what it was for Mama to lose those babies. No wonder she went with the last one; it was more'n she could bear to lose another.

Zeena recalled Daniel Marston's face that October evening when the doctor came down to tell him about Nettie, his wife. "She's gone," he'd said. Her life'd ebbed quick as the tide once the baby was pulled out of the incision the doctor made, and

Zeena, who'd brought the baby down to him, stood holding the child, a girl, in her arms while the doctor explained what had happened and Daniel's face cracked up like so much earth parched in a drought. The only sounds came from him were a grunt and a gulping of air, as if he'd been punched hard in the belly. Zeena approached him with the baby and now she understood the way Daniel looked at the child, the way he stared at the face, looking for Nettie. Zeena now wondered if she could ha' stood in for Nettie. The baby in her arms, it could ha' been hers.

Zeena felt it, a yearning for what she did not have, what those other girls all craved and spent their days preening for: a husband, a baby, one of those little mail order houses that were springing up outside the cities like Springfield and Worcester. Maybe she was not so different as she'd always thought, maybe—

She shook her head. Foolishness.

In Zeena's breast was that needle of pain, Cousin Beatrice's pain, so it didn't bother. What she was doing here, working with her hands, it was more than being a wife and mother. Much more. She was saving a life. In her hands was the healing. It's what she'd lived for.

They stayed there, Cousin Beatrice sleeping, Zeena watching, thinking, the smell of apple peel and core and flesh in the air to soothe her.

"ZEENA."

She felt a hand on her shoulder and her name repeated.

"Zeena."

She jumped.

"You're in a trance or something."

Zeena turned. It was Rebekah, the sun behind her so her face was shadowed. "I been working on these apples," Zeena said.

Rebekah came round under the apple boughs and stood at

Cousin Beatrice's side. She wore a wool skirt and cotton shirt, no cape or hat, perhaps she'd left them out front. "Ethan at the mill?" she asked.

Zeena nodded, still surprised.

"I brought a few more stores," Rebekah said, and gestured toward the house. "I left a basket in the kitchen." She'd kept her eyes on Zeena but now she looked at Cousin Beatrice who lay sleeping, her mouth ajar, her breathing mostly even. "How is she?"

"She's doing fair. I brought her outside. She's been in that room too long."

Rebekah nodded. "Since before last winter, anyway."

"That long?" and again Rebekah nodded. Zeena rose from her chair and beckoned with a hand for Rebekah to follow. She stepped through the tall grass and stopped at the edge of the old kitchen garden. She turned to face Rebekah and asked her straight out, "D'you know about the canker in her breast?"

Rebekah's eyes widened. "Canker?"

Zeena's fingers showed how big it was. "It's been growing some time now."

Rebekah shook her head. "I never heard it." Her eyes cleared then. Her face smoothed. "Last summer—" she started, then stopped. She turned and looked back at the house. "July, it was. Before that, she'd been quiet, always quiet. Since Mister Frome passed on, anyway. Till one day in July when I come. She was altogether different. She'd, she'd turned cranky over night."

"So it's been months now."

"How bad is it?"

"It's bleeding today. It'll be her death soon enough 'less I can heal it."

Rebekah looked over to where Cousin Beatrice lay under the tree. "She know it?"

Zeena nodded.

"Poor thing, she . . ." and Rebekah drew out a handkerchief

and dabbed at her forehead. "She's had bad luck these last years. Was a time, even when I was a girl, the Fromes was on the up. Mister Frome, he had plans for the mill. Course, the train coming through the Flats, 'stead of up here . . . Father said he'd never manage, told him so, but he was stubborn, he had his own ideas. Seems it's been one thing or another."

"Ethan never told you? 'Bout the canker?"

"You think he knew?"

Zeena nodded. "It's certain he did."

"It's like him, to keep to himself. Still, to think I was here all those days last summer and he never showed anything different, never . . . why, I'd never ha' guessed. Course when I was a girl . . ." but she trailed off. She looked at Zeena, eyes distant now. "How'll he manage?"

Zeena's eyes narrowed. "Ethan?"

"Once she goes, Mis' Frome. What'll he do?"

"He should sell. No sense staying when—"

"Sell? Oh, my, he couldn't, not Ethan, not—"

"Why not?"

Rebekah's countenance hardened. Her eyes turned shadowy. Her mouth went into a line. "He might think he'd like to go, but no. You think the Fromes meant for that? Some of us got to stay in these towns, else they'll go to ghosts. We can't let that happen. Mother says—" She looked at Zeena as if seeing her for the first time, then up at the sun.

"What?" Zeena asked.

Rebekah did not answer right off quick. Then, "I could never do it, leave. He's the same as me. His family's got more hold on him than he'd like to admit."

"But they're all gone, they're—"

"They're all right there, at the foot of the hill." She turned in the direction of the Frome graveyard.

"But that's foolishness, to let the dead tell you what to do." She thought briefly of Mama. But Mama was different. Mama gave her courage, strength. Mama was like a light, leading her on. That was altogether different from what Rebekah was saying.

"I must go."

"So quick? Won't you stay for a cup of cider?" She didn't want Rebekah to go. Seemed she had a lot to tell Zeena about Cousin Beatrice and Ethan. Seemed she knew everything.

The afternoon sun was behind them. The lowlands were fogged up with the heat and the sky was a sultry gray-blue. Rebekah's pale skin was damp. She dabbed at her forehead again, then at her eyes. Her shoulders trembled. Was she crying? "Rebekah," Zeena started. "I should never ha' come," Rebekah said, starting back to the house. Zeena followed. "Rebekah—" but the girl kept on around the corner.

Zeena didn't want to leave Cousin Beatrice alone, but she went to the front corner of the house where she could still keep Cousin Beatrice in view. Rebekah stood in the front yard, surrounded by weeds and overgrowth in what must once have been a flower garden. A tangle of stalks and old growth lay against the granite foundation and worked its way along the front path. Zeena called to her, "Rebekah—"

The girl looked stricken. The smooth features, the calm and gentle exterior were gone. "I should never ha' come," she said again, as Zeena approached.

Zeena leaned over. "Did you care so much for Mis' Frome?" she asked.

The girl nodded her head. Tears spilled from her eyes. Her face was blotched with reddish patches.

"Why'd you stop coming to look after her? Was it Ethan, not wanting you to interfere?"

Rebekah's hands went to her face. "Course not. Ethan, he appreciates anything anyone does for him."

Zeena waited.

"It wasn't proper," she cried.

"Proper?" Did appearances count so much folks'd begrudge Beatrice Frome the care she needed?

"Mother, she said it'd sour folks on me if they thought too much about it."

"But your mother, didn't she think on all Mis' Frome'd done for her?"

Rebekah swallowed. She took a moment to get her bearings. She was done her crying. "It wasn't only that."

Zeena had to ask. "Is it Ethan, then?"

She turned shining eyes on Zeena. "It's not that. It's anything but that. It's just—"

"Just what?"

Rebekah folded her handkerchief into a small square and wiped her eyes. "It's just not right, seeing it all go to, to nothing."

Zeena waited. To nothing? What was the girl saying?

"I must go. Mother says I get too wrought up. She says I wear my heart on my sleeve for all the world to see. She says if I don't get hold I'll be a spinster," and she broke down again.

Zeena's chin lifted. Was that such a terrible fate? she wanted to say. But before she could speak, Rebekah said, "You can see why I'd fear that, surely, any woman'd fear that, wouldn't she?"

Zeena was silent. What could she say? Rebekah searched her face, then realized, "Are you . . . Zeena, I didn't know, I just assumed you . . . you're such a motherly sort, but, oh, you'll think I'm a silly child for the way I speak, I never meant to—"

Anyone else would've insulted Zeena, but Rebekah's face showed her innocence. The girl didn't have it in her to be mean. "Don't you fret," Zeena told her, and then, "Are you saying Ethan's the man you want?"

Rebekah laughed. "Certainly not," and she sighed. "He's too old for the likes of me, you can see that. Well, not in years, but in his heart he's an old man, isn't he? Like you said, he holds his tongue. How could a girl fall for someone can't even speak his heart?" She started to laugh then. "But I do worry over him. He's, well, different. You must see it. The poor man, he don't have it in him to go it alone here."

"Folks do what they have to."

"Someone'll manage with Ethan." She looked at Zeena. Laughing, she said, "Maybe you!"

"Oh, for the land's sake, no!" Zeena said. She remembered Cousin Beatrice. "But I must go back." She gestured in the direction of the apple trees. "Come sit and we'll talk. You can tell me about life in Starkfield."

Rebekah held out her hand. "I must go. Mother'll worry. She don't even know I come out here."

Zeena watched Rebekah walk to the barn and unhitch her horse. Before she climbed on the bay, she leaned against the horse, rested her head against its neck. Then she placed one foot in the stirrup and drew herself up to sit sidesaddle, all with great effort. She headed down the lane at a slow pace. For a girl who had to get home to an anxious mother, she sure was moving slow, Zeena thought.

NINE

*T*he kitchen smelled of applesauce and cider. The window over the sink was steamed. Zeena couldn't find the strainer and decided they'd have the applesauce lumpy; then she added the raisins Rebekah'd left for them and set the sauce to cool till supper. Zeena'd cooked up the ham slices Rebekah'd brought and put out the last of her anadama bread along with her biscuits baked fresh at dinner, the dill pickles, and some squash she figured Ethan wanted cooked up because it was lying on the table when she came inside.

She'd found Rebekah's shawl draped over the back of a kitchen chair when she first came in. Zeena had picked it up. It was a soft gray wool with a red ribbon woven through the outer edge. Even without the ribbon it was the kind of finery Zeena'd never had. Was it lamb's wool? She'd wrapped it around her shoulders, had smoothed the fringe out with her fingers. Father always took care that Zeena had what she needed. But fineries, Zeena'd had none.

Foolishness, Zeena'd thought. She'd removed the shawl and

folded it and laid it on the dresser. She'd wondered if she should give it to Ethan to return to the Varnums. But the girl'd said her mother didn't know she'd come. Zeena decided to wait, hoping Rebekah'd get over whatever it was that'd upset her and come again soon. She did seem a tender soul. The sort a girl that'd get tossed hard by life. Zeena liked her, though. There was nothing in Rebekah to harm another soul. Usually young girls, they thought only of themselves. But Rebekah, she was as far from selfish as Zeena'd ever met. And it seemed she knew about the Fromes. Zeena wanted to ask her more. What Cousin Beatrice was like before she took sick. How she'd managed out on this farm, so far from town. And Ethan, why he couldn't sell the farm. Couldn't he do what was practical? His dreams—could he give them up so easily?

Ethan noticed the shawl soon as he came in. He stood just in the doorway and looked at it sitting on the pine dresser. The red ribbon woven through the edge showed clearly along one corner. Zeena wondered if he would recognize it as Rebekah's. Ethan's brow wrinkled.

"Rebekah Varnum come by with some stores," Zeena announced. Ethan looked over at her. "She's a thoughtful enough girl. She didn't want I should trouble too much as I was settling in," Zeena said, deciding to speak up first.

Ethan approached the pine dresser. He touched the fringe on the shawl with just one finger.

"I found the shawl when I come in. She must ha' left it when she brought her basket in. I was still outside with your mother."

"Jotham'll take it to her tomorrow."

"No need. She'll come again."

Ethan stood at the dresser still. Now his hand was on the shawl. "She might be wanting it," he said.

"I don't think so," Zeena returned. "She'll be back soon enough."

Ethan coughed. He reached a hand into his pocket as if in search of something.

"She cares awful much for your mother." She watched Ethan's face for his response, but it showed no flicker. She wondered if he would tell her Rebekah'd been out to set with his mother all summer, but he just nodded his head in acknowledgment. "I guess she cares for any poor soul what's suffering," Zeena went on.

Again, Ethan nodded. His eyes betrayed him. They'd turned dark as midnight, like Cousin Beatrice's. His eyes were focused on her when he nodded, but his gaze was elsewhere. He was thinking of something else. She said no more about Rebekah's visit but turned to the chore of getting supper on the table.

ZEENA'D ALREADY GIVEN COUSIN BEATRICE some biscuits and milk, had settled her in bed and brushed her hair. "Fifty strokes," she'd told her. "And I'll do fifty more before you go to sleep." Cousin Beatrice's eyes that had glared and stared with blue-black intensity were softer now; was it that Zeena knew the truth and was bound to heal her? "You don't need to suffer no more," Zeena whispered before building up the fire to keep the room warm for the evening and going in to the kitchen.

Ethan took longer than he had at dinner to wash up. He stood at the sink and soaped up, lathered his face so he could shave, scrubbed his neck, dipped the rag into the water, and sent it scrubbing inside his union suit.

I didn't know as you was taking a bath before supper, Zeena thought to say from the doorway, but held her tongue. Twice she'd left the room to take something to Cousin Beatrice and twice returned only to find him still there at the sink.

A knock came at the door and a man stepped in to the kitchen behind Zeena. He was older than Ethan by maybe ten years, Zeena guessed. Stockier, he looked ox-strong. There was a dullness in his gray eyes. "I take'n that lumber in to Hale's," the man said.

Without rising from his washing, Ethan said, "I thank you."

And then, "This's Zenobia Pierce from Bettsbridge, what's come—"

"I heard," the man returned with a nod and a gaze from beneath the rim of his cap at Zeena.

Zeena nodded at the man who'd stepped into the room, his cap in his hand now, shifting from one foot to the other. She walked to the cookstove and bent to add some wood.

The cat slinked out from under the stove and brushed against Zeena's leg. She stooped to pat it.

To Zeena, Ethan directed, "This's Jotham Powell. He gives me a few hours at the mill most days, especially now I'm trying to get as much into Hale's as I can before freeze up." Ethan was drying his face now, rubbing the towel round his neck, through his hair. His face was flushed red, from a day in the sun or from the washing, Zeena could not tell. "You staying to supper?" he asked Jotham.

Jotham nodded in assent, as he looked to Zeena. "I got something more to finish up in the barn after," he said, his eyes brightening some. Again he shifted from foot to foot. "Long as you've got 'nough to spare." He scratched his chin. "You found the squash?" he asked Zeena.

"I didn't know where it come from, but I cooked it." Zeena pointed to a bowl on the table.

Jotham nodded.

Ethan approached the table as Zeena pulled another plate from the shelf, some more cutlery, and dug in a drawer for another napkin. Was this Ethan's practice? she wondered. To offer his hired help a meal at night? As Jotham washed up at the sink, Zeena whispered to Ethan, "You might ha' told me there'd be an extra place." She didn't want to be rude, but if she was going to be cook and housemaid along with healing Cousin Beatrice, she needed to know for how many.

The three of them sat at the table, the two men on one side, Zeena on the other. The sun came in on Ethan's and Jotham's faces. The features on Ethan's face, Zeena noticed, they were finely chiseled. His ears, they were set close to his head. Mama always said that was a sign of high intelligence. His eyes, though, that's what drew you, she thought. So sorrowful you felt you should look away, yet you couldn't. They pulled at you. Jotham's eyes, you had to hunt to find them; they were sunk under a protruding brow and he kept them looking down at his plate. What struck her about Jotham, though, was his neck—strong and thick, the muscles pushing out when he turned his head.

"Good biscuits," Jotham uttered between bites as he slathered on butter and jam. He rubbed the back of his sleeve across his mouth before reaching for more. "Cider's good too," as he finished off a cup and wiped his mouth with the other sleeve.

Zeena stared at him. Hadn't she given him a napkin? These country folk sometimes forgot their manners, she knew. Or maybe they'd never been taught.

Jotham looked up as he again wiped his mouth on his sleeve. Zeena's eyes on him set him to shifting in his seat. He pulled the napkin from between his legs and rubbed his mouth. Then he reached for the pickles. "Lost it in my lap," he answered, a half smile forming.

Ethan poured and drank two glasses of water. With emphasis, he wiped his mouth with his napkin. Then he started in on the squash. He nodded his head. "Butternut's good," he said to Jotham.

"Mr. Powell left us plenty," Zeena said.

The applesauce went fast, though Jotham picked out the raisins and left them on the side of the plate. "Can't chew 'em," he said apologetically, pointing to his jaw.

"You don't have nothing makeshift?" Zeena asked, thinking of her own false teeth.

Jotham looked at Ethan first, then at Zeena. He shook his head, then looked back down at his plate.

While the men finished their third helping of food, Zeena

made the tea. "How long's this heat going to keep on?" she asked as she brought the pot to the table, along with a bowl of apples.

"Least a few days, I'd guess," Jotham said, looking to Ethan for confirmation.

Ethan nodded.

"I never saw it so warm this late," Jotham offered.

Zeena held her tongue.

"Saw Miss Varnum," Jotham told Ethan. "She was taking some food to the church."

Ethan nodded.

"She asked after you."

Zeena looked at Ethan; he was nodding his head. His eyes were seeming to glaze over. She'd seen it before.

They ate in silence then, their forks clinking on their plates and in the serving bowls. Zeena chewed her food carefully, counting the number of chews, as she stared out the window. Mama always said chew each bite at least ten times so as to assist the body in getting what it needed. She needed all she could get to keep her hands going and make her breast strong enough to take Cousin Beatrice's sickness and hold it in her own.

Outside and down the hillside the tops of the trees were shining in the gold light. The red maples were shoots of flame in among the gold. But way down the hill, the dark woods looked like a cave. Zeena glanced at Ethan. He was looking out the window too. The light hit his eyes, brightening the blue. Was that water up on his lids? Zeena wondered what feelings had betook him. The surroundings, they seemed to bring on the strongest feelings in him. To her, the hillside of gold and red was pretty, but how could it make a body cry?

Jotham spoke up. "An' how's Mis' Frome coming?" he asked Zeena.

Zeena felt her spine straighten. She lifted her chin and started to answer, but Ethan coughed and said, "Zeena's had her outside every day."

Jotham nodded.

"She's coming along," Zeena offered, sipping her tea and looking at Ethan. His eyes were tearing still. In his face was a bleakness, as if there was no way to put words to the feelings in his heart. Might's well be in a tomb, she thought, as be unable to voice your heart. Might's well lie under the ground, a stone the only thing what'd speak for you.

ZEENA WAS COUNTING ALOUD the number of brush strokes she'd given to Cousin Beatrice's hair when "There's no way round it," Cousin Beatrice suddenly said, the words coming clear as brook water. She paused, and Zeena waited, brushing the gray hair gently as she could. "I been waitin' for this since I was a girl," she said, and Zeena knew she meant the canker growing in her breast. Cousin Beatrice's eyes were wet; they gazed out the window at the branches of the twisted lilac as Zeena kept on brushing her thin hair with a slow and steady stroke.

"It must pain you terrible," Zeena said.

Cousin Beatrice closed her eyes and swallowed.

Zeena wished she had something to give for the pain. Whiskey, or some spirits of any kind, but there was none in the house. The salve she'd used was intended to ease the pain, but Zeena didn't think it was doing its work.

"Auntie Etta," and Cousin Beatrice sighed again, a slow and shivering sort of sigh, "she come here," and Cousin Beatrice tapped the bed with her hand flat, "she come here to spend her last days with a canker."

"Auntie Etta?"

"She was Father's aunt. I take after her. She grew up right here," and again she tapped the bed.

Zeena knew Cousin Beatrice was from Worcester, same as Mama, but she knew Cousin Beatrice's mind was playing tricks on her so she didn't contradict her.

"Mother didn't think she'd last more'n a couple days. They

set her up right here," and again, the tap of the hand, "and set me in a trundle bed there by the window," and she pointed a finger at the space between the bed and the window, "so I could keep an eye on her. There was a night she raised a fever shortly after she come to us. Mother said it'd be her last."

Zeena kept the brush going through the hair, easy, like a leaf drifting down a river, the current pulling it.

Cousin Beatrice swallowed. She squeezed shut her eyes. Her shoulders trembled. "What you're doin' to my hair, I don't re-call how long it's been since . . . more'n forty years anyway. The morning I was married Mother set me on a stool in the kitchen. I held a looking glass while she brushed. Did something fancy to my hair. I never knew how she done it, but she smoothed it and waved it all at the same time."

"Your hair's like silk," Zeena said, startling herself, so like Mama did she sound, like Mama singing Hush, Zenobia, sleep now, just that kind of voice.

"Mother stitched my dress," Cousin Beatrice said, her voice thinning out like spun wool. "The skirt was ivory taffeta. Lace covered the bodice. She'd saved the taffeta since it was given her when she married. She took apart a pearl necklace what'd been passed down from Grandmama, and she stitched those pearls one by one in along the neckline," and Cousin Beatrice's hand went to her chest and made a scooping motion from one shoulder to the other. "From the neckline there was lace up to the neck. Everybody said it was the finest wedding dress they'd ever like to seen." Her face relaxed. Wrinkle lines showed around her eyes.

"Fourteen years passed b'fore Ethan came."

Zeena paused in her brushing.

"I had to wait so long."

"You wanted a child all through those years?"

Cousin Beatrice shifted her position; she grimaced. Her arm was paining, and her back. "Don't every woman?"

Zeena hadn't. Not until coming to Starkfield and cradling Cousin Beatrice like she was a baby.

"What else is there?"

Zeena felt a prickling in her spine. There's other things, she thought. Wasn't it so for Mama? She loved her healing work. Everyone looked to Mama when they had troubles. Wasn't that enough?

"I had several starts, but I lost 'em. I give up hope then. I never give up the wanting, though."

Was that how it was for Mama? Doing her work but always wanting a healthy living child?

"I never guessed I'd have my own baby, being thirty-six, like I was," Cousin Beatrice whispered.

"You were thirty-six?" It set Zeena's heart to pumping. "I'm just twenty-eight," she told Cousin Beatrice. She began to brush the hair again, long and slow strokes.

"Don't you have no children?"

"I never married," and she straightened. "I always done for others, looked after them when . . ." but the words faded.

Cousin Beatrice stared at Zeena. "I'm sorry for that," she said.

Zeena thought to defend herself. I'm not, she wanted to say. But she just sat there. She was sorry too.

Cousin Beatrice changed the subject. The words started coming, a flood of them. "I set up in the trundle bed all night, that night Auntie Etta was dying with the fever what come from the canker in her bosom. Mother set up in that chair," and Cousin Beatrice pointed to the corner as if there were a chair there. "Mother kept the lamp lit. She wanted to see Auntie Etta's face. But in the morning when the light edged in through the window—there was no lilac bush then, just an open space of window looking out to, well, I thought it was maples." She stopped.

Was she seeing it still? That morning light through the open space of window? "But in the morning," Zeena repeated.

"But in the morning," Cousin Beatrice continued, "when the

sun come in, Auntie Etta opened her eyes. 'I won't be dying just yet,' she told us."

Zeena put the brush down on her lap. She stared at Cousin Beatrice. That feeling had overtaken her again. It was hard to keep her hands from touching Cousin Beatrice. They wanted to caress and embrace, to express the bubbling of feeling in her chest. Words, she realized, would not be able to say it. Mama must've felt this same way for me, Zeena realized, recalling the touch of Mama's hands on her hair, the feel of Mama curved against her back on those cold nights. Mama must ha' took her life from those moments, same as she give it to me. But Father, she couldn't remember a moment when tenderness overtook him. On those occasions when Mama pulled him from his chair to dance while Zeena played the piano songs Mama'd taught her, his eyes practically bulged out with pleasure. He laughed out loud then, great gales of laughter. But it wasn't tenderness. And when he laid the babies in their boxes and the boxes in the ground, his hands trembled with something. Sorrow, but no tenderness. But it was in Mama, sure as the night ends when the world's lighted up again each morning at dawn. It's what made Mama a woman.

"Auntie Etta," Cousin Beatrice started up again, "she lived till spring. I stayed every night in the trundle bed and she told me stories of the old times. I never thought she was going when she did, a May morning so beautiful the scent of things grow-ing was everywhere and everything was green, that yellow green what comes first. She didn't think she was going either. On her face was a look of surprise, like as if she knew then—" and Cousin Beatrice's voice turned wobbly.

Zeena reached out and held to her shoulder that had started up its trembling and shivering again.

"In just that last moment, she must've known." Cousin Beat-rice's mouth twisted up.

The sun was setting, the room darkening. There was the sound of wood simmering and burning in the woodstove. From the other part of the house came the sound of a door closing. Ethan, he must be done in the barn, Zeena thought.

"I won't see May again."

"Yes, you will," Zeena said. "Course you will."

Cousin Beatrice was shaking her head. "Auntie Etta made it through, but what good'd it do?"

"Don't think like that. You'll live to see next May and the one after if you just hold on and—"

"I'm awful tired," Cousin Beatrice murmured.

Zeena straightened. She kept her thoughts in. They whirled this way and that. Mama, Father, the babies Zeena never had, the troubles she'd seen to in other folks, the husband she never had, Auntie Etta, Cousin Beatrice, Daniel Marston who lost his wife but held her baby in his arms, Ethan in the barn looking at her when she asked him why he'd not told her about the canker, and Aunt Belle . . . How'd her life come to this very point? For as long as she could remember she never questioned it. Now, the differences between her and all the women she'd known set a fence round her. She stood alone in the middle of a field, their faces peering in at her, pointing their fingers. All except Rebekah. She wasn't like the others. She counted a body's value by something other than what it did. She looked in Zeena's eyes and recognized who Zeena was, the soul inside. She was like Mama.

"Hold on," she said every now and then to Cousin Beatrice. She even wondered if she was speaking to herself. Hold on, Zeena.

Mama, tell me what to do.

But Mama was silent this time.

Zeena stayed there as the room went to dark and until Cousin Beatrice's breathing turned smooth as a breeze.

INSTEAD OF GOING INTO THE KITCHEN, Zeena took off her apron, hung it on the door handle in the entryway, and opened the front door. She stepped out into the night. It was still warm. The air smelled more like spring than what it was, those last tender autumn days before the cold comes.

The tall moose grass brushed against her skirt as she stepped across the yard. It was dark, but Zeena could see the shapes of the elms' trunks and their arching limbs extending into the sky like feathers. The moon would rise before long, and then she could see across the fields and even back to the ridge.

Inside Zeena was a vast and unfamiliar swirling of feeling. She felt like crying. It was a knot in her throat, stuck there.

Crying is foolishness, she told herself. But since sitting in that dark room with only the touch of Cousin Beatrice's hand in hers and her thoughts flying all about in her mind, the crying had been there in her throat. It was like when Mama put the stick down her throat to see were the splotches of red forming that meant the throat distemper'd struck.

In those weeks after Mama went, Zeena'd nearly run wild some days with wanting to cry. When she could, she held it till she was in her bed and could cry into her pillow. If Father found her crying, he said something like, "It's done now, she's gone, you can't cry forever." Zeena sometimes thought Father's silence was a form of crying. He wanted her to stop looking at him with those sorrowful eyes. "What're you looking at?" he'd snapped at her. In school the trembles overtook her. Her hands shook when she tried to do her figuring on her slate. Miss Pratt several times had to take her from her place at the desk she shared with Mina Wilkins and lead her to the back hall. "Go on outside and walk around the schoolhouse ten times, and keep your eyes looking right where you step," she instructed. "Only where you step," she emphasized. "When you get hold a yourself, look up and see what's round you. The sky, the hills, those're what you should look to, to keep yourself steady." Once Miss Pratt walked home with her. "It's time, Zenobia," she said, resting a hand on Zeena's shoulder, "to put your mama to rest and get on with your life."

"She's in my head," Zeena explained to Miss Pratt. "She sings to me here," and she tapped one finger on the side of her head.

Miss Pratt coughed. She shook her head. "Your mama's gone, Zenobia."

It was like tamping the snow down with her boots, trying to quell Mama's voice.

NOW IT WAS BACK AGAIN, the wish for Mama's singing. And the trembling in her limbs. So much trembling, so much wanting to touch Cousin Beatrice, to keep her hands on Cousin Beatrice's hair, her skin, as if that might hold her to life.

All that speaking, Cousin Beatrice'd spoke till she tired herself. So much to say. So much to tell. All those years married, wanting a baby. Zeena could understand now what that must ha' been, that yearning to feel your body flesh out, to know you were giving the world what it'd given you, life. To be wanting to hold it in your arms. . . .

Zeena's arms came up as if to cradle what she'd held many times yet never'd moved her. Now the holding her arms just so, she felt it.

And the waiting. Waiting for this canker to come and take Cousin Beatrice like it took Auntie Etta. Had Cousin Beatrice given up? Zeena wanted to give her back the will to live.

Zeena'd heard of folks with cankers that all of a sudden shriveled up and disappeared. Healers laid their hands and gave their remedies. Folks what'd seemed hopeless in their chances were saved.

Zeena felt it, so many wishes. Cousin Beatrice's, her own, and they were all mixed up. Wishes for time to pass and bring a baby, for time not to pass, for time to go back, for second chances, for the sense that it means something, your life.

Maybe if I walk out to the elm trees, if I can get to the lane and walk along it, the moon'll be up soon and I can see my way then, and maybe I can walk it away, Zeena thought. Miss Pratt'd told her, "Keep your eyes looking right where you step." Zeena kept her eyes on the ground and stepped carefully in one of the tracks that rutted the lane.

"Mama, help me," she whispered aloud. "Sing to me what to do. Not like after you went, when you sang so much I thought my head'd split. Please, Mama . . ."

The waning gibbous moon was just over the line of the woods at the foot of the sloping hillside. She could see the lane clearly now. Everything silver. White shimmering light danced on the leaves. The grass became streaks of silver-black. The shadows were black as boot polish; the light was so many sparks in her eyes.

The trembling increased. Shimmers of it spread all through her. The crying was still in her throat, but she felt light as air, as if she might float off into the sky. Would there ever be an escape? A way to fly above the land so the cold couldn't touch her, so it wouldn't matter if her feet weren't steady, wouldn't matter if her heart was so much softness, wouldn't matter if she cried until there was nothing left to cry because it wouldn't hurt, she wouldn't be able to feel it anymore . . . Mama'd said to save her crying. Was this the night she'd saved it for?

"What's this?" came the words at her.

Zeena froze. She knew the voice.

"I thought I seen something—"

It was Jotham Powell. Zeena had no voice. The knot of crying was in the way.

"I'm just heading home," he said, reaching the place where she stood in the lane.

The moon was rising in the sky. It lit everything up, but with silver and black. The autumn colors, they were silver. The sky, it was black with silver dots of stars and a silver moon. Jotham, he was silver. And black where the shadows were, under his cap's rim, as if his face was gone. All except his chin that lurched out from the black like the bowl of a silver cup. And his hands, the moon covered them with silver. The thumbs were hooked in the pockets so the fingers fanned out.

Zeena was breathing fast. She heard herself crying in her head. But the crying didn't sound itself. She folded her arms and looked at the black place where Jotham's face was.

"I'll be going then," Jotham said, stepping around her, pulling on his cap's rim.

Zeena watched him go round and past her. She stood where she was on the road and watched his figure, silver where the moon lighted it, black where the moon shaded it, and still said nothing. There'd been a kindness in his voice, in the tipping of his cap, but Zeena was unaccustomed to such. It only made her throat tighten all the more.

She raised a hand in the air, a wave, but of course he did not see it. He was already down past the Frome graveyard, on the other lane that skirted the hillside and disappeared into the woods.

ZEENA OPENED THE FRONT DOOR and stepped inside. She stood with one hand on the door handle and listened. There were no sounds from either side of the house. Maybe Ethan'd gone to bed.

Zeena tiptoed through the parlor. Even after the day's warmth, the parlor was cold. She opened the door to Cousin Beatrice's room. The moon gave enough light for Zeena to see Cousin Beatrice lying on her back. The bedcovers covered her slight frame.

Zeena reached for a match and lit a candle with trembling fingers. She leaned over the bed then; Cousin Beatrice's face was pinched up. Her mouth was a crooked line. Her eyelids were thin as parchment. Zeena pulled the covers back, opened the flannel wrapper.

In the dim light Cousin Beatrice opened her eyes.

"It looks better now," Zeena said. She peered at the skin around the sore; it was mottled but dry. No more oozing, no more bleeding. "The swelling's down. S'it pain as much?"

There was no answer for several moments, then, "I don't know."

Zeena sighed. She rubbed more salve on the canker. "Can you take the air on it?"

Cousin Beatrice nodded.

"The air'll do it good," Zeena whispered. "You sleep now."

Zeena added wood to the stove and adjusted the damper. When she stood, Cousin Beatrice whispered, "What's the use? F'you keep me till May and I go then . . ."

"You'll feel different when you see the red maple buds in March. You'll be glad you stayed."

"F'I stay, will you?"

"I—" Zeena started. She bit her lip.

"Will you?"

"I mean to see you up and about."

Zeena stood in the dark and listened to Cousin Beatrice's breathing. It was sharp and fast. She sat on the bed and placed her hand on Cousin Beatrice's forehead. She held it there steady and firm. "Rest now," she sang. Finally the breathing turned low and easy.

She looked at her hands. They were all she had. It hadn't been enough for Mama. Was it enough for her? She sighed. Didn't seem she had much choice. Her time for having a life like other women was over and done. No man'd asked for her; she'd never wanted one either. She had what she wanted: healing hands.

Zeena stood; she pulled the door closed behind her and tip-toed back through the darkened parlor.

The kitchen lights were out now. Zeena had hoped Ethan would still be up. She wanted to tell him: Your ma wants to live.

If he'd listen. If only he'd listen.

* * *

AFTER DRINKING HER LAST GLASS OF WATER for the day, Zeena headed up the stairs to her room. From under Ethan's door came a light. She stopped by his door and lifted her hand, ready to knock, but she heard footsteps within and then the door opened with a noisy rattling.

Ethan was there, filling the door frame, one hand fumbling at the door handle, the other gripping a candle that cast light and shadows into his face. He was dressed in his union suit. His face was flushed; his nose was red as a radish. When he saw Zeena he backed a half step into his room. "I didn't—"

Zeena looked him in the eye. She waited.

"I weren't—"

"If you'd for once finish a sentence I'd follow your thoughts."

"It's . . ." but his voice drifted off.

Zeena stepped toward his door. That close, something softened. "You been here so long, Ethan, so long without a body to talk to, you and your mother, it's taken a toll."

Ethan's eyes widened.

"It don't have to be this way," she added, looking past him through the open door to the bare walls of his room. The room was shaped the same as hers. Sloped ceilings on the front side, a wide bed set up against the inside wall and next to the window. A small chest on the floor at the foot of the bed. A narrow rocker on the outside wall.

"You don't know what it is here, you think—"

"I can guess quite well what it is here. I see it with my own eyes."

Ethan's gaze wandered over Zeena's face.

She felt his eyes like some sadness. "There's every reason she can heal," Zeena said. "She wants to heal, she told me just now she does."

Ethan stared at her.

"It's what I come for, it's what I mean to do."

Ethan looked at the candle flame. "Time was . . ."

"Time was what?" Zeena pressed.

"Folks come by. On their way here and there. Ma, she set on the porch," and he paused, "there was a porch off the ell—" Ethan looked up.

"Whyn't you do it? Get away from here?"

Ethan's face emptied of all expression. His eyes were dark blue holes leading into nothing. There was no shine, no sadness, no nothing. "I'm not saying it for spite," she said, but Ethan stood there helpless as ever. What more could she say? Zeena turned to open her door. Behind her was Ethan's step, followed by a grip to her arm. "You don't know," he said. "I saw you walk down toward the graves tonight. You come back before you got there." A spark came into his eyes. "Next time, you go up close. You read those names. You read those dates. I'll never be more'n them. I am them, don't you see? And nothing, not technological school, not Ma living, not your telling me what to do's going to change it."

He let go her arm then and in a moment was turned and headed back across the hall. Zeena swallowed. The door closed then. The knob clattered in such a way that Zeena wondered if it'd ever open again.

TEN

"ell me how it used to be," Zeena spoke.
Zeena sat in the straight chair beneath the apple tree, peeling, coring, slicing, filling bowl after bowl for applesauce. If
nothing else, she figured, she'd put up applesauce to last the
winter. "These Saint Lawrence is about the sweetest I ever
encountered," she'd told Ethan and Jotham at supper the night
before.

Cousin Beatrice lay in the chaise, covered with a thin woolen
blanket. Her gray hair was spread out like a bird's wing across
the pillow, soft as so much feathers.

It was Friday, not ordinarily a washday and an unlucky day
to start a project, but it would take some doing to get this household into a regular schedule. On a line strung between the back
door of the woodshed to a post in the ground by the chicken
hatch hung the morning's wash, soaked and boiled and wrung
through a ringer. The hem of Cousin Beatrice's muslin nightdress dipped into the tall tips of grass that leaned to the north
in the occasional warm breeze.

It was the fifth day of Indian summer. Zeena'd left off her stockings and undershirt when she dressed that morning, knowing she'd perspired through her flannel wrapper in the previous day's heat. If it kept up, she'd be laundering again on Monday. Already she'd spent two mornings washing Ethan's and his mother's clothing and bedding. "If I don't do it now," she told Ethan, who dug out the kettle and lye, "it'll be spring before someone gets to it."

It was a game she started playing the morning after their exchange in the hall. She didn't see why Ethan had to settle for what his parents'd laid out for him. Any man could do better if he wanted. The inspiration to migrate was just that, a wish for a better life. Folks were finding it every way they turned. And Ethan, he'd almost found it himself. If his father hadn't a died . . . But once Cousin Beatrice was better, why there was no telling what they might do. So she took to saying things like, "In the spring," and then was some description of how it would be; "When your mother's up cooking again" or "Once that ell's rebuilt" or "When the mill pays your debts" or even "When everything comes out right." Neither Cousin Beatrice nor Ethan showed disbelief in her predictions, nor did they affirm them. For Zeena it was a way of letting them know just how much she thought was possible. Father'd always said, Where there's a will, there's a way. Wasn't this what he was talking about?

Cousin Beatrice's eyes were closed, but she was not sleeping. Zeena'd watched her knees come up and then go down, then come up again. Her head'd turned side to side like a window shutter. "Are you paining?" Zeena asked. Cousin Beatrice shook her head. There'd been no talking today, just a steady restlessness.

The day before, Cousin Beatrice'd laid in the afternoon air and slept the hours right away, like a small bird eating the seeds of a sunflower, slow and particular. Late afternoon Ethan dragged the chaise into the kitchen, and while Zeena ironed that morning's washing and prepared supper, cabbage from

Jotham's summer garden along with applesauce and pickles and the brown bread Rebekah'd brought, Cousin Beatrice lay in the chaise and watched Zeena's every movement. "It's the first I seen you in more'n a year," Jotham pronounced at supper, grinning.

The canker was drying up. Several days in the clean air, Zeena figured, had done it, along with the frequent bathings and applications of salve and Zeena's hands that rubbed and pressed into flesh and muscle, taking the clutched-up pain away. Whenever Zeena looked directly at Cousin Beatrice, her own breast ached. She knew it was the sign she needed; the canker was going into her own body, which was strong enough to dispel it.

"We lived with Albert's parents when I first come," Cousin Beatrice suddenly spoke. Zeena held the paring knife still and looked up at her. "Yes," she said. A few seconds passed before Cousin Beatrice went on. "They was parents to me, same as to Albert." One eye twitched, even as it was closed. "I nursed 'em both at the end."

Zeena put down her work and reached for one of Cousin Beatrice's hands. She worked on the hand then, pressing and rubbing the palm and along each finger.

"There was other farms, two of 'em, out here on the ridge."

Zeena'd seen no trace of another farmhouse. But she knew how quick a field'd bush up, once it wasn't cut. How quick a foundation hole'd have a chestnut or an ash growing in it once the weather got to it.

"Was al'ys someone coming by. The Bettsbridge pike, was al'ys someone coming by."

"The trains changed all that, I'd guess," Zeena said. She reached for the other hand and started in to rubbing.

Cousin Beatrice nodded. " 'Fore the train come to Corbury Junction, why this was the pike to parts south. Everybody was al'ys coming or going on this road. Folks'd stop to buy our fresh vegetables."

"Where're the gardens?" Zeena asked.

Cousin Beatrice's other hand lifted and pointed to a field beyond the apple trees. Beyond that was the mowing field, a cow path running alongside one edge where Ethan led the cows out to their pasture. The garden was a mess of tangled scrub and grass. Flattened piles of hay were scattered about. "Weren't just vegetables they bought." Now her eyes opened. "You'd ha' thought here on the hillside, the wind coming strong like it does, nothing'd grow." Cousin Beatrice's mouth spread into a wide smile, showing her toothless gums. "But seemed the wind passed over the ground 'stead of taking the soil clear off. Up on the ridge, it's all rock. I figure the soil was cleared off and carried down here so we'd have ourselves the finest growing ground around."

Zeena smiled.

"They come for my preserves and jams and jellies too. Folks said as how my apple jelly was the best they ever tasted. Then too," and she rose onto an elbow, craning her neck and grimacing with the effort, "there's the syrup." Her hair spilled across her face. "There's a stand a maples down there," she said, looking to the hillside and the woods at the foot of the hill. "Time was the lanes were lined with 'em." Zeena reached out to pull Cousin Beatrice's hair behind her shoulder. "Come sugaring, we all worked together. Even Ethan, young's he was." She smiled even broader. "Tapping the trees with those old spiles Albert's great-grandfather'd used, we all did it. Lugging those same old buckets to the wagon. Used the summer kitchen to boil it down all through the nights even." Cousin Beatrice eased back against the chaise. "Folks," she started, "folks always come for syrup once the roads was passable."

Zeena'd heard Father's mother talk about getting by on the land. Folks worked hard the year round and then they died with thanks from no one. It was merciless work. Grandfather was up every morning at four to milk the cows. Wasn't a single morning of his life he weren't done tending the animals by dawn, Grandmother used to say. Died doing it, too, is how Zeena saw it. They found him on the floor in the cow stall, a bucket of milk filled to the brim and waiting by the door. His heart went getting the second bucket.

"Was one year," and Cousin Beatrice's eyes brightened so the blue was bright as what Zeena'd seen in the sky on a clear January morning, "the sap come early and kept coming and coming like nothing we'd seen. Nights was cold and days turned warm, and it kept on going like that, the sap running like a river, like it'd never end. We got . . ." and her brow furrowed up. She looked right at Zeena. "You ever worked so long your feet swole up like sausage?" But she didn't wait for an answer. "We was sleeping on our feet in the woods. Albert stayed too long one night and one of his toes turned black. He lost it eventual. And Mother Frome, her back snapped one day so she had to be carried home on the sledge." Cousin Beatrice shifted her position. She pushed herself up on the chaise with a groan of discomfort, sunk herself down farther, lifted a knee, eased finally onto her side. She gazed off into the sky, seeing it still, Zeena guessed.

Zeena didn't see how Cousin Beatrice could smile with such a memory. Only once, after Mama was ailing from childbirth and another blue baby, was Zeena sent to stay with Grandmother Pierce. It was planting time, and Zeena spent every waking hour with Grandmother and Uncle Wilfred and his family working that soil so Grandmother'd have her garden like always. If it wasn't cold and rainy, then the midges started in to biting. Grandmother covered Zeena's unprotected skin with a mixture of beeswax and comfrey root and told her to keep on making holes with the hoe just so many inches apart for the corn and then to drop the kernels in just so, building up the soil around it so the corn'd grow, and Uncle Wilfred struck her straight across the back once with his shovel when she set down and cried, so sick from the bug bites and cold from the wet dirt and heartsick for Mama was she.

Cousin Beatrice's voice turned fluttery when she said, "We boiled more sap that year than any before or since. Once a day we laid some out on the snow and et it, fresh and chewy as taffy. Folks could get through come just for that."

Cousin Beatrice grew still. Her limbs settled, as if the straw insides had been taken out of a doll. Then, "That was the year . . ." she started up. Then again, "That was the very year . . ."

Zeena felt it just then. A shiver of cold ran up her back. The sun dipped down behind the trees on the ridge, casting the ground between the ridge and the house into shadow.

"The stones," Cousin Beatrice whispered then.

Zeena's bowl was full. It was time for Ethan to get his mother inside. "The stones?" she echoed, distracted, as she finished up one more apple.

"The gravestones," she answered, her voice low.

Zeena's hands stilled. She looked at Cousin Beatrice. She looked small and old and wrinkled, grimacing.

"They tell it, what we done," Cousin Beatrice said. "They tell it."

ELEVEN

*M*ama's stone, it stood in among her babies. The hands carved on her stone, they took care of the little ones that were gone. There was a space for Father next to Mama, when his time come.

They were all planted deep in the ground in the churchyard. Behind the church, willow trees rose up alongside the brook and next to the far end of the cemetery; their limbs hung down over the graves nearest that end. In summer their leaves brushed against the tallest stones. In autumn they covered the ground with a corn-yellow blanket of leaves.

Mama and her babies were right now under the shelter of those leaves. Probably the babies' stones were even covered up altogether. Last time Zeena was there, the leaves had just turned. Under the willow branches the air shimmered gold.

In summer Father kept the grass trimmed low so the stones wouldn't get choked, but the leaves, Zeena knew they didn't choke. They made a blanket for the snow to lie on.

"Mama," Zeena'd said, the last time she was there, pressing

her hands against the stone ones on Mama's grave, "I'm going 'cross the valley up into those hills. I'm going to bring back Cousin Beatrice." She told Mama what she knew of the Fromes, how she was going there to do a healing.

The babies' stones were lined up, little mounds of marble. Mama's stone was in the middle, rising tall among them.

Mama's life was there before her. All except for Zeena. There was no space for her, since it was long ago figured she'd go with a husband. How could Mama and Father ha' guessed she'd be a healer who worked with her hands to bring folks back instead of marrying and having babies?

Most folks didn't bother with stones for blue babies. The stones were too costly, and a blue baby what never saw the light of day didn't have anything much to be remembered by. Mama insisted though that her babies have stones, tiny as they were. All her babies had names, even when they were blue, but their names were not engraved on the stones. "What's it matter, the year, the day, even their names when they was so young?" Father'd said. "It's enough they got stones."

Mama's stone was nearly pink when the sun got low in the sky and hit it just so. It stood up regal from the ground.

Mama's life, it was carved there. Folks that didn't know her could stand there and see her life spread out before them like a quilt. They'd say: Althea Ann Pierce, Devoted Wife, born July 3, 1805, died November 12, 1836. She went before her husband, folks'd say if they looked at her stone. Five babies, she had. Not one of 'em lived long enough to make a record of its life. Prob'ly they were blue babies. Prob'ly the last one took her.

There were no words saying how she longed for each of those babies or how she nearly died of grief after each one's passing or that she had just one live child to carry on her healing work. No words telling how she loved to sing, how nimble her hands were with a needle. No way to show her beauty, to make her laughter ring in the air. Nothing about her childhood in

Worcester, how she went with Father to Bettsbridge. Nothing about how her husband turned sour when he lost her.

But the essence of Mama's life, her hands, her caring healing hands, folks'd see it right there.

So what was it Ethan and Cousin Beatrice said Zeena'd see in the Frome graveyard?

TWELVE

$\mathscr{Y}$our hired man, he'll be eating his supper here?" Zeena asked, pulling at a loose hair and tucking it in behind her ear. It irked her that he didn't tell her things she needed to know. Didn't he realize what it was to get food on the table?

Ethan turned. He stood at the door, about to go out to the barn. "I don't 'spect so."

Zeena folded her arms. What exactly was he meaning? "So're you saying he won't eat with us?"

Ethan nodded. "Least, he didn't say nothing about it." He looked out the window then.

"I won't set a place for him, then." Zeena leaned over to check the firebox for the cookstove.

Ethan rubbed his neck. "You want I should bring the chaise in here again for Ma?"

Zeena stood. She smoothed the skirt of her apron. She stirred the applesauce as it simmered on the back of the stove. Cousin Beatrice had been tired when they got her settled inside again.

Zeena'd hoped to get outside and walk down to the graveyard, but Cousin Beatrice'd asked her to bathe her again, and then it was time for new compresses on the sore, and then it was time to get supper going, and Cousin Beatrice had fallen into such a deep sleep that Zeena couldn't get her to take a spoonful of supper. "She's sleeping sound," she started. "I guess she needs her rest."

Ethan's shoulders lifted. "Her skin's lost its color."

"She's all tired out."

"She looked poorly," Ethan said, sinking one hand into a pocket.

"She was tired. She was talking all afternoon."

"Maybe it's too much, being outside." He shifted from one foot to the other, withdrew his hand from the pocket.

"The air's what she needs."

Ethan shook his head. He opened his mouth, then closed it.

There it is, Zeena thought. Nothing irked her so much as seeing this man with something to say and unable to say it. "What're you trying to say?" Zeena asked.

"I already said it," and his voice raised just slightly.

"If you want I should go . . ." She stepped over to the drawer that held the forks and spoons. She reached for two plates.

Ethan swallowed. He shook his head. "I already told you—"

"But is it what you mean?"

Ethan's eyes clouded. He approached the cookstove. He stood just feet from Zeena. His eyes were watery and dark and pained. "That's my Ma you're tending," he said, as if to explain.

Zeena nodded.

Ethan was breathing heavily. He pulled a glass from the shelf, filled it with water from the jug, and drank it, slow and steady. He replaced the glass on the shelf. "I'll do the milking, then," Ethan murmured, running his hand across his chest.

"Supper's ready anytime," Zeena replied. The boiled potatoes and cabbage were warm on the stove. The pickles were on the table already. The bread was on the board, ready for cutting.

The late-afternoon sun filled the room. The cat lay in a square of light on the floor. Zeena laid the knives and spoons and plates on the table. She could hear Mama talking to Father in that lighthearted voice she used when she was trying to say something serious: "Don't be short with me." And Father, he could only soften then because Mama wouldn't let him stay brittle next to her. Zeena'd always thought she was like Mama. She was a healer, like Mama. She liked things nice, like Mama. She kept the house neat and tidy, like Mama.

But her words, talking to Ethan, it was like Father. She felt the flush of shame spread into her cheeks. She didn't want to be brittle, like Father. A healer couldn't be brittle. She had to be soft, like Mama.

Zeena stared at the table. Mama never prepared a table so gray and dull as this one.

Outside there was as much color as a body could want. Flames of gold and orange and red covering the ground like it was a scrap quilt. Zeena thought she'd go outside then. Collect some leaves. Make the table pretty.

So Ethan, he won't think I'm such a brittle thing.

THE AIR WAS COOL. Cooler than the last couple of evenings, Zeena thought, returning to the house to fetch her wool shawl.

Back outside again, she wrapped the shawl tightly around her shoulders. It was in the air, the smell of cold coming. And in the leaves rustling overhead, chattering in the breeze coming up from the west. In the sky, a paler sort of blue than the haze that'd settled over the land the last few days. The breeze held an edge; sharp, it was.

Something sounded in the barn—a door slamming, or a plank falling. Ethan'd had the cows out to pasture in the north field all day. Perhaps he was just getting them back in their stalls. Zeena grimaced at the thought of Ethan. He worked harder than she'd known a man could do, and to what end? So he could stand in the kitchen, his heart bursting with some feeling or other, letting the fate of his life direct him like he was a leaf hanging limp from a tree. She shook her head.

Zeena headed to the elms. The ground beneath these towering trees was golden yellow. She bent to collect one or two. As she rose, she felt it, that familiar cranking up in her spine. She stood still a few moments, breathing, working her thumb and fingers into the muscle that covered her hip. It's the cold what does it, Zeena was thinking. All these warm days, she'd thought of it only enough to notice it wasn't causing her any bother.

Zeena started walking down the lane. The larches, a fiery yellow orange, were shining in the afternoon sun. How long, she wondered, till all the trees were skeletons? Another week? Once the leaves were gone, the world'd turn bleak. November was the start of it, just two days off.

Cousin Beatrice, it'd take weeks to see her get strong. Weeks, to see that canker heal up and go away. Even then, Zeena thought, how'll I leave her? Yet she would not stay the winter. It'd be more than she could muster to find that kind of strength in herself. But still, if Cousin Beatrice needed her . . .

Zeena was moving slowly along the lane as it worked its way down the hillside. Just ahead was the lane that climbed to the ridge and met the road to town. And just ahead to the left was the graveyard.

The graveyard. Zeena turned to look at the barn. Was Ethan there, seeing her? She glanced from one window to the next. All she could see were the small black squares of windows. The big bay at the far end was open a crack. Was he there? If he was watching, well, so be it.

Zeena stepped through the tall grass, nearly purple in the sun's low rays, toward the graves. She felt a breeze. Cold fingers were there at her back. She stepped quickly. Beneath the larch limbs, the shadowy air was 'specially cool. She walked round to the gate, hanging from its hinge. It would not budge, so she stepped around it.

It was a contrast, Zeena thought, the care given these graves, these stones. No flowers had been planted here, but it was clean-cut. Even though some of the stones slanted at crazy angles, Ethan'd looked after things as well as he looked after the animals in the barn.

The stones, they were all rough-cut white marble. No fancy spires or elaborate carvings. But the sameness of the stones, the way one marble stone tied to every other stone through the mottled gray of it, the way a body knew without thinking it that the stone had once been under the ground and now it was the folks under the ground and the marble was on top and rising firm; all of this gave an elegance to the Frome cemetery. There was a feel of order, of everything in its place. Zeena liked that. There was a feel of the past, large and solid beneath her feet. She liked that too. All the Fromes that lived on this hillside over the last hundred years, they were all here beneath her feet. It wasn't like standing near Mama and the babies; it was more than that.

It was a homecoming, a family coming home to itself.

Mama's family, they'd never do that since Mama and Aunt Belle went so far from home, and besides, the farm outside of Worcester was sold when Grandfather Higgins opened the men's apparel store and they moved into town. Zeena'd never even seen the farm, or what was left of it. And Father's family was scattered too. His three brothers were all gone to bigger towns, one even to Portsmouth. The Pierce family plot on the farm was no longer tended once the place was sold after Grandfather Pierce died.

Up till now Zeena'd thought of the Fromes as country folk, too poor and too foolish to change their ways. Now she wasn't so sure. They knew enough to come home to this ground. Zeena's head spun. She'd never guessed what it could mean, a family graveyard built on the family land, so the new generations would live in the old generations' shadow. A comfort, that shadow.

Before her were two small stones rising inches from the

ground. The babies, Zeena knew those'd be, and inside her throat it came again, that choking over a knot. Her hands came together at her chest where the emptiness lodged like a new-dug grave, unfilled. No baby'll suckle here, she thought. Zeena shook her head. She didn't want to think on it, what she'd never have. Didn't want to read the names and dates on no baby stones. She'd seen enough baby stones. Least she'd never have no baby stones of her own. She grimaced; is that my comfort?

"It's all here," came at her.

Zeena swung round. Ethan stood at the gate, his hands in his pockets, his shoulders hiked up against the chill air. "I didn't hear you," she said. She pulled her shawl tighter, wrapped her arms in the folds.

Ethan was looking at the stones, his head tilted to the side as his eyes roved. "I tended these stones when I was a boy. Pa said to do my best since it'd be my home someday." He walked over to where Zeena stood by the babies' stones. Above them the larches' leaves shielded the last sun.

Zeena looked at the small stones. "There's five babies' stones where my mother lies. Four sisters and a brother."

"When they go young," Ethan started, shaking his head, "least they don't have to watch everyone else go before them." He walked over to the biggest stone in the center, raised up on higher ground with a low iron fence around it. The name FROME stood in tall letters at the top with a rising sun carved out of the name. Jacob, b. 1764, d. 1847, over the words *And now to join Him.* His wife Birdena, buried before her husband, lay beside him; b. 1771, d. 1809, and the words *Angels will hail us to Heaven our Home* were carved beneath her dates.

"Your family's been here a long time," Zeena said.

"Once you're in the ground—"

"I meant," Zeena interrupted, "they come here to this hillside a long time ago."

Ethan looked at her. He nodded.

"Frome." Zeena said the name aloud and then to herself.

Frome, Frome, Frome. She sounded it with her own name. Zenobia Frome. She shook her head. Foolishness.

"There's been Fromes on this ridge more'n a hundred years," Ethan said, looking around in a circle.

There were other stones, all the same white marble, prob'ly come from Vermont where Mama's stone come from, all rough-cut, but they were of different sizes. Zeena could tell who'd died when by the shape and cut of the marble. Some were tall and thin, plain-cut, and decorated with cherub faces and comforting words about heaven. Those were the oldest, the dates of death occurring at the turn of the century. Jacob and Birdena's children. There were two in one grave, Violet and Lily, a year apart in age with their deaths coming just a day apart in February 1806. Another with just the word *Daughter* carved on it. A son, he was seven in 1808. Another son; he died in February of 1806 with his sisters. Something hit them hard. The typhoid? The pox? Birdena Frome died months later. Worn to pieces from nursing her children? Was her heart broke?

Ethan stepped over to three stones that stood wide and squat with decorative carvings, urns with weeping willow branches flowing. These deaths were in the 1830s, the sons and a daughter of Ethan Frome whose stone was to their left.

Zeena read the words aloud: "Sacred to the memory of Ethan Frome and Endurance his wife, who dwelled together in Peace for fifty years."

Ethan turned and looked back up at the house. Zeena looked too. The gray clapboards were soft where the early evening light fell on them.

"Reverend Munson said when you die you join the ones's gone before you, that they're just waiting for you in heaven," Zeena said.

"That how you see it?" he asked.

"Father said that was just the old talk. He said the church was trying too hard to be a comfort to folks." She looked at Ethan to see his response. His face was pained, but he didn't say anything. "When Mama went, no one said she'd be waiting for me by the gates of heaven. That's the truth of it, 's I see it. When you go, you go."

Ethan stared up at the branches of the larches. Zeena looked at them too. The last leaves made patterns against the sky.

"The only way you last is in the minds of those what survive you," Zeena stated. "Long as I keep talking to Mama, she'll live. Soon as Father's gone and then me, why, who'll keep Mama alive? No one. Her white stone's all there'll be."

Ethan turned to her. "That's what I'm saying," he said.

"But you can't live your life just so—"

"Who'd ever talk to them," Ethan flung out, and he swung his hand wide to encompass all the stones, "if I was to get away?"

Zeena had no reply.

Ethan turned and started back through the gate.

"Wait," Zeena said, following him. She caught up with him and reached for his arm. "I talk to Mama from a distance," she told him.

He shook his head and pulled away. He headed up the lane to the house.

Zeena followed behind him. The leaves she'd been carrying, she tossed them into the air. They floated to the ground. Once they landed, she couldn't distinguish them from the ones that already lay there. She kicked at the leaves. Then she stepped quickly along behind Ethan.

THIRTEEN

_O_nce again Ethan wore his union suit and trousers to the supper table. His smoothed black hair was damp. His skin was shining clean. But when Zeena stared at him, she saw bits of straw clinging to his pant legs. Even after washing up, there were specks of dirt in his hair. You don't know what all you're bringing to the table dressed like that, Zeena almost said. Instead she said, "I fixed a bread pudding for supper."

Ethan looked at Zeena briefly, then nodded as he pulled out his chair.

Zeena checked the firebox and added wood. She shivered. "Can't keep up with it."

"It's coming on cold," Ethan told her. "The way the sky turned gray so sudden and that wind, it's coming."

"Rain?"

"Snow, I'd venture."

Zeena shivered again and pulled her shawl from the back of the rocker before joining Ethan at the table. "I'd hoped it'd hold off awhile. Least till I go."

Ethan shrugged.

"You get all what you needed done at the mill this afternoon?" She retied her apron and smoothed the skirt.

Ethan sighed. "The driveshaft was broke. I spent the afternoon on it. It's still not working good, but it'll carry us through to get that order to Mr. Hale by Monday." He unfolded his napkin and then wadded it into a ball as he pulled his chair up close to the table.

"He give you a fair price?" Zeena asked, her eyes narrowing as she handed the steaming cabbage to Ethan.

Ethan nodded but said nothing. He spooned a large helping of cabbage on his plate.

It's like always, she thought. A man thinks a woman can't understand his work. Course she can. It's her work's hard to understand. Zeena dished some potatoes onto her plate and handed the bowl to Ethan. "These Jotham's potatoes?" she asked.

Ethan shook his head. "Weren't much time for planting last spring, what with Ma taking such a turn. But I did get the potatoes in." His eyes brightened. "Always come up good, potatoes do."

"Your ma, she said everything come up good here, despite the soil being sparse on the ridge."

Ethan gave a blank stare.

"Weren't that so?" Zeena asked.

He ran a hand back through his hair, sprinkling dust and dirt into the air. "I'd guess not." He commenced to cutting his potatoes and mashing them with his spoon.

"Why'd she make such a point in saying the soil was so good, then?"

"Time was, long ago, I heard it was better. But we took what we could from the soil here. It's no good now."

For several minutes they ate in silence. Ethan sprinkled salt on his cabbage and potatoes two or three times. He took a second helping of vegetables, speared some pickles with his knife. Zeena listened to the crunch of pickles in his mouth. He drank three cups of cider down fast, then wiped his mouth with his napkin. "Ma, is she sleeping?"

Zeena nodded. "She didn't touch her supper. Not a bite."

Ethan gazed at Zeena, his dark-blue eyes turning wet. "All that fresh air, it just tired her out." He blinked, squeezing shut his eyes. When he opened them, he looked out the window.

"That canker, it's drying up, like I said."

Ethan nodded.

"How 'bout some more a this cabbage, or shall I save it for soup?" Zeena caught the scent of something burning just then. She glanced over at the cookstove and saw a thin line of smoke trailing upward from the oven door. "Oh," she cried out, "my biscuits," and was out of her seat, "they'll be burned up good," as she stepped quickly to the stove, reaching for a towel to open the door, and withdrew a pan of smoking blackened biscuits. Zeena waved at the smoke with her hand, "I never," she cried, "I never in my life," and she was shaking her head side to side. "These're plain ruined."

Ethan was there beside her. "They ain't so bad, we can just—"

"They're ruined, they're—" She lifted one from the pan, but it was so hot to the touch that she dropped it to the floor with a *crack*. "Oh," she cried, starting for the sink, "they're, why, they're burned so bad, they—"

Laughter, Ethan's laughter, is what Zeena heard. The biscuits were smoking like fired-up charcoal nuggets. He took the pan from her hand.

"What're you laughing at?"

Ethan stepped toward the stove. Zeena followed. "These're so burned, they're . . ." he started, but he was chuckling, and the biscuits tumbled, landing with more *cracks* on the bare wood floor.

"How can you—"

"It's just I never seen biscuits burned this bad, I—"

"Well, I never in my life, I—" but Zeena caught it then too,

Ethan's good humor, and she started in to laughing too, so the two of them stood there with the burned biscuits on the floor between them until Ethan kneeled down to collect them, and he picked them up gingerly since the smoke was still steaming from them, and she bent down to help, saying, "I never in my life—" and then they stood together with the pan full of smoking biscuits, and Ethan lifted the front lid on the cookstove and turned the pan so the biscuits sailed through the air and into the firebox.

Ethan gave a salute of his right hand to his forehead, and the two of them burst out again, and Zeena bent over with the laughter, and the pins that held her pug in place let go so her hair fell loose into her face, and her tears were coming now, tears of laughter, and she felt Ethan's hand on her shoulder as he bent too with the laughing, and then as Zeena stood straight again, wiping her tears, trying again to say it, "I never in my life, I never not once in my life," until she finally got it out, "never burned anything so bad," and Ethan was smiling at her so they didn't hear the knocking at the door, they didn't hear anything but their own gales of laughter until—

"Anybody home?" and someone opened the kitchen door from the back hall, and "I been knocking," he said, stepping into the room, a wide-eyed look showing beneath his fedora. He was dressed in a brown suit that was rumpled and dusty; only the starched collar held its original shape, wedged in under his fleshy chin.

Ethan drew up quickly and composed himself. "Mr. Varnum," he said, stepping away from Zeena. "We just had a problem here, the biscuits, they got burned."

Zeena didn't dare to retrieve her hairpins from the floor, so she ran her fingers through her hair, letting it fall behind her shoulders. She smoothed down the skirt of her apron, then one hand went to the last of the scrape on her cheek. She swallowed her laughter, even as she looked at Ethan and saw it still in his eyes.

The visitor cleared his throat before speaking. "I wouldn't ha' come in but I was knocking and I wanted to leave this—" He held an envelope in the air.

Ethan coughed.

Zeena gestured to the stove. "We had to throw 'em in the fire," she started, "they were burned to charcoal," and she had to stifle a laugh as she glanced at Ethan, but there was no laughter left in him. His face showed a sudden solemnity.

The visitor sniffed at her explanations. "I been to Worcester," he said. "On business," he added. He removed his hat with one hand and with the other held out the envelope.

Worcester, just the mention of this town, it brought Mama to mind.

Ethan approached the man, waving a hand in the air at Zeena. "This's Zenobia Pierce, she's here from—"

"Bettsbridge," the man interrupted, "I know all about it."

Ethan looked down at the floor. "She's here to look after Ma." He turned to Zeena then. "This's Lawyer Varnum, from town."

Zeena nodded at the visitor, then turned to the cookstove, leaving the men to their business. So this was Rebekah's father, she thought. "I got this letter for her," the visitor was saying, but Zeena wasn't listening. In her head was the sound of laughter, Ethan's, hers. She felt the lingering impression of Ethan's hand on her shoulder, warm and solid. She swept the crumbs off the surface of the stove and replaced the lid, then lifted the linen towel that covered the bread pudding to see was it warm enough. She'd separated the morning's cream from the milk, had saved it special for the pudding.

"Zeena." It was Ethan. He was beside her at the stove. "Zeena, Mr. Varnum's got a letter for you."

Zeena turned with questioning eyes. "A letter?"

"I was in Bettsbridge last night, seeing a client," Lawyer Varnum was saying.

Zeena nodded.

"Seems my client's a neighbor to Mr. Pierce," he said, taking a step in Zeena's direction, holding out the letter some inches from his chest.

"Mr. Fullerton?" she asked. He worked at the bank where Father made his payments on the house he'd mortgaged to buy his place in the ice delivery business.

Lawyer Varnum nodded. "I had the opportunity to meet your father when he come in on some business of his own, and when he heard I was heading to Starkfield, he asked would I carry a letter to you."

Zeena approached him. She'd not imagined she'd hear any news for weeks, at least not until he heard from her, but there'd been no time since she'd arrived to write him.

Lawyer Varnum nodded. "He went on home and wrote it right then. I collected it from him when I passed by."

Zeena reached for the letter. Her hand hung in the air.

Clutching the letter, Lawyer Varnum went on, "Mrs. Varnum," and he turned to Zeena saying, "that's my wife," then back to Ethan, "she wants you should bring Zenobia into town one of these days before snow comes."

Ethan looked at Zeena with raised eyebrows.

"I'd hate for Cousin Beatrice to be alone so long," Zeena said. Then, to Lawyer Varnum, after lifting her chin, "Course, I'd like to meet her." She kept her eyes on the letter, though she'd withdrawn her hand. "Might she come here for a visit?" Zeena inquired.

Ethan coughed. He shook his head as Lawyer Varnum spoke, "It's such a ways out here, but I'll tell her so." And to Zeena, "Course if you come in to see us, Mrs. Varnum'd be pleased. The girls don't often meet folks from away. There's so many unsavory types, we don't encourage travel, not when they can find what they need right in town."

"Your daughters?" Zeena asked.

"Rebekah," and he looked at Ethan with narrowed eyes, "and Ruth, she's our baby."

Ethan turned to the cookstove. "It's quite a ways out here for town folk, Zeena," he said, bending to check the firebox.

"Rebekah knows the way, that's for certain, but she's not as sturdy as most. I don't hold with a young girl gallivanting round the countryside, 'specially when she's a sickly sort."

"I'll make sure Zeena gets to town one day soon," Ethan said.

"Mrs. Varnum has some lace curtains she sent all the way to Chicago for. She'd like to show 'em off," the lawyer said to Zeena.

"I'm sure they're lovely." Then quickly she quipped, "But of course, you don't get the view of the mountains into town like you do out here, do you?"

Ethan coughed. "How's Ruth, she getting along after that chest cold?"

Lawyer Varnum nodded. He kept his eyes on Ethan. "She's recovered well enough," he said, and Zeena thought he was waiting for Ethan to go on and ask about Rebekah, but Ethan only coughed and said, "T'was nice of you to bring that letter."

The lawyer still kept his eyes on Ethan. "It was no trouble, seeing as how I was passing by." He replaced his hat and looked around the kitchen. He stepped over to the sink and gazed out the window. "Snow'll be flying any day." Then, "Too bad you didn't get that ell back together this year."

Zeena looked at Ethan's face, saw his features turn stony. "I don't know how he managed at all," she said to the lawyer, "what with his ma taken sick and the mill work he's got."

Lawyer Varnum leaned toward Zeena, so close she could see the dark pupils of his hazel eyes and the cracks in his lips. "The Fromes're tough stock," he said. "His father built that mill with his own hands all the while working in the woods. Ethan here was born to such. It's his duty now to carry on his father's name. Young folks today, they don't—"

"I thank you for my letter," Zeena said, reaching for the envelope and pulling it from his fingers. "And tell your wife I hope she'll come soon. It's always nice to have company." Then she added, "No reason she couldn't bring your girls too."

"DON'T YOU WANT TO SEE what's in your letter?" Ethan asked, smothering his dish of bread pudding with cream.

"I want to finish my pudding first," Zeena answered. The letter lay on the table beside her water glass; she stared at Father's lettering: Zenobia Pierce, the letters crawled across the envelope like a silk fringe. She looked away; there'd be time for the letter once she'd got the supper dishes cleaned up and had taken some food and a new compress in to Cousin Beatrice. Then, "Folks from town, they all so pig-headed?"

"Some are, some aren't."

"And he's one that is," Zeena said. Off in the distance Lawyer Varnum's buggy wove along the lane on the next ridge over. She patted her hair; she'd twined it up into a pug soon as Lawyer Varnum left, but wasn't sure it was secured with her hairpins.

"He needs to think he's so high and mighty, else he'd prob'ly feel same's the rest of us."

Zeena smiled. "Father always said to stay clear of lawyers. They put too much attention to what benefits theirselves."

"Maybe, but he was always good to us. Hired Pa to work on his house. We called it a mansion." He reached for the pudding and spooned some more into his dish. "A man a his standing, he needs to remind a poor man like me how little I have so he can hold on to how much he has. Like his daughters, they're just two more possessions, far as I can tell." His eyes turned cloudy as they stared out the window.

Zeena was unaccustomed to so much talk from Ethan. Had Mr. Varnum's visit brought it on? Or had the laughter over the burned biscuits got him going? She took advantage of the moment and asked, "The rest of the Varnums, they all so high and mighty?"

Ethan's face hardened; he lowered his head and squinted at the darkened window. "He didn't mention the two sons he lost to scarlet fever," and he frowned. "I never once heard him speak about those boys. Or Mrs. Varnum. It was as if they couldn't believe folks as good as them could be struck with such sorrow."

"Death don't care how much gold you carry in your pocket. It's like winter, it comes when its time is due."

Ethan nodded and kept staring out at the dark.

Zeena thought of Mama and her babies. "Life's as fragile as the finest glass." Then, "Rebekah, she as sickly as he says?"

"Until recent, she was."

"How'd a cocky fellow like him get a daughter kindhearted as she is?"

"She's her ma in looks, but she was born to the wrong family. She don't go along with highfalutin ways. Rebekah, she likes all folks. Always has a good word for others, even when there don't seem to be a shred a good anyone else can see."

"How'd she come by this quality?"

"She used to be sickly, all right. Maybe that did it. The scarlet fever, she got it same as her brothers, but she survived, and that was hard to bear."

"How d'you mean?"

"She was all the time wondering why she was spared." Ethan pushed back from the table. He shook his head. "It's all over anyway now."

"What's all over?"

It took several moments for Ethan to answer. "Being sickly. She's good as the next one now."

"How old's Rebekah?"

"She's . . ." he looked at the ceiling, "twenty, maybe."

"Oh. I thought she was younger."

"That's young enough."

"But I thought, well, twenty, that's marrying age."

Ethan reached for his cider and took a swallow. He ran a hand through his hair, sending spears on end. He pushed his chair back from the table. Was he done talking?

Zeena had given herself a healthy serving and was nearly finished. "No matter how much I eat, I stay the same." She paused before saying more, but then went on. "In school they called me 'Bones,' " and suddenly, saying it aloud like that, it didn't seem so awful. Ethan's eyes softened, which sent a smile onto her face. "I hated it. All those other girls, so sweet looking with their pretty curls and their round faces."

"You must ha' had your good points."

"Mama always said—" but she caught herself. She wasn't used to speaking to a man this way, especially him in his union suit and leaning back in his chair like he was the state governor or something, except what state governor'd let his hair stand in spears?

"Your mama always said what?" he asked.

She shook her head. "T'were nothing."

Ethan leaned forward. He looked at Zeena from across the table with eyes dark blue as the night sky and a yearning as deep. He opened his mouth to speak, but paused. Then, "What'd she say?"

"She always said," Zeena went on, sitting up straight in her chair and lifting her chin, "always said beauty's in the eye of the beholder."

Ethan blinked. She could see in his face a flush of feeling, but he said nothing.

Zeena waited. Then, "I'll get some more cider," she said.

Ethan remained as he was, leaning back in his chair, his hair still mussed and standing on end.

"Your head looks like an asparagus patch," she said as she returned to the table.

Ethan's brow furrowed.

"Your hair," she explained, "it's all in spears." She brought the looking glass from the sink over to the table to show him.

Ethan chuckled, "Well, I'll—" He might as well've been a boy then; a grin ran across his face and his eyes sparkled and it made Zeena smile again. He ran his fingers through his hair, smoothing it down. "I never seen it do that before."

"How often you look in the glass?"

He laughed, lightheartedly.

Zeena felt the lightness of it and was seized with a wish to let her hair loose. For those moments when Lawyer Varnum was there and her hair'd hung behind her shoulders, it was like being a girl before Mama went, when Zeena played the piano while Mama and Father danced, and sometimes Zeena shook her head, sending her hair loose. She watched her parents whirl round the room, Mama's feet like tiny birds ready to take flight and Father's arms leading Mama like she was an auburn-haired angel. Sometimes when Father was working and Mama'd been called off, Zeena tried it. She twirled in circles, lifted her arms in the air as if ready to fly. She danced around the room then, arms waving in the air like wings, her hair flying loose.

Pure freedom, it was.

FOURTEEN

$\mathscr{Z}$eena sat on a chair in the near dark of her room to read Father's letter. She'd taken some food to Cousin Beatrice, had bathed her quickly, cleaning the canker and putting another compress on it. Ethan was in the kitchen working on an ax handle. He'd cut himself a piece of ash and was preparing to shape a new handle so he could finish up the woodpile. "What I done so far won't get us past the first full moon of the new year."

Zeena pulled her shawl tighter about her shoulders. It was already too cold to stay for long in her room, but she wanted its privacy to read her letter. The candle on the dresser gave enough light so she could read Father's words. She already suspected bad news. Why else would Father write?

Zeena slipped her thumb under the lip to open the envelope and unfolded the piece of paper. Father's jagged scrawl covered most of the page.

Daughter Zenobia,

This gentlmin says he's going by the Frome farm and can take you this letter. Be sure to thank him for his truble. I'm writing to tell you Aunt Belle has passed from this world. Happened so fast, she were gone before anyone knew she was sickly. She got seezed up with something, it kept her from breathing. She had an apple pie in the oven what burned to crisp. That's what got Uncle Nathan in the kitchen. She was already gone.

Belle always seemed the kind what'd go fast. There's a small blessing in that fact. Widow Danvers, she's been looking in on me, so you stay long as you're needed.

> *Your Father,*
> *Lubin Pierce*

It couldn't be so. Aunt Belle, everyone said she was strong as an oak tree, nothing'd ever cut her down. Aunt Belle wasn't sick a day in her life. When the typhoid came into her home, she took care of the others and didn't fall prey to it, even when she lost her only son. She was that strong. Uncle Nathan, he always said she'd outlive the rest. A seizure—what'd cause such a thing? Zeena didn't know much about seizures.

Mama'd cry an ocean if she knew. Mama always looked to Aunt Belle like she was a pillar of strength. By example she told others how to live, which is why Mama'd said Zeena would go there when she was grown. Mama'd chosen Bettsbridge and didn't seem to mind the lack of advantages in that small town, but she wanted more for Zeena.

But with Aunt Belle gone, who'd I go to? she wondered. Aunt Belle, she was part of the dream.

Aunt Belle, how'll I do it now?

* * *

"ZEENA."

Zeena heard it, but it was so far away. Her name, someone was calling. Was Father wanting her in the kitchen? Something about Aunt Belle.

"Zeena," again softly, but with more insistence.

Zeena opened her eyes. The candlelight from the dresser illuminated a pair of hands, curled in her lap like wood shavings. Whose hands were they?

"Zeena," and this time a knock on the door.

It was Ethan's voice. Now she knew it. And they were her hands. The feeling'd gone from them as she'd slept. She shook them, felt the tingling of blood. And this was her room at the Frome farm. Father's letter, it was on the floor by her feet. She'd fallen asleep in the straight chair by the window. Cold air was seeping in round the cracks of the window. Now it was dark outside. There were no stars showing, no moon to cast its silver light. Only the velvet black of night. And in that night, Aunt Belle was gone.

The knocking picked up. "Zeena, please."

Aunt Belle's gone. This would not change. She would not go to Springfield to see Aunt Belle, to tell her everything about Cousin Beatrice and Ethan, to find a healer to teach her the newest methods, introduce her to the newest treatments. She might not ever go to Springfield again. How could she?

Zeena's neck ached. She rubbed it and called out, "That you, Ethan?"

"Zeena, can you come to the door?"

Zeena stood slowly, giving her back a chance to loosen. Her joints were always stiff after sitting so long, so she held to her hips. She stepped over Father's letter; she would pick it up later. What'd it matter if it was on the floor? She knew its contents. Aunt Belle's gone, she repeated in her head. She rubbed her face as she stepped to the door, then opened it.

Ethan stood holding a candle in the hall. His tall frame cast a shadow back down the stairs and along the sloping wall of the stairwell. "You sleeping?" His voice shook; in his eyes, dark holes, was an agitation. When he saw her face, his brow furrowed. "You ailing?" he asked.

The night's chill had settled in Zeena. She shivered. "I'm just chilled, setting by the window." Aunt Belle's gone. The words stuck in her throat.

Ethan stood there, his head cocked to one side. His hair was mussed and the skin on his face looked damp in the candlelight.

Zeena stared at him. She knew he needed her to say something. "What is it?" she asked, like something she'd memorized.

"It's Ma. Something's wrong."

Zeena straightened. Her voice lacked its usual crisp tone; even she could hear it as she spoke, "How d'you mean?"

"She's white as a winter rabbit. And her eyes, they just stare. Even when I snap my fingers."

Zeena told Ethan she'd need a cup of tea. Then she'd go to Cousin Beatrice. She wanted to tell him about Aunt Belle, but the words, Aunt Belle's gone, they were down in her throat. She didn't dare try to speak them. She blew out the candle instead.

As she followed Ethan down the narrow stairs, he said, "It's spitting snow."

"Already?" she managed to ask.

"First snow, it's always too soon."

The words sank in. Snow. "Guess it snuck in on that warm spell. Like I say," she quipped, "Indian summer's no more'n a tease."

In the kitchen, she waited at the sink while the tea steeped. She wanted to tell Ethan about Aunt Belle, but he was so intent on his own worry. He paced and ran his hand through his hair and rubbed the back of his neck. "You want tea?" she asked him, and he shook his head. She poured a cup for herself and stood at the dark window that faced west. Ethan paced. Then suddenly he stopped and asked, "You read your father's letter?" Zeena told him yes. Was he well? Ethan asked. Zeena told him yes. Then she said, "But Aunt Belle's gone," the words coming out in a sort of croak. Ethan said nothing, so Zeena added, "Mama's sister, from Springfield," and Ethan said, "The one you planned on staying with," and Zeena said yes.

Ethan approached her, stood behind her. Zeena could hear him breathing. "It's all right," she said, leaning on the sink for support. She could feel his hand almost touching her shoulder. If he lays that hand on my shoulder, she thought, I'll go to pieces.

But he didn't. "That'll be a sorrow for you," he said.

Zeena swallowed. "It's all right," she repeated. The cup clinked in its saucer as Zeena put it in the sink.

"You sure?"

"I'll never see her again," Zeena said.

"No," Ethan confirmed.

Zeena had the sense she could lean into Ethan then, could lay her head against his shoulder and he'd hold her and maybe that'd ease what was going on inside her. Her mind saw it happen. But it was foolishness to imagine such. "Let me see your ma now." She led the way, then, Ethan following behind with the candle.

ousin Beatrice, she was like Ethan said. The skin on her face, it was porcelain white. Cousin Beatrice's face, it was like it'd started shriveling. Where before'd been a few wrinkles, now they were everywhere. Her shoulders were bony rises. And her eyes—the way they stared, it was impossible for them to be seeing anything. They were like marbles, no pupils.

Zeena imagined Aunt Belle's eyes when Uncle Albert found her. Were they wide in a death stare? She shook her head. Mustn't think on it, she told herself. Mustn't think about what she'd do once Cousin Beatrice was healed and Zeena could go. Where'd she go now? Mustn't think on it.

Ethan put a hand on his mother's shoulder. "Ma," he said, a heavy sound, like an iron set on a piece of clothing to press it. He scratched his head, and when he spoke again it was with a voice soft as water, as if maybe that'd get a response. "Ma, look at me, will you?"

Cousin Beatrice continued to stare unseeing at the ceiling.

Ethan bent and touched her cheek. "Her skin's cold, like I said." He turned frightened eyes to Zeena.

Zeena stepped in as Ethan made way for her. "Cousin Beatrice," Zeena said, sitting beside her on the bed. She ran a hand through the air over her face. The eyes blinked. "You saw that, didn't you?"

Ethan came close.

Zeena waved her hand again in the air. Cousin Beatrice blinked again. Then she closed her eyes. "I'm listening," she croaked out.

Ethan thrust his hands in his pockets as he turned and paced by the bedside. "Don't start that again, please, Ma," and he caught Zeena's eye with a shake of his head. "I don't want she should start that."

Zeena stared at Ethan, then back at Cousin Beatrice. She placed her hands on Cousin Beatrice's eyes, palms down. She held them there, like Mama'd long ago showed her. She gave a little pressure, then let her fingers work on the forehead. She made little sighing sounds, which to her was singing. Then slowly she let her fingers trail down over the eyes. "You're just tired, isn't that it?" she directed at Cousin Beatrice. "You had too much fresh air, I'd venture, you—"

From behind her Ethan whispered, "It's more'n that, look at her."

Zeena heard him speak, but she didn't listen to the words. She knew by his tone that he was scared. It was his Ma, course he'd be scared. But Zeena, she knew Cousin Beatrice just needed rest, and she didn't want Ethan upsetting his mother. A man could turn everything sour at a time like this.

Zeena stood up so she could pull back the covers. She withdrew an arm. The fingers were white. Zeena held the hand in hers and stroked it, saying, "Are you cold, Cousin Beatrice?" as gentle as she could. "Remember what I said, you got to love this hand," Zeena started.

"What's happened to her?"

Zeena's lips pressed together. She shook her head. "Ethan, you'd best go right along while I check some things."

He nodded, already withdrawing.

"Bring me a basin of hot water. And a clean rag. And some towels."

His eyes grew large.

"And my apron, from the back of my chair."

The door closed behind him. It's always better for a man to have something to do, she thought. A man without something to do is like a pig brought inside a parlor. He slams into things and looks uncomfortable.

Just then Zeena noticed the wind. A fine whistling whirling sound, it enclosed the house. She looked to the blackened window and shivered. She couldn't see the snow, but she knew it was there. That was the thing about snow. It come up behind you. You went to bed seeing stars out your window and woke in the morning to a white cloud settled on you. Too, you might go in a room expecting to see Mama and she'd be gone. Or you'd open a letter, and Aunt Belle, she'd be gone. Just when you're thinking things're going your way, you find out otherwise.

But there was no point in thinking on sorrows right now. Zeena knew she must train her mind on Cousin Beatrice.

"Cousin Beatrice," Zeena said from where she stood at the window, "I'm going to tell you straight. There's snow out there. In the morning, you'll see it. Time morning comes, you'll be telling me you want to go outside again and I'll be saying, No, we can't, not today."

Zeena returned to Cousin Beatrice. Even with the snow coming, a tremendous warm feeling was growing inside her. Her senses were heightened. Her hands covered the eyes again, worked on the forehead, soothed the cheeks, and Zeena felt every pore of the skin. She felt the blood clogging in the veins at the temples. She worked to free the blood, to let it flow smooth again. With her fingers pressing on the skull, she felt the brain beneath, little sharp impulses like needles, the tiniest combustions. "You're all riled up," she told Cousin Beatrice, as she worked her fingers in tight little circles to break apart what Zeena was sure were Cousin Beatrice's hopeless thoughts.

"Imagine it's that night long ago when you collected so much sap and your feet were swole up, and you come to bed so you could rest, and when you laid yourself down you felt all your tiredness seep out and with each breath you took in the life you'd given out so in the morning you were ready again," Zeena whispered in her ear. It seemed to Zeena she could breathe her own life in through the skin if she could only get close enough.

Zeena heard rattling sounds in the other part of the house. Ethan's fetching the basin, she thought.

She opened the bodice of Cousin Beatrice's clean nightdress and removed the bandage. Cousin Beatrice cried out. The canker'd swelled up again, hot and ugly. It gave off a sickly odor. "Ethan's bringing water, I'll clean this all up," Zeena told her. The canker radiated heat, but everything else on Cousin Beatrice was cold. "You're chilled," she said, covering Cousin Beatrice again and rising from the bed, then stooping to load the stove with more wood. She opened the damper to let the fire roar. "Better to listen to the fire roar than the wind," she whispered to Cousin Beatrice.

Zeena took her hand. She laid it palm to palm against her own. She placed her other hand on top of Cousin Beatrice's. "Auntie Etta, she laid in this bed and got herself cured," Zeena whispered, even knowing it was not this bed, not this house that Cousin Beatrice was a girl in, but she hoped to bring that youthful hopeful time into the room so it'd circulate into Cousin Beatrice's blood. "You can be cured. I'll just clean that sore up and get it warm in here."

Cousin Beatrice looked at Zeena. There was a flatness and a cloudiness to her gaze, as if her eyes were filled with muddied pond water.

"You can see me, can't you?" Zeena asked.

Cousin Beatrice blinked. She stared at Zeena with those clouded eyes.

"Once we get you fixed up, there's no telling—"

"I'm listening," Cousin Beatrice interrupted.

Zeena drew back. Maybe it was more'n she figured, that swollen canker. Maybe it was twisting her mind. Keeping her outside these afternoons, maybe she got so wore out, like Ethan said, and it was setting off something else. Watching Zeena slice apples, maybe it crossed her eyes.

Ethan pushed open the door then. He looked questioningly at Zeena.

"Put that over here," Zeena instructed, standing. He rested the basin on the stove so the water'd heat up near to boiling, then looked at his mother. Zeena held to his arm. "You go on now," she said, turning her back to the bed so she could look directly at him. His brow wrinkled as he opened wide his eyes, nearly black in the dim light. "That canker's worked up again," she said. Ethan's shoulders slouched. "I'll set up with her tonight," she told him, holding tight to his arm.

Ethan leaned toward her, his face tilted down so his cheek was almost touching hers, so she could feel his breath against her face. If she lifted her chin, her lips would touch his. Zeena froze. Ethan's head lowered still more, till—

Ethan pulled away. He closed his eyes. His hand went to his forehead. "I shouldn't—" he started.

Her knees had turned to trembling, and his arm, where she held to it still, was shivering ever so slightly, but "Don't think on it," she whispered, though she wasn't sure whether she meant Cousin Beatrice or the fact they'd almost kissed. She let go his arm.

Ethan reached for her arm and nudged her, his eyes still closed, to the door. With his head bent so his chin brushed her hair, he voiced, "I don't know how I'd do without you."

Zeena's heart was going in her head now. The trembling, the

warmth, they were spreading through her. She couldn't think of a word to say. Her hand went to her cheek. Had his lips touched her there? She wasn't sure. Her cheeks were flushed now, hot.

"I mean to . . . to bring her back," she said, though the words themselves were not at all what was working inside her. The unfamiliar feelings that tossed her about, shook her from all she'd known into another place; they were as broad, as wide as the sea, or maybe the sky.

They stood like that, staring hard at each other, Ethan's eyes bright with water, Zeena's with heat. So soft, she felt herself. Woman soft.

ALL DAY IT'D BEEN FORMING. This sense of herself as healer, as woman. It'd been building inside her without her knowledge. The place inside her where Mama lodged, and now Aunt Belle, their voices formed a chorus, their eyes gave off a light. Their hair, it was a bluster of fire. Mama's hands, they were held together over Zeena's in prayer.

Father, all his admonishments, he was far away. His voice was a tiny sizzle sound at the edge of her mind. His faultfinding, she couldn't find it inside herself anymore. His sorrow, it was dead, but not Mama and Aunt Belle.

Aunt Belle, she was lying on the kitchen floor, her cheek pressed against the pine floorboards and the apple pie burning. Zeena could smell it. She could almost touch Aunt Belle's legs that were sprawled, misangled, across the floor. But it didn't matter. Her voice and her eyes, even her hair, thick and lush, it was all inside Zeena now.

Mama, she lay on the bed with Baby wrapped in gauze, but it didn't matter. What was inside, Mama's voice, her hands, her eyes, these pulled Zeena into all she ever hoped to be.

As the darkness settled in deeper and the wind rattled the windows and the sky spit snow, Zeena knew what to do.

Her mission, to bring Cousin Beatrice back, and that other feeling, that yearning in her flesh for what she'd never known, a merging of two into one, and that heat spreading through her, that heat of her life, it wound the strands of herself into one.

The lilac branches were scratching on the window and the woodstove was radiating its heat. Everything in the room was hot to the touch except the window's glass panes. They stung Zeena's fingertips when she tapped the glass. But the bedcovers, and the water in the basin, and the wood frame of the bed, Zeena felt the heat there.

Hands, drink in that heat till you turn red.

She was thinking about Ethan and the moments when their faces were so close she could see nothing but his eyes, could feel nothing but his cheek against hers, barely, barely. It washed away in the water. Now there was only Cousin Beatrice.

Zeena felt not a moment's doubt that she would bring Cousin Beatrice back once and for all. Heal that canker so in the morning there'll be little trace of it. Ease those swollen joints so Cousin Beatrice'll move without wincing.

Hands, she said, listen to this night. Let it seep into your pores. It's there in the night, what you will do.

They were trembling, those red-palmed hands, as they uncovered the swollen breast. The canker was purplish black. Zeena fixed a steaming compress and laid it over the sore. Cousin Beatrice whimpered. Zeena held it there. She inhaled, then exhaled in little bursts, lifted the compress, rinsed it, and laid it on again. Over and over she repeated the process, passing the minutes this way without a pause, against the background of the wind. She listened to Cousin Beatrice's quiet cries. She left the compress on for longer periods then, and while it heated the canker she pressed her fingers into Cousin Beatrice's scalp; she laid her palms against the eyes; she trailed her fingers down the cheeks; she pressed at the back of the neck, running her fingers up in the small indentation. On the shoulders, her fingers pressed, kneaded, rubbed. Zeena's breathing deepened; she kept her fingers working until she and Cousin Beatrice were one.

The breast was blood red now. Yellow pus drained into the compress. Zeena got fresh water from the kitchen and started in: she rinsed, pressed, rinsed, pressed. On and on the pus came. Its odor pinched at Zeena's nose. On and on the night went, Cousin Beatrice crying, Zeena breathing, Mama's hands guiding her, Aunt Belle's arms supporting her, and when the shooting pains started down her legs and her head nearly fell in exhaustion, she fetched more water and started in again.

On and on.

When there was no more pus, though, the swelling continued. The canker was filling with blood. When the bleeding started, there was no stanching its flow. The room was so hot, Zeena's clothing was dampened, her hair sopped. Cousin Beatrice's skin glowed with perspiration.

Zeena knew to open the window then. Wide. To get the life-giving air in and the death-inducing air out. Snow, it was swirling in among the lilac branches. Specks of it flew into the room. She leaned over, let her face get the full feel of it. "Snow," she whispered to Cousin Beatrice, laying her snow-cooled hands on Cousin Beatrice's face. She fanned Cousin Beatrice as the blood seeped from the canker. She cleaned it up, fetched more water.

Was it just before dawn that Zeena found she could not keep up with the blood? It was that hour when the dark turned darker than black and Zeena lit the third candle of the night. Cousin Beatrice lapsed silent about then. Her eyes closed and rolled back in their sockets. All color drained from her lips. When Zeena returned to the room with fresh water, she found the blood'd seeped down between Cousin Beatrice's breast and her arm, soaking the bedcovers, the sheet, the mattress in a pool.

Zeena closed the window. "Hold on, Cousin Beatrice," she

whispered. Cousin Beatrice's features blurred. It could've been Mama, her auburn hair making a fan around her face. "Hold on," she said again, letting her hands go to work.

But the bleeding kept on.

One second it was Cousin Beatrice, then it was Mama, and Zeena was saying, "Hold on, Mama, don't go like this," and Zeena's fingers pressed and kneaded the forehead, the face, the shoulders, the neck. Her thumbs pressed on the neck, pushed, pushed, pushed, and her fingers dug in deep until—

Cousin Beatrice opened her eyes. From their dark sockets, her eyes were blue-black pools of water. They looked right at Zeena, focused hard, but their gaze went straight through her. What Cousin Beatrice was seeing, Zeena could not guess. What she was knowing, Zeena could not know.

A long, low sigh came from those lips that had no color.

"No," Zeena cried out. But she couldn't stop it. Cousin Beatrice's life'd been draining away, and in that sigh was the last of her.

SIXTEEN

*Z*eena was on her knees by the window. She recited the words "What'd I do?" over and over. It was hard to think what they meant, though. She pressed her face against the glass and watched the darkest hour fade. The dark was not so dark then. It was just black.

Then it was gray.

The gray came up behind the pine trees up on the ridge. She saw their tips poking at the still-black sky.

The gray spread, then, filling the sky with a ghostly tint. Everything was gray until there was enough light to see white. Snow covered the ground with a thin blanket. It lay in the crooks of trees like cotton. The last orange leaves still on tree limbs glared. Red maples against the snow were an exaggeration, too much for the eye.

Gray and white, it was everywhere.

"Why couldn't you do like Auntie Etta?" Zeena said aloud. She turned quickly. Maybe it was true, Cousin Beatrice'd sit up and say, "I guess I won't be going just yet." But Cousin Beatrice lay there, a stone. And what'd I do? Zeena asked.

Ethan, she thought, if he'd just asked for help months ago. How could she've helped someone what was already half gone from the start? But Ethan didn't know. Did he?

But what'd I do? cried in her head. It was hard for her to settle on these thoughts. They flitted in, out, in, out and she wasn't sure she could say just what it was she was thinking.

Zeena's hands folded together. She unclasped them and looked at the palms. Long ago they'd been soft, but now they were etched with lines. She studied the fingers. The skin was rutted where once it'd been smooth. She looked at her knuckles and the backs of her hands. Not much flesh, but it was loose. Just hands, getting-old hands. Mama's never got this bad, she decided. Even when Mama's hands aged, they were different from these.

You are no healer, her hands told her.

Zeena's head dropped. What'd I do? She could think it no longer. She could look outside no longer. The gray and the white were a prison.

You are no healer.

Truth.

You are a spinster.

Truth.

Zeena's head was bowed, but she could not turn from the window. Aunt Belle and Mama, she feared they were behind her. Mama, on the bed beside Cousin Beatrice. Aunt Belle, sprawled on the floor. Their eyes were shut, all of their eyes were shut. Mama and Aunt Belle, their hair was a fire. Cousin Beatrice, hers was the color of the sky. Gray. They'd lost their voices.

Mama, tell me what to do, please, she begged. Mama didn't answer.

Aunt Belle, tell me I should come to Springfield. Leave this hillside, this gray land, and come to Springfield. Aunt Belle didn't answer.

Cousin Beatrice, come with me. I'll take you—

It was no use. They were all of them gone, and there was no healing in her hands.

ZEENA DID NOT HEAR ETHAN'S STEP on the parlor floor. She did not hear the door open.

But she heard the sound he made when he entered the room even before she turned to see him. It had no shape, that sound. It was low and high all at once; it was a sigh and a cry and a moan, all at once, lasting just a second. It shook her from the vacillating thoughts that'd plagued her. Now she could think on something: Ethan.

Zeena rose to her feet. "Ethan, I—" but the sight of him, his face twisted, his hands already shaking as they came to his face, she dared not speak. She went to him. He turned to the closed door behind him and leaned into it.

She remembered when Mama went. Remembered standing by Mama's bed, remembered the way her body shook like tall grass in the wind, the way everything inside her turned sick, all the things she wanted to cry out but kept silent, all the words that would do no good, and the way Father ordered her out.

She placed a hand on Ethan's shoulder. It was shivering, like her knees had shivered when she stood by Mama. His shivering made her legs strong.

Zeena looked at Cousin Beatrice. Her mouth was askew; her eyes, half open; her chin, thrust up and gray. The canker, the blood, it was a scarlet splash on the bedding. Like one of those hibiscus from Florida. Zeena acted quickly, pulling the covers up over Cousin Beatrice.

"She just now went," Zeena whispered, a hand on Ethan's arm. His shivering increased. "I was by her side. I was holding her." Ethan let his head bump against the door. "Don't," she said. "She went peaceful." He sighed, and Zeena recalled Cousin Beatrice's life as it had passed in that final sigh. "She went just like that, in a sigh."

Ethan looked at her from the corners of his eyes, his head butted up against the door. "She feared the snow. Hated its coming. Winter was more'n she could bear these last years. She must ha' known." He gestured to the window and the white snow that covered everything.

"I tried everything." The words came easily. "I heat-packed that canker. I worked on her, I—"

"You done everything."

They stood there, then, Ethan leaning against the door, Zeena with a hand on his shoulder. Zeena realized how tired she was. She felt the asthma coming on. When she breathed, there was a rattling sound. But there was so much to do. She had to clean Cousin Beatrice, get her ready. She had to—

"I want to set with her," he said.

"Let me clean her up first. Make her presentable."

Ethan nodded, reached for the doorknob. He turned then and faced Zeena. He kept his eyes from straying over to the bed. A confused look settled over his face. "What'll I do now?" he asked.

Zeena smiled. She smoothed her hair down. "You go get the cookstove roaring and start some water to boil. You tend to the animals, like always. You eat some a that bread I left on the breadboard and get some oatmeal cooking. When I say so, you come set with her. Then, Ethan," and she whispered, "you must go for the undertaker."

He nodded, like a boy assigned his chores.

What'll I do now? Zeena considered the question for herself only momentarily. For the time present she had plenty to do. She had more to do than she imagined having time for. There was the laying out of the body and the undertaker to come and the cleaning of the house and the cooking for tomorrow's funeral and there was the burying.

After that, when all of that was accomplished, then she'd have to answer: What'll I do now?

SEVENTEEN

Cousin Beatrice is small as a child now. Her feet extend only halfway to the foot of the bed. Her head rests on a pillow that's covered with a piece of black veil that Zeena found in the chest at the foot of the bed in her room. A clean brown blanket comes to her chest. Her arms rest on her chest under the blanket; her hands fold together. Her fingers are slender icicles. She wears the black serge that Zeena found in her chest, wrapped up in paper to preserve it. Prob'ly it'd been her mourning dress after Mr. Frome went, and others before them. Black jet buttons are its decoration, along with crepe cuffs. Soon as the undertaker comes and packs ice under her, the smell of passing away will diminish.

The room is bright with sunlight. Soon after Ethan left to fetch the undertaker, the gray skies lifted. A dazzling white landscape spread in all directions. The snow-sparkled light filled the room while Zeena washed the body and prepared it. Even now the light is harsh.

Even so, Cousin Beatrice's skin is like china. Zeena washed

it, oiled it, powdered the face and hands so they are smooth and white as a baby's. Her features are delicate, like a china doll's. The nose, the mouth, the chin, even the eyelids, they would break off if she was dropped on the floor.

Cousin Beatrice's suffering hardly shows. The wrinkles in her face are smoothed and her eyes are closed. She looks like someone that lived long and realized it was time to go and accepted it with an uncommon grace. Even welcomed it. Her dying, there is little evidence of it, unless one was to open her nightdress and examine the blue-blackened breast. The festering is over, though. Even that is calm now.

Zeena is calm too. Through the process of washing, cleansing, dressing, of cleaning the bed, of arranging Cousin Beatrice just so, Zeena's heartsick mind was cleaned and arranged also. She will not think about her failure for now. Long as she has someone to do for, and Cousin Beatrice, until she is laid in the ground, will be that someone, Zeena feels herself intact. And after Cousin Beatrice, there'll be Ethan to do for. For a few days, anyway.

Even her hands are calm. They stopped their fluttering, their twisting, that sense that they could not come to rest anywhere. Now they rest in her lap like children sleeping.

She'd had to be calm for Ethan. "Do you want I should wait here?" Zeena'd asked him when she found him in the kitchen and told him his mother was ready for his visit. He shook his head. His eyes showed feelings she could only guess at since he couldn't speak them. She felt no irritation with him anymore. Her own feelings shriveled up next to his unspoken ones, and in that was her saving. When he stood at Cousin Beatrice's side, he still said nothing, just stared at his mother's face for several long minutes before swallowing and backing up, out the door. Zeena followed him to the kitchen. "You going to be all right?" she asked him. He nodded vacantly and then turned his gaze to the windows that faced the hillside. "Will you go for the undertaker?" she nudged. He'd forgotten, clearly, because he snapped out of his reverie and repeated it, "Mr. Willoughby?" as if he'd had no idea of it. Then, "Ma said as how she wants us to keep her here after she goes, she said don't let them take her into town for the laying out." Zeena was not unaware of his use of "us," but she passed it by. "I'll talk to him when he gets here," she said. "You go right along now," she said, putting a hand on his shoulder. She hoped the ride into town would jar him from the stupor that seemed to've taken him. She kept her hand on his shoulder until he finally said, "Well, I guess I'll be going to town then."

After he left and before she returned to Cousin Beatrice, Zeena stood by the table where Ethan had sat only minutes before. She reached her hand out in the air to the place where his shoulder had been. He was a large man, with broad, strong-looking shoulders, but the feel of that shoulder, it was soft. It'd surprised her. She recalled the evening before when they'd stood at Cousin Beatrice's door. The same stirring she'd felt then came again. It was a fluttering inside her, and it sent her heart to thumping in her head. She felt she might faint and sank into Ethan's chair. A strange feeling overtook her. Light-headed, sick almost. A wish so strong to be near to him it consumed her.

When she was able, she made her way to the sink and the water pitcher. She filled a glass and drank it. She filled another. And another. Finally she got her bearings.

Now Zeena has pulled the chair to the window and is sitting in it, back to the lilac branches. The snow is starting to melt. By afternoon, it will be gone. But now the snowlight makes a glow behind her, illuminating the room.

Zeena sits with hands folded. She is so tired her eyes sting and her head wobbles when she blinks. Her shoulders ache, and the shooting pains down her left leg make her foot numb. Her back pains her, but that is no surprise after all the time she's been on her feet, bending, lifting, carrying water. She can't remember when she last ate, when she last bathed herself or brushed her hair. Yet she couldn't eat if she wanted to. In the pit of her stomach is a gnawing that doesn't want food. She couldn't sleep if she wanted to; her veins are fairly dancing. Yet she is calm.

Zeena gazes at Cousin Beatrice. Zeena's seen enough death to know that when Cousin Beatrice moves her head to one side, it is only fanciful. When it appears that Cousin Beatrice's eyes will open, Zeena does not start up. The dead keep moving in our eyes, she tells herself. Even until the lid is closed on them.

When Cousin Beatrice is laid in her box, she will not struggle to escape. She will not cry for someone to help her. She is gone. All that remains is her tired-out body. The hands, Zeena thinks she's never seen such delicate, beautiful hands. Small as seashells and carved with such care as angels must take in decorating heaven. She shakes her head; where'd such notions come from? Mama talked about angels after Grandfather died, how they'd sing to him for eternity so he'd never be alone. But even as Mama said it, Zeena knew she didn't believe it.

Zeena's seen enough dying to know heaven is in the minds of those who stay behind. The minister, he says most everyone will go to heaven. He forgets it's the earth that takes the dead.

Zeena does not let herself think about what she will do after the undertaker comes, after Cousin Beatrice is laid in her box and is planted in the ground at the foot of the hill. A picture of herself on the train almost comes to mind. A picture of Father at the station, and though he won't say it, she sees it in his eyes, that she's no healer. She can't go home to Father now.

So how can she take a train? Where would she go?

EIGHTEEN

*Z*eena was still sitting there, her hands clasped in her lap, when a gentle knock came at the door. "Come in, Ethan," she called, rising from her chair.

A woman some years older than Zeena pushed open the door. The woman had rounded shoulders and plump hands that fluttered in the air. She had tired dark eyes and smooth pink skin; the way she looked at Zeena with her head tilted gave a warmth to her face. Rebekah, small and slender and white-faced, stood behind her mother and stared at Zeena with eyes that said pretend you don't know me. Zeena acknowledged the request with a slight nod of her head.

"You're Zeena," the woman started. "I'm Lucy Varnum," she said but waited to be invited in. "You met my husband, Lawyer Varnum, the other day."

Smoothing her hair, feeling for her hairpins to see were they secure, Zeena asked, "Where's Ethan?"

"We come back with him. Mr. Willoughby'll be along

shortly." She took a step into the room, avoiding the bed where Cousin Beatrice lay.

Zeena approached them, led them back into the parlor.

Lucy Varnum turned serious eyes to Zeena. "I've known Beatrice Frome since I was a girl. All my life, she's been the one to—" but she faltered.

Rebekah looked at the floor, then peered up at Zeena from under her brow. Her thick hair was pulled back, but strands of it had escaped the confinement; she pulled at them with thin fingers. Under one arm was a knitting bag, the tips of the needles poking out.

"This's my daughter Rebekah," the woman said.

Zeena nodded a greeting. She could see the resemblance between the girl and her mother that Ethan'd referred to. They both had the oval-shaped face, the mouth that curved up at the corners, the small delicate nose and high forehead, and the thick dark hair that waved away from the face.

Rebekah said, "Pleased to meet you," and smiled. Her dark eyes darted about until they came to rest on Zeena's.

Zeena's hands went to her pug; was it coming loose? She adjusted her hairpins again.

The mother said, "We're all thankful you're here. Ethan, he's had such a lot," and her head tilted toward the kitchen. "Times I thought he wouldn't hold up. So much to bear," the woman said, looking at her daughter.

A worried look formed on Rebekah's face. She fidgeted with her knitting bag. She looked everywhere but at Zeena and her mother.

Zeena studied the girl's face. Rebekah, she was a serious sort, like her mother, but she knew sorrow in a way her mother did not. Zeena could see it in her eyes and in the fidgeting of her fingers. She hadn't seen it when Rebekah was there without her mother. Now it was painted all over the girl's face.

"Such a pity," the woman said, shaking her head.

Zeena pulled back her shoulders. "I done all I could, Mrs. Varnum."

"Call me Lucy, please," she said with her intense stare. "Course you did all you could. We all knew she didn't have long." She looked at Rebekah, then Zeena. "I'd have come myself, but it's such a long way," and then she sniffed, "and it's, well it's not what it used to be." Then, lowering her voice, she added, "Time was this house was as clean as—" she looked around at the stuffed chairs, their arms worn thin, the fabric nearly gray; at the sofa, its cushions flattened, its seat lumpy; at the lamp with the ripped cover; at a stuffed owl on a corner table, its feathers dusty. "It's gone to pieces these last years and was only so much I could do. Mr. Varnum, he hired Albert whenever—" then she stopped, but only to get her breath. Then, "Never seemed right, Beatrice out here nursed by Ethan." She sighed. "We heard you were coming and were greatly relieved."

"She went peaceful." Zeena felt that fluttering in her hands again, a jitteriness, but it passed when she clasped her hands at her waist.

"So many times, Ethan'd come to town and I'd ask, 'Can I do anything,' and he'd shake his head, no, and I never knew if it was the truth. After Albert passed, Beatrice, why, she just, well, it started long before that, I'd guess . . ." and her voice trailed off. "Rebekah," she started up again, "she rode out with Ethan's hired hand some days and set with Beatrice." She stared at her daughter then. "Wasn't much else she could do. Course she brought food."

Rebekah fidgeted again with her knitting bag.

A silence fell. The late-morning sun glared on the bare floor, emphasizing the room's spareness. From the other side of the house came sounds of activity. "Whyn't I see if Ethan needs anything," Rebekah said, her eyes watering.

"I'll be along in a moment," Lucy said.

Zeena watched Rebekah step across the floor. Most young

girls moved with the freedom of youth, their feet falling firmly on the floor and with little doubt they'd meet with anything but a warm welcome, but Rebekah's step was labored.

"She feels so for him," Lucy said, her voice lowered as if to bring Zeena into some intimacy, and she gazed in the direction of the passage.

Zeena waited. Clearly there was more.

"We all worry after Ethan," and now she was almost whispering. "Beatrice and Albert, well, things turned sour for them so sudden, it seemed, when he was kicked in the head. He didn't act right after that. Gave money, and Lord knows they had little enough to give, to folks less fortunate than them. Then when Ethan first came home from Florida, he had a chip on his shoulder, and the girls in town, girls of his station," and now her voice rose again, "they couldn't get him to turn his head. Now, though, maybe things'll be different. Maybe he'll see there's several girls in town'd be—"

Zeena's eyes widened.

"I'm not meaning Rebekah, you understand."

Zeena waited.

"She's too delicate, don't you know."

Zeena shook her head.

"She's not like other girls."

"No?"

"She wants to be, Lord knows. Just last month she had some foolish idea about leaving these parts. She announced it to Mr. Varnum and me at Sunday dinner."

"Leaving?"

"Off to find a new life, s'what she said."

"Alone?"

"Certainly not. No, there was a young fellow she was sweet on," and Lucy lowered her voice again, "but not the sort her father and I could approve of. She forgets her place sometimes."

Zeena stared. "Her place?"

Lucy kept on. "It's what all the young folk are doing. Up and leaving their families. History. How can you know your history when you're in some strange land?"

"Was she wanting to go west?"

"Gracious, no, it was south, but she's given it up. Her father set her down and put some sense in her. Told her no daughter of his would up and leave his home that way. No one'd have any appreciation for her in faraway places. She's a fragile sort. She could be down with a fever and gone before we knew she'd took sick. No, sir, Mr. Varnum and I, we lost enough," and she looked mournfully toward the room where Cousin Beatrice lay. "No, our Rebekah, she's not like the others."

Zeena nodded, as if in sympathy of Lucy, but what she felt was an understanding of Rebekah. Isn't that what'd been said of herself? "Zeena's not like the rest," she'd overheard Father say to Aunt Martha. It was in the eyes of her cousins, her aunts and uncles, town folks, everyone who knew Zeena'd looked at her askance. The odd thing was that here in Starkfield no one'd given her that look. Since she'd come to the Fromes, folks'd treated her like anyone else.

"Oh," Lucy said, her voice rising, "I shouldn't be speaking of this now," and her eyes watered. "It's just, well, you must see what I'm saying. I mean, is he going to lose the farm, it'd be such a shame, after all his grandfather did to raise the place to profit, and then to see it all go when Albert tried to build up the mill just when the trains was coming, why . . ."

Zeena shook her head in sympathy.

"Poor Beatrice, she did her best with Ethan, but once he came back to Starkfield, well, what with Albert going and then herself turning sick, course, I always wondered if Ethan'd be happy anyplace."

"Oh?"

"Ethan's carried the burdens of the world on his shoulders since he was this high," and she held her hand at her waist. "You could see it in him even then. Rebekah was poorly when she was a child, and Ethan, he brought flowers to her when he come to town, before he went off to college, that is. Such a nice gesture. Why, he'll get caught up here with the mill and then there'll be no more of this worry about the farm. Course you know all this, I don't have to be telling you."

Zeena just stared at her.

Lucy sighed. "Such a shame."

Zeena lifted her chin and held her hand out toward Cousin Beatrice's room. "You want to look in on her?"

"Well, I don't want to intrude, if it's too soon or—"

"She's near ready now, though the undertaker'll bring the ice." Zeena turned back to the room and opened the door. Lucy Varnum stepped past her and walked to the foot of the bed. "Oh, my, I—" she started when she turned to face Cousin Beatrice. Her lips quivered. She drew her hands to her face. "I just never saw Beatrice so, so . . ." and she paused and looked at Zeena. "So beautiful," she finished.

Zeena was thinking of Rebekah and Ethan in the kitchen. Rebekah's young presence, it'd fill the room. Her voice, soft and warm as it was, it'd soothe Ethan.

"You made a miracle here," Lucy was saying. "I never saw Beatrice so fine looking, you wouldn't ha' thought she could ever look so peaceful, not after all she's been through, why," and then she started to cry.

Zeena tried to shut out her imaginings of Ethan and Rebekah in the kitchen. She folded her arms. She squinted at Lucy. There was a heaviness in her limbs, a sense that she could not move if she wanted to. Thoughts of Ethan and Rebekah in the kitchen, they kept coming back.

Then: Where'll I go now? The question formed in her mind and stayed there like a stone, the water running over it.

AT DINNER ETHAN WAS DISTRACTED. "Have some more of this spiced pork," Lucy told him. He still had a plateful of food that he'd picked at but hadn't gotten through.

Rebekah was more gentle. She sat beside Ethan and laid a hand on his forearm when she turned to him and said, "Maybe you need time to yourself." Zeena knew then that Rebekah Varnum was more knowing than her mother ever could be. The girl'd seen that inward look of Ethan's and had correctly understood it. There was a kindness to the girl that Zeena'd seen only in Mama. "Maybe you'll want to get over to the mill or the woodlot. Mother and I can help Zeena with anything needs doing." She looked over at Zeena with a warm smile.

"I'll talk to Mr. Willoughby about the arrangements," Zeena told him. "I saw Jotham and arranged for him to prepare a place down the hill, next to your father. He'll be tending to that this afternoon."

Ethan nodded, looking at his plate.

"He'll make the box too," Zeena told him.

Ethan stood. "I'll be tending to that this afternoon," he said, catching Zeena's eye.

"Can you do it?" she asked.

Ethan's gaze sharpened. He nodded. It was the first time all day he'd taken his inward gaze and let it move outside himself. His eyes were more black than blue as they stared at her; it was as if there was a river in his eyes and he was being carried by a current and could barely keep his head above the water. Out of that river, though, came a look of gratitude. She knew then, without his saying it, that he could not do all that she'd done, that he could not talk to Mr. Willoughby or arrange with Jotham about the place of burial, that he could never have handled his mother's body, that these were things he could not do. But she could. Everything she'd done since she arrived, he was grateful for. The straightening of the kitchen, the washing of clothes, the preparing of food, the tenderness she showed his mother. In that one gaze was all of Ethan's helplessness and all of his relief at her coming and all of his fear for the future and all of his sadness.

Zeena smiled back. Everything she had to give was in that

smile. A small and tender smile, Lucy would've missed its import had she seen it. Rebekah saw it. Zeena felt the girl's eyes go from herself to Ethan and back. Ethan saw it too; he received Zeena's smile with a slow blink of his eyes and a barely perceptible nod of his head.

Lucy said, "Now Zeena, you tell us what we can do to help," but Zeena did not answer her. Her ears were roaring. Her heart was pounding, reverberating in her temples. The heaviness she'd felt all through dinner'd lifted. Now she felt light-headed. The softness that was inside her, she thought it might send her to a collapse. But it didn't. It bolstered her up. She'd seen pictures of those giant balloons floating in the sky, carried here and there by the wind. That's what it was like for Zeena. As if she was floating in the sky and could see for miles and there was nothing to pull her down.

LUCY AND REBEKAH STAYED all through the afternoon to help prepare the funeral biscuits and cakes. Rebekah unpacked the food they'd brought: spiced meats, bottles of cider and rum, a whiskey cake. "For tomorrow," Rebekah explained. When she was done, she sat at the table and knitted, her head bent over as her needles clicked, while Lucy started in to baking. When she looked up, she caught Zeena's eye and smiled at her. Later, when Lucy was in the parlor, she said, "Thank you for not letting on about my coming out here," and Zeena said, "It's for the best." Then Rebekah said, "Ethan's been needing someone like you a long time," and her eyes were watery.

"I just tried to do my best for Cousin Beatrice, seemed unfair she had to suffer so."

Rebekah sighed. The clicking of her needles stopped. "Nothing's fair, I guess. He's suffered too. Tried to do the right thing."

"I never guessed she'd go this fast."

"I'm surprised she lasted this long." The needles started up again. "Ethan's got so much to bear, what with the farm going down. It's nearly broke his heart."

"Is he so beholden to his ancestors?"

Rebekah smiled. She nodded her head. "He loves the land so. He might talk about leaving, but he won't, not Ethan. D'you ever see him grow speechless over the hills and the sky? It touches his heart, these sights."

Zeena wondered at the girl's wisdom. Her mother'd talked about how sorry she was for Ethan, but Rebekah wasn't giving him her pity. She had understanding beyond her years.

"He needs someone like you," she said, and again her eyes watered.

Zeena shook her head. Foolishness.

"I think you should stay."

"Stay?"

"With him. I think you should stay."

The girl was voicing what Zeena'd not let herself think. "I couldn't. Not now. Why, it wouldn't be—"

"Proper?" The softness drained from Rebekah's face. "There ought to be more'n proper that dictates what we do. What about human suffering? Don't that count more'n appearance? A family's hopes, they can become a burden. Seems as if . . ." and her voice trailed off.

Zeena looked at her. The youthfulness and innocence were gone. Instead was a face that knew too much. What'd the girl suffered? Zeena wondered. And why was she telling Zeena this?

"Seems as if there're some'll get what they want no matter what they do. Others can do right all their lives and end up with nothing."

"My father always said those what work hard'll get their proper due." Wasn't that what she'd always tried to do? Wasn't that what'd kept her going?

Rebekah shook her head. Her dark eyes watered. "I don't go

along with that. That's just what we try for so to keep from the truth."

Zeena just stared at Rebekah. The girl wasn't bitter, though her words could've been taken that way. "Are you saying—"

"I'm saying you should do what you can to stay. It's the only way he'll—"

A knock on the front door stopped Rebekah's words. Seconds later a man appeared in the kitchen.

Rebekah's face was washed of what it knew. Now it held its girlishness again. And now Zeena thought she understood the girl's kindness. There was nothing shallow or false about it. Nothing selfish. It came from knowing the world'd never cater to her, that to see the world from another's eyes was her way.

Lucy returned from the parlor. "Why, Mr. Willoughby," she said.

He pulled on his cap. His demeanor was serious, sorrowful. He talked to Lucy while Rebekah leaned close to Zeena. "I don't ever want an undertaker doing for me," she whispered. Zeena looked her in the eye, saw a spark there. "They're too solemn," she whispered ever lower. Zeena nodded. She thought she understood. When she'd started the laying out of Cousin Beatrice that morning, she'd found herself speaking with Mama's voice: "Nothing to fear now," she'd told her. "Where you're going, it's peaceful." Death, it didn't have to be so awful, she'd realized.

Zeena left Lucy and Rebekah in the kitchen and took Mr. Willoughby to Cousin Beatrice's room.

"You done most everything," he told her.

"Cousin Beatrice don't want to be taken to town," she instructed. "She wants to stay here in this house till tomorrow."

Mr. Willoughby nodded his understanding.

They stood on either side of the bed, then, separated by Cousin Beatrice. Just then something showed in the crookedness of Cousin Beatrice's eyebrows. Or was it in the contrasting shadows and shining patches? Zeena bent down and stared.

"Some folks," Mr. Willoughby started, "they think the dead'll speak to them."

Zeena pulled up. "Foolishness," she returned. But her smile faded and she stood back. Maybe so, she wanted to say. And if so, she wanted to hear what Cousin Beatrice had to say.

ZEENA MADE JOHNNYCAKES and served them with milk for supper. Ethan ate slowly, chewing for long seconds before swallowing. Unlike the other days, when his work left his face flushed and his eyes dull with tiredness, this night his skin looked almost gray and his eyes were bright as they stared at the darkened window. Once he withdrew an old silver turnip watch from his pocket and stared at it, blinking, as if he could make no sense of it. He pulled out his pipe and his tobacco pouch, filled the pipe, leaned toward the candle, but did not light it.

Zeena did not speak at supper. She felt it best to let the silence be. She rose to make the tea while he finished his food. When she poured out two cups, she said, "I'm planning to set up with her tonight. You'll want your rest," and she took her seat across the table from him.

Ethan looked at his tea, then up at her. "You was up all last night, you—"

"I slept this afternoon." Zeena'd bathed herself. Rebekah'd helped to wash her hair by the cookstove. She let it dry sitting by the window in the parlor where the afternoon sun fell on it. Rebekah came with a towel every so often and rubbed her hair with it, then ran a brush through. "You need to rest," Rebekah told her, so Zeena'd gone to her room and had fallen into a sudden and deep sleep for over an hour.

"Rebekah went through the house like a whirlwind," and Zeena looked at the scrubbed floor, at the pile of folded bedding, Cousin Beatrice's, in the basket by the door, "and Lucy, she dressed up the parlor for folks to set in tomorrow."

"The Varnums've always been good to us."

"Rebekah, she's a sweet girl."

Ethan nodded.

Zeena swallowed. "She'll make someone a good wife."

He reached for his tea.

"There must be plenty of young men in town who'd—"

"There ain't but a couple, none good enough for her." Ethan leaned back in his chair.

Zeena remembered what Lucy Varnum had said that morning, but still she asked, "Whyn't she get away, then, like most girls? There's work in Lowell for girls her age."

He shook his head. "Mill work'd never do for her."

"It'll do for anyone, far as I know."

"Rebekah, she's—" and he pushed his chair back, started to rise. "She's different, s'all."

Zeena did not pursue it. She'd heard it from Lucy. Rebekah was from a higher family than'd let a daughter go to a mill, and Rebekah was fine spirited, maybe too much, so to work long hours'd wear her down. Prob'ly she'd get sick, is what'd happen. "But still," she said, "if your choice is to stay in Starkfield where there's no chance of a husband because you're too good for the locals, why . . ."

Ethan was up from his chair. He pushed it in to the table. He waited for Zeena to look up at him. "You done so much for Ma."

Zeena shivered. She sat forward and held to the saucer for fear the trembling in her hands'd show. There were flashes of Cousin Beatrice's last moments, the way Zeena'd worked her hands at Cousin Beatrice's neck, the way there'd been that last long sigh and then . . . She shook her head. "I should ha' done more, I should ha'—"

"You done everything except see how bad off she was." He leaned onto the table. His fingertips lightly brushed the back of her hand as it held to her saucer, then he quickly withdrew his hand and coughed, standing straight.

Zeena shook her head. That tightening in her throat came again.

"If you'd known her before, you'd ha' seen how bad off she was."

Still Zeena shook her head, but she said nothing.

Ethan, his eyes'd never been so bright. "She deserved better. But in her last days, you was there to—" he couldn't go on. "Now I don't know what I'll, I—" Ethan walked over to the cookstove and back. He paced the room again.

"I'll stay to go through her things," Zeena offered. To herself, she wondered: And then what?

Ethan stopped. He stared at her, uncomprehending.

"Your mother's things, I'll go through them, send them where you want them to go."

Ethan shook his head. "I, I don't even know—"

"And her sewing machine. What'll you do with it?"

A look of realization passed over his face. "I never asked."

"There any cousins on your father's side?"

Ethan shook his head as he returned to the table, slumped in his seat.

Zeena waited a moment before asking, "Anyone here in town she liked special?"

It was too much for Ethan. He sat there, his head shaking side to side. Again that helplessness overtook him; his eyes sank into the current again.

Zeena stood. She held to the edge of the table with one hand. She looked at Ethan, who fidgeted with his suspenders, whose hair was mussed, whose eyes were swimming. "Don't think on it now," she said, softly. Then, the words came out of her mouth before she'd had a chance to consider them, "Whyn't I wash your hair?"

Ethan looked up at her, startled.

"So tomorrow," and she pressed on, though cautiously, "you'll look your best."

He ran his hands through his hair and left it standing on end. "I guess it's—"

"I could take the scissors to it too."

She was already at the cookstove. "There's plenty of hot water," and looked back at Ethan with a small smile. She motioned with her hand, "Over here, come on," Zeena was saying as she cleaned out the dishpan. Like an obedient child, Ethan rose from the table, and then he was standing there by the sink and she was helping him off with his work shirt and he was leaning over the sink, his suspenders hanging to his sides, and Zeena was pouring hot water over his hair so it filled the pan. "Set here," she said, pulling a stool to the sink, "so I can cut off what's too long," and he did as he was instructed, and she combed out and then snipped away the hair that curled at his neck and trimmed the sides and the front. When he stood up and turned to lean over the pan of steaming water so she could commence the washing, his face was flushed with color. Zeena's hands went to work then. They worked in the soap, pressed at the scalp, kneaded the back of the neck, at which Ethan made a little sound, "Uh," just barely audible, but it told Zeena to keep on with it and so she did, letting her fingers work at every inch of the scalp, and then she began the slow and steady rinsing, all the while letting her fingers work through the hair and along the scalp, ridding it of all the soap, and then she rinsed again with more water from the stove until the hair squeaked with clean. "Wait there," she told him and stepped over to the basket of folded laundry and pulled out a towel still smelling of the last of the autumn leaves and the first snow, and she wrapped it round his head and gently dried his hair, and the minutes passed as she held the towel and worked at the hair and caught the last droplets that dripped down his forehead or down the side of his neck.

Zeena ran a comb through the hair. Over and over she ran that comb, letting it gently scrape the scalp, until, "Guess I'm done," though her hands didn't feel ready to stop, and the nearness of him, it made it hard to get her breath. Her hands, they were trembling again, but with something else, the wish to touch him, just to touch him.

"Guess I'm done," she repeated, though her fingers kept stroking the hair.

Ethan didn't attempt to move. He sat on the stool, his eyes closed, letting Zeena's fingers play over his hair until he said, "I want you should go through her things and keep what suits you."

"Oh," she started, "mercy, there's nothing I need."

"She used to wear combs in her hair," and his voice cracked then, but he sighed and got hold of himself and said, "I want you to have her combs."

Still Zeena's fingers stroked the hair.

"There's a shawl, she always kep' it wrapped in paper, it's black, for best," he said. "I never seen her wear it. I want you should have it."

"What'd I do with a fine black shawl? You'd ought to find—"

"I want—" and he stopped. There was a shivering through him. He took one of her hands then as it came down by his ear and held to it. "I don't know what I'd'a done . . ."

Zeena felt her hand in his. Hers was cool, while his was damp and hot. She felt fluttery all over. Almost sick. A feeling of wanting to be near him, so strong it took her breath and trapped it in her chest. She rested her other hand on his shoulder. "You must get some rest now, Ethan. Tomorrow's coming and you need your rest."

"What about you?" he asked, letting go her hand.

"Don't fret about me," she told him as he rose from the stool. She was content to stay up with Cousin Beatrice. Zeena knew the dead could not speak. But she couldn't get it out of her head that Cousin Beatrice had something more to say.

NINETEEN

*T*he night Zeena stayed in the parlor
where Cousin Beatrice'd been laid out was longer than any day.

After lighting a candle and settling in on her chair, Zeena remembered when she was a child and Aunt Belle'd come to visit; on one occasion she'd worn a black velvet dress. The skirt was so full Zeena could sink into its folds and there'd be nothing else but the smell and feel of velvet. Usually she liked this, but once the folds got so deep she could not find her way out. When she wailed in fear, Aunt Belle's voice came through the folds, "You lost in there?"

Such was this night. Black and sweet-smelling and velvet-smooth. So many folds there was no escape.

Across the room the candle's flame was the room's only light. From behind the candle the stuffed owl stared with dusty and shadowed eyes. The pine casket lay on the long table in front of the window. Zeena sat in a straight chair beside it and looked out at the dark, moonless night. Or she studied Cousin Beatrice and watched her face start to move, though Zeena told herself she knew better. The dead don't move nomore, she told herself.

But maybe Cousin Beatrice's different.

Lucy Varnum'd brought dried rose petals and spices and had arranged them in bowls around the room to sweeten the air, but there in the dark night, it was too much. The sweetness, the heaviness of those scents, it turned Zeena's mind around.

First there was the sense of Ethan in the room with her. The smell of him, of wood and perspiration and the horse and the mill, it must've stuck to her hair and gotten in the fabric of her shirt because it lingered in the air around her, stronger in waves than the rose petals and spices. "That you, Ethan?" she voiced, but no one was there. The feel of his wet hair, his forehead, his neck, it was on her fingers. His voice, soft as it was, but with a roughness to it, she heard him whisper, "Zeena," but again, when she lifted up and looked around, no one was there.

The way her heart was going, a steady and loud palpitating, it nearly made her sick. When her breathing turned asthmatic, she placed a hand on her chest and tried to let it settle into a quiet rhythm. This feeling Ethan'd started in her, a gnawing inside her, she'd never known it before. Some moments it was a giddiness; is this what those girls felt when they carried on?

Ethan, he wasn't the only one troubled her during the night. Mama, she started in to crying, like after she'd lost one of the babies. A mournful sound, it came from upstairs. Mama, I can't feel bad about it anymore. I'm as sorry's I ever was about the babies, but I can't be no more sorry than that.

Mama didn't understand. If you're not sorry about the babies and me, how'll I live? she asked.

I don't know, Mama. I just can't think on it anymore. It's all I done for so long, and I'm tired.

Father too, he came. Seems you'd ought to leave healing to the others, he whispered at the corners of the windows.

Ethan says I did fine, she defended. He says I did all I could.

You'd best get on home, Father said. Get back here where you belong. It's not proper, you being alone with him.

Then it was Ethan again. Just the scent of him, but he wouldn't come out where she could see him, wouldn't say a word.

Aunt Belle, she even had something to say: It's just as well you go on home to your father now.

Don't you see I can't? Zeena returned.

It don't matter what you see, it's what you must do.

Did Zeena sleep then? All she knew was the candle'd burned down and her head was leaning against the casket when she heard the voice. At first she could not understand the words; they kept repeating in her head without any meaning to them: Stay here with Ethan.

Then Zeena took it in. It was Cousin Beatrice. Zeena told her she was dead and not to trick her.

This's no trick, Cousin Beatrice said. This's me, going to the earth, but not till I know you won't leave him. He won't stand it. I know the boy's heart. He won't stand it.

Zeena told her Ethan didn't love her, she couldn't stay if he didn't love her. Cousin Beatrice said it's not a matter of love, it's a matter of life. Zeena asked what did she mean by that? but the voice'd stopped by then.

Zeena thought on the words, forgetting they were spoken by Cousin Beatrice lying dead in the pine box. Her head started spinning and spinning until finally she collapsed on the sofa and lay without moving until the night was over.

IT WAS THE WIND that woke Zeena. The wind whining, the wind encircling the farmhouse like a twister, the wind rattling every window in a chorus, the wind creeping through unseen holes under the eaves like floodwater.

She looked at Cousin Beatrice. The face was settled into the

wrinkles it would hold forever. The mouth, so small and delicate, was like a flower's bud. The brow, with her hair pulled back
off her face, was long and narrow and worn with lines. "Least
you can't hear the wind," Zeena told her, shaking her head.
Mama'd always said the wind'll take your mind and twist it. Father, when the wind came to stay, he went from room to room,
from chore to chore, unable to settle on anything. Zeena didn't
like the wind either. She didn't like being unable to get away
from it.

Zeena stood up too quickly; her back cranked up with the
movement. She gasped at the strength of it, right up the length
of her spine. She breathed slowly, knowing she'd only rankle it
more if she became jittery with the discomfort.

Zeena blinked. She rubbed at a crick in her neck. It was late,
she realized. Folks'd start coming in a few hours. The burial was
to be at two, after Sunday services in town. She was dressed in
yesterday afternoon's calico wrapper; it was wrinkled and
mussed.

She listened for Ethan, but other than the twist and whine
of the wind, there was nothing. Was he still sleeping?

The smell of the rose petals was not so strong in the light of
day. Zeena rubbed her hip and walked around the room, sniff-
ing at the bowls of petals and spice. She poured some into her
hand and took them over to Cousin Beatrice. She sprinkled
them over Cousin Beatrice's chest.

Vaguely she remembered Cousin Beatrice's voice in the
night. Foolishness, she told herself. The dead don't speak. But
the words, it's a matter of life, they stayed with her.

Mr. Willoughby'd left ice packed in sawdust in the barn.
Zeena would need to repack it under Cousin Beatrice before the
service.

First she went to wake Ethan. She stood outside his door and
knocked, calling his name. The wind was rattling the windows.
Could he even hear her call him? Zeena pushed in the door.
Ethan lay on his side; he was curled up on the far side of the bed,

facing the wall. The wind ruffled the bedding that hung loose by the window. Zeena watched to see was he breathing. "Ethan," she said, stepping over to the bed. Still he did not answer. Zeena leaned over and laid her hand on his shoulder. "Ethan," she said again, lightly shaking him. He started up then, wild-eyed. When he saw Zeena, he flopped back down on the bed.

"You're all wore out," she said, thinking it explained everything.

He nodded.

"Come along to the kitchen."

He closed his eyes and seemed to go far away.

Zeena went to the door. "We'll be needing water." She waited to see if he'd gone to sleep, but he turned and pushed back the covers and sat on the side of the bed, rubbing his face. His union suit was stained and ragged. His hair was mussed, but clean. "Ethan, I know what it is to bury a mother."

He looked at her then, his head at a tilt.

"It's a great sorrow," she said.

Ethan looked out the window. "Winter's coming early," he said.

Zeena looked too. The sky was gray as wood clapboards left so long unpainted they shine. The field, the garden, and the south pastures were overgrown and neglected; soon they'd bush up and turn back to wild. Zeena had a picture of the house lost in a tangle of growth; giant bushes and tree limbs claimed what the Fromes'd called their home for over a hundred years. Tree roots'd broken up the foundation, sending the granite slabs to odd angles. Vines'd curled in through the window frames and dislodged them. The center chimney'd given way so roof and rubble were in piles; tansy and mint grew wild over the piles.

Zeena shook her head. For the land's sake, I'm losing my mind, she thought.

But when she looked at Ethan, she had the feeling he'd been seeing the same thing.

* * *

ETHAN WAS MORE OUT OF SORTS than the previous day.
He couldn't seem to keep it straight what was happening that
day. "When'll the hearse bring her back?" he asked. Zeena reminded him, "She's right in the parlor like you said she wanted,
don't you remember I arranged it with Mr. Willoughby." Ethan
nodded. "I'll get a place ready for her," was another thing he said,
and Zeena shook her head, "Jotham, he saw to that yesterday."
Was he trying to test her, to see if she'd done what she'd said?

As they ate their breakfast of cornmeal mush, Ethan asked,
"You been through her things yet?"

"I'll see to that tomorrow," she said.

"What d'you think we should do with the sewing machine?"

Again, he'd used "we," and again Zeena paid it no outward
attention. "There someone in town needs one?" she asked.

"Or we could keep it here awhile." His voice was wavery and
his eyes darted about. "What'll you do after seeing to her things?"

Zeena felt her face flush. "I don't know just yet," she told him,
clearing the bowls and starting to lay food out on the table for
the funeral. Ethan looked out the window. "Snow's coming," he
said, "before the week's over." "You think so?" she asked. "It's
in the air," he said, and turned his eyes to her with a questioning look.

"I guess I'll be going, like I said," she said softly.

Ethan just stared at her, unblinking, until some thought
roused him. He turned back to his breakfast, then went to the
barn, then filled the woodboxes in the kitchen and the parlor.
He came back in the kitchen, washed up, combed his hair, and
sat in the rocker while Zeena dished pickles and preserves into
bowls and set them out with the bread and the fruit sauces
Lucy'd left. Ethan checked the cookstove several times and
watched Zeena go back and forth between the kitchen and the
parlor where she built up the woodstove.

The cat lay on the floor beneath the cookstove and Ethan

gave her a bowl of milk. Then he took his place in the rocker and fidgeted as he rocked.

The wind was wailing now, so the trees bent and their limbs swam wildly in the air and clusters of leaves lifted up and followed the currents of air. Zeena looked out the window by the table. The little snow that remained from the day before lay in pockets at the base of trees or by the protruding rocks in the dooryard. "Seems as if the wind'll carry us all away," she said, searching Ethan's face for something to hold to.

Ethan nodded.

She looked out across the sloping hillside to the road that ran to town, then back to Ethan. "You think folks'll still come in this wind?" Ethan's shoulders lifted. But his eyes settled on her. Fear is what Zeena saw. He said, "Winter's coming." Ethan stared out the window, wordless. Suddenly, Zeena reached out with a hand to his shoulder. "Ethan, you tell me what you want I should do." He looked confused, so she added, "I can iron a shirt for you or fix you something more to eat." He nodded. "Just now," he said, "I'll go outside, if you don't mind."

She watched him walk down to the graveyard. He wore a clean shirt, unironed, and a pair of wool trousers, for the occasion. He walked as far as the graveyard and stood by the open grave, his hair flying up, his shirt billowing. He did not seem to notice the trail of three carriages and a wagon coming across the ridge and down into the valley until they were there beside him.

Folks from town, they brought baskets of food. There were the Varnums and the Hales and the Wileys and the Richardsons, and the minister, Mr. Hartman. They left their carriages and horses tied to the graveyard fence at the foot of the hill and followed Ethan on foot to the house. Zeena watched their approach, a slow column of black-caped folks, the women wearing black hats, some with veils, and the men with their fedoras trimmed with black crepe. When Ethan came in the kitchen, Rebekah and Ruth Varnum were beside him, gazing up with their darkly serene eyes; their girlishness was emphasized by Ethan's solemn slope of shoulders and the way his large hands hung at his sides. Lucy Varnum came in behind them and introduced folks to Zeena as they entered the room. Each one studied Zeena carefully and shook her hand. Mr. Hale brushed the back of his mustache as he said hello to Zeena. A diamond stud that fastened his shirt caught the light and sent a stream of color through the air. Mrs. Hale lifted the black lace veil that covered her eyes to reveal a long and narrow face and a pinched mouth. "My dear," she said, "I never expected someone so young," and she lowered her head to look over her eyeglasses at Zeena, and continued, "The way I heard it, Ethan's older cousin, I thought you'd be, well . . . older." Zeena took it as a compliment. "Why, thank you," she said, and gave a smile broad enough to be appropriate, given the sorrow of the day. "Come into the parlor," Zeena announced, and they followed behind her. Only Lucy cried aloud when she stood by the casket and gazed at Cousin Beatrice, but her husband placed his hand at her elbow and she gathered her strength so she could step over to her seat. Mrs. Hale, who'd done more doctoring in town than any other woman, whispered several questions about Cousin Beatrice's sickness to Zeena. "Did her heart give out?" and "Was it a fever that drained her?"

Mr. Hartman motioned it was time to begin. He held his Bible in both hands, opened on his palms like an offering as he read these words, "In thee, O Lord, do I put my trust," and then, "Make haste, O God, to deliver me." The minister paused then, making certain all eyes were directed at him. He waited even longer for Ethan to turn his eyes from the window; then he said, "Beatrice Frome awaits the Lord's calling. Let us now remember her as God gave her to us in life." He looked around the room again, from one face to the next, pausing with a melancholic stare at Ethan. "Who can say they never partook of Beatrice's charity? Her home was anybody's home that needed it. She lived by the Word and kept Jesus in her heart; her reward is the

Eternal Rest granted by her Holy Father and her husband Albert who awaits her," and he looked out the window and in the direction of the graveyard and then from one to the other sitting and standing in the room as he said, "We will sorely miss her." Ethan had turned his gaze back to the window, though all Zeena thought he could see was gray sky and maybe treetops waving. Rebekah sat on one side of Ethan with Andrew Hale on the other. Ethan fidgeted as the minister continued reading from the Bible, Corinthians and then Matthew; Ethan's chair creaked and his hands jittered and his eyes darted from outside the window to the casket to his own hands that lay curled in his lap and back outside again. Zeena sat on a straight chair in the corner nearest the door so she could get to the kitchen if she needed to. She watched the minister's face; his long nose twitched as he spoke and his eyelids fell down over his eyes like window shades. His hands, Zeena noticed they were the same color as one who's passed on, a grayish white; his fingers entwined beneath the Bible whenever he called Cousin Beatrice by name. Then in closing the minister read, "Finally, brethren, whatsoever things are true, whatsoever things are honest, whatsoever things are just, whatsoever things are pure, whatsoever things are lovely," and as he paused one last time Zeena felt herself sink into another time, as if the years had vanished and it was that other time, "think on these things. So sayeth the Lord our God."

Mr. Hartman bowed his head in a solemn pose.

Zeena bowed her head. If she closed her eyes, it would have been Mama who was going to the earth and not Cousin Beatrice. Time shrank and shriveled so yesterday was the same as nineteen years past and today was only the future, impossible to know. The minister's voice, it was the same as that other minister, droning on with a vibration to it, like a harp; and if the words were different, Zeena couldn't say. She knew it was the sound of it that mattered. Zeena'd never felt Mama's passing into the earth so clearly; Cousin Beatrice, she and Mama were going together. Zeena wondered if maybe the earth wasn't the greatest comfort a body'd ever know.

As Mr. Hartman concluded, Zeena looked over at Ethan. He showed himself in physical pain, as if it was his kidneys or his lungs that pained him and not his soul. His eyes gave off no brightness. They were dark holes that had no bottom, like Aunt Belle's velvet skirt and the velvet black night when Zeena sat up with Cousin Beatrice. She stared at him hard, willing him to look at her, and he did.

It was not a grimace that crossed his face, but something akin to it. A yearning, it looked to be. His brow furrowed and his eyes softened, watery. His lips moved. What was he saying? Zeena looked at the others, embarrassed. Had they noticed? Their countenances were held in attention to the minister. Zeena looked back at Ethan. His mouth opened as if to speak.

Zeena put her first finger to her lips as if to say "Hush," and she hoped he heard her unspoken words: When this is over, tell me.

"ARE YOU READY, ETHAN?"

Ethan looked at Mr. Hartman and gave no indication of anything.

Andrew Hale stepped over to him. "Ethan," he said, "it's time."

Ethan rose on unsteady feet. His head shook side to side. Andrew Hale looked at Zeena and nodded toward Ethan. Lucy whispered to her, "You'd best help him."

In her own heart was a heavy weight, the weight of being left when another has gone, but there was something else. Ethan, his sorrow, Zeena wanted nothing more than to be his comfort. She stepped forward and approached him, and as she did she knew her face glowed, knew there was in her a womanliness that softened the lines in her face and the bones in her shoulders; she felt it, a warmth of flesh. "Ethan," she whispered to him, and he looked at her as if from another realm, so far that he could not reach her, but she said, "We're going now," and slipped her arm through his and nodded to the others as she lifted her chin and led them all from the room, Ethan at her arm, the men bearing the weight of Cousin Beatrice, the women falling behind, out through the front door that young Ruth came forward to hold, so Zeena said, "Thank you, dear," with an unfamiliar graciousness, but it felt good and right to be so gracious, and Zeena realized then there is no grace where there is no softness of spirit and flesh, and these were hers now.

The wind awaited them.

It swirled her best brown merino skirt as they stepped across the dooryard and onto the lane and down the hillside. It shook the limbs of the regal elms so the few remaining leaves tinkled above them like glass. It whined up from the valley and down from the ridge.

Zeena looked back only once at the bent figures of the men who carried Cousin Beatrice and strained to stay steady in the wind as their jackets flapped and their hair stood straight, all except Lawyer Varnum who'd had the sense to adjust his fedora before stepping out into the cold, blustery afternoon. Zeena wrapped her shawl tighter around her shoulders and willed away the shivering that would ordinarily have sent her back to the house for her cape.

At the open grave Pastor Hartman intoned words about God, the Father; God, the Son; and God, the Holy Ghost; but it was only because of the familiar rhythm of those words that any of what he said was heard as the wind moaned and the men worked the ropes that let the box into the ground. Some took a clump of dirt in their hands and threw it in on the box then. With each *thunk* Ethan shuddered and Zeena held tighter to his arm. She wanted to reach for some dirt but dared not let go of his arm, and Mrs. Hale nodded to her as if she'd chosen correctly.

Then it was done and the dirt was shoveled in.

"Ashes to ashes," Mr. Hartman shouted, the words nearly lost.

Rebekah approached them. "Ethan, you done all you could."

Zeena looked at Ethan. He stared at Rebekah.

"I should know," Rebekah said. Her eyes were brimming with tears.

Ethan nodded.

"Take care of him," Rebekah whispered in Zeena's ear. "Don't leave him alone."

When they returned to the house, their clothes and hair were askew, their faces were windburned, their eyes were red and watered. Zeena busied herself with the food, making sure everyone had what they wanted. Back and forth between the kitchen and the parlor she went. Dishes came in with more food that someone'd brought. The heated cider was poured into cups, the rum into glasses, all of it sipped and swallowed away.

The sunlight glared on the bare floorboards as it passed to the west.

There was quiet talk, gentle murmurings, as folks recalled Cousin Beatrice's younger days. "She was a saint," Mrs. Richardson said. "You ever taste her apple jelly?"

Others nodded as their forks clinked on their plates.

Mr. Wiley said, "I always think of her setting out on the porch there, waiting to see folks. Many a time, she waved me up the lane and give me a cool glass of lemonade or a piece of pie."

Others murmured in assent.

Ethan appeared not to hear these reminiscences. He stared right at the person offering the recollection but gave no response, no sign of having heard. "I recall," Andrew Hale offered, "when you was just a boy, Ethan, and you had the mastoid," and everyone started nodding and rolling their eyes, "how she took you clear to Worcester."

Ethan stared vacantly. Was he even listening?

"She never was one," Andrew Hale went on, "to let a body suffer."

Zeena listened to these stories about Cousin Beatrice, most

of them describing a woman she didn't know. But she wanted to contribute, so she said, "We had her outside during the warm spell," and she looked round to see was everyone listening and they were, "and she told me about spring sugaring and how they boiled it straight through the night, and one night Ethan," and Zeena looked to see was he listening, but he was looking at her with an intensity of expression, clearly with something else on his mind, "he was just a boy," and she held her hand up to show just how little he was, "and he even was out in the woods with them."

The others nodded. "She always worked by Albert's side when he needed," Mrs. Wiley said.

They all noticed when the sun no longer stretched its fingers across the floor; it was time to go. The wind was still whining as they stood and looked out at the waning afternoon's gray skies. "It'll be raining by the time we get home," Andrew Hale said, and everyone nodded their heads, yes, rain was coming.

"Least it won't be snow," Lucy offered.

Ethan spoke for the first time, "It'll come soon enough," and looked up from beneath his furrowed, bent brow.

Silence fell over them all as they collected their capes and hats and scarves.

"You're a wonder," Mrs. Hale told Zeena as she prepared to leave. She pulled a scarf over her head and wrapped her cape tightly about her. "He's had such a hard time, poor man," she added, shaking her head. Then, "I shudder to think of him staying on alone, but it won't do for you to stay, will it?"

Zeena said, "I don't know what you mean."

"The two of you, alone," Mrs. Hale whispered under her hand at Zeena's ear.

"I mean to look after him a couple more days," Zeena said, lifting her chin.

This information gave Mrs. Hale relief. "Ah, yes," she said. Then, "But won't you let us wash these plates?"

Zeena looked at her, standing there in her cape, her scarf, her gloves, and said, "No, I mean to do it."

Mr. Wiley, as he pulled his fedora down onto his brow, said, "He's had one bad turn after another, least he hasn't had to go this alone."

Zeena thanked him for his kind words.

Lucy Varnum took her aside. "You can bring your things along to our house and stay anytime. You'd be near enough to come out days and look after him."

Zeena drew up her shoulders. "I won't be staying that long," she told her.

"Someone from town," Lucy added, "can bring food out and do his washing once a week—"

Rebekah said, "Mother, please," and bit her lip. She looked at Zeena and rolled her eyes. Zeena knew again that Rebekah was her friend as she'd never had one. She smiled at Rebekah. "Will I see you before I go?" Zeena asked. Rebekah pursed her lips. She shook her head. Zeena knew her meaning: Don't go.

Jotham Powell, last to leave, offered her this: "I wouldn't go home tonight less'n you was here," and he shook his head as he gestured to where Ethan stood at the window, watching the others walk down the lane to their horses and carriages. "Tell him I'll be at the mill first light to get things going, no need for him to get to it too soon."

And then they were alone.

Ethan stood at the window on still-shivering legs.

"You're chilled," Zeena told him. She led him to the kitchen and made him sit in the rocker by the cookstove with a cup of tea while she worked steadily, carrying plates and dishes into the kitchen, lugging the hot water to the sink, washing everything, wiping everything, carrying what needed cold storage down cellar, filling the milk jugs and storing them on the stairs, wrapping everything that needed wrapping.

Ethan rocked in his chair, occasionally leaving it to stoke the fire. Then the creaking of the rocker took up again.

The rain, it started in with a vengence. Pattering, ticking, spattering, the large droplets of water pinged against the windows, doused the clapboards, then washed over the roof like floodwaters. A dampness invaded the house, though the cookstove roared. Ethan shivered in the rocker and watched the gray skies darken.

"Shouldn't you see to the animals?" Zeena nudged him when her work was nearly done.

Ethan did as she'd suggested while Zeena put the parlor back to order. He was shivering all the more when he returned from the barn, his face damp. "It's gone dark," he said to Zeena.

"I don't know where the day went," Zeena sighed.

Ethan nodded.

"I'll get us some supper," she suggested.

Ethan shook his head. "Not on my account." He stood then by the cookstove, his legs trembling, his great shoulders falling away, and spoke to Zeena's back. "I don't like rain," he said.

"Could be snow," she said, turning. Then Zeena told him the snow wouldn't come for a while yet. "Maybe two more weeks, maybe more. Some years—" but she stopped. He wasn't listening. He was somewhere else, that inward gaze having pulled him away from time and into that other realm where moments are like drops of rain, falling, falling fast to seep into the earth, and all that's left is the night sky, dark and vacant and never ending.

TWENTY

$\mathscr{T}$wo more days the rain lasted. Two days Ethan went to the mill to get as much timber planed out as he could before the workings froze up with winter's cold. Two days Zeena stayed inside, went through Cousin Beatrice's things and made piles: piece bags, peddlers, the almshouse, what Zeena'd keep. Ethan appeared at noon both days for dinner where he sat, silent, and ate his food. Then just before dark on the second day he reappeared for supper and the tending of the barn animals, silent and hesitant in his actions. After washing up, he came to the table shivering, his teeth nearly chattering. When he pulled out his chair to sit down at the table, he paused, as if trying to remember something and lost himself to thought. "Ethan," Zeena said finally, startling him, so he looked at her apologetically. At supper they finished up the spiced meats brought for the funeral and the last of the funeral cake. Twice he opened his mouth to say something, or else he was given over to trembles, Zeena couldn't tell.

"Drink this," she said, bringing him a cup of steaming cider into which she'd poured a spoonful of rum. "You're chilled through to the bone. Were you in the rain the whole day?"

Ethan took the cider and let the steam run up into his face. He took a swallow, sighed. His shoulders shrugged. "Jotham worked in the mill, I got in more timber."

"How much more time before it freezes up?"

Ethan's shoulders shrugged again.

Zeena tried to get him talking. Would he use the winter to cut and haul timber? Would Jotham work through the winter with him? Would he have enough firewood to last the winter once he got what was out in the dooryard cut and split? With each question came a nod or a shrug. Then she said, "I been through all your mother's things. Would you like me to take the things to the almshouse to town when I go?"

Ethan had no response to that either. Zeena could see it: he was defeated already and winter hardly begun. She could not tell him she did not want to go home to Father, that she had her own defeat. Nor could she tell him that his nearness to her sent her insides to twisting, that her hands wanted only to touch his shoulder, his face, his hand.

Ethan came out of his reverie to stare into her eyes and looked as if he would speak, but his brow wrinkled with hesitation and then he looked away.

Zeena cleared the plates to the sink and placed them in the basin. She turned to the stove for some hot water and filled the basin, wishing for something to say that would end his troubles, and hers. Ethan rose out of his chair. She looked over her shoulder at him and saw something different in his eyes. They were focused. He had a purpose. His shoulders broadened as he took a deep breath. "Will you have more cider?" she asked, dipping the forks in the rinse water, though she already knew he wouldn't answer, which he didn't. Instead he said, "Zeena," his voice fogged. He approached her. She heard his steps and knew he was heading for her. She kept on with her chore, washing the knives and letting them soak in the rinse water. She knew what he was coming to her for, knew the words he would say, knew she should turn to meet him, but her knees were like jelly and her heart was pounding in her throat so if she wanted to speak, she couldn't.

"I want you should stay," came his words.

Zeena did not turn from the sink. She was drying her hands on her apron, turning them over and over, feeling the linen's roughness against her skin. When he repeated the words, she pulled up. "What're you meaning?" she asked. On the shelf over the sink was the looking glass and her reflection; her face was flushed red and her eyes were dark as pockets.

He swallowed and sighed, so his shoulders lifted up again. "I want you should stay as my wife."

Zeena could not speak, dared not try. Still she faced the wall and the looking glass, could not turn. If she looked at him, what then?

"If you don't want to—"

Zeena shook her head. She held to the sink for support. She could not speak. There was something big as the sky, the same sky she'd seen in his face, only this was a beneficent sky, sun streaked, inside her.

Ethan's shoulders sagged. Zeena could see his face in the looking glass. His eyes seemed to droop. "I shouldn't ha'—"

Zeena turned. His face was so close she could see the lower lashes of his eyes, dark and moist. "I'll stay," she said.

The rain was spattering the windowpanes beside them. The wind sent fingers of cold damp air in through the cracks. Cousin Beatrice, she was whispering it's a matter of life in Zeena's ear. Zeena answered: Not just Ethan's. Mine too.

"I want to stay."

Ethan reached out and held the palm of his hand against her cheek. To Zeena it was more comfort than she'd ever known. She couldn't get a deep breath. So light and fluttery it was, breathing. The wind what'd batted the house three days now, it was inside her. She started to fall. Ethan was there, though,

211

to hold her up. His arms, they slipped around her and held her. One of his hands, it pressed her head against his shoulder; the other, it wrapped round her waist.

The sinking feeling, the sense of everything turning dark in her head, the wind inside her, and the sound of the rain *plink, plunk, plink, plunk* against the windowpanes, it nearly set her to crying. The sobs, she could feel them in her throat, scrabbling at her. Comfort, it wasn't something she thought she'd ever have.

But Ethan was whispering and murmuring. "You were good to come out here," he was saying, and "I couldn't stay another winter here, I couldn't—" and her head was pressed against him, and he was rocking side to side with her, his own crying coming out in little half-swallowed sounds.

Her hands, they came up to Ethan's face. They were in his hair, around his neck. And Ethan was kissing her then and rocking her and crying in with the kissing and she was lost to it. There was nothing then she wouldn't't've done for Ethan. Everything inside her, everything she was, she gave over to Ethan as they stood there at the sink and swayed and kissed and shivered together.

HOW LONG DID THEY STAND THERE?

Time didn't exist. Time wasn't something that passed; it wasn't something that'd been; and it wasn't ever going to be any different than it was right then. The remainder of her life could've passed there in the dark with the rain and the wind and she wouldn't have minded.

Something was happening. Lost in Ethan's arms, entranced by his whisperings, nearly ill with longing, Zeena felt things inside her change. Where before had been bone and joint and muscle now was something fluid and pliant. Where before were tightness and aching now was only something soft. Her spine, a watery current was running through it, softening her. Her back, it would bend as she needed it to. Her limbs, they would sway and flow if she asked them to. Her lungs, they were free to breathe.

She stood outside herself momentarily and noticed it, the way she swayed, the way she let herself be pressed in against him, and she knew: She'd stepped into a new body.

"It's late," broke through her thoughts. It was Ethan. She pulled back and looked at him.

"We must get to bed now."

If he asked her, she would go with him to his room, would lie with him through the night. Then they would be as married as they needed to be. She'd always thought to lie with a man would be distasteful, but now it was natural, even urgent. How could she go to her own room tonight? Sleep in her own bed? It was unthinkable.

If he asked her, she would go right now to town with him, would wake up Mr. Hartman so he could marry them, if that was what Ethan wanted. Then they would ride back together in the dark with the rain pelting them, and then they would go to his room and then they would be truly married.

Ethan scratched his head. He was gazing at Zeena. Her hair'd come undone and fell loose to her shoulders. Would she ever bother to do it up again?

"I think we should get married soon's we can," he said.

She nodded. "I'm ready," she offered, thinking he would know she meant she was ready right then, that very moment.

He swallowed and then coughed. He was still breathing deeply. "We'll go together to town," he said. "Tomorrow."

After he filled the woodboxes and she cleaned the lamp, he followed her up the stairs. At her door he hesitated. Would he start it up again? The kissing, the holding her, so his hands would touch her again? "I—" but he paused. "It don't seem right," he started. "With Ma just passing."

Zeena nodded. "She only wanted your happiness," she said.

"But folks, what'll they say?"

"They'll say it's good you got a wife." She smiled. Ethan leaned across the space of air between them and kissed her again, lightly. *If he asks me to come with him . . .*

"Tomorrow," he whispered.

And then he slipped into his room, leaving Zeena leaning against the door frame to her room with her insides all aswirl and her heart all aflutter, thinking, *if he'd a asked me . . .*

TWENTY-ONE

*T*he ride to town was dreamlike.

Just a couple of weeks ago she'd sat in the same place beside Ethan in the wagon, listened to the same *clop-clop* of the sorrel's hooves in the rutted lane, seen above her the same sky, though now it was a gray morning sky instead of the blackening darkness she'd come in under. On that night Ethan's shoulders had slumped and his eyes had roved the darkness with a melancholic slant, yet his voice, when he'd motioned to the landscape and said, "These hills," had been rich with feeling. Now his gaze swept the morning's landscape with a stain of sadness, yes, but his eyes were bright as he shook his head and again said, "These hills," leaving the reins in one hand and grandly encompassing it all with the sweep of the other hand through the air.

Zeena looked where his hand swept. Yesterday's rain had left tree trunks, leaves, and grass shining and dark. Hills, purplish gray against the gray sky, sheltered patches of forest green where the pines were congregated, and dots of red and yellow, the stubbornnest of autumn's leaves. Along the ridge the treetops were black lace against the sky, which stretched a solid sheet of gray in all directions.

On that night when she'd first passed the graveyard where Cousin Beatrice did not yet lie, the stones gleamed white in the onsetting darkness. Now the marble showed gray. Now Cousin Beatrice's fresh-mounded grave was a scar on the earth. Zeena pictured Cousin Beatrice in her box under the ground, her eyes closed to the darkness; her tiny hands, small as quails' breasts, clasped together in prayer. Mr. Willoughby made sure about that. Zeena looked up into the sky where she hoped Cousin Beatrice's soul was floating free. Ethan did not turn his head to look; whatever his thoughts were, he kept his gaze on the road, and Zeena smiled at the difference between them.

On that night when she'd first arrived, Ethan'd sat beside her. She saw nothing more than his irritating habit of being unable to let his thoughts take shape in words. Now she thought she understood. He carried those stones on his shoulders as if they were his bones, as if from his broad back and shoulders the stones rose like trees from the ground. All the Fromes in that graveyard, they weighted Ethan's shoulders and kept him silent. And the land. There was no separation between his heart and the land.

Time, it had fallen away. In a matter of days the thing that'd pulled at her life had let her go. A healer like Mama, she would not be. A woman, she would. It was not without a sense of loss that she greeted the day; Cousin Beatrice, Aunt Belle, Mama, her dreams, these were laid away now. Mama was with Aunt Belle and Cousin Beatrice. She would enter her new life with the old one buried. Time, it would have no end now, no way of being measured as it had, hour by hour, day by day, everything counted from when Mama went. Now it stretched out all around her like the sky.

The wagon wheels creaked as they passed through the gate and turned left onto the road to town and left the graveyard behind.

Zeena looked at Ethan from the corner of her eye. In the creases around his eyes, in the thin line of his mouth, in the color of his skin, gray like the sky, there was grief. But Zeena was staying to be his wife; he would not be alone. Each would be the other's comfort.

That morning before breakfast, while Zeena'd steeped the tea and stirred the hot cereal, Ethan'd sat sleepy-eyed in the rocker, the cat at his feet. His mind was occupied, Zeena could see. Every time she started the conversation, he stopped it. "This rain, just think if it was snow," she'd said. Ethan turned to look at her with a blankness in his eyes. Ethan's inward look, she called it. "Young Ruth Varnum, she sure is a thoughtful girl," was another try, but Ethan held his pipe, turned it side to side and stared at it, offering no reply.

"Rebekah, if she isn't the sweetest," she said. "Where's she going to find a husband?"

Ethan stared out the window. "Her father'll find her one, no doubt."

Zeena went to the sink and patted at her hair as she glanced in the looking glass. She'd wound it up and secured it while dressing but wanted to see was it sagging on one side. Her face, it was shining. From her eyes, from her skin came a sparkle. It gave her an entirely different look: younger, lighter, not so bony and sharp-angled. She undid her hair, ran Ethan's comb through it, then pulled it back and up into a pug.

Zeena'd gotten up before Ethan to get the stove going and the water heating so she could get a bath before the dawn showed its gray light. Today she and Ethan would say their vows, and she wanted to shine with cleanliness. She hadn't expected her face to shine with . . . exuberance? Prettiness? That's how she looked; the realization sent a flush into her cheeks. She looked down at her calico wrapper. Her brown merino that she'd worn for Cousin Beatrice's funeral was hanging behind the stove; the steam from the kettle'd take out any wrinkles that'd set in. It would have to do for the day's event. Ethan, she noticed, wore his same white shirt and woolen trousers. A woolen jacket was hung over the seat back. A worn fedora—"It's Pa's, I got it out of the chest"—sat on the dresser.

They ate together at the table, like the other mornings, only Zeena'd prepared cranberry muffins to go along with the cereal and the stewed applesauce. "Father don't care for mountain berries," she explained as she uncovered them, steaming, in a basket. "They're my favorite, though."

The cookstove gave off a steady heat. The smell of fresh-baked muffins and the stewed fruit sweetened the air. The table'd been scrubbed clean.

Finally Ethan spoke. "This house weren't always so quiet." He was spreading butter on a muffin, but leaned back in his chair then.

Zeena leaned forward. She could've said the same thing about her house after Mama died and Father turned silent. "Tell me how it used to be," she asked.

"There was always someone visiting, a cousin or an uncle or someone passing through."

Zeena noticed the gray mist that hung in the lowlands. It didn't bother. Nothing could bother, not on this day.

"Or there was a peddler here in the dooryard, or someone from town doing business with Pa."

Zeena smiled.

"I first heard about Florida from a man passing through. He thought Ma was the finest cook he'd ever known, and Ma give him some of her apple jelly, and he was telling us about going to Florida and then he asked me, 'Son, you ever heard of Florida?'" Ethan looked right at Zeena then.

"That's what set the idea in your head?"

He nodded. "I'd never ha' got Ma to Florida."

"She loved it here on the hill."

Ethan leaned forward, one corner of his mouth drawn in. "She never loved it here. I don't know what she told you, but she never loved it here."

Zeena passed him the basket of muffins. She recalled Cousin Beatrice's words, days ago, about sugaring in the spring.

"What she felt, it were in her eyes," he said. "She soured on the place long ago."

Zeena remembered Cousin Beatrice's eyes, how they could look one way, dark and pained, and how they could look another way, joyful even. For a second, she saw Cousin Beatrice's eyes open in the dark of her casket under the ground. She shivered. Foolishness, she told herself.

"We could go, though," he said.

Zeena looked up. "Go?"

"To Florida."

Zeena sipped at her tea. Rebekah'd said he could never leave. "Florida?"

His eyebrows rose. "Come spring, we could sell the farm if I get the bills straightened round."

But Florida was a long way off. How long would it take to get there? she asked. And the heat, wasn't it unhealthy in those temperatures? Spiders, weren't they giants? And swamps, weren't there nothing but swamps? Zeena said she'd heard folks got all sorts of ailments. Ethan ate a second muffin while he listened to her concerns. He told her how once you got there, it was worth it. There were opportunities for work there. "Besides, you'd like the flowers, they're great big," and he held up his hands to show the size.

"But—" she started.

"In Florida, you get decent wages. There's not enough hands to do the work. We'd have savings from the sale of the house and in a year we'd be on our feet."

"What about Worcester. Or Portsmouth? They're not so very far."

"If we're going, we might's well go."

Zeena thought of what Rebekah'd said about the gravestones, all his forebearers planted out there. "How could you leave this place?"

Ethan took a swallow of tea. "I could do it," he said, hooking his thumbs in his suspenders and looking at her with serious eyes.

"I'd like to go," she said. The spring was a long way off. By then, why, everything might be different. There might be a baby on the way. She put her hand to her heart, felt its quickening. She swallowed. It was frightening to think it. Mama'd gone with a baby; so many women did. So could Zeena.

But that was all in the future. Time, it'd spread out for Zeena. A year seemed forever since there was nothing in it to dread. Half a year, it was a long way off. Who could guess at all that'd come to pass in half a year?

THEY STOPPED FIRST at Andrew Hale's office, a shed at the yard. Ethan had some business to tend to. "Shall I wait?" she asked as he stepped down, but he was coming round the wagon to offer his hand so she could step down. "I want you should come too."

Andrew Hale was at his desk, papers strewn all around. Behind him, a stove roared, and as they entered, he rose and adjusted the damper. Immediately the roar subsided. His diamond stud sparkled in the morning's gray light as he turned and said, "Can't keep the heat even." Then he right off offered his condolences. "Your mother, she was fine as they come."

Ethan had removed his hat; now he held it at his waist as he lowered his head.

To Zeena, Mr. Hale said, "Everyone's glad you were there so she didn't have to suffer alone, and Ethan, it'd been no good . . ." his words went on, but Zeena wasn't listening. She was noticing the flush building in Ethan's cheeks, and his blue eyes when he raised them.

Ethan showed Mr. Hale some figuring he'd worked out. "If I was to get that wood you just got in planed 'fore snow flies . . ."

and on he went while Zeena looked at him, wondering if he'd tell their plans.

They set out some arrangements, then Mr. Hale turned to Zeena, "Glad you could come into town, see some folks. I imagine it gets awful quiet out there even after a few days."

"We're going to see the minister," Ethan said.

"Pay a visit on Mr. Hartman, well, that's a fine thing," Mr. Hale returned.

Ethan coughed. Zeena looked at him. "So she can be my wife," he said.

A silence fell. Mr. Hale looked from Zeena to Ethan. "I'm not sure I—"

"We mean to be married," Zeena said.

Mr. Hale pulled on his mustache.

"Zeena and I, we're going to ask Mr. Hartman if he can do it right off."

"But you," and then, "you thought this over?"

Zeena stared right at Mr. Hale. "We talked it over."

A silence fell. Ethan coughed. Zeena stared at Mr. Hale, who looked back and forth between the two of them. Finally, "If it's for the best," he said, extending his hand and smiling. "You young folks, I can't keep up with you," he said, chuckling.

Minutes later, as they approached the hemlocks that lined the Varnums' property, Zeena told Ethan to stop. "I want to speak to Rebekah," she told him. Ethan looked doubtful, but Zeena said she would stay only a moment and he could go on to find Mr. Hartman to make the arrangements, that way she wouldn't have to wait while he spoke to the minister. Ethan said he had one thing to tend to so that would suit him well enough. "But please see me in," she asked. "S'not right I should just appear by myself on their doorstep."

They were greeted warmly in an elegant entryway. The walls were lined with polished walnut. An elaborate hat rack and mirror were attached to the left wall. An oval-shaped table was in the corner, with a fringed lamp in its center. A narrow red-patterned carpet ran from the door to the stairs that twisted their way up to the second floor. A grandfather clock stood on the other wall, tall and imposing, its slow tick emphasizing the slow passing of moment to moment. This was like Aunt Belle's house: spacious, comfortable, built for two worlds, one for welcoming company, the other for the Varnums' private lives. "Come in, do," Lucy Varnum said, opening the door wider, then noted, "you're all dressed up, wherever are you going?"

Ethan and Zeena stepped inside.

"Why, you're not leaving so soon?" she asked Zeena.

Before Ethan'd removed his hat he told her. "Zeena and I mean to marry."

Lucy took a step back. She looked from Ethan to Zeena and then to Rebekah who came into the entry with a warm "Hello."

Ethan took off his hat, opened his mouth, but then looked at the floor.

Lucy spoke right up. "You mean to marry?"

Rebekah stopped in her place and looked at them with widened dark eyes. She blinked several times and then studied Ethan's face.

"But," Lucy started as she looked at Zeena who smiled evenly, and at Ethan who shuffled on his feet, "why, it's just so—" and she paused a moment before finishing, "so sudden."

"It's only right," Ethan said, and Zeena looked at him, wished he'd say more than that, but that was as much as he could muster.

Zeena looked at Lucy and Rebekah, fashionable in their dark gray skirts and black shirts, their lush thick hair pulled back, their complexions pink and white. Lucy wore a watch on her breast; Rebekah wore a cameo pin at her neck and a dark brown wool sweater. The buttons on their shirts were black jets that shimmered when they moved. And their hands, Zeena noticed the softly white skin on the back of Lucy's hands, how it was as youthful as Rebekah's, and their nails were carefully trimmed.

Aunt Belle'd had a china figure brought from Europe by her husband's brother; she stood erect and clean and handsome, like Lucy and her daughter.

Ethan shuffled some more. He looked up with a corner of his mouth pulled in and his brow furrowed. He stared at Lucy, then gave Rebekah a glance. "Zeena wanted to tell you the news," he said. "I'll leave her while I make arrangements with Mr. Hartman."

"Why, yes," Lucy said. "Rebekah, see to some tea, please."

Rebekah was staring at the floor.

"Rebekah," Lucy said. She put her hand on Rebekah's arm. "You'll see to some tea, won't you?"

Rebekah gazed at her mother. "Yes, course," she said. The pink'd gone out of her face.

Ethan had a pained look on his face. "I might be a while," he said. "I have one errand to run so—" but he didn't finish the sentence as he backed out the door.

Zeena watched him through the window as he adjusted his hat, turned, and stepped away. His hand waved in the air, the way Father's did when he was off somewhere. Men knew about going off, while women knew about waiting.

Lucy opened a door to another room and said, "Come in here, Zeena, we'll have tea in here."

The parlor was rich in furniture and fabric. Side tables, end tables, lamps on tables, lamps standing, footstools, a love seat, a sofa, two plush chairs, several straight-backed chairs, a piano. A large soapstone stove radiated heat. Zeena hadn't realized anyone in Starkfield lived so well. Ethan'd said they called it a mansion, but she hadn't thought it would be so grand.

Rebekah came in with a tray of white china cups and saucers that had rims of gold with blue flowers across them, and a pot of tea; she laid the tray on the table by her mother. "Sit down, dear," Lucy told her, then lifted the cover off the teapot and peered inside. "We'll let it steep," she said, perched on the edge of her chair to wait with her hands clasped in her lap.

Rebekah sat on a footstool near her mother with her knitting in her lap. She felt distant to Zeena, after their various whispered conversations. Perhaps it was because her mother was in the room.

"Well, what a surprise this is," Lucy said, smiling. "You look so happy, dear."

Zeena nodded. She smiled. She was happy.

"I hated to think of Ethan there, so alone on the farm," she said. "I never guessed he'd find anyone who'd go out there—"

Zeena's eyebrows raised.

"—it being so far from town," Lucy finished.

Zeena was tempted to say, We won't stay past the spring, but decided she'd wait until there was something more definite in their plans.

"Maybe you can get Ethan to work on the place, get that ell built. Why, everyone says, if Ethan Frome'd get that ell back, the place'd feel like a farm again."

"He works every hour of the day, more even," Zeena defended.

"Well, I know, but after all, it's been—" She turned to Rebekah, "How many years since the ell came down?"

Rebekah was knitting and didn't answer.

"Rebekah?" Lucy asked.

"It hasn't been that long," Rebekah replied.

Lucy went on then about the farmhouse, how it needed this and that bit of work, how the flowers and bushes in the dooryard'd all turned to scrub, how the vegetable garden needed planting if he was to get through winter after winter. "Folks share their plenty, but I'd ha' thought a man'd have more pride than to take from others." She went on still and Zeena looked over at Rebekah once and caught her eye. "Where's Ruth?" Zeena asked her, cutting off Lucy's complaints.

"Gone to school," Rebekah answered.

"She's at the top of her grade," Lucy boasted. "And you were too, don't forget now, Rebekah." Lucy leaned forward to put a hand on her shoulder. "She'll make some young man a very fine wife, don't you think, Zeena?" and she gave Zeena a probing look. "A lawyer, maybe, or a shop owner, someone of stature."

Rebekah leaned into her knitting.

Zeena swallowed. "I'd guess, yes, you got two lovely daughters, I'd say."

"It's such a surprise about you and Ethan, dear," Lucy said, changing the subject. "I'd never've thought, well, you being cousins . . ."

"Distant," Zeena quipped. "Cousin Beatrice was Mama's aunt's cousin."

"Still . . ."

"I think it's fine," Rebekah spoke up, her eyes glistening as she smiled at Zeena. "Every girl's had her eyes on Ethan Frome. Zeena's the only one—"

"It's just," Lucy interrupted as she lifted the strainer and began to pour the tea, "aren't you quite a few years older, dear, not that that fact alone'd keep him from being sweet on you, but—"

"Seven years," Zeena said, just to keep from being bothered about it.

"So that'd make you—"

"Mama," Rebekah exclaimed.

"I know, dear," Lucy answered, sighing and looking up from under her brow at Zeena as she handed her a cup. Rebekah put down her knitting and offered her some sugar, but Zeena shook her head. "I like it plain."

"But are you sure—" Lucy started, then stopped under Rebekah's glare.

All Zeena's life she'd had to explain herself—to aunts and uncles, cousins, neighbors, townsfolk, anyone who looked at her with raised eyebrows as if to inquire, And what do you do with yourself if you're not a wife? I'm a healer, she'd sometimes answered, and folks'd nod as if to say, Weren't that nice. Now Zeena was going to be a wife. She had every reason to be a good wife, she told herself. Every good reason to give herself to some-one who needed her as much as Ethan did. She could help him get his debts paid by keeping an orderly home and by tending to his wants. She would go to Florida with him. She'd give him children to pass on his name. Maybe one of them would come back to Starkfield and buy back the farm and live that hard life, but Ethan wanted to migrate, like so many folks, and she'd be the one to help him do it. But she wasn't going to tell Lucy Var-num any of this. It wasn't anybody's business but hers and Ethan's. "Ethan and I'll do just fine," she stated. She would not let Lucy's questions rankle her. Not on this, her wedding day.

IT WAS REBEKAH who found the bit of lace for Zeena's hair. "Come with me," Rebekah'd said after tea, leading her up to her room. She fished through a drawer and pulled out a strip of ivory-colored lace. She arranged the lace on Zeena's hair, then pulled her to the dresser and held up a looking glass. "You need some finery like this," Rebekah said.

Zeena smiled. It did look nice.

"It softens everything," Rebekah said, almost breathless. "You never looked so pretty."

Zeena said nothing. No one but Mama'd ever spoken to her this way.

"Pinch your cheeks, like this," and she worked at her own. "It'll give more color."

Zeena shook her head; the embarrassment she felt sent a heat into her neck.

Rebekah laughed. "It's coming a little more pink now."

"Will you come to the church?"

Rebekah replaced the looking glass on the dresser, turning her back. "I won't, Zeena."

Zeena felt her cheeks color. This business of marrying, it put a body into a new position. Under what other circumstance would she have asked something of Rebekah?

"You don't need me there," Rebekah continued, still with her back turned.

Zeena wanted to say, You're as much a friend's I ever had, but instead, "I don't know why you'd want to anyway."

Rebekah turned. Her face was pale. "It's not that."

"I understand."

"No, you don't, you can't," she said, blinking several times.

Zeena waited. Her fingers fussed at the lace. Rebekah's sorrows, they kept her from things, and it wasn't Zeena's way to try to change someone. "Folks are the way they are and there ain't nothing you can do about it," Father'd told her often enough. But she recalled the way Lucy had spoken of her daughter to Zeena. Did Rebekah need encouragement to see herself differently than her parents did? Zeena thought she would talk more to the girl at another time. Now was not the time.

"Like this," and Rebekah adjusted the lace, then reached for some pins to hold it. "Don't touch it now. It's just right." She turned to her dresser, pulled open another drawer. "Something blue, you need something blue."

Zeena laughed and shook her head. She looked at Rebekah, tiny framed but well rounded. Her waist was small enough for two large hands to encircle. Ethan's, for instance. It could ha' been Rebekah in her place, marrying Ethan. Zeena wondered who the young man was that Lucy had spoken of. When they had their talk, she would inquire about him.

"What about this?" and Rebekah held out a handkerchief, white with embroidered blue cornflowers. "Put this in your pocket," she said.

"I don't need it, it's foolishness, it's—"

"It's not," Rebekah said. She looked at Zeena, her eyes starting to water, but she blinked it away. She reached for the cameo at her neck, unhooked it, and said, "I want you to have this," and pinned it to Zeena's collar. "Oh, no, Rebekah, I won't—"

"It's my wedding present to you."

"No, I couldn't, it's a family piece, surely—"

"My Aunt Charlotte wore it at her wedding and gave it to me before she died. Now I'm giving it to you. It's meant for a wedding, and that's that. It's your wedding day, Zeena. And you're beautiful as a bride should be. Make it everything it should be."

Zeena nodded. Rebekah was right. She felt young, she felt as full of life as she ever would. And she loved him. Surely she loved him and he loved her. "I will," she said.

AS THE WAGON BUMPED ALONG THE ROAD, leaving the village behind them, Zeena sat beside Ethan and fingered the gold ring on her left hand. A narrow flat band, it fitted her finger as if it had been crafted just for her. Smooth and gold, unmarred, it glistened in the light of day. That was the errand Ethan'd tended to.

"It's not real gold," Ethan'd confided after helping her into the wagon. "When we get away to Florida, I'll find you a proper ring," he promised her. "I'd ha' kept Ma's but she always said to bury her with her wedding ring," he said, and for a moment a heaviness fell on his shoulders.

Zeena felt his sorrow like it was her own. "You always done your best by her," she told him. Ethan shrugged. "And I like the ring just as it is." She held out her hand to admire it. "Your hands'll get cold," Ethan warned her, but Zeena didn't care. She wanted to study the ring, gaze at it, touch it, bring it up close and then look at it far off. Was this what those young girls felt that giggled and gadded about and seemed so simpleminded to Zeena? A fluttering was in her heart, light and airy, and a sensation inside her so strong it made her nearly ill. Lovesick. She'd heard it said of others but always thought it foolish. How could a body be sick with love? Now she knew.

The last minute before entering the church, while they awaited Lawyer Varnum who'd arrived just as Ethan was collecting Zeena and insisted he serve as their witness—"The Lord knows, it's the least I could do"—Zeena asked Ethan, "You sure you thought enough about this, like Mis' Varnum asked?" If Ethan told her no, she knew she'd sink, but still, she had to ask. She didn't want to be accused later of some dishonesty, preying on Ethan when he was at his weakest. Ethan looked down into her eyes and she felt herself turn soft and knew whatever beauty was in her was at that moment shining from her face. Ethan leaned close to her, almost so their lips touched, so she could feel his breath on her face. His cheek brushed against hers and he said in her ear, "I couldn't face tomorrow alone." To Zeena it was the tenderest confirmation. She wanted to speak her feelings, tell him how she thought she'd be happy now, now that she had someone to look after, but Lawyer Varnum was beside them, grinning and saying, "You've made a good choice, Ethan," and Ethan pulled back, his face red as a sunset sky.

For Zeena the unfamiliar sensation of love was like dancing, being twirled round and round by a man's dancing arms. Barriers that'd once kept her in check, they fell before this sensation. To dance, to embrace, to kiss, to . . . Zeena feared it, but now, simply because of how she was feeling, what once she'd viewed with disgust she now saw with a hunger to know.

The wedding vows, spoken in the minister's office since there was such a few of them and their voices would've been lost in the upper reaches of the church's arched ceiling, lasted ten minutes. Zeena stood tall by Ethan's tall frame and listened to Mr. Hartman's every word. She drew her head up when he asked would she take Ethan for better or for worse, for rich or for poor, and said "I do" proudly, but Ethan, when asked the same, had to repeat it, "I do," so low was his voice. Zeena stole a quiet look at him when he said the words again and saw a face flushed and watery eyed. Was he scared as she about what it would be like?

The ring was pure surprise. Zeena'd never expected such an indulgence but was instantly proud of it. Ethan withdrew it from his coat pocket and unwrapped it. He held the ring between his thumb and first finger and the light caught it, sending beams of light this way and that. She held out her hand and he slid the ring onto her finger and Zeena felt herself turning woman soft. In that moment beauty was hers.

When they were pronounced man and wife, Ethan stepped close to Zeena and without holding her, bent down to kiss her lightly. Lawyer Varnum said, "Congratulations," and patted Ethan on the back and bowed earnestly to Zeena so she decided maybe he wasn't as stiff and high-minded as she'd once thought, maybe he couldn't help the airs he put on, and then it was done.

Zenobia Frome. Zenobia Frome. Zeena repeated her new name to herself as they left the church. If only Mama could know . . . and Father, she'd write soon. Course, he'd tell her he'd been right all along. I told you he was needing a wife, he'd say. She didn't want to hear it. It'd diminish what was between her and Ethan.

She looked at Ethan; his face was still flushed and he was smiling, but his eyes held that inward sorrowful look and Zeena wondered a moment what he was thinking, but by the time they were settled in the wagon and heading home, Ethan's sadness was forgotten and there was only the ring and the road ahead, leading them home.

TWENTY-TWO

*T*he first flakes of snow were spitting by the time they turned onto the lane. Zeena looked up into the branches of the larches, bare after the rain and wind had taken most every last leaf, and watched the big heavy flakes float down like lily pads on water.

The graveyard was off to their right; again Ethan did not turn his head. And again Zeena looked at the fresh plot that was Cousin Beatrice's. The earth was black with the rain that'd soaked the ground during the night. She wished she had some flowers or some pretty thing to draw the eye away from the lumpy earth that would, by next summer, be a green grassy cover. "Will you purchase a stone?" Zeena asked Ethan.

"When I can," he said, lowering his head.

It was turning cold. When they'd left early that morning, it'd seemed there was a chance the sun would come out and dry everything. But as they left the church the sky was billowy gray and damp again. But snow, Zeena'd hoped it would come as rain if it had to come at all.

"Seems early yet for snow," Zeena remarked.

Ethan nodded.

"Guess if it snows early spring'll come sooner."

"I never saw no justice in the seasons," Ethan said.

"It all evens out, though, don't it?"

Ethan shrugged his shoulders. "I never noticed that."

Under the elms and then the house was before them. The unpainted clapboards were dark where the rain'd soaked in. With no curtains, the windows were black holes; the house looked unlived-in. Where the ell had been, Ethan'd stacked most of his wood and covered it with canvas strips, but it looked a meager supply. The dooryard was unkempt; there was just the scrabbly dirt and piles of scrap lumber and some old buckets piled up. The makeshift steps from the house, at what had once been the juncture with the ell, did not look sturdy enough to support a good-sized man. The granite slab step at the front door stood out in a way it would not had there been lilac bushes and bleeding heart and pansies and tansy to fill in around it.

Ethan helped Zeena down from the wagon and started to unhitch the sorrel. Fly whinnied as Ethan led her inside the barn to brush her down and give her some water. "I'll get dinner on the table," Zeena called to Ethan, and he waved a hand at her.

Zeena stood at the door on those makeshift steps and looked out at the landscape. Cold, dreary, damp, there was nothing but twisted black tree branches and wet decomposing leaves and grass that never was gotten to by the goat so it lay in uneven clumps. On any other day such a scene would've weighed on Zeena. But this day held something poignant; Zeena fancied Cousin Beatrice was there in that ground, sweetening it. Mama, too, lay in earth now sweet and sacred with her bones.

The sky was settled low over the land; it released the snow in unsteady bursts, so one minute it seemed to let up and then the next it came down hard. Soon the snow would only come down hard. By night the world'd be white and cold and settled.

But it didn't settle hard on Zeena. There was too much warmth inside her to feel cold on this day.

Zeena thought of the night to come. She'd move her things into Ethan's room that afternoon. She'd change out of her brown merino and into her flannel wrapper. She'd take time to brush out her hair. She'd left Cousin Beatrice's best black shawl out on her bed, thinking she might wrap it round her shoulders after supper when they sat by the stove. She could do some mending while Ethan worked on one of his projects, the ax, or the planer that'd come apart. Then it would be time to go upstairs.

Inside her chest was that fluttering. Her stomach was all riled up. Time, now it settled on her like snow clouds and left everything to chance. Waiting had always come easy, but now she wondered how she'd fill the minutes of this day, in wait of what was to come. There were chores, tasks she'd start in on, but how would her mind stay still?

What Ethan would ask of her that night, would she have it to give? This morning, she'd felt so sure. Last night when he was kissing her, she'd felt only certainty. Last night she'd have lain with him if he'd pulled her with him into his room, never doubting what it'd be.

But now there was time to think on it. Even as they'd headed up the lane, Zeena'd felt an anticipation swirling inside. When Ethan helped her down from the wagon, she'd shivered at his touch. Now her hands trembled as she reached for the door handle.

For what did Zeena know of love? She turned and stared at the hillside before her and thought, I know nothing of love. The trembling went through her. She'd seen it, on the streets of Bettsbridge after a church affair, couples leaving together, arms entwined, giggling and laughing, ducking under the limbs of an old tree to whisper and embrace. Zeena'd hurry by them, disparaging their intimacy. Foolishness, she'd called it. It's not right to cut everything else out and see only the one you love, she thought.

At home there was Mama twirling in Father's arms while Zeena played the piano. Mama and Father dancing, that was love, she told herself. That twirling and dancing, Mama's eyes like fire and Father's so intent. They must have known this sickness, this lovesickness, in their dancing. Father's face turned red and Mama's breath'd come fast, and even after they stopped dancing it was there between them, something private that excluded even Zeena. Nights, after the dancing, she'd hear those sounds if she got up and crept out into the upstairs passage. Like Mama crying, only Zeena knew it wasn't the kind of crying Mama did after losing a baby.

Mama must've felt it. Lovesick.

A sense of calm spread through her. It eased into her limbs. Her mind settled. The trembling ceased.

Zeena decided she would dance with Ethan, not actually pull him from his chair and dance the way Mama did with Father, but in how she would act, how she would speak to him and look at him. She would let herself glide, swirling and twirling in her imagination, and when he reached for her, she would be there, and what he asked of her, she would have it to give.

AFTER DINNER ETHAN LAID OUT HIS PLANS for the afternoon. "Jotham's taking lumber in to Mr. Hale after I help him load it. While he's in town, I'll be at the woodlot. The lower lot needs thinning."

Zeena listened and nodded as she soaped the dinner plates at the sink.

His voice was almost lighthearted as he added, "Your cooking sets me up good."

"You're in high spirits today, I'd say," she said, turning with a smile.

Ethan stopped and turned, filling the door frame. "I guess I got reason enough."

Zeena twisted round and saw in his face that yearning that

looked less like sadness and more like what she'd seen in Father's eyes after he danced with Mama. He uttered some words as he approached her, "Now you're my wife." One of his hands went round her waist as he edged closer to her. The other came around in front and held to her shoulder. He smelled like hay and fresh air and perspiration, and Zeena, who'd once have found that distasteful, now leaned into him and his smells. He kissed her ear. He undid the pins in her hair. His fingers wrapped about her hair. And then they were kissing again. Zeena's soapy hands wrapped around his neck. If he were to've asked, right then, that they go upstairs, Zeena'd have left the dishes where they were in the basin with the hot rinse water cooling.

But he didn't. He kept holding her, kissing her, until that half-swallowed crying started again, even as he kissed her, and then he pulled away and told her she was so good to him, who else'd stay out here with him, who else'd keep the house running smoothly and maybe they'd get to Florida in the spring.

"We'll see," she answered, feeling her swollen lip with her tongue.

She watched him head off into the steadily falling snow, his cap pulled low over his head, a scarf wrapped round his neck, and his big hands hanging stiffly at his sides as he walked to the barn. He looked so sorrowful Zeena wanted to call him back. Don't go, she'd've cried. Stay warm with me. But he already had the bay out and was halfway down the hill and there was Jotham Powell coming down the road with the work sleigh.

Zeena's tasks kept her inside for the afternoon; her concentration stayed in her hands as she cleaned the dinner dishes, as she went through the cupboards in the back passage, cleaning the shelves and rearranging the dishes. She cleared a place down cellar where the milk could be stored for the winter months; keeping it on the cellar steps was just asking for trouble. Everyone knew milk should be kept separate, in a clean place. She cleaned the butter churn and prepared it for the next day. She filled the woodboxes, cleaned the kitchen lamp, went through the candle basket and sorted out the stubs that could be melted with the tallow to make more candles. Tomorrow she would bottle the spices Ethan'd hung down cellar.

Her back didn't even bother. Bending, stooping, lifting, scrubbing, carrying, all things that ordinarily'd send her back into a clutch, this time did not. Her breathing, when she went down cellar where the dampness was, didn't get ragged on her. By the time supper came round she was calm and ready.

Zeena had her and Ethan's places set for supper. She'd found a faded tablecloth, which she aired and spread out on the table. Then she'd gone through the china closet in search of some fineries and had found a pair of glass candlesticks. These sat between the two plates with the candles already lit.

She primped at the sink, leaving her hair loose, then winding it up, then loose. Finally she settled on her regular pug, but she didn't pull it as tight as usual. Crimping pins is what the younger girls did with their hair; it set it into waves. Zeena would get some at the store when she could. She rubbed juice from the beets she'd cooked for supper into her cheeks for color. She found an apron in the bottom dresser drawer and tied it round her waist. It had a ruffle at the skirt's hem and the two deep pockets; had Cousin Beatrice used it in years past for special occasions?

Zeena was lighting the candles when Ethan came in with Jotham Powell following behind him. "Can you set another place?" Ethan asked as he went to the sink to wash. When he was done, Jotham washed up too.

The two men sat at the table and watched Zeena bring the food on, beans and biscuits, and beets. She tried to catch Ethan's eye. Had he told Jotham they were married now? Ethan seemed intent on discussing with Jotham the work needed by Mr. Hale, so it wasn't until partway through supper that he even looked at Zeena.

"D'you tell Jotham?" she asked, smiling, making sure to hold her hand just so, so he could see the gold ring on her finger.

Ethan coughed. He turned to Jotham who was taking a second serving of beans. "Zeena and me," he started, and waited for Jotham to pause and look up from his food, "Zeena and me, we got ourselves married today."

Jotham stared at Ethan, unblinking, for several seconds. He looked at Zeena then, noticed her hand held out and saw the gold ring. "Well," he finally said.

Zeena smiled broadly. "We want you should keep on with us, course."

Jotham's eyes blinked now. He looked at Ethan who'd dropped his napkin to the floor and was retrieving it.

"Yes, I'm Mis' Frome now," Zeena was saying.

Ethan reached for the beets and handed them to Jotham. "Have some more."

Silence settled on the table for several minutes. Finally Jotham pushed his chair back. "I'm full up."

"Won't you have some pudding?" Ethan asked.

"I had enough," Jotham said, wiping his mouth and rising from the table. He carried his plate to the sink. He stopped by the table on his way to the door. He shuffled his feet and looked at the floor. "I wouldn't ha' stayed if I'd ha' known," he started. "An' I wish you happiness here. Ethan couldn't do no better," he said, pulling his hat on and peering from beneath the brim.

"You'll always be welcome," Zeena said, feeling generous.

Jotham backed himself out of the door with a raised hand of farewell.

After he left, Ethan said, "What's got into him?"

Zeena laughed. "For the land's sake, Mr. Frome, it's our wedding night." She rose from the table and stood by Ethan. "He had the good sense to know he shouldn't ha' stayed."

"I wasn't looking at it like that," Ethan said.

"No, but he was. And I was," she said.

Ethan reached for her hand. "I guess it's good you married me. I need someone who knows these things."

There was silence then between them, until Zeena said, "I moved my things into your room this afternoon."

"Well," he said.

More silence. "Was that what you wanted?"

"I hadn't thought on it."

Zeena drew back. She waited. When he took another serving of pudding onto his plate, she cleared some dishes to the sink and began washing. She could smell Ethan's pipe tobacco. She turned once and saw him smoking his pipe and staring out the window. "Ethan," she started, turning, "didn't you want I should move my things?"

"I just hadn't thought—" he said.

Zeena stared at him. Was that possible? "Well, now you think on it, what's your decision?"

Ethan rested his pipe on his plate. He rose from the table and came to the sink where Zeena stood. "Don't you see," he started, "I, I—"

Zeena turned and starting scrubbing a dish when Ethan could go no farther.

Ethan put his hands on her shoulders. She felt a wrench of longing. Her knees weakened. She turned then and fell against him. The kissing, it started again. Her hair came undone. Ethan held her to him. "I don't know what I'd do," he muttered. "I'm here," she whispered. She wanted him to lead her upstairs to their room. She wanted to lie with him and know what it was.

Ethan was breathing hard. His brows lifted, sending lines across his forehead. Then they smoothed. She stepped close and leaned against him. He smelled of soap and woodsmoke and pipe tobacco. He took her hand and turned. He collected one candle from the table and led her to the door, then through the passage. "D'you check the stove?" she whispered. He didn't answer. He led her up the stairs behind him, the candle sending flickerings of light along the sloped ceiling. He paused at the door to his room and stepped aside for her, still holding to her hand.

Zeena stepped over the door's threshold. She thought she might slump to the floor. Ethan blew out the candle, leaving them in the dark.

TWENTY-THREE

issing is like dancing. They sway and lean and turn in a circle, and the music is their breathing and the sounding of her heart. Zeena imagines she's in a ball-room, like the ones she's seen in pictures. She's in a dress of white bengaline with Hamburg lace at the neck and the cuffs. She wears jet and crystal beads like in the pictures. Her hair is wound up with lace and on her feet are delicate white dancing slippers.

They spin and twist and turn. Then they are no longer danc-ing, they are sinking into each other as into water. A river car-ries them. Ethan pulls off his shirt and trousers, wears just his union suit now, and starts shivering. His teeth are chattering. "You're cold," she whispers, which she is not. She is warm from the inside out. Her arms and legs are tingling with it. She rubs his shoulders, his back, his arms.

Then Ethan's fingers are pulling her flannel wrapper off her shoulders. It falls to the floor and she does not pick it up. He is kissing her again and she holds to him to keep from falling. He sits on the bed and she stands beside him and they kiss. In the dark he tries to get her clothes off but she has to help him. She loosens the camisole at the waist and his hands go up under the flannel undershirt. No one has ever touched her there, not since Mama plastered her chest with camphor. He slips off her camisole and undershirt so she is naked to the night's dark cold but she feels only warm, only warm. His hands go all over her. They wrap around her back; his fingers trace her spine.

His face buries into her bosom and then he is crying.

She holds tighter to him. "What is it?" She leans into the bed and holds him, cradles his head. She is swimming in her love now. "Tell me," she whispers. "Is it your grieving?"

He coughs. He sputters. Then he falls to crying again.

"What is it?" she whispers.

He falls back against the mattress. He stops crying and just lies there. "I'm sorry," he finally says.

She lies against him, cradles him. "Can't you tell me?" she begs.

He turns onto his side, away from her. She lies against him and rubs his back as he breathes, breathes, then falls to sleep.

She does not sleep. When she gets cold, she pulls the bedcovers around them and buries her head in against his neck. She keeps stroking his arm and his back.

WHEN HE WAKES AND TURNS TO HER, she is waiting. He doesn't kiss her. He pulls off her petticoat and she slips her drawers and stockings off, and then she can hardly follow what happens. That river overtakes her again and she is awash in it and she knows she will give in to it. His breathing is loud and urgent in her ear; his hands are tentative for a moment, but then they go all over her. He is sweating and breathing and she is too. But she is not prepared for what comes next. He lifts on top of her and then a sharp pain comes where he pushes inside her. He pushes like that two more times and then he is shuddering against her, his face in her neck.

If she could, she would cry after he goes to sleep. But she can't. She can only lie at his side in the dark and wonder what it was that happened and hope there is not something awfully wrong that made it hurt so.

IN THE MORNING she awakes to pain. She watches him dress. She wants to ask him why he cried, but this is not the time. She tells herself it is his grieving.

She wishes she could cry. She cannot understand what happened between them during the night. She cannot believe the pain she felt is what loving is. Mama wouldn't ha' wanted Father to hurt her that way, yet when she looked at him with love, she must ha' known what was in store.

In her back and down her legs, the pain throbs. Then into her belly. The red stain she finds in her nightdress after he has gone downstairs shocks her. It is her monthly flow, come early. What he did brought it early, she figures. The bleeding is like an injury now where before it was something to ignore and wish away.

Somehow he knows. Without her saying anything, he does not kiss her and hold her that day or any of the four days it lasts. She has never had so much discomfort with her monthly flow before. It is hard to stand up, much less do her work. The shooting pains in her legs make them almost useless. She drags herself through the days, baking early, washing, ironing, cleaning, mending. Once when she carries the supper dishes to the sink she stumbles. A plate falls to the floor and breaks. She grabs hold of what's nearest to her, the rocker. When he asks her what it is, she says, "I got my shooting pains," and holds to her hip and thinks it is his fault, what he did.

When it is over, he seems to sense it. That night when they go upstairs she is fearful. It is not like dancing when he helps her off with her clothes and they kiss and then they lie on the bed and he lifts on top of her and again there is the pain inside, but it is less than the first time, and she doesn't have time to think maybe it will get better each time because then it is over and he is crying those silent sobs. She strokes his back. "Is it your grieving?" she asks. He does not answer. "You been through so much," she says, remembering what folks in town have told her. He falls asleep while she rubs his back, strokes his shoulders. Her own yearning grows stronger. The tingling in her limbs, it returns.

She is always warm now, waiting.

She waits for him. She has always waited for things and she will wait for this, Ethan's touch. For the kissing, for his hands, the feel of his hands on her skin, all over her. It comes on her, this thought: If she can give him a child, he will stop crying and she will feel like a woman.

IT IS THE SAME EVERY NIGHT. They start by kissing in the dark and then either she is helped off with her clothes or her nightdress is pulled up around her shoulders and then he lifts on top of her and then she feels it again, that sharp thrust as he loves her. Sometimes he cries first and then falls asleep and she just holds him and rubs his shoulders.

Sometimes the wind blows, rattling the window frames. Sometimes the night is still as the surface of a pond, glassy and quiet. Sometimes it rains, the droplets pelting the glass in the window. Sometimes it spits snow, a quieter pattering against the glass. Sometimes there are the wolf calls, eerie and shrill. Sometimes there is the distinct sense that deer are at the apple trees. Sometimes there is the scuttle of squirrels in the eaves, or the quieter pluckings of mice behind the walls. Sometimes the night is so black she thinks she is under the world.

As the moon approaches a new cycle and fills the room with its light, she looks down at her nakedness when it is over and feels she should cry. He is already sleeping and she is alone in the night with her white legs, her white body, her white breasts.

She sees a corpse, not her own living flesh. She wants to cry, but it doesn't come. She pulls up the bedcovers and tries to forget what she has seen. The window is her friend. So long as she can see it, she knows there is a world waiting for tomorrow.

One last time she asks him, "Why do you cry?" It is on a moonless night after it is over and she is stroking his shoulder. When he falls asleep, she knows not to ask again.

Days, she comes to feel her own yearning for him less and less. In her mind is the memory of the nights before. It isn't just the physical pain it causes her. She has the dim sense it could be otherwise. But how to make it so? It seems to her yet another confirmation that she is not like any other woman who swells with love like a blossom, who looks to her husband with a knowing smile that says: Because of what we do in our secret moments, I am a woman. In their faces Zeena does not see what she feels inside. There is no look in their eyes that speaks of such loneliness as she suffers. The moments in which a man and his wife are most tender and close are to her the most brutal and distant.

She lies awake into the night. Finally she sinks into a bitter sleep.

But this sustains her: When the full moon wanes and she is with child, then she will know she is as much like other women as she needs to be.

TWENTY-FOUR

On Thanksgiving morning, there was an ominous red strip along the horizon. The moon, nearly full, had showed a ring the night before.

"Snow's coming," Ethan told her as he slipped his trousers over his union suit and stared out through the window.

Zeena saw his breath in the air. "It's too cold up here," she wheezed. "It tightens up my lungs."

Ethan pushed his arms into the sleeves of yesterday's work shirt and began buttoning them.

"Whyn't you bring the stove from your mother's room up here?"

"I already told you, if we stay another winter . . ."

"I thought you was planning on selling."

"That's why I need the stove downstairs, so I can do my planning. I got to get back to my studies if I want to find work."

Zeena breathed in and started coughing. There was that clutching in her lungs as she doubled over. "The cold is what brings this on," she sputtered between coughs.

Ethan stood beside her with a glass of water.

When she stopped coughing, Zeena reached for her teeth and then took the water. "Thank you, but I don't see as this'll—" She broke into coughing again. "It's the cold what—" but her coughing cut off her words and when she looked up, Ethan was gone. He had a habit of disappearing now. He'd hover over her, make suggestions about something, then when she blinked her eyes, he was gone.

Nearly a month it was since they'd said their vows. The days were filled with hard work starting before sunrise and ending when they collapsed into bed at night and Ethan turned to her and she felt the pain again. Now the sun went down at about the time they sat down to supper, a quick repast, followed by more work. For Zeena it was mending and piecework; she was starting a hooked rug, something to bring a little color into the kitchen. For Ethan, it was repairing tools that'd broken during the summer and fall, sharpening knives and saws so he could get to the woodpile before the sun was up.

Zeena looked out the window. The apple trees were bare, save for a few lingering red apples that hung on limply. The fields were frosted; the bushes and grasses glistened white. Down the hillside the lane and the road south were crusted with it. Her coughing had stopped, even the wheezing.

Bathing was her morning routine, though the cold water in that cold air was unpleasant. She shivered as she pulled on her underclothes and her stockings, pulled on her petticoat and camisole, then her black calico wrapper as she slipped into the hall. The coughing overtook her again as she went down the stairs and out to the backhouse.

After tying on her apron she stood at the cookstove and breathed the steam from the kettle. That often relieved her symptoms. When Zeena carried plates of sausage patties and eggs and cornbread to the table, Ethan said, "That steam cleared your coughing up good," and smiled at her.

Zeena sighed. "Yes," she answered.

"But your face is white as milk."

"Oh?" Her hand went to her cheek. "It's just all the coughing, I'd guess. That room's so cold."

"You sure you're up to going to the Varnums'?"

Zeena pinched her cheeks. Her eyes brightened. "For the land's sake, yes. I ain't ventured off this land since the day we married." She was planning on wearing Cousin Beatrice's black shawl to show Lucy that Ethan could provide very well for a wife. And she looked forward to seeing Rebekah, who'd not been to visit since the weather'd turned cold.

Ethan asked was she baking anything to take to the Varnums for dinner. Zeena reminded him she'd done it yesterday so as to be ready and pointed to a basket where the biscuits and cranberry bread and pickles and pumpkin pie were wrapped and ready to go. "I also packed my prize."

Ethan looked at her with raised eyebrows.

"The red pickle dish."

Still he looked questioning.

"What Aunt Philura Maple sent us as a wedding gift. Mama's aunt from Philadelphia."

"You're taking that?"

"I want them all to see we got beautiful things like they do."
Ethan nodded.

Zeena smiled. "I packed it careful."

After breakfast Ethan got ready to finish his chores in the barn and go to the mill for a couple of hours. "I'll be back at noon," he said.

"That leave you time enough to clean up?"

Ethan paused. "Better be back before noon," he said. Then, "I can't keep my mind on time like you do." He smiled. "It's good I got someone to get me places."

Zeena stood at the stove, sipping her tea as she watched him go. Seemed she had to think of everything. Seemed he'd forget just about anything if she didn't remind him. It bolstered her pride. She lifted her shoulders and smiled, to think how much good she was doing him.

Then she stepped over to the sink to do the dishes. She glanced in the looking glass to see was she all that pale. She was. Her skin had a pasty look. For the last weeks she'd been flushed and shining whenever she looked at her reflection.

She knew being with child'd drain a woman of her color, especially early on when her insides turned sick. Food would be hard to swallow. Nothing would taste right. Pains in the chest could come. Some women said they felt it within days. Some even the next morning.

Zeena took a last sip of tea. She realized she wasn't feeling well. It wasn't just the wheezing and coughing. She leaned against the sink as she washed and wiped the dishes. Her head felt light and airy. Her stomach was fluttery. She wasn't feeling well at all.

IT WAS SNOWING HARD by the time they left the ridge road and turned onto the road to town. The wagon lifted and then swerved on the slick ruts that'd frozen solid. Zeena held to her seat; she braced herself with one foot pressed against the wagon. Her stomach heaved with the wagon's shiftings. She shivered under the blankets Ethan'd brought. "I don't know when I felt so cold," she chattered.

Ethan nodded.

"I'm thinking maybe it's not my asthma."

Ethan straightened up. He held the reins in one hand and looked at her. "You want to turn back?"

"Land, no, like I said, I wouldn't miss this."

The wagon's wheels slipped up over and then down a rut. The wagon jogged sideways.

"It's snowing like it's January. We'll be wishing we had the sleigh by the time we go home," Ethan said. They came up over a ridge then and the road dipped down. The town was before them. Ethan looked around him and his eyes sparkled. "Look at it, though."

Zeena was shivering. She leaned against Ethan. "I thought you hated to see the snow come."

Ethan pulled his cap down onto his ears. He sniffed the air. "Something about these hills, though, going white."

Zeena looked at the landscape. The green of the firs and pine trees stood out against the gray and brown woodlands that were filling in white. The sloping hillsides had a velvety quality, purplish, with a lace white covering. The sky was silver gray. It was pretty, all right, but what good does prettiness do when it's all there is? That was her view. But Ethan was different. He was touched by prettiness. "How can you think of Florida when you feel so strong about these hills?"

The wheels crunched and the wagon clanked several minutes before he answered. "I'm just trying to get by. A man can't get by in these hills no more."

Was that it? A matter of economy? "You'd stay, then, if you could get by?"

The silence lasted several minutes. Finally, "I ain't sure."

"Maybe we don't need to go so far. Maybe Worcester, or Portsmouth, or some city where there's plenty going on."

"Maybe," he answered. He hunched down onto the seat and stared straight ahead at the road. The snow was collecting quickly.

Zeena was thinking. She'd treated Ida May back in Bettsbridge when Ida was first in the family way and was so sick she couldn't do a thing. Ida'd complained about a sick headache and a constant pain in her chest when she ate any food.

Zeena strained to feel what was different, if anything. She thought about how the eggs she'd had for breakfast hadn't tasted right. The applesauce, heated the way she liked it, it almost tasted like it was turned, but Ethan'd said no, it was fine. And her head, she felt a sick headache coming on.

As they drove under the Varnums' row of hemlocks, Zeena felt she might faint; she saw stars wherever she looked. Her mouth'd turned dry. When she stepped down from the wagon, one foot slid on the snow. She caught herself by holding to

Ethan. Lucy was on the porch, waving. "Come along, come along," she called. Zeena waved back. She reached for the basket of food that Ethan was carrying. "Don't you try to take that," he said, turning. "I'm just checking," and she peered into the basket. "I wanted to make sure the pickle dish's there."

Lucy welcomed them at the door with handshakes and her warm smile. "I'm so glad you've come," she said. "We couldn't leave you out there all alone, not with your mother passing such a short time ago."

Zeena pointed to the basket. "We brought some food," she said. Then she reached for the wrapped-up dish. "And my pickle dish. All the way from Philadelphia," she said, looking to see Lucy's response, but there was just a nod and a "Well, how nice," and then Ethan left her in the hall to tend to the sorrel.

Lucy kept smiling. Lawyer Varnum was in the parlor, waving to her. Rebekah had come in and was taking Zeena's cape. There was a tiredness in her face that was dispelled when she leaned close and said, "My, but you look well, Zeena."

Zeena started to say she'd been feeling poorly the last few days. There was her wheezing, and maybe she was getting a chest cold, or a sick headache, or maybe what she'd hoped, a baby to carry on Ethan's name. It was so cold at the farm. But Rebekah was smiling, her hands sunk in the deep pockets of her sweater.

"Marriage suits you," Lucy said.

Zeena had a momentary flash of memory: her white legs lying naked on the bed after Ethan'd loved her and had sunk into sleep beside her. How hard it was to reach down and pull the bedcovers up over herself. How hard to look at him first thing in the morning when he lit the candle to dress, so she lay on her side now and stared out the window at the darkness. After he'd done his chores in the barn and she was busy at the cookstove, it was easier. She could look him in the eye and see he was the same as ever. What happened between them in the dark, he didn't seem to think on it, or wonder what it was that was wrong about it. He just went about his day, heavy limbed, plodding, his shoulders as sloped as ever, with not so much as a word about how things'd changed.

Rebekah and Lucy waited for Zeena to say something. They smiled and waited. Lucy's dark eyes were piercing; Rebekah's held that sadness, despite her smile.

Finally Zeena said, "Yes, I guess it does."

They smiled at each other and at Zeena. "How wonderful," Lucy said. "I'd never ha' guessed," and she glanced at Rebekah. "I mean, it's just so good the way it's worked out."

"You got yourself a fine husband," Rebekah said, sighing. "Many of us in town, we wished he'd take notice. I guess he was all the time waiting for you."

Zeena smiled. Rebekah put words in such a way as to make everything right. She felt it again. The glow inside her that spread out and made her eyes shine. When she next saw Ethan, it was as if everything was as she wished it to be. She stood and went to his side. She slipped her arm in his. The yearning came again. She felt it so strong, her legs went weak. She stood beside Ethan, her husband of a month, and wondered how long she would wait to tell him she was with child.

ETHAN ASKED HER, "You feeling all right?" as they stepped into the dining room.

She returned his question with a blank stare.

"This morning—" he started.

Zeena shook her head. "I was just tired." She pulled Cousin Beatrice's black shawl around her shoulders and looked at the group of people before her. There were eleven to dinner. Zeena and Ethan, the four Varnums, a variety of Varnum aunts and uncles, and a sister of Lawyer Varnum's from Worcester, come to stay a month. The sister was dressed in mourning, with a black veil covering her hair, and a death's-head ring on one finger. She twirled the jet beads that hung round her neck. She sat to Lawyer Varnum's left, somewhat across from Zeena.

"Worcester's where my mother grew up," Zeena told her. The sister nodded. "Her father was Joshua Higgins. They lived on a farm down in the valley, near the hamlet." The sister nodded again. "There's a stream runs through the land and the weeping willows, Mama said there never was a finer stand of weeping willows than them. She said everyone come in the summer to set out under those willows."

"I don't believe I ever heard of 'em," the sister said.

Zeena lifted her chin. "No?"

"I'm from the town. I never knew the hamlet folk."

To Zeena's left was Lucy's uncle. He was quite deaf. "Eh?" he asked Zeena. She told him, "I'm talking about my grandfather from Worcester," but "Eh?" he asked again. "My grandfather," she repeated.

"Eh?"

Zeena smiled. She nodded. "Weren't that nice."

He smiled and buttered a roll.

Zeena watched Lucy get up from her chair and go to Rebekah. "You'll overheat in this sweater." Rebekah protested she was too cold. "You can't be cold, child." Rebekah looked at her lap. "Let her be," Lawyer Varnum told Lucy. He looked around the table. "A mother doesn't know when to stop," and he chuckled.

Zeena had never seen such a fancy table. A sparkling white linen tablecloth covered it. The china was elegant. "Lenox," Lucy said when Zeena complimented it. The water glasses sparkled. "Hereford crystal," Lucy explained. "Mr. Varnum's brother sent them from Germany."

"From Germany?"

Lawyer Varnum said, "He went to Austria after the war to study medicine. Hasn't been home since."

Zeena reached for her red pickle dish and handed it across the table to Lucy's aunt. The red dish was the most colorful item on the table. Zeena thought it stood out and gave her and Ethan a place at the table. "This's mine," she said. "It's from Philadelphia."

The aunt passed it on to Lawyer Varnum's sister. "It's cunning," she said.

On the table were meat pies, smoked venison, a roasted chicken, dressing, squash, potatoes, creamed onions, beets, jellies, relish, fruit sauce, cranberry sauce, and of course biscuits and Zeena's cranberry bread. Zeena'd never seen such plenty.

"Mis' Frome," a voice came at her. It was the first time someone'd spoken it aloud. It was another aunt. "How you think you'll like living out a town?"

Zeena looked to Ethan. She wasn't sure she should speak about their plans. Ethan kept a steady gaze at her that seemed to say she shouldn't. "Ask me in May, when I been through a winter," causing a gentle laughter at the table.

"It's wonderful, the way Ethan holds on to what's been in his family so long. So many folks're migrating west. I say, there'll be no one left but us old folks," the aunt said, looking round the room. There were murmurings and sighs of agreement. Lawyer Varnum spoke up. "Long as folks think there's better worlds, they'll go after them. What's wrong with being satisfied with what you have?"

"Long as you got enough," Zeena said.

"But who's to say what's enough? Maybe we have enough now."

Ruth, sitting to Zeena's right, held a platter of chicken and dressing out so Zeena could spoon what she wanted onto her plate. Ruth's hands were trembling. She coughed. "This's too heavy for you," Zeena said. Ruth's face was flushed. She shook her head. Zeena studied her face. Was she ailing? As the conversation continued, Lawyer Varnum making his points about why Americans migrated and how, since the war, everyone'd traded their heritage for something else, gold, and the hope of making a fortune, Zeena half listened and half watched Ruth. Once she spoke up, "What's so wrong with wanting a fortune?" and gazed around the room at the elegance that surrounded them.

"If it means giving up our history, then I say no. Gold doesn't guarantee comfort," the lawyer returned. "The comfort that comes from tradition, from knowing where your neighbor stands in relation to you."

Zeena was taken aback and looked to Ethan, but he was studying the food on his plate. Zeena was aware of Ruth's picking at her food and coughing. "Where your neighbor stands?" she asked the lawyer.

"It's a question of class," he said.

Silence fell on the table. Lucy cleared her throat and avoided Zeena's eyes. Zeena caught Ethan's eye and saw it, that sorrow, heavy on his shoulders and in his gaze. Rebekah changed the subject. "I hear the *Farmer's Almanac* says we're in for a snowy winter." Looking out the window she said, "I guess it's starting like they said it would. This's the last we'll see of bare ground, I'd venture."

Zeena turned to Ruth. Her face was flushed, and her hands trembled. "You don't look well," Zeena said, putting her hand to Ruth's cheek. "The child's burning up," Zeena said, pushing back her chair. Lucy put down her fork. "Ruth?" she asked. Ruth raised her eyes from her plate. They were glassy. "She's just over a chest cold," Lucy said.

"Let me take her upstairs," Zeena said, rising. She helped Ruth from her chair. Lucy started to get up. Zeena motioned with her hand for Lucy to stay. "You got guests, I'll see what's ailing her." The girl leaned into Zeena, coughing. She was shivering and trembling. Zeena'd seen the throat distemper before. The sudden flush, the dry cough, the loss of strength.

Ethan said, "Zeena'll know what to do."

Lucy said, "She's a marvel, Ethan."

As Zeena and Ruth left the room, there was silence again. Zeena heard the clatter of forks and knives on the beautiful bone china as she crossed the parlor and headed to the carpeted stairs.

AFTER SETTLING RUTH IN BED, Zeena went to the kitchen and told the hired girl to fry up some onions and mix in molasses, and to bring it right along. This is the only nourishment Ruth should take, Zeena told her. She got the stove going and set a pot of water on top to get moisture in the air. She applied a plaster of chicken oil to Ruth's neck and chest and wrapped a cloth around her throat. She applied cold and then hot water to Ruth's forehead. But she didn't work on her the way she had with Cousin Beatrice. Her hands itched to try it, but her heart told her no.

You're no healer, she knew now.

Zeena sat by her bed and listened to Ruth's breathing. First it was light and quick, then heavy and slow, then light and quick again. Zeena looked round the room at the papered walls, the curly maple dresser and matching mirror, the plush chair covered in flowered damask, the carpet on the floor and rugs thrown across it, the green glass lamp. A large chiffonier stood on one wall. In a miniature rocker sat a china doll with auburn curls and blue eyes, wearing a lace pinafore over a velvet dress. Zeena sighed. Course Lawyer Varnum can say folks have enough. He has more'n enough for him and his family. It irked her that he could judge others for wanting what he had. Hypocrisy, is what she'd call it.

Ruth lay still as the doll. Zeena would not begrudge the girl for having so much. T'weren't her fault.

She and Ethan would go off to find their own fortune some day, and Lawyer Varnum could say what he wanted. Zeena would look him in the eye and say, I only want what you want. Don't I have the same rights's you?

Rebekah came upstairs and into Ruth's room. "She's got the throat distemper," Zeena told her. "She might get some sick with it, it's come on so hard." Rebekah pulled a small rocker over to the bed. They watched Ruth and listened to her erratic breathing. "Several folk're suffering from pneumonia," Rebekah said. "You're sure it's not that?" Zeena told her no, but it could turn into that, "the way she's breathing and all."

Rebekah got up. She pulled Zeena's arm. "I want to show you something in my room."

Zeena followed her into her room. The stove was out, and the air was cold.

"I don't want anything to happen to my sister," Rebekah said, pulling the door closed behind them. That serious look was on her face, her eyes darker than usual.

"She'll be all right."

"The scarlet fever, it took my brothers."

Zeena told her she knew.

Rebekah lowered her voice. "It happens so fast, someone you love goes—"

Zeena nodded. She knew about that.

"They always said I was the one should ha' gone."

Zeena said she hadn't heard that. "How long ago was it?"

"Eight years. John, he went first. We thought Henry'd stay it through, but spring came and it brought a flare up and then he was gone. Just like that. And folks'd look right at me and say, 'We thought it'd be you.' And now Ruth, and they're all downstairs thinking, It should be Rebekah, she's the sickly one."

"You ought'n to think that way."

"I always wondered, why'd I live when they went."

"There's no reason for these things."

"But do you think Ruth—"

"This won't last. Don't you fret for Ruth."

"If you say so, I won't." Rebekah was shivering. She opened a chest and pulled out a woven shawl, dark purple, and wrapped it around herself. She smoothed her skirt. "But what about you?" she asked.

"Me?"

"Marriage. How's it suit you?"

"I guess it's fine." Zeena thought to say, It's not what I imagined, but she kept that to herself. "There's more work than I realized. Ethan, he gets at it before dawn and don't stop till he falls to bed."

"I'll never marry."

"What're you saying, course you will, look at me, for the land's sake."

Rebekah lifted something off her dresser and turned to Zeena with it. It was pressed violets behind an oval glass frame, just inches tall. "I pressed these when I was a girl."

"You're still a girl," Zeena teased.

Rebekah shook her head. "I was poorly then. One whole summer I recovered from the scarlet fever that took my brothers. Ethan, he brought me these violets. All that summer he stopped by and left me flowers. Yellow daisies and white daisies and pansies and asters and violets, was always something sweet looking, tied with a ribbon."

"It's pretty."

"I want you to have it."

Zeena shook her head. "Why, I couldn't, it's, it's yours."

"I think it's more yours now."

"You're more generous'n anybody I ever knew." Then without considering her words, Zeena asked, "D'you love Ethan?"

Rebekah laughed. "You think I'd give this away if I did? You think I'd see you as the only friend I have?"

Zeena waited. She watched Rebekah's face. It was smooth and serene. Even the sadness was gone.

"I'll be truthful. I had a girl's crush . . . who wouldn't?" and she leaned against Zeena's arm and smiled. "There's others I loved. But not Ethan. Not like you love him."

"No?"

"You look after him. He doesn't need some foolish girl to tend to. You're strong enough to give that to him. You're, you're a woman." Her face was serious again, and solemn. "Look at him. I see how it is. He's happy like I've never seen him. Mother noticed it right off. Even with his mother's passing, you could see it. Hope."

Zeena held the framed and pressed violets in her hand. "Still seems this is yours."

Rebekah shook her head. She went to the door then. "But don't let Ethan know they're the same violets he gave me. He'd know I'm no more'n a silly girl then." She smiled as she held the door for Zeena.

"Wait," Zeena said, deciding to plunge into another subject. "Who's the young man you're pining after?"

They heard Lucy calling from the stairs then. "Mother won't want me going in to Ruth," Rebekah said. "She says I'm too delicate to be around folks' sicknesses. Don't tell her I was in Ruth's room."

"What about my question?"

Rebekah seemed to consider it for a moment. Then, "He's no one to talk about, not now."

There was Lucy, calling again. Was she coming up the stairs?

"Come out to visit sometime soon," Zeena said. "Maybe we can sit over a cup a tea." Maybe she could get Rebekah talking then. Maybe she'd have some news to share with her. Isn't that what women did? Share their troubles and their joys?

DOWNSTAIRS THE GOOD-BYES WERE SAID QUICKLY. With the snow coming so strong it was wise to get started right away. Lucy and Rebekah accompanied them to the hall. Lucy held Zeena's hand and looked her in the eye. "We need the likes of you around here," she said. "Mrs. Hale, she's always done the doctoring, but she's not liking to go out so much." Zeena said she'd been doing it all her life. "Mama trained me," she said. Doctoring, she could continue with that. Anybody can do that, she thought. It's healing that's done only by some.

"Folks'll hear of you," Lucy said. "I can promise you folks'll hear of you." To Ethan, "This town needs the likes of her. Isn't it good she stayed?"

Ethan half smiled at Lucy, then looked at Rebekah.

Rebekah was knitting even as she stood in the doorway. She looked up at Ethan, then quickly to Zeena.

"Course, I wish she'd stay here with us tonight," and Lucy looked anxiously at Zeena, "and look after Ruth."

Zeena'd considered staying, had thought to offer it, but really, Lucy could do what Zeena'd tell her was necessary. "Ruth'll be fine and I'll be back," she said. Ethan added, "Jotham or I'll be in tomorrow, 'less the snow's too deep, and we'll bring her."

"You're sure you don't want to leave that dish?" Lucy pointed to the basket and the pickle dish wrapped in flannel. "Till then," she added, looking out beyond them at the snow.

Zeena shook her head. She wanted to get the dish home and back to its place in the china closet.

"It was kind of you to bring it," Lucy said.

Rebekah nodded. "It's such a fine piece," she said. Her needles were clicking.

Lawyer Varnum was in the parlor with the other guests but he called a good-bye.

Zeena thanked them as Ethan led her out the door.

She huddled beside Ethan on the ride home. The snow was steady, and with a driving wind. Fly worked to pull the wagon through half a foot of wet, heavy snow. Ethan got out and led the horse up the first steep hill. "I never seen anything like this," Zeena told him when he climbed back in beside her. The wind was so strong she almost had to yell. "Not this early, anyway." She was shivering already with cold.

"You don't know a Starkfield winter," he yelled back, pulling on the reins to guide Fly to the left more.

"I seen Bettsbridge winters, can't be too much different."

He just looked at her from beneath his cap. His blue eyes were startling against all the white that surrounded them. Ethan pointed to the left suddenly. "That's the coasting hill," he told her, but he had to repeat it in order for her to get the words.

She looked at where he pointed. White swirling snow, and a drop-off.

Ethan leaned close. "We'll go coasting soon," he said.

"I ain't coasted in years."

"One a these nights soon, we'll go."

They continued on in silence, along the ridge out of town, through the tunnel of woods, over to the next ridge, down the hill, and finally onto their lane. The graveyard, now that the snow'd covered the ground and was leaning up the stones, looked different; the stones could've been floating in a sea instead of marking the final homes of Ethan's ancestors. The wind'd let up and the snow was just lightly falling, settling where it landed.

Zeena looked at the farmhouse. It was almost pretty in the snow, all white, softly lined, homey.

"It's not much," Ethan said.

Zeena felt his shame. Didn't seem fair, she thought, him working so hard and barely getting straightened round, while Lawyer Varnum'd amassed his fortune doing lawyer work, which Father said was taking advantage of folks' weaknesses. Zeena leaned her head against Ethan's shoulder. In a gush of generosity she said, "It's enough for my needs."

Ethan laughed. "I know that ain't true."

Zeena slipped her arm in his. She felt almost girlish.

Ethan's shoulders hunched up. His arm tightened against Zeena's. The snow was spitting in their faces now and he lowered his head.

They were under the elms, approaching the barn. Ethan drew on the reins and settled the wagon by the first bay. He slipped the reins around the post and came round to help Zeena. When she stepped down to the ground he pulled her close. Zeena's hat fell into the snow but she hardly noticed. The snow was settling on their heads, their shoulders, and she was listening to Ethan, "How'd I do without you, I couldn't, I—"

Zeena felt her knees go soft, but Ethan held her. She was numb now to the cold and the snow.

"We'll get away from here," he murmured. "I'll work harder this winter, you'll see . . ."

Fly whinnied. The snow came down and the darkness was rising.

"You'd best get inside," Ethan said, letting her go.

She thought she might sink. She gripped his arm. She wanted to tell him her hope, that a baby was already growing inside her, but instead asked, "D'you love me?"

"You're my wife," he said.

Her legs were trembling. If she let go his arm, Zeena thought she'd go down.

He kissed her then. It was his way of saying it. She let him kiss her. She kissed him back. Surely he loved her, she told herself.

THAT NIGHT WHEN HE LOVED HER, Zeena knew it was not going to change.

This is what loving is, she told herself. This feeling like she was going to turn to molasses, it took all the barriers away, it made it seem as if there was nothing but good in the world, as if the way she felt was enough to carry her through life and there was nothing to worry over, not money, not the past, not sorrows, not all the work that was needed to get through a single day.

A river is what it was. It carried her along so easy, carried her along so time fell away, so life might turn to dying and it wouldn't be any different, it was all the same, the passage of day into night into day, a comfort.

But when it was over, with her left feeling still like molasses and him sleeping like a baby, back to her, the barriers came back piece by piece. Tomorrow loomed as more drudgery. The past was the voices that had for a little while been silenced. The sense of having too little, of not being recognized for what she was or could be so that others held more importance by virtue of their last names or the house they lived in or the judgments they'd passed, all of this clouded her mind.

Zeena pulled down her nightdress. She reached for the bed-covers and pulled them over Ethan and herself. She lay in the dark and looked out the window at the snow falling. She had the idea it might just snow and snow and never stop, burying them.

There was one comfort. She would carry a child and birth it and then she would have what she needed. Then she would be somebody.

TWENTY-FIVE

*R*uth was sitting up in bed when Zeena next saw her. "I'm all better," the girl told her. Her cheeks had a healthy color to them, not the flush she'd had when she first took sick.

"I wouldn't ha' thought you'd be so quick about it."

Ruth chuckled and sounded like her father. "It always happens like this." Then, "Mother says I can't get up."

Zeena asked, "You been drinking plenty of water?"

The girl nodded. "And eating those onions with the molasses. Mother made me."

Lucy stood on the other side of the bed. "Zeena said it'd help."

"And looks like it did," Zeena said. "To tell the truth, I feared it might be worse than throat distemper." She shook her head. "I'd ha' been here days ago but the sleigh's needing repairs and the walking's not easy, what with all this snow."

"I'll send you back in a sleigh with the hired hand."

Zeena nodded her thanks. To Ruth she said, "You ought'n to get up just yet."

Ruth frowned.

Lucy looked at her daughter. "You do just what Zeena says."

Zeena looked at Ruth's hands. The palms were dry, the skin not puffy. She looked at her eyes. No sickly shine. Her heartbeat was regular. Her skin temperature was a little cool. There really wasn't much reason to keep the girl in bed but for Lucy's sake. "At least another day," she said.

Lucy walked her downstairs. "Will you have a cup of tea?" she asked.

"Why, yes." Then, "Is Rebekah here?"

"She had some digestive troubles this morning, said she thought she'd stay in her room today."

"Oh?"

"I think she's just tired. She's bent on finishing the scarves and mittens she makes for the church and she stays up late nights even when I tell her no." She shook her head. "Daughters. You never know just what's in their heads."

Zeena smiled. She could smile at that now where before she'd've had to look away. She was sure she was with child. The last few mornings she'd awakened with that dryness in her throat and an aversion to the smell of fruit sauce steaming on the cookstove. Now she was part of the female world. When a woman complained about the pains of childbirth or the discomforts of carrying a child, or if she fretted over her children or complained they didn't know what was best for them, now Zeena'd be able to smile knowingly. I understand, her smile would say.

IT WAS TWO WEEKS to the next snowfall.

It'd been in the air since morning. The view from the kitchen was desolate. Winter's barren colors were clouded in mist. Zeena'd wakened with a sick headache. Her joints'd been acting up all day. She'd done her ironing, pausing every so often to rub her hip or sit in the rocker while the irons heated. She washed the floor in her and Ethan's room, not bothering to get under the bed as far as she knew she should. She cleaned the lamp and filled the water jugs to take upstairs, carrying only one jug instead of two. Ordinarily she'd have fetched water from the spring, but she didn't think her hip'd hold up. At dinner she told Ethan, "Snow's coming. My spine's been cricked up, and this knee," she said, pointing to her right leg, "can't hardly stand on it."

Ethan nodded. "The sky, it's gray as a cat," he said.

Zeena asked if he'd get the water for her. "It's just more'n I can do today."

The dark settled in early. After a supper of broth and biscuits and fruit sauce, Ethan went out to check on the animals. When he came back, he announced, "It's started."

"The snow?"

He nodded.

"I'd hoped to get to town tomorrow. I want to see how is Rebekah doing."

Zeena'd been back to look in on Ruth two or three times, had left a tincture for her throat and a remedy for the fever that'd come back a couple of days after her first bout, renewed. At Zeena's last visit Ruth was recovering but Rebekah was in bed. Lucy was afraid Rebekah was turning sick. "I'm just tired," Rebekah explained. Zeena'd sat on the rocker by her bed and told her, "Your color's no good," thinking it was her spirits that were suffering. Rebekah said, "It never is in winter," and stared at Zeena with a look of resignation.

"I wonder if the girl's low in spirits 'cause she's just turned twenty and no sign of a husband," Zeena said. Ethan said Rebekah wasn't like most girls, it'd take someone extra good-hearted to fit the bill. "Then, too, he'll have to be of a proper standing. The Varnums won't hold with no common sort for their daughter." He was whittling a block of wood. The wood chips spilled onto the floor at his feet. When Zeena was Rebekah's age, she remembered a kind of panic. What everyone

else had, she would not. "Took till I turned twenty-five to settle into being a spinster," she told Ethan. "Father always said it's
best to accept what God give you, but it's hard to believe being
a spinster's what He intended for Rebekah. She needs to leave
this town and get to where there's other young folk."

Ethan kept at his whittling. Then he stood. "I'll be in Ma's
room, see if I can do some studying. That's why I set that desk
up in there."

Zeena looked at him.

"Mr. Hale give me some books on the new machines. I want
to see what I can make out."

"Can't you do that out here?" she asked.

He shrugged.

Zeena spent most of her days alone and looked forward to the
evenings when Ethan'd sit by the cookstove with her, she in the
rocker doing her mending and piecework, he at the table doing
his figuring or some chore, leatherwork for the horses or the repair of a tool or whittling wooden spoons. Even if they didn't
talk, which is the way Ethan liked it ("I'm too bone tired to
talk"), she liked his presence and felt some comfort and com-
panionship in that.

"It'd be good if you'd fill the woodbox before you go," she told
him. He nodded. "The shooting pains in my legs are about
more'n I can bear," she said. At first he had been solicitous of
her ailments; now, though, Zeena had to repeat things. It irked
her that he did not listen. She tried not to complain, knew complaints were a weak person's choice, but she was finding the
work more than she could do. She wanted to help him, but how
far could she push herself?

That evening Zeena mended Ethan's socks. He was so hard
on his socks. She found a bit of flannel in Cousin Beatrice's piece
bag to make over a sleeve on Ethan's shirt that'd got ripped
while hitching the sorrel up the day before. One of her aprons
needed mending; the bib'd come loose. Her calico wrapper
needed stitching along the side seam. She worked busily, get-

ting through all the tasks she'd set aside for the night. While she worked she thought about Rebekah. She'd get to see her soon and have that talk with her. You need to be with other young folks, she'd say. Then she'd ask again was there a young fellow that she loved. She'd tell her that parents try to hold a child back out of love but that it didn't mean the child always had to listen.

Then Zeena thought about writing a letter to Father. She'd received a congratulatory letter from him along with the news of Bettsbridge, the most important bit of which was that he'd been ailing nearly three weeks with a chest cold and feared it'd turn to pneumonia like it had those other times. His lungs were his weakness, for certain. He didn't ask for her help, and Zeena didn't think to offer it, but she knew she should write back and tell him they couldn't come just yet to Bettsbridge. Ethan didn't want to lose the days at the mill. Maybe Father'd visit them come spring, she would suggest. But her eyes were crossed with tiredness; the small stitching had strained them. Prob'ly it was time for eyeglasses.

The wind was starting to blow. It edged through the floor-boards from down cellar and made drafts around her feet. The back wall of the kitchen rattled. Zeena pulled her knitted shawl around her shoulders. She stood and took the broom to the front door. She stepped outside. The wind swirled under her skirt, flapped her shawl. She swept the doorstep and a little beyond, but very quickly it was apparent her efforts were fruitless. Whatever she swept away came right back with the wind.

She thought of the winters Cousin Beatrice'd watched come in. Such a little creature she was, but she must ha' been tough as nails. But would she ha' hated to see it come again? Had Ethan been right, she was ready to go? He didn't want to talk about his mother, now she was gone. Didn't have a word of his father to say. It was different with Zeena. Mama and Father, the things they said, they were always with her.

The snow was flying every which way. If she stepped across

the dooryard, she'd never find her way back. She couldn't even see the elms, though she thought she could hear their limbs straining.

Zeena returned to the kitchen. She lit the lamp and filled the cookstove with wood, then turned down the damper. She gave the floor a last sweep and laid some things out for the morning: cornmeal for mush, flour for biscuits. Then she went to bed.

She listened for sounds of Ethan but fell to sleep before he came to bed.

THE NEXT MORNING it was still snowing. The hillside was a white lake that stretched into a gray sea sky. The ridge up back was a white wall; the pine trees rose black along the top. The wind had stopped and now the snow fell steady as rain in fine gentle flakes, kind-looking when you were on the inside looking out. But Zeena knew there was no kindness in snow like this. It was the sort that, when it cleared, left the ground several feet under and no hope of seeing it again till spring.

At breakfast Ethan looked tired. His eyelids were swollen and his skin was pale. But his eyes were bright. And he started talking the minute Zeena came down to find the fruit sauce simmering and eggs cooking. "I slept down here," he said. "I didn't want to wake you. I got to reading and couldn't stop."

"What was you reading?"

"There's new ways of making things. Machines that make cloth, machines that fire bricks, anything you can think of."

Zeena stood by the table and looked out the window. "Don't look like it'll be stopping any time soon."

Ethan handed her a bowl; two poached eggs on toast.

"Can you be getting me to town today?"

Ethan shook his head just as steps were heard in the back passage. Jotham stepped in. "Whew!" he said, "I tell you." He brushed more snow off the back of an arm. "I ain't seen snow like this since—"

"Sixty-four?" Ethan said.

"Where the third blizzard come in on the others?" He lifted his cap to Zeena. "Mornin', ma'am."

"It were December, just like this, weren't it?" Ethan asked.

"I recall it were, yes."

"School closed down over a week. The roads couldn't be rolled, nothin'."

"So when'll it end?" Zeena asked.

The two men looked at her. Jotham coughed. Ethan said, "No way a telling that."

"But I want to get in to see Rebekah."

Jotham shook his head. "She been poorly. Her pa told me so last night 'fore the snow took on so."

"That's why I want to see her."

Jotham said nothing but his mouth went into an O.

"I got a sense about it. Something's wrong with the girl," she said.

Neither man inquired further but kept up their reminiscences of the storm of sixty-four. Zeena remembered it. She was snowed in at Vera Marston's with her three children who were down with the pox. The house was quarantined, of course, so it was Zeena had to tramp down the snow and shovel it out so Vera could get to the barn where the last cow hung on. Was it any worse'n any other storm? Two of the Marston children died; the third gained his strength. The mother took to bed with shock and grief. Zeena'd seen such suffering before. All storms hampered the life in these hills.

"Soon's you can, will you get me to town?" she asked Jotham.

He nodded. "Soon's the horses get it tramped down enough so I can drag a small load to Mr. Hale."

Ethan stared at Zeena's plate. "You ain't touched those eggs."

Zeena wrinkled her nose. "I can't stomach 'em this morning."

"I'll take 'em," Ethan said. And to Jotham, "There's more in the pan for you," and he pointed to the spider on the cookstove.

The men bantered about the weather, the food, the day.

"Enjoy them eggs, 'f our chickens freeze like last year when the north wind tore off the henhouse roof, you won't see eggs in that spider for some time to come." Or "Did your parsnips come up good this year? It's one thing about winter, you can look forward to parsnips simmered in maple syrup in early April." And "Ol' Man Hale, you think he'll notice if the load's not full today?" "Not 'less another short load catches his attention first."

Zeena was clearing the dishes when Ethan came up behind her and said, "Tonight's the night," and he put his hands on her shoulders. Zeena felt a dread. "Coasting," he said.

"Coasting?"

Jotham brightened, became almost giddy. "Could be the best of the winter. The children'll be out all day. That hill'll be packed down so good they'll be sliding on their backsides." He chuckled and headed to the door. A wave and a pointed index finger to the west indicated what he was planning with his day. Ethan nodded. "Ten minutes," he said, meaning, go on.

"We'll go after supper," Ethan said.

"Go?"

"Coasting."

"You mean it? Ain't we a bit old for it?"

"Folks all ages go coasting. My grandfather watered the runs, swept 'em even, kept 'em fresh and clear all season. Gramma and him took their toboggan out till they was too stooped to take a step. Grandfather went that winter. They set up torches so he could be taken in along the ridge, past the coasting hill, to the church for a midnight funeral."

"I can't go coasting." She was thinking of her condition. It was important to stay quiet and not overdo.

Ethan shook his head. "Just wait." He grinned widely.

"It's foolishness," she said, but the idea of it pulled at her. The young women, they all did it. Mama'd said it was like dancing. You spin and twirl until you leave the ground altogether. Then you're like starlight, shooting through the dark on a journey that separates time out. The rest of the world, it measures minutes and gets places on time and thinks of yesterday as something that happened before today. When you're coasting, there's the moment before you and nothing else, Mama'd said.

Zeena remembered being small enough to fit up front on the sled between Father's legs while Mama kneeled behind and held to Father with her arms round his neck. "Not so tight," he'd yell, and she'd shriek with laughter and pull all the tighter. Father steered the sled like it was part of himself. He leaned just to the left and the sled righted its path. He leaned back and pushed on the right and the sled glided to the left. "Watch that," Mama called, and Zeena saw it, a drop ahead, the one Father led them to every time, and then Mama was shrieking and then they were flying straight through the air, gliding on starlight or the beams of light from God's eyes. That's what Mama said, anyhow.

"Well, maybe," she said.

Ethan grinned again. "You'll see."

"And maybe we can stop in and see Rebekah first."

"Maybe. We'll see what the walking's like. You might not want to walk all the way in to town."

"We'll see. Sometimes that's just the thing."

Ethan frowned. "I can't figure—" and he stopped. Zeena asked him what. He didn't answer, and the frown smoothed.

Never can understand how his mind works, Zeena thought.

ETHAN CARRIED A LAMP as they stepped on the trampled snow. They followed Jotham's tracks far as the lane that went down the other side of the ridge where he lived. Tracks had been made along the ridge road since the snow stopped in the afternoon, and they followed these. There were some stars out, but Ethan carried a lantern, held high so Zeena could watch her footing. She held to his arm and began shivering before they even reached the ridge road.

Ethan'd looked at her boots as she put them on. "The leather's near worn through," he pointed out. She nodded. "You need to get 'em to the shoe shop," he said.

"I didn't know there was one in Starkfield. I seen so little of it."

"Jotham'll take 'em in one day and leave them."

Now those boots were already damp through to her toes. How would she last the coasting? Her feet'd be froze to ice. "How long since you used that sleigh in the barn?" she asked and could feel Ethan bristle. "I had it out last winter. One a the runners needs tending."

Zeena sniffed. "I guess we'd better not go all the way to town," she said.

By now the town was in sight. It fit snugly in the valley, set in among the hills. Lights dotted the sloping hillsides and clustered in the center. Wood and coal smoke filtered the air. Zeena heard music. "What's that?" she asked.

"The church."

"What's going on?" The building was throbbing with the music, with stamping feet, with voices calling.

"There's a dance most Saturdays, some Fridays even."

Zeena wondered why Ethan hadn't taken her to a dance. "I could ha' met folks," she said.

Ethan's breathing was smooth. Hers was rough, tested.

"It's mostly the young folks. They carouse and carry on. Specially after a day of snow. I don't think you'd enjoy it."

"I enjoy sociability, course I do. I never done much dancing, but then . . ." and she coughed, "I was so busy what with doctoring folks."

Zeena's feet were starting to ache when they came to the coasting hill. Behind her was the town, the music, a glow of light reaching almost up to where they stood on the ridge. Beyond them was near black, the stars giving a silver haze to the snow. Ethan stopped, so she did too. "I thought there'd be other folks," she said. "Usually there's others," he answered. Then after a pause, "It's early yet. After the dancing, they'll be up here. Lanterns set out and everything."

"Maybe we should go to the church, warm up, and wait."

Ethan was already pulling her on. "Hold this," and he handed her the lantern. "Wait," and he left her standing by a large fir as he dug around underneath its branches and withdrew a sled.

"We can't sled in the dark."

"I done it years and years."

"You can't see what's down there," and she peered into the darkness. "I can't see, I, I can't even tell where it drops off."

Ethan laughed. "I can see well enough and I done this all my life."

"It's foolishness," but she stepped closer and held to his arm.

"I'll take a couple runs, see it's laid out," he told her. "You stay here with the lantern."

Zeena listened to him go. There was no sound but the runners swishing along the snow, a higher then a lower pitch. "Ethan?" she called when there was no more sound of runners. He didn't answer. "Ethan?" louder this time. When he got to the top he was not even out of breath from pulling up the sled. "I'll do one more."

"I'm ready," she said, handing him the lantern to set on the ground.

Though she could not see his face she could tell he was looking at her and that he liked it, that she was ready.

"You set up front," he said, giving her a hand.

"Let me kneel behind you." Somehow that seemed the safer to Zeena. He climbed on and she took her place. Above them were a few dim stars. The snow that'd fallen for twenty-four hours without letup was done now, but you could still feel it hazy in the air. By morning it'd clear off. But for now there was just the faint slight hint of snow in the air.

"Hold on," Ethan said.

Then they were moving. Quickly they built up speed. Zeena's

arms wrapped tighter around Ethan's shoulders. She could feel the strength of his muscles through his coat. The sound of the runners in the snow was familiar . . . it could've been all those years ago and Mama could've been shrieking "Faster." Now they were rocketing down the hill into darkness, and now it was Zeena's voice that was shrieking, it was fear . . . and delight, delight at going so fast and having no idea where she was headed, no sense of where they would come out, but it didn't matter . . . until she remembered the tree limb. She saw it in her mind's eye as they descended the second steep slope. "Ethan—" she started, but just then, "Hold on," Ethan called, and the sled dug to the left.

Zeena shrieked again. Her cry could've come from someone else. She'd never made a sound like that. Only Mama . . .

On and on, faster still, over another rise and even into the air for seconds and then they slowed and came to a stop.

Ethan was breathing deeply. Zeena was already up, gasping for air. "Let's do it again!" she cried.

Ethan was chuckling, but he took the rope and started up the hill. Zeena held to him, working to breathe, laughing, crying even. "I never," she said. "I just never knew such—" but she could not go on. "You're sure you're up to it?" he asked, and she just answered, "Yes, yes." Slowly they made their way to the top and repeated the run. Racing, rocketing down through the darkness with that slight dim light of the stars in the air, not enough to distinguish much but enough to indicate patches darker than others. Zeena started shrieking the second they began. The air, it was in her face, all through her, and the snow spun up under the runners, and the fear, the sense they might take off and never land on solid ground again, it fired her up.

"Once more," she said.

Ethan chuckled again. He put his arm around her. "I never know—" but he stopped.

"Come on," she said, starting right back up the hill. Long ago Father'd held her on his shoulders and pulled the sled and

Mama'd walked behind them. Now she was Mama, walking beside her husband as he pulled the sled. In a couple years there'd be a little one to go down the hill with them and then ride on Ethan's shoulders up to the top.

The third time, Zeena kept a looser hold. She wanted to feel the air around her, to imagine what it might be to . . . fly, which is what she was doing, after the sled jogged left and maybe because she held on so tight there Ethan couldn't get the balance, but the sled leapt up over the rise, and then it turned in such a way as to send Zeena off, flying through the dark night, and there was only silence then, the air silent in her ears and then she was coming down, down, and then *flump*, onto a patch of soft untamped snow, knocking the wind right out of her.

"Zeena?"

She heard him calling her and thought she answered, but it came again, her name, and it was Ethan calling her with an edge to his voice.

"I'm here," she finally heard outside her head.

He was beside her. "What happened?"

She was breathing now. In, out, in. He waited, silent. "I went flying," she said.

"I thought something terrible, I called—"

"I was a bird and I . . . flew off."

"You must be froze, let me help you."

"I'm not cold at all," she said, sitting up. She expected a crick in her back when she stood, but it didn't come. "I'm warm. Even my feet."

They walked home then. It was the first time she could remember having fun in the snow, liking the snow. She told him this.

"We'll come again. When the moon's full, or there's others coasting. It's never like this, just no one. Not on a night like this."

Zeena smiled. She felt she was floating, that her feet weren't even touching the ground. Lightheaded. Giddy. "Ethan," she giggled, "it's lucky I came down at all. I could ha' kept going. I could ha' gone straight to the stars."

AS SHE STARTED UP THE STAIRS she felt it. A sharp, searing pain in her spine that went down her legs. She gripped the railing. Stars were shining around the edge of her vision like the ones in the sky as she'd gone flying through the air.

Another pain struck. This one was deep inside. Had she injured something when she landed? Her kidneys, maybe? Or—

She wouldn't think it.

Never mind, she would go to bed. Tonight, when Ethan came and reached under her nightdress, she would turn away. He would understand. "I'm getting a sick headache," she'd tell him, which wasn't all that far from the truth. She'd take a remedy, and in the morning she'd be better.

Landing so hard on the ground, it just knocked the air out and left her bones needing to readjust.

Zeena climbed the stairs, one at a time. The pain grew worse. She sucked in her breath. No, she willed it. No pain now. No.

TWENTY-SIX

She is floating in liquid. Warm and moist, the fluid supports her. She does not have to try to stay afloat, like she would if she was swimming. This is something different. She is just floating, effortlessly.

Mama is there too. I left you all these years but now I'm back, she says.

Zeena floats and cries, like she used to when Mama held her and rocked her. The tears are warm and moist. They add to the fluid that suspends her. Mama, I missed you, she says.

Not like I missed you, she says.

Zeena reaches a hand to touch her face. It is Mama's face, the last year she was alive.

Mama says, I missed seeing all the things you done. Never saw you grow into a woman.

There's a current now in the fluid. It pulls at Zeena. It is her own crying, a river. She holds to Mama's hand, but it's slippery as oil. I never saw you grow old, she tells Mama.

I'm not old, Mama says. I never will be. You'll go before me.

How to tell her she has already gone? Zeena feels something pull at her. Now it is herself that goes. Mama stands firm and Zeena starts to float away.

She cries out, "Hold on to me, Mama."

When she opened her eyes, Ethan was there with a candle held over her. "Zeena?" His eyes were dark holes. His brow was furrowed. His shoulders were wider than usual, and his hand, when he held it out, it was like a night creature, flying.

Zeena moaned. It hurt. Inside her, the pain rose and fell in waves.

He placed the candle on the dresser and came to the bed. He stood by the window and said, "What is it?"

Zeena felt her cheeks. They were dry. She hadn't been crying after all.

The window was rattling. Would the glass panes fly out? Would the snow come in on them?

Zeena lifted onto one elbow. Then she felt it. A gush of liquid between her legs. The river, it was real. She pushed back the covers. Her nightdress was already stained. The blood, it was bright red, hot and sticky.

Ethan stared at the blood, then at her. There was fear in his wide dark eyes. "Should I go for Mrs. Hale?" he asked.

Zeena shook her head. She tried to think. I need hot water. I need something to stanch the flow. The pains set in again and Zeena doubled over. She didn't want Ethan there, troubling over her. This was woman's work. "Just bring me hot water and some towels." She would try to contain it here. "And my remedy bag," she called, as he went down the stairs.

Ethan returned and left her everything she'd asked for. He slipped out the door. He didn't need to be told: There'll be no baby just yet.

IN THE MORNING Zeena made her way downstairs with the dirtied bedclothes in her arms. Her back rang with throbbing at each step. Sharp fingers of pain clenched the muscles and sent the shooting pains down her legs. She paused at the foot of the stairs. Would the flow of blood start up again? She saw stars and held to the railing. They cleared.

Mama'd always told her not to dwell on sadness. "There'll always be more," she'd said. "Save your tears."

Did this warrant her tears? Mama'd lost full-term babies, four of them. Wasn't that worse than her loss? A baby just started, could she cry for that? Pain in her spine. Mama had worse'n that. Mama was ripped apart with each birth, was laid up weeks till she could gain her strength. What was a clutch of pain in her back compared to that?

Zeena took a deep breath. She told herself it was not yet time to cry. Small steps took her to the kitchen. She leaned against the door frame to rest. So much to do; how would she get it done? It was Wednesday and she had baking to do, then she had to finish yesterday's ironing. She had to clean the kitchen; the oilcloths were grimy. She had to take the last of the apples and dry them. She still had to bottle the spices that were drying in the cellar. She had butter to make before the milk soured. Christmas was just a week away. She had to start in cooking: puddings, a braided bread, maybe start some wine. She'd cut some greens and had to arrange them. And she wanted to finish the vest she was making for Ethan for Christmas out of fabrics from Cousin Beatrice's piece bag.

Her head spun. How could she do any of it?

The cookstove was roaring. The woodbox was full. Water'd been drawn already, the jugs lined up by the sink and at the foot of the stairs. Cornmeal mush was warming on the back of the stove. The wash pot was filled and simmering on the stove.

Ethan was nowhere to be seen. He'd gotten up early to do for her, then had cleared out to work.

It was starting to snow again, but the wind'd died. When Zeena looked out the window by the table, she saw white. A white dooryard with a drifted peak extending from the corner of the house. Elms with half white trunks rose languidly from white mounds that lay up against one another. The white hill-side extended to the lower white hillside. The woods were white, patched with black and forest green. And the sky was white as milk.

But over it all was a film of red. A red peony in the sun. The red splotch on her nightdress. The red rags she soaked and rinsed and soaked and rinsed in cold water and still stayed red. The pain in her back was red. Blistering red. But her face, when she peered in the looking glass, was white, not gray; it was white. The life'd drained clear out of her.

Zeena dragged herself to the stove. She sunk the bedclothes and her nightdress in a basin and poured cold water over them. She worked at them, rinsed the water, then filled the basin again. Time to time she saw stars. She ran to the backhouse and sat on the cold seat and let her blood run. She stared out the small window that looked to the north, up on the ridge where the sky showed some clearing.

Out of a patch of blue in the sky she listened for Mama's voice but got only a ringing in her ears.

TWENTY-SEVEN

*I*t was hard to be patient. So long she'd lived with pain in her spine. When had it started? Was it after Mama died, the next spring? One morning she woke up and she noticed it. Father told her not to think on it; it would go away. Or it would stay, which it did. Either way, wasn't anything she could do for it. A spine had a mind of its own, Father said.

On days when she couldn't walk to school for the pain, she lay in bed and tried to think what Mama'd said about spines. She thought she remembered Mama telling Leila Mae Dutton that a spine knows its own perfection and will find it on its own. Waiting, Mama would ha' said, is the way for a spine to heal. But Mama would ha' given her touch to it. Mama would ha' helped her spine to find its way.

So Zeena had to treat it herself. She tried to stretch her hands to her back and give it the comfort it needed. She'd make a treatment for herself, a remedy or a liniment or a salve, and try to work it in to the muscles. Then give herself time to recoup. But it wasn't the same, giving comfort to herself.

And now she couldn't take that time. Every day there was enough housework for two women. Carrying water was a constant chore. She was forever losing her footing on the snow in the dooryard and spilling the water. She took to pulling it on a sled from the pump, but she couldn't pull it smooth enough to keep it going. When the ground sloped down, it butted her in the ankles. Father'd always carried the wood and the water. It wasn't that Ethan wouldn't help if she asked. But he had all he could do just to get his own work done. He spent longer days there now, coming home after dark by lamplight for supper, even too tired to eat much some nights. " 'Fore the workings freeze up," he said.

Zeena wanted to do her share. She'd taken to milking the cows twice a day. She climbed up a ladder to get the hay for the horses and pitched it down. She filled the water troughs. She spread the feed for the chickens. If this's what she had to do to help Ethan, then she'd do it.

But when her spine went, what'd she do? You can't do your work when you're forced to bed. Can't fetch water, can't carry wood, can't do the washing, can't get down to clean the floor or reach to dust a spider's web from a corner. Even your needlework and sewing. How can you do that laying down?

ZEENA SENT A LETTER to Rebekah with Jotham the next day. She told Rebekah she could not come to town just now as she was feeling poorly. She hoped to see her soon, though. In another few days, perhaps. She hoped Ruth's fever was down for good and that Rebekah was up and about.

She was surprised, then, while sweeping the kitchen floor the following day, to see a lone horse and rider weave along the ridge and down into the valley on the road that Jotham and Ethan'd packed down with their comings and goings.

Zeena's anadama bread was rising, set back of the stove. A broth was simmering. A bucket of soapy water was waiting so she could clean the floors.

She went to the door and waved to Rebekah who was hitching her horse. "Work your way round the wood here," she called. "When Ethan gets that ell back . . ." but she didn't finish the thought. It was as if she'd lived here all her life now.

Rebekah stepped through the snow and then stomped her feet in the dooryard to kick off what clung to her boots. She wore a long brown cape with a hood that covered her hair. She swept the hood back as she approached the step. She'd wound a blue ribbon through her hair; her cheeks were flushed red, her eyes squinted against the cold. She was carrying a basket. "I thought you'd be to bed," she said.

"Someone's got to see to things," Zeena said.

"That's why I'm here."

This silenced Zeena. She was used to doing for others; long as she could remember, since Mama went anyway, it was Zeena took charge and kept a household, hers or someone else's. "What about yourself? You weren't feeling too awfully good last I was at your house."

"Today I'm better." She stood at the foot of the steps, smiling.

"What've you got there?"

Rebekah climbed the makeshift steps, out of breath, eyes blinking. "I thought you'd need some stores."

Zeena opened the door wide and stepped back to let her in.

"I thought sure you'd got the throat distemper from Ruth," Rebekah said, still out of breath.

"No, no, nothing like that." Zeena looked away, through and past the stars that still lined her vision. Her head was swimming again. Her hand reached out to the door frame for support as her knees turned soft.

"What is it?" Rebekah asked, unbuttoning her cape with one hand.

Zeena shook her head. "You don't want to hear my troubles."

"But I do."

Zeena didn't know what to say. She'd never talked about her female troubles with anyone, and it'd been years since she'd looked for comfort for her spine's flare-ups. 'Sides, she wanted to talk about Rebekah's troubles, not her own. The girl needed her, and Zeena wanted to help.

"You been feeling faint recently? Sickly in the mornings?"

"No, no, it's not that."

"You can tell me, Zeena, I'm no gossip."

"Course not."

Rebekah waited.

It was dark in the passage, a likely place to share a secret. "I thought it might be . . ." and she paused, swallowed, then went ahead, "but Ethan took me coasting and I landed hard. I been bleeding steady three days."

"Oh." Rebekah set down the basket. "Oh, I'm sorry, Zeena, I didn't really think, well, Ma said," and she looked up, "no matter what Ma—"

"What'd she say? I'm too old?"

Rebekah's lips went into a straight line. She shook her head. "You must excuse my mother. She comes out with the most outlandish things. She means well, I'm certain, but she don't see times're different from when she was a girl."

"I'm not even thirty," Zeena said. "I helped many a woman older'n me birth their babies."

"Many of 'em wish it weren't so, I'd wager." Her eyes filled suddenly with tears. "If they got a brood already, that is."

"Some can't even have a one . . ." Zeena leaned against the wall. Her legs'd turned weak.

"Don't think that way, Zeena. Next month you'll see. It doesn't always happen right off, it—" She stopped then and started for the kitchen. Zeena followed and went to the cookstove to prepare some tea. "You set yourself in that rocker," Rebekah said. "I have my bread to do," Zeena returned. Rebekah put out a hand. "I can do that too, you know. I've made bread before."

Zeena sat in the rocker and watched Rebekah punch down the bread, knead it, and set it in two pans covered with a damp cloth. Then she carried a cup of tea to Zeena and another to the table where she began to unpack the food. Beets, beans, and mincemeat in jars. "For when you run out of store." Zeena didn't tell her there was no store other than the potatoes Ethan harvested and what Jotham shared. "Pumpkin soup and sausage," Rebekah went on.

When she smiled, it was like a warm breeze coming Zeena's way. "You remind me of Mama," Zeena said.

"Your mama?"

"She was soft-spoken like you, and kindly, and . . ." and Zeena hesitated before saying it, so unfamiliar was she with this sort of exchange, "and pretty to look at."

Rebekah's cheeks turned redder still. "Why, that's sweet of you to say, Zeena." She drew a chair to the cookstove and sat down. They talked then of the goings-on in town. What Mr. Eady was doing with his store to attract more customers. "He's talking of adding ready-made clothes. That'll get folks going." Then how many'd come down with pneumonia. "Ma's been giving your name," she said. "You'll get called." Finally, "We missed you at church again."

"Ethan says there's no time for church."

"Course not."

"And I been poorly, like I said."

"Mr. Hartman gave a fine sermon. Everybody said so." Her eyes filled. "He talked about charity, how it's everybody's duty to look after those what's less fortunate. And he talked about the poor in spirit, how they have less than the money-poor. He said those folks don't need charity, they need to examine their hearts and ask is God in them. He said those were the ones'd come out on top."

"I guess I hope God's in me, then," Zeena told her.

Rebekah stared off. "But don't everyone turn poor in spirit some time in their life?"

Rebekah wasn't seeking an answer. She was leaning forward, perched on the edge of her seat, and around her eyes, those eyes that were darkly sweet and mysterious, were shadows Zeena'd never seen. Tiredness. Or crying. Now Rebekah looked Zeena in the eye. "D'you ever do something sinful?" Rebekah asked her, leaning still farther forward. "I mean, you don't have to tell me what it was, but you're someone I respect, someone I think's done so much good for others, so I want to know, d'you ever commit a sin?" and she looked at her boots that poked out from under her serge skirt.

In Zeena's mind she was on her knees on Mama's bed. Her hands were at Mama's neck, the fingers probing, pushing. Or was it Baby? Or Cousin Beatrice? Just a flash, and then it was gone. But the flash, it gave her a cold feeling. She shivered, reached for her wool shawl to pull around her shoulders.

"I think you did, like I think everyone does." Rebekah folded her hands around her knees. "It makes no sense some folks's always good and some're always bad. Does it to you?"

"Some folks may be just plain bad," Zeena offered. "But seems most everyone has a little good in them."

"That's what I think. I think those what turn bad or fall into a poor spirit, they have a reason for it, don't you think?"

"Prob'ly."

"And those what are held up as good, only good, isn't it just we don't know their sinning, what bad thoughts they had, what failures, what poverty?"

"Prob'ly."

"So how can one body judge another?"

The kettle steamed lightly, almost a song. The broth simmered. The firebox pulsed with heat. The cat scratched at the door to go out.

"Zeena, help me." The placid serenity, the light smile, the gentle good nature, these were gone. What was left was supplication, an iron grip. "Please help me."

"I, I don't know what you're saying," but she did, she already knew.

"I don't know where to turn. There's no one, least of all Ma or Father." Rebekah slipped onto her knees and took Zeena's hand.

"I'm one a them what's poor in spirit over a sin I committed."

"How d'you mean?"

"I need to go away," she said, emphasizing the words "go" and "away" by saying them deeper and slower than the others.

Zeena knew. It's the way women talked to one another. A code, words used to mean one thing, but in a certain context they meant another, and the secret meaning, it all had to do with those secret female things that never saw the light of day. How many times had she been at someone's bedside having a conversation that was interpreted by the husband passing in and out as mindless chatter, when in fact it was the woman's heart she spoke of. "I see," she said.

"You must have cousins, friends, folks from away who'd give a home to a girl who's poor in spirit for what she's done, who'd see her through it."

Aunt Belle's the one to care for such a girl, but Aunt Belle's gone. Aunt Martha Pierce? Zeena'd already considered that Rebekah could go to Father's sister so as to meet other young folks, and with Uncle Eben gone since last spring, Aunt Martha's home would be the only substitute for a girl in her condition. There're those women who can't have babies. God's turned his face from them, and all the world knows it and sees it. The lucky ones got the babies born to girls like Rebekah, girls whose fathers couldn't take the shame it'd bring their name, whose mothers'd sink and never regain themselves. Zeena knew without asking the Varnums were such.

" 'Less you know of some other thing I could do."

Zeena knew what she was meaning. "I don't," she said. She told Rebekah of a girl who'd come to her once seeking a potion to rid herself of what she couldn't keep. Zeena had no such potion. Then the girl said she'd heard of another way: You take a knitting needle. I won't do that, Zeena told her. The girl did it herself. Her blood got poisoned and her lungs filled up. She was gone within two days, despite the efforts of a doctor called in.

"But if it was done right?"

"There's no right way to do it, don't you see?"

"What'd her family say?"

"I didn't tell 'em the reason for it. But the girl suffered awful."

"Why couldn't you do it right?"

"How far along are you?"

"Three months."

Zeena shook her head. "It's too risky, Rebekah, surely you can see."

Rebekah was shaking her head. "But I don't know how it'd be, going somewhere else."

"I heard it you wanted to go. I heard—"

"But not alone. Not like this, no."

"What that girl did is no answer."

"Course, course not," she murmured.

Zeena could see this was too much for her. Rebekah was destined for a home like her mother's. A well-to-do husband with children and hired help and curtains on every window of her house and goodness all around her. Tears came to Rebekah's eyes, spilled. She covered her face. "It's wrong I should talk to you, it's—"

"I'm glad you come to me. Anyone else in town, it'd get around, you know how folks are."

"But you, I shouldn't be asking you."

"What d'you mean?"

Rebekah bent over, rocking. "You're so kind, why'd I want to hurt you?"

"Why couldn't you stay with me and Ethan, we could look after you, we'd—"

"It'd never do."

"No one comes up here, Ethan says no one comes—"

"No!" she cried out. "Not here."

Zeena sighed. The girl was hysterical. Zeena'd seen it go this way. The best thing was to get her to Bettsbridge soon as she could.

"Promise me you won't tell Ethan."

Zeena agreed. "I promise you."

Rebekah lifted a face of angles and shadows and splotches. "I didn't ever think such a thing'd happen to me. Other girls, but not me. It, it shouldn't ha' happened, but it was only just the once, and only because I wanted him to know I cared same as him, or, I don't know, I don't even know—"

"There's no need to explain."

"Tell me what to do, Zeena."

Zeena took Rebekah's hands. "Aunt Martha," she said. She explained about Aunt Martha who lived in Bettsbridge, and how Uncle Eben'd died last summer. "You can go as her companion. I'll take you myself."

"What'll she think of me?"

"Aunt Martha Pierce, she's seen it all. She won't judge. Once she sees the sort a girl you are, she'll understand you're innocent, she'll—"

"But I'm not, I'm not."

"The way I see it, no man a good standing'd leave a girl such."

Rebekah sank to the floor, weeping. "No, Zeena, you must understand, it weren't like that, I, I loved him."

Zeena thought, That's what I mean, you loved him, and he should ha' known. But what she said was, "Poor girl, I do see, course I see." She waited a moment, stroked Rebekah's shoulder, then said, "I'll take you to Aunt Martha Pierce myself."

"Oh Zeena, no, I couldn't do that, leave Ethan here all alone, why—"

"I won't send you alone. Folks'd wonder at it."

Rebekah stared at Zeena with dark, frightened eyes. "And you won't tell Ethan?"

Zeena gave her word.

"WHERE'D ALL THIS FOOD COME FROM?" Ethan asked Zeena later.

"Rebekah, she come to see me."

Ethan paused.

Zeena nodded. "She wanted to see was I all right. She'd heard I was poorly. I'd ha' been laid up if there wasn't so much to do." Zeena told him how Rebekah'd done some housework, how she'd got dinner ready, had finished up some ironing, had even brought in more wood before she left. "It's more'n I'm used to, a day's work here."

Ethan washed up. He soaped and scrubbed and sloshed at the sink, then rubbed his face dry with a towel. "I wouldn't a thought she'd ha' come all the way out here," he said, as he came to the table.

"Well, she did."

Ethan put his hands in his pockets and stood looking out the window. "Jotham'll be along any minute. We worked ourselves an appetite. We got us enough wood to last the winter now, I'd say."

Zeena nodded. "Weren't that nice." Then she blurted out, "I told Rebekah about the hired girl Aunt Martha wants. Not a common girl. She wants a companion. She's been poorly since Uncle Eben died."

Ethan gazed at Zeena, his head tilted to one side.

"I told Rebekah it might be just the thing for her."

"Just the thing for her?"

"That she go to Aunt Martha's. Rebekah's been saying there's no fellas here, and I was telling you I thought she needed to get away to where there'd be—"

"Will she go?"

"She said she'd like to, and I said I'd take her. I'll see Father, since he's feeling poorly, and I can collect the rest of my things. I'll be gone only two nights."

Ethan just stared at her.

"When you go to town tomorrow, you stop in there and see what Lawyer Varnum says. Tell him it'll do a world of good for Rebekah. Tell him I think she needs some society. Besides, who could be more trustworthy than Aunt Martha Pierce?"

TWENTY-EIGHT

$\mathcal{Z}$eena sat in Lucy Varnum's parlor and gazed at the wallpaper. Swirls of leaves and vines danced over the walls. Heavy damask curtains, dark red, hung at the windows, pulled to the sides with silken tasseled ropes; behind them were lace curtains. An ornate gold clock with angel figurines ticked on the marble mantel in front of an enormous looking glass.

She had decided she would speak to Lucy herself. It would give her a chance to look in on Ruth too. "You well enough to go to town?" Ethan'd asked. "I'm well enough to carry water," she retorted. She rode on Fly, while Ethan walked beside them.

Rebekah'd ushered Zeena in. "You still want to go to Betts-bridge?" Zeena asked quickly before Lucy came in to the room.

Rebekah said yes, there was no other way.

"I'll bring it up to her first as a proposal," Zeena suggested. "She'll call you in and offer it." Rebekah left to find her mother. When Lucy appeared at the door, she looked distracted. "Why, Zeena, how nice a you to call, but I'm doing my correspondences."

Zeena rose from the straight-back chair. She started in explaining that it wasn't a social call, though she'd surely like to visit, but that she had an aunt in Bettsbridge who needed a companion for a time, her husband having recently passed on, and she wondered would Lucy consider letting Rebekah take the position. "It wouldn't be like she was a hired girl. Aunt Martha has a hired girl to do for her already." Lucy's eyes focused on her. "Rebekah'd be her companion. To help with her correspondences, read to her. Go out calling with her. It might be a way to meet a young gentleman of proper standing."

Lucy hesitated. Zeena could see her mind figuring. Lucy looked at the clock on the mantel, did some more figuring. "Sit down," she told Zeena, taking the other straight chair.

They talked several minutes. Lucy asked about Aunt Martha's house. What sort of a person was Aunt Martha? Was she kindly? Was she likely to work Rebekah too hard? Few realized how fragile Rebekah was. "She's not got a strong constitution. Ruth's been the sickly one recently, but usually it's Rebekah. It's just this last year," she said, "Rebekah's been as strong as she is," and she paused. "Only, Rebekah's a tender-hearted girl. Things affect her. She's had spells of . . . heartsickness, I'd call it. These last weeks, for instance, she hasn't been herself. I don't know if it's because a that outlandish idea she had to go south. She thinks we hold her back, but it isn't that at all, you'd understand that, being . . . well, doctoring like you do and seeing folks and all they do to raise their children good and proper."

Zeena suggested how Aunt Martha's position might be a perfect solution. "It'd give her the feeling of being someplace new and there'd be other young folk for her to meet. Aunt Martha's quite cultured; she'd offer Rebekah a chance to see something beyond Starkfield."

They talked some more. Lucy expressed her concerns at sending Rebekah away from home, and Zeena told Lucy about Bettsbridge and how most folks were fair-minded and knew right from wrong. "And Rebekah can come home if it don't work."

Lucy agreed, then, sooner than Zeena expected, and went off to fetch Rebekah. Zeena listened to Lucy call for Rebekah, then, "I'll try upstairs," and Zeena listened to the swish of her hem on the carpeted stairs. She hoped the plan would go without mishap. She looked around the room again. An upright piano stood on one wall, with an elegantly carved stool before it. Mama's piano was still in the parlor at home, though it hadn't been played in nineteen years. Zeena'd cleaned the keys once a month. Father'd long ago said he'd just as soon sell the piano, but there it sat, same as always, for Zeena to dust.

Zeena stood and went to the piano. She looked at the musical score resting on it. She could not read music. Mama'd taught her to play by ear. She was tempted to play one of the keys. Middle C, she held her finger over middle C and pressed it slowly, so it did not sound, but so she could imagine the sound. Middle C. She and Mama'd played duets once. Zeena'd got laughing so hard she slipped off the bench to the floor. "You girls are a sight," Father'd said.

Something outside caught Zeena's eye. She looked through the lace curtain. Ethan was back already from Mr. Hale's. Usually these visits took longer than was expected because Mr. Hale had a habit of telling stories. Maybe he wasn't there, Zeena thought. Now she would probably have to wait while Ethan talked with him later.

Ethan raised his hand in greeting. Zeena leaned closer to the lace curtain. Who was he smiling at? She pulled the curtain aside, careful not to upset the arrangement of the damask curtains. It was Rebekah. That was Rebekah's back, and Ethan was bent now, talking to her, his cap under one arm. His other arm swung out, to make some point, and his mouth was going. Whatever could he have so much to say to her? Then he was listening. Rebekah must've been talking to him, though she looked at the ground. She was without her cape or a shawl. Her arms were wrapped around her waist. Then her head tilted up at him.

The expression on Ethan's face held Zeena spellbound. She'd

never seen it so soft, with an affection that showed in his eyes and around his eyebrows and in the way he smiled. Even the way he stood, light on his feet, and he kept drawing his shoulders up and his arm swung forward to touch her arm, then let it go, then touch it again ever so lightly. Even when he was kissing Zeena, he didn't look like that. Sorrowful, he looked at those times. Needing kindness. But was that love?

Rebekah looked down again. He bent lower to see her face.

It came on Zeena then like a cold wind that Ethan loved Rebekah.

And then she knew: The baby, it's Ethan's.

ZEENA WAITED IN ANDREW HALE'S OFFICE while the men conversed about business. She'd have preferred to wait outside, but it was too cold so she'd gone in with Ethan and had turned straight to the small window that faced the yard where piles of logs were stacked up and ready for the mill. Hardwood, some softwood, everywhere she looked there was more.

Zeena wasn't thinking about the wood, though. After a minute or two she wasn't even seeing the wood. In her mind she was still at the Varnums', was still looking out the parlor window, was still seeing Ethan standing there, one hand holding his cap, his other hand touching Rebekah's arm, then letting it go, then touching it, all the while his face was bent and there was that affection in the way his eyes looked down at her, and she was standing stiff and proud, or trying to, because even from behind there was something delicate and breakable in the line of her shoulder and the way her head was tilted up and then down.

Lucy Varnum'd returned to the parlor, saying, "I can't locate the girl," and Zeena'd said, "She's there, talking to Ethan," and Lucy turned to call her daughter in, but Zeena stopped her by saying, "Lucy, answer me something," and Lucy approached her, perhaps because of the tone in Zeena's voice, a cold strain that even Zeena could hear. "Whyn't they never marry?" she asked.

Lucy crossed her arms. Her hair was swept up behind her face, every hair in place, like always. Her eyes, dark like Rebekah's, darted here and there, then came to rest on Zeena's shoulder. "Mr. Varnum'd never agreed to her stepping down like that."

Zeena lifted her chin and kept her eyes on Lucy, even if Lucy wouldn't return her gaze.

"Why, going out to that farm where there's been nothing but bad luck these last ten years, and the house looking so lonesome there on the hillside. Beatrice, she told me the soil'd just dried up. Nothing'd grow in that ground, not vegetable, not barn animal, not even human. To think of Rebekah out there, it'd been like . . ." and she paused, swallowed, then went on, "like sending the girl to her death."

Zeena could've been slapped and felt it no less. Her eyes stung but stayed tearless. Had she gone to her death? Is that what Lucy thought?

"The girl being so fragile, don't you know."

Zeena nodded, but no, she didn't know. Her eyes squinted as she waited for the next words.

"It's another thing entirely for Ethan to've asked you for his wife. You're not like the rest of us, you've had to do for yourself, no man to look after you and all. No man to call your own, why I couldn't ha' done it, but you, you're different." Lucy seemed to have forgotten Zeena as she went on, "Besides, a winter out there alone after nursing his mother so long, watching her mind go . . . he couldn't ha' stood it. We used to wonder if his mind'd go, 'specially after we knew Beatrice wasn't long for the world, and he got so tangled and Rebekah'd say, 'He can't stay out there, not alone,' and Mr. Varnum reminded her of her station, being higher than most, don't you know, and he told her, 'It won't be you'—" and then she looked up and saw Zeena.

Zeena smoothed her skirt. She was taller than Lucy so she looked down at her. Yet her height gave her no advantage. Zeena was aware of her own bony limbs, her lank frame, her flat bosom, her sallow complexion, all in contrast to Lucy's soft and supple lines, her rounded shoulders, rounded bosom, rounded hips, even her hands were softly rounded, and her face, the chin and cheeks smooth as a baby's and as pink.

"A girl like Rebekah, she needs to be looked after. You wouldn't know it, from just looking at her. It's in here," and Lucy tapped her heart. "Like I said, she's fragile. She'd never ha' stood up to that life." She sighed. "Her father explained it to her and she took it."

Zeena could've told Lucy then about Rebekah's predicament. She could've said it in such a way as to sound like she was caring for Rebekah by revealing her secret, that Zeena didn't want the girl to suffer alone. But Zeena knew that would not've been the reason. She knew the urge to tell was vindictive. Lucy'd hurt her by what she'd said; she'd hurt Lucy in return.

But she said nothing. She swallowed the blows Lucy'd thrown her. She didn't want to consider whether she herself had "stepped down," as Lucy put it. She didn't want to consider the impossibility of life there on the hillside, as Lucy'd suggested. She didn't want to consider that her marriage was born of Ethan's dread of a winter alone in the farmhouse where he'd tended his father in his last days and had watched his mother's mind go, knowing he was all that was left.

Instead, Zeena lifted her chin and said, "It's a life only some could appreciate."

"Or bear. Leastwise you won't be raising young ones out there, it'll be just the two of you since—"

Zeena gave her a hard stare that said, I mean to have young ones, I do.

Lucy's eyes widened. "Oh my, I hadn't thought . . ." Then, "Better you than another."

They stood in silence a moment. There was nothing else to say. Lucy called Rebekah into the parlor and the plan was presented. Zeena was unable to move from the window; she felt her feet might remain planted in that carpet next to that piano and the window that'd showed her the truth until the day she died. At first it was hard to look at the girl. She's carrying Ethan's child, was all she could think. But then it struck her: The girl's innocent. Zeena knew enough of love to know it was a man determined what happened in these matters. It was Ethan who was responsible. Ethan who'd taken her . . . where? To the room he now shared with Zeena while his mother lay dying downstairs? It sent Zeena to reeling.

The girl's innocent, repeated in her head. The girl'd done what he wanted and now she bore the results. Zeena could do no more than to help her. Help her get to Bettsbridge.

But Ethan. How could Zeena look him in the eye again? How could she go to their room and sleep in that bed? How could she—

"Yes," Rebekah was saying. Yes, she'd like to go.

"Zeena says you can come home if it don't suit you."

Rebekah nodded. "It's a fine idea," but the flush she'd brought in with her was draining and she looked faint.

"It'll be a chance to meet some young gentlemen, Zeena says," Lucy was explaining. "You wouldn't be a hired girl, she already has a hired girl."

Rebekah kept nodding. She avoided Zeena's eyes until the end. "How good of you to think of me," she said, her eyes wells of dark water.

Zeena's heart went out to her. You're the innocent one, she wanted to say. You committed no sin. Instead, "When'll we go?"

"With Christmas coming so close," Lucy started, "you'll wait, of course . . . say, into the new year."

"Eighteen seventy-four," Rebekah stated.

Lucy stared at her daughter. "Yes, dear."

"We could go sooner," Zeena said.

"After Christmas," Rebekah answered. "Two days after Christmas would be the day."

Lucy continued talking of the various plans she'd made for Christmas. The aunts and uncles, the cousins, the supper parties, the gatherings.

"Two days after Christmas," Rebekah repeated. "If that suits you, Zeena."

Ethan appeared in the doorway then. Lucy rose from her chair and went into the front hall, obviously not wanting Ethan to step inside in his work boots and clothing, leaving Rebekah and Zeena together in the parlor.

As sympathetic as Zeena felt for Rebekah, there was an uncomfortable distance between them. Zeena could've hated her for seeking her help, for carrying Ethan's child. But Rebekah was like no one Zeena'd ever known. Selfless is what she was. Some in Rebekah's condition that she'd known in Bettsbridge appeared that way until Zeena came to see they had some other motive for their behavior. Mina Milton, she just wanted folks to feel sorry for her, and Esther Woods, she acted that way so as to get the chatter about folks that she needed in order to settle a score. But Rebekah, there was none of that.

"You don't need to take me there," Rebekah started in. "I don't want to be a bother, least of all for you."

Now Zeena understood the last of Rebekah's words. But she would not ever let Rebekah know she knew the truth. The girl wouldn't bear up under it. "I won't send you off alone. Your mother wouldn't agree to it in any case."

Rebekah nodded. She studied Zeena's face. "I never knew anyone like you."

"I was thinking the same of you."

Rebekah's face was like the land, sunken beneath a cover of snow. Her eyes were the night, deep and dark.

"It'll all turn out," Zeena told her.

"You must be wondering who the father is," Rebekah whispered.

"I'm wondering no such thing," Zeena answered, feeling a twist in her stomach. "It's none a my business."

"The father won't know," she said, firmly. "That's one thing I'd never do. Bring him down too."

"You must love him then."

Rebekah's eyes filled with tears. She blinked them away. "I do," she whispered. "I very much do."

Zeena felt a peculiar emptiness. Rebekah should've been the one said her vows to Ethan. But now she would leave Starkfield, shamed, the father not knowing what he'd caused.

"But I can't go to him. He, he has someone else. Someone much better than me."

Zeena blinked. "Not better."

"I don't guess God sees it that way. What Mr. Hartman says—"

There were Lucy's and Ethan's voices in the hall to interrupt them. "Don't think on what he says," Zeena said. As she stood, her spine clutched. She rubbed at her hip. Then, with an effort at conveying a knowledge of human suffering, Zeena leaned close to her and said, "God forgives those that ask." Rebekah looked startled. "Just ask," Zeena said. "You'll see."

ZEENA STILL STOOD AT THE WINDOW in Mr. Hale's office, staring at the log piles and replaying the scene at the Varnums'. Rebekah's pale face, her lips quivering, Ethan's face flushed when he led Zeena out to the sorrel and they started over to the Hales', it was all before her. "I hadn't thought she should go away," Ethan'd told Zeena. "She's always stayed close to home. She's that kind a girl."

"She said she wants to go."

Ethan shook his head. "I wouldn't ha' thought it."

Zeena tried not to think on the fact she was married to a man who loved a girl who was with his child, that Zeena was helping the girl to get away to her Aunt Martha Pierce's so the girl could give the baby up to some poor unfortunate woman who could have no baby of her own.

Even when behind her was Ethan, talking to Mr. Hale, all she could hear were her own thoughts. Ethan's voice held an edge to it. Probably Mr. Hale wouldn't notice, but Zeena heard it. Ethan claimed not to understand why Rebekah would go. If he knew the truth, what'd it do to him? Would it be the burden to sink him, knowing he was the one put the girl to such straits? Or would he take Rebekah and flee?

Zeena tried not to think on what she would do the next time Ethan turned to her at night. "I'm not Rebekah," she'd wish to say. Or, "Was this where you loved her too?" But she'd hold her tongue. Her promise to Rebekah could not be broken. Mama'd taught her that. And if Mama wasn't buried underground with Cousin Beatrice, she'd tell Zeena what to do. Would she say: Go now, while you can. Back to Father. S'no sense in staying where you're not wanted.

But how could Zeena go now? No one'd know the truth and she'd suffer their mean thoughts the rest of her life. And Father, he'd never let her know the end of it; there'd never be a word spoken on it, but it'd loom between them every minute of their days that she'd failed at the one thing a woman was born to.

More'n likely Mama'd say: You got yourself a husband, you must do for him. For better or for worse is what you vowed. Your test is coming sooner'n it usually does, but every woman meets it sooner or later.

Mama was like that. She turned an unpleasantry into something welcome just by the way her words echoed in your ears long after. When she walked into a dying woman's home, Mama helped the woman to open her arms and meet death like it was a long-lost friend come to stay for good. When she found disease in a small child's brain, she turned the parents' moans into cries of thanks to God for giving them the child at all. Mama could do that with her eyes, and her laugh, and the touch of her fingers on your cheek, and her words that sang to you.

Zeena would stay with Ethan.

But she would not give Ethan a child. She would not let him turn to her in the night. No one would fault her for it. They would say she was too old. They would say, Zenobia Frome, she done her best by him.

MUCH LATER, ZEENA WONDERED if there was something more she should've done for Rebekah. If there could've been another way out for the girl, something less fearsome. But what would it have been? The girl couldn't have come to stay with her and Ethan.

It was Christmas Eve day, before the sun was even risen, when there was a knocking at the door. Zeena heard it and knew it'd be someone needing her, someone from town who was down with pneumonia. She listened as Ethan came up the stairs, two at a time, calling, "Zeena."

Zeena was washing by candlelight. "Zeena," he called again as he opened the door. "Zeena, hurry and dress, it's Rebekah."

Zeena held her calico wrapper to her breast and stared at Ethan.

"Something bad's happened. She's taken sick."

"Sick?"

Ethan was backing out the room. "She's out of her mind delirious with a fever. She's going. Zeb, the hired man, he says to come quick, see if you can keep her from going."

THE SUN WAS JUST RISING to a gray day when Zeena got to the Varnums'. Ethan'd rushed her out of the house so fast she hadn't eaten a morsel, hadn't even run a comb through her hair. But when she saw Rebekah, she knew why she'd been hurried.

The girl was barely recognizable. Her eyes were hollow dark holes. Her lips were cracked. The pink skin was gray as dishwater. Her lungs seemed clogged; breathing was with great effort. Just then she was shivering, her body giving over to a series of convulsions. Minutes later she was still, her limbs sinking into the mattress like they would never be lifted again.

Lawyer Varnum'd met Zeena at the door with a pipe in his hand, waving it. "Were you stopping to look at the scenery?" he said, pulling his robe tighter around his wide waist.

"I come fast as I could," Zeena said.

Upstairs Lucy Varnum paced and cried while Zeena looked at Rebekah. "Do something, please, Zeena," she moaned. "She took sick so sudden, I woke yesterday and found her on the floor here. Her insides've been draining out since then. I never saw so much blood."

Zeena knew what it was. The bleeding, coming in clots and gushes, the high fever, the filling of the lungs, the shivers and shakes, the weakness of limb, the way the girl'd gone behind some cloud. She'd tried to get rid of the baby herself, what Zeena'd told her not to do.

Rebekah couldn't be reached. This sent Lucy to distraction. She fell to her knees by the bedside. "I lost my boys to scarlet fever. Don't let Him take my child," she begged, hands clasped right up under her chin.

"Has no doctor been called?"

"We sent for a doctor from Corbury Junction, but he ain't come."

"Get me some cold water," Zeena instructed.

Once Lucy was out of the room, Rebekah's shivering started again. Her limbs flailed. She tossed and twisted on the bed, moaning. Her breathing was rough. Zeena knew the pain was bad; she'd seen it before. She sat beside Rebekah and leaned down to her ear. "You tried to take it yourself?" she asked.

"I thought I . . ." she started, slurring the words.

"Rebekah, I told you this was no good."

"I don't want to go away."

What was she meaning? She didn't want to die? Or she didn't want to go to Bettsbridge and that's why she'd done it? Zeena knew there was nothing to be done for her. The bleeding would drain the girl of life. Her mind would twist. She would flail her way to the end. Her lungs would fill and she would suffocate.

Zeena took Rebekah's hand in hers. It was cold, damp like the earth what's gone cold with frost. Her face settled into a grimace. Even in her stillness she suffered. Zeena placed her hands on Rebekah's forehead. Beneath her palms Rebekah's face was hot. If her hands could heal the fevered flesh, at least she'd go in peace.

Tell me, Mama. Let me at least help her find peace when she goes.

Mama didn't answer.

I won't try to heal her, Mama. Just let me help her in this pain. I can't bear to see her so pained.

Mama gave her only silence. Mama was gone, buried with Cousin Beatrice. Mama would not help her. Zeena sat at the bedside, holding to the hand as it grew colder, colder. If Mama'd speak to her, maybe the girl'd be saved. Mama'd performed miracles, brought folks back from worse'n this. But there was only the silence, a cold, hard silence that told her the Lord was no better'n any living man; He was cruel as the next one. Living, what was called a gift by some, it was no more'n a curse.

Lucy came with the water and Zeena washed Rebekah down. Maybe the fever would abate. But Rebekah turned worse, now crying out, now moaning, now throwing her arms in the air, and one last flurry of a rising fever caused Rebekah's eyes to fly open and wildly search the room. But when she fell back on the pillow, her face was colorless and her eyes turned back in her head and she groaned a sigh.

Lucy fell to crying, praying to God, first plaintively, begging God to spare her eldest daughter, then hurling insults, "You only take away, you never give."

Zeena laid a hand on her shoulder and told her it was no good. "Your daughter's going. You want to sit with her in these last minutes or carry on your argument with the Lord?"

"I don't even know what's taking her."

"A woman's generative organs can turn to hemorrhage," Zeena explained.

"But why?"

Zeena gave no answer.

"Is there nothing can be done?"

"A doctor'd try a mineral acid solution, or acetate of lead, but there're dangers with those, poisons to the blood. 'Sides, I don't think there's time."

Lucy went to the door. "John," she cried out. "Ruth."

Lawyer Varnum and young Ruth came to the room then.

With Lucy on one side of the bed, Lawyer Varnum on the other, Ruth leaning onto the foot the bed, and Zeena standing back to watch the last blood drain from Rebekah's face, the girl went.

Lawyer Varnum left the room like someone in a trance. Ruth cried softly, bent over Rebekah's feet. Lucy's cries were worst of all. There's nothing to match a mother what's lost her child, Zeena knew.

TWENTY-NINE

*D*eath comes silent as the new dawn.

The hills, washed clean by autumn rain and then covered with winter's snow, that just yesterday appeared kind in their softness, in the new dawn's light now show themselves as harsh friends.

The sky, painted a clear crisp blue, blue as only a winter sky can be, that yesterday appeared to stretch in all directions for all time with soothing hands, now sinks down on the land suffocatingly as the sun rises onto the land.

The snow is no longer a soft blanket. It forms a shroud over the earth.

The voices of folks once loved now sound strident, harmful. Their eyes, once generous with love, now remain downcast. If they look up, there is no life.

HERE IT WAS AGAIN. That sense that the world had changed overnight. Zeena remembered it from when Mama died.

Zeena lay in bed and watched the day's new light fill the room. The sky was already blue and crisp, but to Zeena it was flat and fearsome. The night before she'd lain stiffly on her back and waited for Ethan's hands to pull her to him, which they did not do.

Now Ethan lay still in bed. Ordinarily he'd have been up for an hour by the time the sun rose. Now he was a stone beside her, lying on his stomach. Zeena could not even hear his breathing. Last evening—Christmas, it was—he'd come to town to fetch her after she'd spent another day at the Varnums'. She'd been asked to do the laying out. For Zeena it had been a distinctly painful duty. It was Rebekah's voice, Rebekah's presence, and her way of righting things before they turned bad that were absent from the house. The pattern of things had shifted. Lucy's cries'd turned to whines; she came to the door and told Zeena, "I don't like the way you've folded her hands, they should rest at her sides." Lawyer Varnum, ever on the edge of things, disappeared to his study and stared obliquely at anyone who disturbed him, as Zeena did when she asked him did he want to see Rebekah now she was ready. Ruth grew to a woman overnight. "What can I do to help?" she asked Zeena every few minutes.

Was that it? The complete shifting of familiar patterns to something unknown, unfamiliar? Nothing at the Varnums' was the same. Nothing in her own home was the same.

Now it was time to rise. Zeena had work to do before the funeral at two. It was Thursday. If she stuck to her schedule, she would clean the kitchen today, wash the floors in the back and side passageways, sweep the stairs, and make butter. It tired her even to think it.

She rose onto her knees. She wanted to wash, but not with Ethan right there. "You'll want to wake up now," she said to him, shaking his shoulder.

His eyes flipped open, telling her he'd been awake already.

"The funeral's at two," she said.

Ethan sat up and reached for his trousers. "I won't be going to the funeral."

Zeena did not respond immediately. She remained where she was on the bed, her feet drawn up beneath her. She watched Ethan pull on his shirt and button it, tuck it into his trousers, and adjust his suspenders. Finally, "The Varnums come to your ma's."

"I got work at the mill before I shut it down for the winter. I'm weeks late with it already. I can't just leave it to Jotham."

"It'd mean so much," she started. "Besides, it's not right I should go alone."

Ethan ran his hands through his hair. He went to the window. "I done enough grieving."

"I don't think it'll look right."

"I'm not thinking how it'll look."

"Folks in town, they'll—"

"How'd she go, anyway?" It was the first he'd asked of it.

"It were the bleeding done it, a woman's generative organs, they can act up something terrible and take her . . ."

Ethan glared at her. "What caused it is what I'm asking."

"She was so fragile. It could ha' been . . . anything."

Ethan's jawbone was working.

"Folks'll wonder," Zeena said. "If you're not there, they'll suspect something."

"What're you saying?"

"You know how folks can be, they imagine things, they might conjure up some story about you and the Varnums, they might—"

"Folks'll think what they want."

"If you don't care what folks think about me, then I guess it don't matter."

Ethan stepped to the door. He turned and looked back at Zeena. "If you want I should go, I'll go."

She knew enough to say nothing. She just nodded, yes.

* * *

FUNERALS TAKE FOLKS TO THE EDGE of what they don't want to know. Their mortality stares back at them when they stand at the edge of a grave and watch the casket lowered in. It's one thing if the one who's gone is old. A life fully lived, it reassures them. But the life of a young woman, too young yet to've married and borne her own young, it almost pulls them in with her when they throw in the frozen clods of earth and listen to the hollow thunks.

The ground in December is almost frozen through, but if the snow comes early, as it does some years, it can still be dug even up to Christmas. This is one of those years. Not so much cold, but plenty of snow. Drifts up to the windowsills and tree trunks skirted with it.

Folks don't just mourn her passing. They wail and keen, on the inside if not the out. They rail against the injustice. They grieve the unlived life. They fear for their children. Don't take mine, oh, please, no.

They look away or they stare intently at the mother supported by her husband and only remaining child into the church. Either way they are afraid. How to live with such a horror as life handed that mother? They make promises and pacts. Let me live and I'll hold in my pride. I've known passions; I can forgo them from now on. Give my child a long life and I'll wake early to pray in the mornings before I rise.

As many as could come attended Rebekah Varnum's funeral. They walked, they rode their horses, got out their sleighs. Solemnly they collected at the church, wondering at the fate that had spared them but had struck the Varnums.

Afterward folks couldn't remember the hymns. They'd hardly heard the minister's words. "There is kindness in an early passing; the Lord giveth and the Lord taketh away," he'd said, but they all wondered at the kindness. Mostly they listened to Mrs. Varnum, sitting in the front pew, bent over, then sitting upright, bent over, then upright, and all the while giving out a cry that played itself in the rafters and came down onto the next cries like a swallow that soars up then sinks back down to join its flock.

Make her stop, most of them thought. It was too much to bear, so much sorrow.

AFTER THE SERVICE Ethan approached Lucy Varnum as she held to the railing out front of the church and waited for Lawyer Varnum to bring round the sleigh. "We won't be coming back to the house," he told her when the folks ahead of him'd had their say. She would not catch his eye, even when he said, "It's a terrible shame." Her tremblings began anew. Ethan stepped back. He joined Ruth, who put her hand to his arm and said, "Ma don't know what she's doing."

Zeena came forward. "I'll come to call in a day or so," she told Lucy.

Zeena sat sidesaddle atop Fly while Ethan led the horse past the church, down the hill, and up onto the first long ridge. She wore her cape over her brown merino and wool jacket. The snow that'd come through during the night had left the hills freshly white under a dazzling blue sky. A light snow, it still clung to the sweeping branches of the pines and firs on the ridge. The air was light, warm for a late December afternoon; it was more like a January thaw. Ethan trudged along, his boots sinking into the snow. He wore his cap pulled down onto his forehead and thrust his head and shoulders forward as he walked, as if the weight he carried on his shoulders needed an extra effort to keep from wearing him into the ground.

At the top of the ridge, Ethan stopped. He looked at the hill that sloped gently away to the right and back to the town and steeply to the left. "We used to go coasting."

"I don't know who you mean."

Ethan stood at the crest and looked at the hill.

Zeena stared at him.

"There was a bunch of us. They're mostly gone west. I'm the only one left in Starkfield."

They continued on in silence. Along the ridge, then down the lane and finally past the Frome graveyard where only the tops of the stones showed gray against the snow that threatened to swallow them. Then up toward the house until Ethan stopped, and Fly, carrying Zeena, stopped behind him. Above them the cloudless sky was blue as a pond in summer; it made an almost sickening contrast with the silver gray clapboards and roof shingles. The low pale sun shimmered on the snow that stretched far as the eye could follow. The snow was banked up on all sides of the house and barn like the frothy waves of the sea. Between the two buildings the snow'd been tramped down into a meager path by Ethan's comings and goings.

And the elms, they draped their arms in a mournful gesture to the sky.

This is how it will be, Zeena realized. The two of them in that house, the path to the barn for Ethan, the animals, all of them waiting. Waiting.

For spring?

Zeena knew it was more'n spring they'd have to wait for. She knew the seasons'd come and go and turn into years the same way snow collects, flake by flake, day by day, that the cold'd freeze their blood solid even through the summer, and that their lives would extend no farther than the graveyard at the foot of the hill.

Zeena tried one last time to call on Mama. What'll I do? she cried to Mama.

Mama didn't answer.

Only the blue sky spoke to her as it sank onto her shoulders: This's all there is. And the snow: You'll never get away. And the elms: Save your crying.

The house before them, it reached out its cold gray arms and pulled them up the hill.

1904

$\mathcal{T}$he cookstove was cold; not even a glow showed through the crack below the firebox door. The kitchen floor was icy under her feet. Zeena stood on the threshold and held to the door frame.

The windowpanes were white squares. Outside the sea of snow had risen, even covered the window boxes where it'd drifted in. The lanky frames of the old elms were black bodies rising out of the sea.

The room was illuminated with the moon's light. The shapes were gray and black and white, somehow dismal. The oilcloth on the floor by the sink glistened white. The metal jugs of water set in the sink sparkled silver. The stove was a bulky black; the stovepipe rose like a snake and disappeared into the chimney, which glimmered gray and white.

The chaise was pulled up alongside the cookstove so its head was back to the door where Zeena stood. Mattie's bare feet protruded from under the feather quilt at odd angles like two silver fish. The rest of her was black and gray, in shadow. Zeena could hear her breath coming ragged in short little gasps; was it making white clouds in the night air? It sounded like a wolf what's been running in chase all night.

Zeena stepped off the threshold and into the shadows. Her knees'd turned to jelly. Her legs shook and trembled. Waves of trembling shot through her chest. It was more'n the cold, she knew. It was the hatred what'd boiled so many years inside and now she couldn't hold it. Her hands jerked with it.

When Mattie whimpered then, it nearly sent Zeena reeling. She caught herself by holding her arms out into the air for balance. The room was swirling. The stovepipe was cocked to the side and the water jugs were turning every which way. The floor, it was heaving. Zeena thought she'd sink straight into the frozen ground. Mattie's whimpering, it made Zeena sick.

But the room settled finally. Zeena made her way to the chaise. She stood behind it and to one side. Mattie looked smaller'n ever in the moonlight. She was slumped way down. During the day when Mattie was in the chair, Zeena strapped her up to keep her from sliding, but Mattie didn't like it. "My skin's near to raw," she complained. "Why can't you just hoist me?" Thirty times a day'd wear my spine to nothing, she'd wanted to tell Mattie, and, You know there ain't nothing wrong with your skin, I checked it again last night. Instead, Zeena just wrapped the belt around the chair and under Mattie's arms. In the evenings, after supper and while Zeena did her mending and piecework, she'd leave Mattie unstrapped, but even that was no good. "I'm like to slide clear to the floor," she whined.

Now Mattie tried to shift her position by lifting herself with her one good arm, but she only slipped back lower into the chaise. Her breathing turned deeper, raspier.

If Zeena just let Mattie go on like this, would she choke herself?

It irked Zeena to see Mattie like this. Whimpering, like she had the right to heartache and suffering, when it was Zeena whose life'd been turned to final sorrow the day Mattie arrived.

Zeena knew from the first moment what the girl was meaning to do. It showed in her cheeks that deepened to rose when Ethan was in the room, in her eyelashes that fluttered, and in that way she had of throwing her head back when she laughed. Forward, is what Zeena would've called it, if she'd ever've spoken about it to another soul.

Zeena tried not to think on those first weeks and months after Mattie came. This had been her survival. But tonight it was back, and with it was the other hurt, the one Zeena knew could bring her down faster'n snow sinking the land in white. The girl, Rebekah—and Zeena hadn't thought her name in more years than she could count, so much did it start the sorrow building again—she died by her own hand, trying to rid her body of the baby, Ethan's baby, and not another soul than Zeena knew the truth. It near drove her crazy that first winter with Ethan, having to hold her tongue. But hold her tongue she did, in remembrance of Rebekah. The secret, it was held so well, it 'most died in Zeena's heart as the years passed. By the time Mattie came, Rebekah was near forgot and her own ailments had taken over her attention.

Zeena knew what she became in those first years of marriage to Ethan. Watching Rebekah die had taken more out of Zeena than she had to give to sorrow. She could see it in Ethan's eyes too, a begrudging look when Zeena told him she needed help with this or that, needed to see the doctor, needed a remedy or a tonic. Occasionally he'd found sympathy in his heart for her. But Zeena knew how hard he had to work to find it. It only made her own suffering all the worse.

Zeena stared out the window at the expanse of gray and silver fields and black hills that stretched off into the sky and wondered what her life would have been if she'd never come to Starkfield, if she'd never let her heart go soft for Ethan.

It would've been a challenge if she'd stayed in Bettsbridge, in her father's home. It wasn't that she fancied otherwise. She remembered all too well the slap to her spirit whenever Father came in the room. But she wondered if she could've stood up to that better'n to live with the secret of Rebekah's death stored in her heart, a hidden hurt.

And then Mattie. Nothing was worse'n tending this one. Day in, day out, she was faced with the truth. No secret here. Ethan had chosen even death with Mattie rather than live the life he'd fallen to with Zeena. How was a spirit supposed to stand up to that?

And there was no one to turn to. At first Zeena called on Mama for help. Tell me what to do, she begged. Once, right after the smash-up, she even hoped for Mama to tell her to go home to Father. She yearned for the words: You don't need to stay with this burden. But Mama'd gone silent, leaving Zeena to her troubles and the memory of Mama's words: "Save your crying."

And so she had.

Now, though, Zeena felt her eyes stinging. She blinked; the room was blurring. She blinked again till things came clear. Crying, she wouldn't turn to that now. Not now, not after all this time.

Mattie's breathing came yet harder. Again she tried to lift herself and again slunk lower still. Her face went into moonlight now. It was like a small white plate with purple asters on it, only the flowers were her eyes pinched close and her mouth a jagged hole. Her cheeks glistened silver with tears. The point of her chin trembled like the clenched fingers of a newborn child.

A child . . . Zeena felt it fresh, a wrenching in her chest at the thought of the child she never had, what would've been the proof of her womanliness. If Ethan hadn't wronged her so, if she hadn't had to bear Rebekah's secret, surely . . .

But the nagging in her heart, she couldn't tolerate it now. Not again now.

Zeena took a step. She knelt and reached out to touch the feather quilt. She pulled gently at it until it slipped off and to the floor. Maybe the girl'd freeze to death, right there in the kitchen. Maybe folks'd know what Zeena'd been up against all these years. Ethan could get only so much wood in, never enough to keep them warm, and food was scarce as a warm summer day. Time and again the water'd be froze in their jugs in the sink when she came down in the morning. Cold such as she'd never known in Bettsbridge.

Zeena hadn't seen Father since the last time she'd been to the doctor, a year or so after the smash-up. He'd sent a few letters, even asked her to come home and look after him in recent years. She was amazed he'd held on this long. Lung trouble didn't usually let a man live into his eighties, but Father was stubborn. That last letter he'd said he was ready to join Mama and would she come. But how could she leave Ethan and Mattie? Long as she stayed, at least she gained the satisfaction of knowing they didn't have each other. And besides, how could Ethan care for himself and the girl? He needed her. After all these years, he still needed her, even if he didn't love her, hadn't ever loved her.

Mattie lay like a corpse, her withered legs stretched out lifeless beneath her flannel nightdress. She didn't seem to notice the quilt was gone. But her crying and the ragged breathing got all mixed up together.

Zeena stood. Her hands were itching in the dark. She could reach over the back of the chaise, pull the pillow out from under Mattie's head and hold it to her face. The girl'd struggle, but how much? With her one good arm and her shoulders? It'd only take seconds . . .

"I know you're there." The words came out in a whine.

Zeena's hands kept up their twitching. Her arms trembled in their sockets. Her chest was a flutter of heartbeat. But she didn't move. And she said nothing. Her shallow breathing was soundless while Mattie's breathing filled the room.

"You trying to scare me?" the whine went on.

Zeena swallowed. Her hands gripped the back of the chaise. "You don't scare me."

It was like water was running through her now. Everything

was aflutter. She held her knees together to combat the shivering. She realized she could jiggle the chaise, send Mattie's teeth to rattling in her head. That might scare her. She could turn the chaise on its side, so Mattie'd hurl to the floor. If she snapped her shoulder or broke her neck, she'd go in a minute. She wouldn't be able to breathe. In the morning they'd find her. Poor thing, she must've tried to get up, whatever'd she do such a thing for? folks'd say.

"You can't even hurt me."

Or Zeena could turn the chaise the other way. She could send Mattie into the stove so she'd crack her head. The idea was enough to turn Zeena to such shivering that she could barely stand. She could hold in her thoughts no more. "Hurt you?" she hissed. "What about me? You ever think on what you done to me?"

Mattie barked a laugh. "Maybe you never thought what it'd be like to be me, beholden to you and your meanness for every thing."

Zeena's breath left her. "Meanness? Why, why—" but how to go on? Zeena would say it, the thing that'd lurked in her mind for all the years since the smash-up, the thing she'd dared not say for its meanness, the thing if Mama even knew she thought would make her 'shamed: "It'd been better if you'd'a died."

Again Mattie laughed. "You ain't the first. I thought it myself a thousand times."

Zeena kept on. That wasn't all. "It'd been better if you both ha' died. You think I cared for him after knowing what he done?"

"Folks thought that too, surely you seen it in their eyes. Pity. Nothing but pity. Why you think no one comes to call?"

Zeena felt the water inside her, flooding her chest so she couldn't breathe, filling her head till she couldn't see straight, sending her limbs to a shaking she couldn't control. She sank to her knees, her hands still gripping the back of the chaise. She would tell her about Rebekah, the other girl Ethan'd loved, the girl who'd . . .

Mama's voice, it came out of the air: But you promised. Oh, Mama, Zeena thought. After all this time, now you're speaking again?

"There ain't a soul can bear to see it, what's become of us," Mattie went on.

"You're the evilest soul I ever—"

"I'm an echo of yourself, if you ain't noticed."

Zeena might as well have been slapped to the floor, kicked in her chest. "No, you're, that's not so, I hate you, I—"

"Then you hate yourself," she said.

Tell me, Mama, tell me what to do. Hold your tongue, Mama said. Wait just a little more. You'll know what to do. You'll know.

Silence. Even Mattie's noisy breathing stopped. There was nothing. No sound. The cookstove stone cold, the air numbing, the house a tomb.

"ZEENA, GET UP," a voice told her.

There was a bursting of water inside her then. The river that ran through her, it seeped out one tear at a time until there were more and more and more. She covered her face as it flowed. Zeena's silent river.

Was that it? Mama telling her it was time to cry? Mama said nothing and Zeena's weeping continued.

"She's just looking for pity," came Mattie's voice, clear and smooth.

Zeena felt someone's hands set her upright.

The other voice, the one that'd said for her to get up, it didn't speak.

"Don't she know folks pity her already?" came Mattie's whine. "Everyone knows why you married her. There's pity enough for her there. She don't need no more."

Zeena lifted herself to a sitting position. "It were more'n that," she cried.

Mattie barked another laugh. "Hear that? She says it were more'n that," and she fell to chuckling.

Seconds passed while Zeena's weeping kept on. Then, "It were," the other voice said.

Zeena did not dare to look into the shadows behind her where the voice had come from. She dared not look to the chaise. Her eyes went to the white squares of the windowpanes. The snow, it reflected the moonlight. Everything was white, shining, brilliant. She rose to her feet. Her crying kept on, but silent, tender. She tightened the shawl around her shoulders and smoothed the fringe with her fingers. Everything, even inside the kitchen, glowed with moonlight and snow.

Had she heard it right? Zeena repeated the words to herself: *It were.* Yes, that is what he'd said. *It were. It were.* The words, they were what she needed, what she'd always needed, and he'd given them to her. She repeated them. *It were. It were.*

Something inside her loosened. The desperation, the terrible desperation of her life, could those words have eased it? Was it as simple as that? Zeena lifted her chin and stepped to the nearest window. She looked out at the landscape that'd formed her surroundings for more than thirty years. This had been her home since that day she came to care for Cousin Beatrice and Ethan met her in town where the stage left her off and he brought her back in the wagon over the rutted roads and past the graveyard at the foot of the hill. It'd been her home so long. But it'd never felt like home.

Mama had said Zeena would know what to do.

Zeena stared out at the land and waited.

ZEENA WAS DRESSED IN HER BLACK CALICO when Ethan came down to get the cookstove going. The cornmeal mush heated on the stove. Water steamed from the kettle. She was at the table, setting the plates and spoons in order. He glanced at her from a half-turned face but said nothing.

Mattie'd been washed, dressed, set in her chair and strapped in, and had already been given her breakfast. Zeena'd arranged her chair so Mattie was near the cookstove but could also see out the windows to watch the rising sun. Mattie was slumped against the belt that held her seated. She was snoring lightly.

"Breakfast's ready for you and the visitor," Zeena told Ethan. She couldn't help but look out the window. So many dawns following a storm she'd seen it just like this: a wide blue sky, clouds puffed on the horizon, and the slopes of white hills a glare. Until now it'd been a trouble to look out; the hills'd been her separation from the world. This morning, though, she knew it would be otherwise. Time, it'd gone in circles and come back to where it'd begun.

There was the day she'd come to this house. There were all the countless days till now. And there was today. Mama'd told her the truth. Zeena would know what to do.

Ethan stood just inside the door. His good side leaned against the door frame. His blue eyes were dark as a midnight sky, as they often were in the morning until he was up and about his work.

"You'll be taking the visitor to town?" she asked him.

He nodded. "Soon's I can get the sleigh out." He passed through the kitchen and out to the back passage. Zeena heard the door latch after him. She stayed by the window and stared at the hills. They were less fierce this morning. Could she love them now?

The visitor opened the door. "Morning," he voiced and looked out the window. "Looks like the storm's passed." Zeena nodded and went to the stove. "I can give you tea to start," she said. The visitor stood by the window while Zeena busied herself at the stove. "That's a lot of snow out there," the man said.

Zeena said, "Yes," as she brought the food to the table.

"He going to be able to get me to town? Mrs. Hale'll be wondering if I'm buried in the snow somewhere."

"I s'pect so," she said. Mattie's snoring grew louder momentarily. Ordinarily it'd set Zeena off. But she didn't even hear it. Zeena sat in her rocker by the cookstove and waited for the men to eat their breakfast.

It won't be long now, she thought.

IT WAS NEARLY TIME FOR DINNER when Ethan returned from town. Zeena was in her room; she sat in the rocker by the window and watched Ethan lead the bay into the barn. Some minutes later she heard his uneven step in the kitchen. He spoke briefly to Mattie, whose whine rose through the floorboards. Zeena hardly heard it, though. She was waiting for Ethan to come upstairs, which she knew he would, to see was she planning to fix some dinner.

She had changed into her old brown merino and faded flannel shirt. It was the same clothes she'd worn for those long-ago trips to the doctor in Bettsbridge or even the one all the way to Worcester years ago. The same clothes she'd worn to every funeral service, even she'd worn for her wedding to Ethan. Her same old satchel was packed with her scant possessions: her few articles of clothing, the comb and brush set that had belonged to her mother and her grandmother, the hair comb that had belonged to Cousin Beatrice, and the two gifts Rebekah'd given her, the cameo, and the pressed and framed violets.

Finally Ethan's slow step was heard on the stairs. He paused before opening the door to their room. He did not step over the threshold but leaned into the room from the hall. He looked at Zeena, at her traveling clothes, her satchel on the bed. An unease showed in his eyes.

"I want you to take me to the Flats," Zeena said.

Now Ethan's eyebrows raised up.

"I'm going home to Bettsbridge," she said.

"You going to see—" a look of dread settling into his eyes.

"I ain't going to a doctor, no. There won't be no fee for you to pay."

Ethan stepped into the room then.

"I'm going home," she told him. "Father needs me." She'd been thinking about it since she'd raised herself from the kitchen floor during the night and had gone upstairs to lie in bed until the dawn came. Then she'd laid on her side and watched the first light of day stream across the tips of the hills and straight through the window to rest on her face like soothing fingers. Father'd had hired help these last eleven years. Though she didn't relish the thought of caring for him, she knew it wouldn't be forever. She would wait him out. She would ignore his pity. She would avoid looking into his eyes where most of his judgments lay. She'd done harder, much harder.

Ethan was shaking his head.

"You'll be all right, the two of you. I wrote a letter to Ruth and explained it. Folks from town, they'll see she gets her care." Mama wouldn't't've wanted Zeena to leave Mattie to her death. Mama always said to do what was right by the other person. Mattie would be cared for proper. And Ethan, maybe he'd do better with only one woman pecking at him.

Ethan was staring now, taking it in.

"I left your mother's black shawl wrapped in tissue in the top drawer of the dresser. It's the way she always kept it." Zeena'd worn the shawl the day she married Ethan. She didn't want a reminder of that day, 'sides, it was right to leave the shawl where it'd lived so long. And it was the only way she could think of to tell Ethan she wasn't coming back. She was going home to Bettsbridge, to see Father to his grave, yes, and then to stay in the house where Mama gave Zeena life.

"Zeena—"

Zeena put up her hand. "I don't want to hear it now. I waited too long to hear what I needed from you." She would've liked to thank him for what he gave her, but her throat was tightened up and she didn't want to start in to crying again. The words, *It were*, they'd been ringing in her head all night. He hadn't married her simply to avoid the winter alone after his mother died.

It were more'n that. Love? Zeena wasn't foolish enough to try to put a name to it. She accepted it wasn't only pity or fear, and that was enough.

Zeena knew Father'd look at her with shame if she let him. But she wouldn't let him. She had it inside her now that Ethan'd had some feeling for her despite what happened with the girl who died, Rebekah was her name, and that small feeling, whatever it was, was enough.

Ethan's face was flushed. His eyes were still dark in color, watery, with no begrudging in them, nothing to hold her. Had he finally seen what it was she'd lived with, caring for Mattie? His hands, when he'd set her upright on the floor during the night, was it kindness she felt in them?

"You can do that much for me, can't you?" Zeena said.

He swallowed.

"When you're ready, you give me a call and I'll come down."

Again he swallowed.

"I'm beholden to you then," she told him. There, she'd thanked him. There was nothing more to say.

Zeena listened to Ethan's ragged steps as he went down to the kitchen. She stared out the window and thought about going home to Bettsbridge. Father, he'd pass on soon enough, and then she'd have the only thing he would ever give her: the house where she was born, the rooms where Mama's hands did their wondrous work, the air Mama's voice once filled with the song of angels.

All this time she'd stayed with Ethan and Mattie, thinking it was the right thing, believing she had no other choice than to do right by the two of them who needed her, certain Mama would've agreed. Now she wondered if it wasn't something mean-spirited that'd kept her. A stubbornness born of bitterness, hers and Ethan's and even Mattie's. Mama wouldn't ever have agreed to that. Course, what would folks've said if she'd left after the smash-up? Pride, pride'd kept her as well. No wonder Mama'd grown silent.

Zeena'd thought it all through. By the first light, she knew what to do. After Father died, she would do some doctoring to get by, but mostly she'd be with Mama. Mama's hands would look after her. Mama would sing to her. Zeena would be at home.

She sat in the rocker and stared out the window at the hills, the hills that would lead her away, and waited.

Zeena was used to waiting, after all.